U0037389

前　言

　　大約十五年前，當我還在高中教書時，我就想編一本像這樣的單字學習書了。一般準備大學入學考試的高中生，還有準備各類英語檢定的考生，必須記憶大量的英文單字。事實上，我認為許多人在背單字時，的確浪費了許多不必要的時間，例如，記 **"visit"**（拜訪）與 **"visible"**（看得見的）這兩個單字時，經常把它們當作兩個完全不同的字來記。如果每個字都照這種方法來讀的話，在背幾千個單字之前，恐怕就已精疲力盡了。其實，**"vis"** 這個字根是有它的意義的，指的就是「看」的意思，而 **"visit"** 是親自到對方家中，「看」到對方的拜訪，而不是透過電話或電子郵件的拜訪。那麼，對於 **"vis"** 這個字根有了這樣的認識之後，看到 **"visible"** 這個單字，就可以知道是 **"vis"** 加了 **"-ible"** 這樣的組合單字。而 **"-ible"** 與 **"-able"** 都同樣屬於「可能的」之意。還有，如果加了形容詞語尾 **"-ual"** 的話，就會產生 **"visual"**（視覺的）這樣的單字。另外，若加**-ize**變成動詞的話，又可以變成 **"visualize"**（視覺化）這樣的單字。因此，在背誦單字時，如果能在心中暗自描繪單字的主要印象，你會發現單字很快就記起來了。

　　本書簡要地介紹構成單字的零件─字根、字首與字尾，教你怎麼把零件一個一個拼裝成單字，使背誦英文單字不再是件難事。本書並不是專業性的語言學書籍，編寫方式非常易懂、易讀，適用於準備大學入試和各類英檢的考生、或對英文有興趣的自學者。此外，本書收錄的單字（含衍生字）全都附有音標。

　　在第1章「字根的意義」中，我們把像 **"vis"**（看）這樣具有特定意義的字根整理歸類，把它們跟60個不同的字首字尾拼裝組合，並將其他相關字與衍生字一口氣整理出來供讀者記憶。在第2章「單字加字首字尾」中，我們把單字基本形加上不同的字首或字尾，衍生出許多單字串。這樣可以省下許多時間，在短時間之內，毫不費力地記下大量同類的英文單字。在第3章「不能拆的單字」中，我們集結了一些不能拆解，但同時也是大學入試常出的單字。在附錄1「60個常用字首字尾」中，介紹了20個英文字首與40個英文字尾。你一定會感到很訝異，因為單單這60個字首字尾，就組成了大部分的英文單字。

另外一項可使本書發揮強大效力的就是書中所舉的例句，例句部分是由我的同事、也是本書的另一作者Sarah Haas所編寫。本書的例句是以閱讀的理解力作為出發點，不需牢記。在研讀本書的過程中，你會發現許多例句甚至具有故事性。這種研讀例句的練習，可成為日後閱讀較長文章的基礎訓練。因此，本書不但可以學習大量的英文單字，更可以加強閱讀的理解力。Sarah Haas所編寫的例句字裡行間充滿了幽默感，非常有趣，請你愉快地閱讀。

　　此外，藏本惠美為本書所繪製的插畫也是功不可沒的。但請不要把書中的插畫當作裝飾，插畫擔任了一個很重要的角色。請你利用這些圖像，與單字作連結，仔細地看插圖，再將單字用「視覺的圖像」記起來。

　　最後，在本書出版之際，容我說幾句感謝之辭。首先，我要感謝河合出版社的東浩二先生，對本書的編排給予許多寶貴的意見。此外，還有Phaedra Atkins, Eloise Paterson, Bettina Begole, Lisa Mandziak, Sarah（Jones）Wringer等人對於本書的英文表達語句所提出的寶貴意見。我也要感謝我的伙伴Sarah Haas的愛貓Momo，總是在Sarah膝上陪伴、鼓勵著她。還有巴哈（J. S. Bach）的樂曲「無伴奏大提琴組曲」，總是無間斷地撫慰著我的心靈。感謝我的愛狗—道爾傑與卡布力斯，在我疲憊的時候，牠們的撒嬌總是讓我精神為之一振。而最要感謝的，還是不惜一切栽培我、教育我的雙親，謝謝你們！

12月18日 內田浩樹記於降雪不斷的鳥取縣

本書特色與使用方法

◆ 收錄單字數：考試必備的3800字

本書收錄了大學入學考試必備的3800字，這些都是在考試中出現頻率相當高的重要單字。此外，本書單字的整理歸納具有條理，易於學習記憶，也很適合準備TOEIC或其他各類英語檢定的讀者。

◆ 第1章「字根的意義」

我們必須先有一個概念，除了單字本身具有意義外，單字分解之後，這些較小的部分(一般稱為字根、字首或字尾)也同樣具有意義。把這些部分拼裝組合，便可以構成相當龐大的單字數量。在本章中，將單字具有特定意義的部分取出並加以分類，這些具有特定意義的部分多為所謂的「字根」。字根底下歸納含有字根的單字，你可以注意看看，單字裡面有沒有出現附錄中所介紹的字首字尾？這些單字的零件是怎麼組裝成單字的？只要理解了，單字就好記了。同時，也可以將字彙中含有同樣意義的單字一併記下來。這樣，就可以把過去在不同時期零零散散所學過的單字，一口氣通通記下來，這是一個相當具效率的單字學習法。

◆ 第2章「單字加字首字尾」

首先，列出關鍵單字的原形，以此單字為基礎，可衍生出不同詞性的單字串。你可以利用附錄2「快查表」來查閱單字加了什麼字首或字尾，同樣也是理解過後再把它記下來。你會驚喜地發現，自己可以輕鬆愉快地把單字記得又快又牢。

◆ 第3章「不能拆的單字」

這一章的單字雖然沒有包含附錄中所介紹的字首字尾，但它把大學考試中出題頻率較高的一些單字做了整理，單字量並不多。前面提到，英文單字幾乎是由附錄1中所介紹的字首字尾所組成，本章就是最好證據。

◆ 附錄1「60個常用字首字尾」

附錄1介紹構成單字的基本元素。單字的元素有放在字開頭的字首與字尾端的字尾，這裡整理了常見的20個字首與40個字尾。建議各位在進入本文先可從這裡開始讀起。不過，並不需要將其中列舉的字首字尾全部背下來，只要先大略看一下有哪些內容就可以了。其實，附錄中所介紹的單字元素，在第1章跟第2章的單字中，都會陸續出現，記得隨時翻到附錄確認。只要能夠經常反覆查閱，自然而然地，就能記住這些字首字尾所代表的意義和功用。一旦有了這些知識，記憶單字的效率就會變得又快又好。

此外，為了讓讀者理解字首字尾的意義，也列舉了一些簡易的例字。這些單字中，有一些是在第1章－第3章中所沒有出現的，也有一些單字的中文翻譯和第1章－第3章不同，這是因為一個英文單字可以有多樣化的翻譯所致。

◆ 附錄2「快查表」

快查表是「60個常用字首字尾」整理成的精簡表格。看過附錄1的內容之後，在學習本書單字的任何時候，都歡迎多多利用快查表來查閱。

◆ 例句

本書所編寫的例句主要是作為記憶單字意思的輔助，並學會單字的用法。也可作為閱讀理解力的訓練，打好閱讀文章的基礎。

本書所使用的符號

◆ 單字的配色

● 第1章

contradictory（標示紅色的是字根的部分，標示藍色的則是其他部分）

● 第2章

shame（綠色代表關鍵單字的原形，以此單字為基礎衍生出不同詞性的單字）

ashamed（藍色代表字首或字尾的部分）

● 第3章

swallow（不能拆的單字用紫色標示）

◆ 音標

本書所有的單字（含衍生字）都附上音標供讀者參考。

◆ 詞性的標示

形 形容詞，名 名詞，副 副詞，動 動詞，介 介系詞，感 感嘆詞

◆ 音軌

音軌符號以 ☆ 001 表示。

本書所有的主要單字與例句皆收錄在MP3裡。

本書的版面構成

例句
不用熟記例句，但必須知道單字的意思及用法。以閱讀較長文章時可以理解為目標。

音軌符號
方便讀者在MP3裡搜尋到對應的主要單字及例句。

字根編號
單字中具有特定意義的部分，一般稱為「字根」的編號。

音標
本書所收錄的標題單字(含衍生字)全都附上音標。

字根+字首或字尾
代表字根與60個字首字尾的拼裝組合。

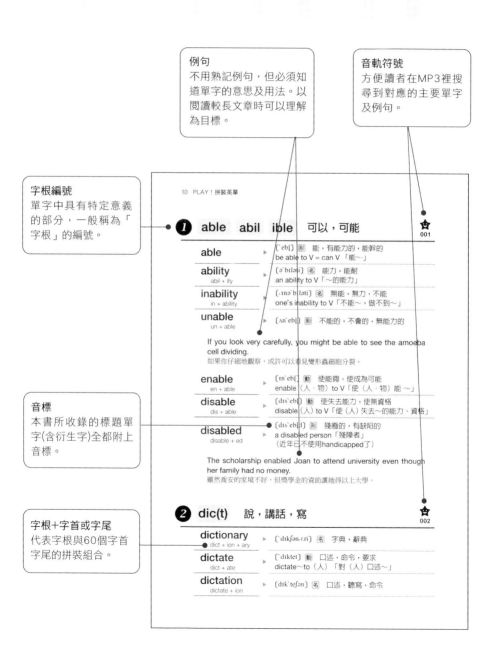

10 PLAY！拼裝英單

❶ able abil ible 可以，可能

☆
001

able
〔`ebl〕 形 能，有能力的，能幹的
be able to V = can V「能～」

ability
abil + ity
〔ə`bɪlətɪ〕 名 能力，能耐
an ability to V「～的能力」

inability
in + ability
〔.ɪnə`bɪlətɪ〕 名 無能，無力，不能
one's inability to V「不能～，做不到～」

unable
un + able
〔ʌn`ebl〕 形 不能的，不會的，無能力的

If you look very carefully, you might be able to see the amoeba cell dividing.
如果你仔細地觀察，或許可以看見變形蟲細胞分裂。

enable
en + able
〔ɪn`ebl〕 動 使能夠，使成為可能
enable（人．物）to V「使（人．物）能～」

disable
dis + able
〔dɪs`ebl〕 動 使失去能力，使無資格
disable（人）to V「使（人）失去～的能力、資格」

disabled
disable + ed
〔dɪs`ebld〕 形 殘廢的，有缺陷的
a disabled person「殘障者」
（近年已不使用handicapped了）

The scholarship enabled Joan to attend university even though her family had no money.
雖然喬安的家境不好，但獎學金的資助讓她得以上大學。

❷ dic(t) 說，講話，寫

☆
002

dictionary
dict + ion + ary
〔`dɪkʃən.ɛrɪ〕 名 字典，辭典

dictate
dict + ate
〔`dɪktet〕 動 口述，命令，要求
dictate～to（人）「對（人）口述～」

dictation
dictate + ion
〔dɪk`teʃən〕 名 口述，聽寫，命令

目 次

- 前言
- 本書特色與使用方法
- 本書所使用的符號
- 本書的版面構成

第1章

○ ○ ○ ○ ○ ○ ○ ○ ○ ○ ○ ○ ○

字根的意義

① able　abil　ible　可以，可能

001

able	▶ ［ˋebḷ］［形］能，有能力的，能幹的 be able to V = can V「能～」
ability abil + ity	▶ ［əˋbɪlətɪ］［名］能力，能耐 an ability to V「～的能力」
inability in + ability	▶ ［ɪnəˋbɪlətɪ］［名］無能，無力，不能 one's inability to V「不能～，做不到～」
unable un + able	▶ ［ʌnˋebḷ］［形］不能的，不會的，無能力的

If you look very carefully, you might be able to see the amoeba cell dividing.
如果你仔細地觀察，或許可以看見變形蟲細胞分裂。

enable en + able	▶ ［ɪnˋebḷ］［動］使能夠，使成為可能 enable（人‧物）to V「使（人‧物）能～」
disable dis + able	▶ ［dɪsˋebḷ］［動］使失去能力，使無資格 disable（人）to V「使（人）失去～的能力、資格」
disabled disable + ed	▶ ［dɪsˋebḷd］［形］殘廢的，有缺陷的 a disabled person「殘障者」 （近年已不使用handicapped了）

The scholarship enabled Joan to attend university even though her family had no money.
雖然喬安的家境不好，但獎學金的資助讓她得以上大學。

② dic(t)　說，講話，寫

002

dictionary dict + ion + ary	▶ ［ˋdɪkʃənˌɛrɪ］［名］字典，辭典
dictate dict + ate	▶ ［ˋdɪktet］［動］口述，命令，要求 dictate～to（人）「對（人）口述～」
dictation dictate + ion	▶ ［dɪkˋteʃən］［名］口述，聽寫，命令

dictator
dictate + or

▶ 〔`dɪk͵tetə〕 名　獨裁者，口述者，發號施令者

The secretary found it difficult to take dictation while her boss paced the room mumbling under his breath.
秘書覺得要將老闆在房裡踱步時咕噥的話記述下來很難。

contradict
contra + dict

▶ 〔͵kɑntrə`dɪkt〕 動　反駁，和⋯矛盾

contradiction
contradict + ion

▶ 〔͵kɑntrə`dɪkʃən〕 名　反駁，矛盾，抵觸

contradictory
contradict + ory

▶ 〔͵kɑntrə`dɪktəri〕 形　矛盾的

What she says and what she does are often contradictory.
她說話和做事時常自相矛盾。

indicate
in + dic + ate

▶ 〔`ɪndə͵ket〕 動　指示，指出，表明，暗示

indicator
indicate + or

▶ 〔`ɪndə͵ketə〕 名　指示器，指針，指示者

indication
indicate + ion

▶ 〔͵ɪndə`keʃən〕 名　指示，表示，徵兆，跡象

Jill gave us no indication that she would change her mind on this matter.
關於此事吉兒並沒有向我們表現出改變主意的跡象。

3 pre　pro　在前，前方，預先

003

predict
pre + dict

▶ 〔prɪ`dɪkt〕 動　預言，預料，預報

prediction
predict + ion

▶ 〔prɪ`dɪkʃən〕 名　預測，預言，預報

Nostradamus made a lot of amazing predictions, but have any of them come true?
諾斯特拉德馬斯曾經作過許多驚人的預言，但是當中有任何實現的嗎？

Everyone is predicting that Brazil will win the World Cup again.
每個人都預料巴西將會再次贏得世界杯冠軍。

prolong pro + long	▶	〔prəˋlɔŋ〕 動　延長，拉長，拖延
program pro + gram	▶	〔ˋprogræm〕 名　節目單，節目，計劃，方案

Luigi tried to prolong the date with his dream girl by walking her home instead of driving.
為了延長和夢中情人約會的時間，路易走路送她回家而非開車。

 4　view　vi(s)　vy　vid　**看見**
004

view	▶	〔vju〕 名　視力，視野，觀看，景色，看法， 　　　　　觀點，觀察 動　看，觀看 a room with a view「景觀佳的房間」
review re + view	▶	〔rɪˋvju〕 名　復習，（電影、戲劇的）評論 動　再檢查，復習，回顧，批評，評論
preview pre + view	▶	〔ˋpriˌvju〕 名　預習，（電影，戲劇等的）試映會 動　預習，試映，試演

She reviewed all her notes before the test.
她在考試前復習了所有的筆記。

vision vis + ion	▶	〔ˋvɪʒən〕 名　視力，視覺，洞察力，眼光，幻覺
visible vis + ible	▶	〔ˋvɪzəbḷ〕 形　可看見的，顯而易見的， 　　　　　明白清晰的
visual vis + ual	▶	〔ˋvɪʒuəl〕 形　視力的，視覺的，可見的
visualize visual + ize	▶	〔ˋvɪʒuəˌlaɪz〕 動　使看得見，使形象化，想像
visit vis + it	▶	〔ˋvɪzɪt〕 動　參觀，拜訪，探望，訪問

This tiny organism is not visible to the naked eye.
肉眼是沒辦法看見這微小生物的。

---

revise
re + vis

▶ 〔rɪˋvaɪz〕 動 修改，校訂

revision
revise + ion

▶ 〔rɪˋvɪʒən〕 名 修改，校訂，訂正，修訂本

After the potential buyers complained that the price of the house was too high, the real estate agency revised the estimate.
在可能的買主抱怨房價過高之後，那位房屋仲介修改了估價。

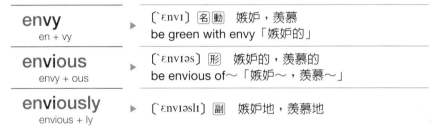

envy
en + vy

▶ 〔ˋɛnvɪ〕 名 動 嫉妒，羨慕
be green with envy「嫉妒的」

envious
envy + ous

▶ 〔ˋɛnvɪəs〕 形 嫉妒的，羨慕的
be envious of～「嫉妒～，羨慕～」

enviously
envious + ly

▶ 〔ˋɛnvɪəslɪ〕 副 嫉妒地，羨慕地

Hannah was green with envy when her friend won a scholarship to study overseas.
漢娜的朋友贏得海外留學獎學金，對此她感到非常嫉妒。

Rick looked enviously at his brother's new baseball bat and glove.
瑞克羨慕地看著他哥哥新的球棒和手套。

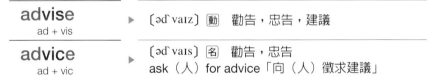

advise
ad + vis

▶ 〔ədˋvaɪz〕 動 勸告，忠告，建議

advice
ad + vic

▶ 〔ədˋvaɪs〕 名 勸告，忠告
ask（人）for advice「向（人）徵求建議」

Don't ask me for advice. I don't know anything about cooking.
不要向我求取建議。我不知道任何關於烹飪的事。

It is highly advised that you bring your camera into the cave.
強烈建議您將相機帶入洞穴。

---

evident
e + vid + ent

▶ 〔ˋɛvədənt〕 形 明顯的，明白的，顯然的

evidently
evident + ly

▶ 〔ˋɛvədəntlɪ〕 副 明顯地，顯然

evidence
evident + ce

▶ 〔ˋɛvədəns〕 名 證據，證人，證詞

To commit the perfect crime, one must destroy all the evidence.
為了達成完美的犯罪，必須摧毀所有證據。

The tire tracks were clearly evident on the muddy road.
輪胎痕跡清晰明顯地印在泥濘的路上。

---

provide
pro + vid

▶ 〔prəˋvaɪd〕 動 提供，供給，供應

provision
pro + vision

▶ 〔prəˋvɪʒən〕 名 供應，預備，條款

The hotel provides towels, but you need to have your own soap and shampoo.
旅館有提供毛巾，但是你需要準備自己的肥皂和洗髮精。

---

⑤ inter　互相，中間，在…之間

005

interview inter + view	▶ 〔ˋɪntɚˌvju〕 名 面談，會面，面試，訪問，採訪 動 接見，採訪，對…進行面談
international inter + nation + al	▶ 〔ˌɪntɚˋnæʃənl̩〕 形 國際性的，國際間的
internationalize international + ize	▶ 〔ˌɪntɚˋnæʃənlˌaɪz〕 動 使國際化
internationalization internationalize + tion	▶ 〔ˌɪntɚˋnæʃənləˌzeʃən〕 名 國際化
interdisciplinary inter + discipline +ary	▶ 〔ˌɪntɚˋdɪsəplɪˌnɛrɪ〕 形 各學科間的

interchange ▶ 〔ˌɪntəˋtʃendʒ〕 名 交換，交替，交流道
inter + change 動 交換，互換，交換位置

The course is interdisciplinary, combining religion, psychology, and sociology.
課程是跨學科的，結合了宗教、心理學以及社會學。

---

interact ▶ 〔ˌɪntəˋækt〕 動 相互作用，互動
inter + act interact with～「和～交流，和～互動」

---

interactive ▶ 〔ˌɪntəˋæktɪv〕 形 相互作用的
interact + ive

---

interaction ▶ 〔ˌɪntəˋrækʃən〕 名 互相影響，互動
interact + ion

In a language classroom, it is important for learners to interact with each other.
在語言教室裡，學員間彼此的互動極為重要。

---

6 **ee** 被動從事者

006

employee ▶ 〔ˌɛmplɔɪˋi〕 名 受雇者，雇員，員工
employ + ee employer employ+er 〔ɛmˋplɔɪə〕 名 雇主

Reliability, punctuality and trustworthiness are qualities that employers look for in prospective employees.
可靠、守時以及可信是雇主在未來員工身上尋找的特質。

---

interviewee ▶ 〔ˌɪntəvjuˋi〕 名
inter + view + ee 被接見者，受訪者
interviewer interview+er
〔ˋɪntəvjuə〕 名
接見者，採訪者，面試官

*spec*tator

-ee
-er
interview

During an interview, the interviewer is not allowed to ask the interviewee personal questions.
面談時，面試官不可以詢問面談者私人的問題。

 (s)pec(t)　spise　(s)pic　看見
007

spectate spect + ate	▶ 〔`spɛktet〕動　出席觀看，觀賞（比賽等）
spectator spectate + or	▶ 〔spɛk`tetɚ〕名　旁觀者，目擊者，觀眾

The spectators were delighted with the players' great show of sportsmanship.
觀眾對選手們展現的運動家精神感到非常開心。

speculate spec + ate	▶ 〔`spɛkjəˌlet〕動　思索，沈思，推測，推斷 speculate about～「思索～，推測～」
speculator speculate + or	▶ 〔`spɛkjəˌletɚ〕名　投機者，思索者，推理者
speculative speculate + ive	▶ 〔`spɛkjəˌletɪv〕形　思索的，推測的，冒險性的， 不確定的，投機的
speculation speculate + ion	▶ 〔ˌspɛkjə`leʃən〕名　思索，推測，投機， 投機買賣

We can spend hours speculating, but we'll never know the outcome until we give it a try.
我們可以花費數小時思考，但是在嘗試之前，我們永遠不會知道結果如何。

expect ex + pect	▶ 〔ɪk`spɛkt〕動　期待，預期 be expecting a baby「懷胎」be pregnant的委婉 說法
expectation expect + tion	▶ 〔ˌɛkspɛk`teʃən〕名　期待，預期，期望， 預期的事物

expectancy
expect + cy

▶ 〔ɪkˋspɛktənsɪ〕 名　期望，預期，期望的事物

I'm afraid I didn't live up to my teacher's expectations.
我害怕沒有達到老師的期望。

I'm expecting a box of baked goods from my parents as a birthday present.
我正期待我父母送我一盒烤點心當生日禮物。

inspect
in + spect

▶ 〔ɪnˋspɛkt〕 動　檢查，審查，檢閱，視察

inspection
inspect + ion

▶ 〔ɪnˋspɛkʃən〕 名　檢查，檢驗，審查，視察

inspector
inspect + or

▶ 〔ɪnˋspɛktə〕 名　檢查員，視察員，督察員，巡官

Each product is inspected carefully before it is packaged for sale.
每項產品在包裝出售前都受到仔細的檢查。

suspect
sus + pect

▶ 〔səˋspɛkt〕 動　懷疑，不信任，猜想，料想，猜疑
〔ˋsʌspɛkt〕 名　嫌疑犯
形　可疑的
a suspected person「嫌疑犯」

suspicious
sus + pic + ous

▶ 〔səˋspɪʃəs〕 形　猜疑的，多疑的，可疑的，有蹊蹺的

suspicion
sus + pic + ion

▶ 〔səˋspɪʃən〕 名　懷疑，猜疑，嫌疑

I suspect that the young boy stole my bicycle but I can't prove it.
我懷疑那個年輕男孩偷走我的腳踏車，可是我無法證實。

perspective
per + spect + ive

▶ 〔pəˋspɛktɪv〕 名　透視圖法，透視圖，看法，觀點，洞察力，遠景，前途

Miraculously getting out of the collapsing building without a scratch has given Raymond a new perspective on life.
奇蹟般地從那棟倒塌的大樓中毫髮無傷逃出，讓雷蒙對生命有了新看法。

spectacle
spect + acle

▶ 〔`spɛktəkl〕 名 場面，景象，奇觀，壯觀，
眼鏡，光景

spectacular
spectacle + ar

▶ 〔spɛk`tækjələ〕 形 壯觀的，驚人的，公開展示的
名 奇觀，壯觀，豪華的節目

Laura thought it was an odd spectacle to see her father dressed up as a woman in the play.
蘿拉覺得看見她父親在戲劇中男扮女裝是很奇怪的光景。

There was a spectacular meteor shower last night.
昨天晚上有一陣壯觀的流星雨。

retrospect
retro + spect

▶ 〔`rɛtrəˏspɛkt〕 名 回顧，回想，追溯
in retrospect「回顧（過去），回憶（過往）」

retrospective
retrospect + ive

▶ 〔ˏrɛtrə`spɛktɪv〕 形 懷舊的，追溯的，回顧的

In retrospect, it was really not a good idea to smoke in bed.
現在想起來，在床上抽菸並不是個好主意。

special
spec + ial

▶ 〔`spɛʃəl〕 形 特別的，特殊的

specially
special + iy

▶ 〔`spɛʃəlɪ〕 副 特別地，專門地，特地，尤其

specialize
special + ize

▶ 〔`spɛʃəlˏaɪz〕 動 專攻，專門從事，專門化，限定
specialize in～「專門從事～，專攻～」

specialization
specialize + tion

▶ 〔ˏspɛʃəlɪ`zeʃən〕 名 特別化，專門化，限定

This store specializes in winter camping equipment.
這間店專賣冬季露營配備。

especial
e + special

▶ 〔ɪs`pɛʃəl〕 形 特別的，特殊的，特有的

especially
especial + ly

▶ 〔ə`spɛʃəlɪ〕 副 特別，尤其，主要，專門地

My whole family, especially my mother, gets excited about Christmas.
我的家人對聖誕節感到非常興奮，特別是我的母親。

species spec + ies	▶	〔ˋspiʃiz〕 名　種類，（生物的）種 many species of snakes「許多種類的蛇」
specify spec + ify	▶	〔ˋspɛsə͵faɪ〕 動　具體指定，詳細說明
specification specify + tion	▶	〔͵spɛsəfəˋkeʃən〕 名　載明，詳述， （產品的）說明書，明細單
specific specify + ic	▶	〔spɪˋsɪfɪk〕 形　特殊的，特定的，明確的，具體的
specifically specific + ly	▶	〔spɪˋsɪfɪḳlɪ〕 副　特別地，明確地，具體地

The teacher did not specify which questions she wanted us to do for homework.　老師沒有明確說明我們功課要做哪幾題。
What, specifically, is your complaint?
你到底是在抱怨什麼事情？

respect re + spect	▶	〔rɪˋspɛkt〕 動　尊敬，敬重，重視，遵守， 關於，涉及 名　尊敬，敬重，敬意，問候，重視，關係，方面 with respect to～「有關～」
respective respect + ive	▶	〔rɪˋspɛktɪv〕 形　分別的，各自的
respectively respective + ly	▶	〔rɪˋspɛktɪvlɪ〕 副　分別地，各自地
respectful respect + ful	▶	〔rɪˋspɛktfəl〕 形　恭敬的，尊敬人的，尊重人的
respectable respect + able	▶	〔rɪˋspɛktəbl̩〕 形　值得尊敬的，名聲好的， 體面的，可觀的，相當的

When she greeted her old teacher, her voice was filled with warmth and respect.　問候年邁的老師時，她的聲音充滿溫暖和敬意。
He was offered a job with a respectable salary.
他得到一個薪水相當可觀的工作機會。

| **despise**
de + spise | ▶ | 〔dɪˋspaɪz〕 動　鄙視，輕視，看不起
（同義）look down (up)on～「看低～，看不起～」
（反義）respect＝look up to～「尊敬～，敬重～」 |

despicable
despise + able

▶ 〔ˋdɛspɪkəbl〕 形　卑鄙的，卑劣的，可鄙的

Rosemary and Fred were in love, but Fred's mother was so despicable that Rosemary couldn't go through with the wedding.
蘿絲瑪莉和佛烈德彼此相愛，但是佛烈德的母親實在太過卑鄙，所以蘿絲瑪莉無法完成婚禮。

prospect
pro + spect

▶ 〔ˋprɑspɛkt〕 名　指望，預期，可能性，前景，景色，視野
in prospect「考慮中」

prospective
prospect + ive

▶ 〔prəˋspɛktɪv〕 形　預期的，盼望中的，未來的，即將發生的

He searched for a job for weeks, but found no interesting prospects.
他找工作找了好幾個禮拜，可是沒有找到適合的工作。
She did not impress her prospective employers by being late for the interview.
她面試遲到，並未讓未來的雇主留下深刻印象。

8　rupt　斷，破，破壞

008

interrupt
inter + rupt

▶ 〔͵ɪntəˋrʌpt〕 動　打斷（講話），中斷，打擾

interruption
interrupt + ion

▶ 〔͵ɪntəˋrʌpʃən〕 名　阻礙，打擾，干擾，休止

It's usually considered rude to interrupt someone while he or she is speaking.
一般認為在他人說話時打斷談話是不禮貌的。

corrupt
co + rupt

▶ 〔kəˋrʌpt〕 動　墮落，腐敗，貪污
形　墮落的

corruption
corrupt + ion

▶ 〔kəˋrʌpʃən〕 名　墮落，腐化，貪污，賄賂

Everyone knew that the politician was corrupt, but no one could find the evidence to prove it.
每個人都知道那個政客貪污，但是沒有人能夠找到他貪污的證據。

bankrupt bank + rupt	▶	〔ˋbæŋkrʌpt〕 名　破產者 形　破產的 動　使破產，使貧窮 go/become bankrupt「破產」＝go into bankruptcy＝fall into bankruptcy
bankruptcy bankrupt + cy	▶	〔ˋbæŋkrəpsɪ〕 名　破產，倒閉，徹底失敗

The company fell into bankruptcy after several years of poor management. 由於數年來的經營不善，那間公司宣佈破產。

erupt e + rupt	▶	〔ɪˋrʌpt〕 動　噴出，爆發
eruption erupt + ion	▶	〔ɪˋrʌpʃən〕 名　火山爆發，熔岩噴出， （感情的）爆發

Mt. Fuji has been dormant for many years, but it may erupt again some day.
雖然富士山維持休火山的狀態已經好幾年了，但是它將來還是有可能會再爆發。

⑨ lat(e)　傳送，運送，轉移

009

relate re + late	▶	〔rɪˋlet〕 動　講，敘述，有關，涉及 be related to～「和～有關」 relate～to...「使～和…有關聯」
relation relate + ion	▶	〔rɪˋleʃən〕 名　關係，關聯，（國家、團體之間的） 關係，血緣關係，敘述的事 in relation to...「關於…」
relationship relation + ship	▶	〔rɪˋleʃənʃɪp〕 名　關係，關聯，人際關係， 親屬關係，戀愛關係

The professor tries to give real-life examples that students can relate to.
那位教授試著舉出現實生活中跟學生相關的例子。

relative relate + ive	▶	〔ˋrɛlətɪv〕 名 親戚，親屬 形 相對的，比較的，相關的，相應的
relatively relative + ly	▶	〔ˋrɛlətɪvlɪ〕 副 相對地，相當地，比較而言
relativity relative + ity	▶	〔͵rɛləˋtɪvətɪ〕 名 相關性，相對性，相對論 Relativity「相對論」

Although they both have the last name of Jones they are not relatives.
雖然他們兩個人都姓瓊斯，但是他們不是親戚。

---

⑩ terr　　陸地，土地，地面

010

territory terr + ory	▶	〔ˋtɛrə͵torɪ〕 名 領土，領地，版圖，地區， 區域，領域，範圍
territorial territory + ial	▶	〔͵tɛrəˋtorɪəl〕 形 領土的，土地的，地區的， 區域的

American street gangs often mark their territory with a symbol or a sign.
美國的街頭幫派常用標誌或是記號來劃分地盤。

terrestrial terr + ial	▶	〔təˋrɛstrɪəl〕 形 地球的，陸地的，人間的，俗世的 terrestrial animals「陸棲動物」
extraterrestrial extra + terrestrial	▶	〔͵ɛkstrətəˋrɛstrɪəl〕 形 地球外的，大氣圈外的 extraterrestrial beings「外星人，地球外生物」

Some terrestrial plants will die if they have too much water.
有些陸棲植物如果澆太多水會造成它們枯萎。

---

⑪ terr　　怕，驚嚇，驚恐

011

terror terr + or	▶	〔ˋtɛrə〕 名 恐怖，驚駭，引起（別人） 恐懼的事物或人 terror＝對實際危險事物感到的恐懼 horror〔ˋhɑrə〕＝對超自然事物、無實體的事物感到 的恐懼

terrorism
terror + ism

▶　〔ˋtɛrəˌrɪzəm〕 图　恐怖主義，恐怖行動，
　　　　　　　　　　　 恐怖統治，恐怖手段

terrorist
terror + ist

▶　〔ˋtɛrərɪst〕 图　恐怖主義者，恐怖分子

Her eyes were open wide with terror as the car suddenly went out of control.
車子突然失去控制時，她因為恐懼而睜大雙眼。

terrify
terr + ify

▶　〔ˋtɛrəˌfaɪ〕 動　使恐怖，使害怕
　　terrify（人）into V-ing
　　「使（人）受到恐懼威脅而～」

He let out a terrifying scream when the mouse ran over his foot.
老鼠從他腳上跑過去時他嚇得驚聲尖叫。

terrific
terrify + ic

▶　〔təˋrɪfɪk〕 形　可怕的，嚇人的，極度的，
　　　　　　　　　　 非常好的，了不起的

I felt terrific pain in my side, but I had to keep running. The men in black were just behind me.
我感到肋邊劇烈疼痛，但我得繼續跑，因為黑衣人在我身後緊追不捨。
We had a terrific time in New Zealand.
我們在紐西蘭渡過了美好的時光。

terrible
terr + ible

▶　〔ˋtɛrəbl〕 形　可怕的，極度的，嚴重的，糟糕的，
　　　　　　　　　 令人討厭的

terribly
terrible + ly

▶　〔ˋtɛrəblɪ〕 副　可怕地，非常地
　　terribly也可用在具正面意義的句子。
　　（例）speak English terribly well
　　　　　英語說得非常流利

I had the most terrible nightmare last night, and I woke up in a cold sweat.
我昨天作了個非常可怕的惡夢，醒來時出了一身冷汗。
I'm not terribly happy about it, but there's nothing that can be done.
我不是非常滿意，但這也是沒辦法的事情。

12 over 超過

overcome
over + come

▶ 〔ˌovɚˋkʌm〕 動
戰勝，克服，勝過

*over*come

She had to overcome her fear of flying when she travelled to Australia.
她到澳洲旅行的時候必須克服她對飛行的恐懼。

---

overeat
over + eat

▶ 〔ˋovɚˋit〕 動　過食，吃得過多，吃得過飽
overeat oneself「吃得太飽」
「吃太多～（蛋糕、肉等）」的說法，並不能用
「overeat～」，要用「eat～too much」才是。

I always overeat at Christmas dinner, and then I feel sick afterwards.
我總是在聖誕節晚餐的時候吃得太多，然後在那之後感到不舒服。

---

overhear
over + hear

▶ 〔ˌovɚˋhɪr〕 動　偶然聽到，無意中聽到，偷聽到
eavesdrop〔ˋivzˌdrɑp〕 動　竊聽（刻意的）

Did you overhear what she just said about you?
你有聽到她剛才怎麼說你的嗎？

---

overlook
over + look

▶ 〔ˌovɚˋluk〕 動　眺望，俯瞰，忽略，漏看，寬容，
照顧，監視

I'm afraid you've overlooked some important points.
我擔心你漏看了一些重點。
Does your hotel room overlook the ocean?
從你的飯店房間可以看見大海嗎？

---

overtake
over + take

▶ 〔ˌovɚˋtek〕 動　追上，超過，突然侵襲，突然發生

I was last in the race on the second lap, but by the time I got to the finish line, I was able to overtake three of the four other runners.
比賽進行到第二圈的時候我只是最後一名，但是到達終點線時，我成功追過其他四名選手中的三位。

overwhelm over + whelm ▶	〔͵ovɚˋhwɛlm〕動　戰勝，征服，壓倒，覆蓋，淹沒，使不知所措 overwhelm（人）with～「～使（人）不知所措」
overwhelming overwhelm + ing ▶	〔͵ovɚˋhwɛlmɪŋ〕形　壓倒的，壓倒性的，勢不可擋的

The actress was overwhelmed with emotions when she won the prestigious award.
那位女演員獲頒榮譽獎項時感動得無以名狀。

overseas over + sea + s ▶	〔ˋovɚˋsiz〕形　（在）海外的，（在）國外的 副　在（或向）海外，在（或向）國外

Sue has been living overseas for nearly five years now.
蘇在國外已住了將近五年。

⓭ pos(it)　pon(e)　pose　放置　★ 013

position posit + ion ▶	〔pəˋzɪʃən〕名　位置，地點，姿態，地位，身分，立場，態度

I'm thinking of applying for a position as the general manager of marketing.　我正考慮申請行銷總經理這個職位。

postpone post + pone ▶	〔postˋpon〕動　延期，延遲，延緩
postponement postpone + ment ▶	〔postˋponmənt〕名　延期，延緩

The party will be postponed due to bad weather.
由於天氣惡劣，派對將會延期。
Janice had to postpone her trip to Greece because she lost her passport the day before she was scheduled to leave.
由於在預定出發的前一天遺失護照，珍妮絲必須延後前往希臘旅行的計劃。

pose

〔poz〕動　擺姿勢，假裝，提出，造成
▶ pose as〜「假裝、冒充是〜」
pose a problem「引起、造成問題」

The group of tourists posed for a picture in front of the Eiffel Tower.
那群觀光客在艾菲爾鐵塔前擺好姿勢準備照相。

Sam going out of town will pose a slight problem for our plans of a surprise birthday party for him.
山姆出城會為我們替他辦生日驚喜派對的計劃帶來點問題。

The committee had a lot of complaints, but when I posed the question "how do we fix the problem?", they had nothing to say.
委員會有許多抱怨，但是當我提出「我們該如何解決問題」的疑問時，他們卻又默不作聲。

propose
pro + pose

〔prə`poz〕動　提議，建議，提出，求婚
▶ propose to（人）「向（人）求婚」
propose a toast to（人）「提議為（人）乾杯」

proposal
propose + al

▶ 〔prə`pozl〕名　建議，提議，提案，求婚

I would like to propose a toast to the new couple.
我想帶頭向新人乾杯祝賀。

suppose
sup + pose

▶ 〔sə`poz〕動　猜想，以為，認為應該，假定

supposedly
suppose + ed + ly

▶ 〔sə`pozɪdlɪ〕副　大概，可能，據稱

supposition
suppose + tion

▶ 〔͵sʌpə`zɪʃən〕名　想像，假定，看法，見解

Who do you suppose made all this mess?
你覺得是誰造成這一團糟的？

compose
com + pose

▶ 〔kəm`poz〕動　作（文章、曲等），組成，構成

composer
compose + er

▶ 〔kəm`pozɚ〕名　作者，作曲家

composition
compose + tion
▶ 〔͵kɑmpə`zɪʃən〕 名 寫作，作曲，作品，樂曲，構成

component
compose + ent
▶ 〔kəm`ponənt〕 名 構成要素，零件，成分

The Moonlight Sonata is one of Beethoven's most popular compositions for piano.
月光奏鳴曲是貝多芬最受歡迎的鋼琴曲之一。

expose
ex + pose
▶ 〔ɪk`spoz〕 動 暴露，接觸，揭露，（底片）曝光，使看得見

exposure
expose + ure
▶ 〔ɪk`spoʒɚ〕 名 暴露，曝曬，揭露，陳列，曝光

The investigative reporter exposed the politician's evil plan.
調查的記者揭發了那個政客的邪惡計劃。

positive
posit + ive
▶ 〔`pɑzətɪv〕 形 確定的，確信的，絕對的，正面的，陽性的
（反義）negative

positively
positive + ly
▶ 〔`pɑzətɪvlɪ〕 副 明確地，堅決地，斷然，肯定地，正面地

This is positively the best onsen I've ever visited.
這肯定是我去過的溫泉中最棒的了。（onsen=hot spring）
If you look at things in a positive light, you might find that things are not as bad as you thought.
如果你用積極的觀點看待事物，你可能會發現事情沒有你想像的那麼糟。

dispose
dis + pose
▶ 〔dɪ`spoz〕 動 配置，佈置，處置，處理
dispose of～「解決、處理～（事情或問題），除去、扔掉～」

disposable
dispose + able
▶ 〔dɪ`spozəbl〕 形 可任意處理的，用完即可丟棄的，一次性使用的
a disposable cigarette lighter「拋棄式打火機」

disposal
dispose + al
▶ 〔dɪ`spozl〕 名 處理，處置，配置

Be sure to dispose of the packaging in the proper receptacles.
請務必將包裝紙等廢棄物丟棄在正確的垃圾箱內。

Disposable goods are very convenient, but very harmful to the environment. 拋棄式商品非常便利，但是對環境傷害甚劇。

purpose pur + pose	▶ 〔`pɝpəs〕 图　目的，意圖，用途，效果
purposely purpose + ly	▶ 〔`pɝpəslɪ〕 副　故意地，蓄意地

She purposely forgot to wash the filthy frying pan, hoping that her mother would not notice.
她故意忘記洗髒掉的煎鍋，希望她的母親不會注意到。

What is your purpose for visiting Hong Kong?
你到香港的目的是什麼？

14　op　反對

014

oppose op + pose	▶ 〔ə`poz〕 動　反對，反抗，妨礙，使對抗 be opposed to～「反對～」
opposition oppose + tion	▶ 〔͵ɑpə`zɪʃən〕 图　反對，對抗，敵對，對立
opposite op + posit	▶ 〔`ɑpəzɪt〕 形　相反的，對立的，對面的，相對的

I oppose the death penalty. = I'm opposed to the death penalty.
我反對死刑。

If there is no opposition to this plan, then we will go forward with it.
如果對這個計劃沒有任何異議，那麼我們接下來將按照計劃進行。

opponent oppose + ent	▶ 〔ə`ponənt〕 图　對手，敵手，反對者

The boxer shook hands with his opponent, and then as the bell rang, punched him in the face.
賽前那位拳擊手跟他的對手握手，但是當比賽鈴聲一響起，他馬上朝對手的臉揮拳猛擊。

⑮ fence　fend　fens(e)　打擊，保衛 ⭐ 015

fence	▶ 〔fɛns〕 名　柵欄，籬笆 　動　用柵欄圍起來
offend of + fend	▶ 〔əˋfɛnd〕 動　冒犯，觸怒，犯錯 offend against～「違反～，犯～」
offense of + fense	▶ 〔əˋfɛns〕 名　犯法，過錯，冒犯，進攻 a traffic offense「違反交通規則」 a first (previous, repeated) offense「初犯 　（前科犯，累犯）」 commit an offense against～「違反～，犯～」
offensive offense + ive	▶ 〔əˋfɛnsɪv〕 形　冒犯的，唐突的，討厭的， 　進攻性的
defend de + fend	▶ 〔dɪˋfɛnd〕 動　防禦，保衛，為…辯護 defend～from/against…「保護～免於…的傷害」
defendant defend + ant	▶ 〔dɪˋfɛndənt〕 名　被告 （反義）plaintiff〔ˋplentɪf〕 名　原告
defense de + fense	▶ 〔dɪˋfɛns〕 名　防禦，保衛，防護，辯護 the Self-Defense Forces「自衛隊」
defensive defense + ive	▶ 〔dɪˋfɛnsɪv〕 形　防禦的，保護的，防禦用的

I hope I didn't offend you when I said you had gained weight.
我希望我說你變胖時沒有冒犯到你。

She became very defensive when she was accused of taking money from the company.
她被指控盜用公款時變得防衛心很重。

⑯ medi　間，中間 ⭐ 016

medieval medi + eval	▶ 〔ˌmɪdɪˋivəl〕 形　中世紀的，中古的，老式的 medieval times＝Middle Ages「中世紀」

People often think of medieval times as romantic times with castles and knights, but in actuality, life was quite hard.
提起中世紀，人們常認為那是個有城堡和騎士的浪漫時代，但實際上當時的生活頗為困苦。

---

medium
medi + um

〔`midɪəm〕名　中間，適中，媒體，工具，手法
形　中間的，適中的
（名詞複數）media〔`midɪə〕名　大眾傳播媒體＝ mass media（訊息來源和觀眾兩者之間的媒介）

Medium is the size that falls between small and large.
M號是S號和L號中間的尺寸。

Hiro Yamagata has adopted the medium of silkscreen for most of his works.
山形博導大多數的作品都是用絲幕的手法作成。

---

intermediate
inter + medi + ate

〔ˌɪntɚ`midɪət〕形　中間的，中型的，中級的

Katie has been placed in the intermediate German class.
凱蒂被分到中級德文班。

Mediterranean
medi + terr + nean

〔ˌmɛdətə`renɪən〕名
the Mediterranean
地中海（陸地跟陸地之間的海）

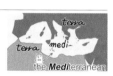

The Mediterranean Sea is a sea between two large landmasses.
地中海是位於兩大陸之間的海洋。

---

immediate
im + medi + ate

〔ɪ`midɪɪt〕形　立即的，目前的，當下的

immediately
immediate + ly

〔ɪ`midɪɪtlɪ〕副　立即，馬上，直接地

She took an immediate liking to her new colleagues.
她馬上就喜歡上新同事了。

If you get a flat tire, you need to stop the car immediately.
如果你的車子爆胎，你必須馬上停車。

(si)st　立，站立

017

stable st + able	▶ 〔`stebḷ〕 [形] 穩定的，牢固的，可靠的
stability stable + ity	▶ 〔stə`bɪlətɪ〕 [名] 穩定，安定，堅定，恆心
stabilize stable + ize	▶ 〔`stebḷ⸴aɪz〕 [動] 使穩定，使穩固
unstable un + stable	▶ 〔ʌn`stebḷ〕 [形] 不穩固的，不牢靠的，動盪的

His condition will soon stabilize if he stays in the hospital overnight.
如果他在醫院住上一晚，病情應該很快就會穩定下來。

insist in + sist	▶ 〔ɪn`sɪst〕 [動] 堅持，堅決認為，堅決主張
insistent insist + ent	▶ 〔ɪn`sɪstənt〕 [形] 堅持的，持續的，急切的
insistently insistent + ly	▶ 〔ɪn`sɪstəntlɪ〕 [副] 堅持地，強求地，緊急地
insistence insist + ence	▶ 〔ɪn`sɪstəns〕 [名] 堅持，強調，堅決要求

Lisa insisted that I stay for dinner.
麗莎堅持要我留下來用晚餐。

obstinate ob + st + ate	▶ 〔`abstənɪt〕 [形] 頑固的，固執的，頑強的， 不屈服的
obstinately obstinate + ly	▶ 〔`abstənɪtlɪ〕 [副] 頑固地，固執地
obstinacy obstinate + cy	▶ 〔`abstənəsɪ〕 [名] 頑固，固執，頑強

She obstinately refused to answer the phone even though she knew her boyfriend was calling to apologize for being late.
她執拗地拒接電話，儘管她知道那是她男友為了遲到而打來道歉的。

assist as + sist	▶	〔ə`sɪst〕 動　幫助，協助 名　幫助，棒球的助殺
assistant assist + ant	▶	〔ə`sɪstənt〕 名　助手，助理，輔助物
assistance assist + ance	▶	〔ə`sɪstəns〕 名　援助，幫助

If you need assistance, please call the receptionist at the front desk.
如果您需要任何的幫助，請打電話給服務台的接待員。

consist con + sist	▶	〔kən`sɪst〕 動　組成，構成，一致，符合 consist of～　由～構成
consistent consist + ent	▶	〔kən`sɪstənt〕 形　前後一致的，相符合的 be consistent with～「與～相符合」
consistency consistent + cy	▶	〔kən`sɪstənsɪ〕 名　濃度，黏稠度，一致，符合
consistently consistent + ly	▶	〔kən`sɪstəntlɪ〕 副　一貫地，固守地
inconsistent in + consistent	▶	〔ˌɪnkən`sɪstənt〕 形　不一致的，不協調的， 前後矛盾的
inconsistency inconsistent + cy	▶	〔ˌɪnkən`sɪstənsɪ〕 名　不一致，不協調，前後矛盾
inconsistently inconsistent + ly	▶	〔ˌɪnkən`sɪstəntlɪ〕 副　不一致地

Mayonnaise consists of egg-yolks, oil, and vinegar.
美乃滋的成份包含蛋黃、油以及醋。

The recipe cautioned that the batter should have a thick consistency, or the muffins would not bake properly.
這份食譜強調麵糊要濃稠，否則馬芬會烤不成功。

instant in + st + ant	▶	〔`ɪnstənt〕 形　立即的，迫切的 名　瞬間，一剎那
instantly instant + ly	▶	〔`ɪnstəntlɪ〕 副　立即，馬上
instance instant + ce	▶	〔`ɪnstəns〕 名　例子，情況，場合 for instance＝for example「例如」

The fireman heard the bell, and in an instant, he was out the door.
那位消防員聽到警鈴響起，轉眼間人就已經在門外了。

distant di + st + ant	▶	〔ˋdɪstənt〕 [形]　遙遠的，久遠的，疏遠的
distance distant + ce	▶	〔ˋdɪstəns〕 [名]　距離，路程，遠處，疏遠

They could see the lights of the city off in the distance.
他們能看見遠方城市的燈光熄滅。

institute in + st + itute	▶	〔ˋɪnstətjut〕 [動]　創立，開始 [名]　學校，學院，大學，研究所
institution institute + ion	▶	〔͵ɪnstəˋtjuʃən〕 [名]　制度，習俗，機構，建立
institutional institution + al	▶	〔͵ɪnstəˋtjuʃənḷ〕 [形]　制度的，機構的，習慣的
institutionalize institutional + ize	▶	〔͵ɪnstəˋtjuʃənḷ͵aɪz〕 [動]　使成為機構，制度化， 將…收容在公共機構內

Timothy goes to school at a technological institute.
提摩西在一所科技大學唸書。

Bill was finally institutionalized for repeatedly attempting to set his hair on fire.
比爾最後因為一再企圖放火燒自己的頭髮而被送到收容所去。

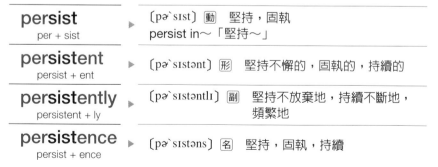

persist per + sist	▶	〔pɚˋsɪst〕 [動]　堅持，固執 persist in～「堅持～」
persistent persist + ent	▶	〔pɚˋsɪstənt〕 [形]　堅持不懈的，固執的，持續的
persistently persistent + ly	▶	〔pɚˋsɪstəntlɪ〕 [副]　堅持不放棄地，持續不斷地， 頻繁地
persistence persist + ence	▶	〔pɚˋsɪstəns〕 [名]　堅持，固執，持續

Persistence seems to have paid off; Lana finally agreed to go out with Troy when he had asked her out for the 25th time.
看來堅持不懈終究是有代價的，拉娜在特洛伊第25次約她時終於答應跟他出去約會。

resist re + sist	▶	〔rɪˋzɪst〕 動 抵抗，抗拒，忍耐
resistible resist + ible	▶	〔rɪˋzɪstəbl〕 形 可抵抗的
irresistible ir + resistible	▶	〔⋅ɪrɪˋzɪstəbl〕 形 不可抗拒的，富有魅力的
resistant resist + ant	▶	〔rɪˋzɪstənt〕 形 抵抗的，防…的 water-resistant 防水的
resistance resistant + ce	▶	〔rɪˋzɪstəns〕 名 抵抗，反抗，抵抗力，阻力

She just couldn't resist eating the last piece of the chocolate cake, even though she knew her brother hadn't had any.
即使她知道弟弟還沒吃到巧克力蛋糕，但她就是抗拒不了把最後一塊給吃掉。

18　liter　(近似letter) 字母，文字　
018

literal liter + al	▶	〔ˋlɪtərəl〕 形 照字面的，原義的，如實的
literally literal + ly	▶	〔ˋlɪtərəlɪ〕 副 照字面地，逐字地，正確地，實在地
literary liter + ary	▶	〔ˋlɪtəˌrɛrɪ〕 形 文學的，文藝的，精通文學的，文言的
literature liter + ture	▶	〔ˋlɪtərətʃə〕 名 文學，文學作品，圖書資料

When I said I was so hungry that I could eat a horse, I did not mean it literally!
當我說我餓得可以吃下一匹馬的時候，我不是真的有那個意思！

literacy liter + cy	▶	〔ˋlɪtərəsɪ〕 名 識字，讀寫能力，知識，能力
illiteracy il + literacy	▶	〔ɪˋlɪtərəsɪ〕 名 不識字，文盲，無知，未受教育

literate
liter + ate

▶ 〔`lɪtərɪt〕形　能讀寫的，有文化修養的

illiterate
il + literate

▶ 〔ɪ`lɪtərɪt〕形　文盲的，未受教育的，
語法錯誤多的
his illiterate letter「他錯誤百出的信」

Despite the complexity of the writing system, the literacy rate in Japan is very high.
儘管日本的書寫系統很複雜，但其識字率卻非常高。

19 flow　flu　flood　流動
019

flow

▶ 〔flo〕動　流動，湧出
名　流，流暢，漲潮
flow chart「流程圖，作業圖」

fluid
flu + id

▶ 〔`fluɪd〕名　液體，流質
形　流動的，液體的

fluidity
fluid + ity

▶ 〔flu`ɪdətɪ〕名　流動性

flood

▶ 〔flʌd〕名　洪水，水災，漲潮，大量
動　淹沒，泛濫，充滿

In one fluid motion, she snatched the child from the flames and put out the fire by throwing her jacket on it.
她以流暢的動作，迅速地將孩子從火焰中救出，並用她的夾克把火撲滅。

fluent
flu + ent

▶ 〔`fluənt〕形　流利的，流暢的

fluently
fluent + ly

▶ 〔`fluəntlɪ〕副　流利地，流暢地

fluency
fluent + cy

▶ 〔`fluənsɪ〕名　流暢度，流利度

Wilma has studied several foreign languages, and has reached fluency in three of them.
薇瑪學過好幾種外國語言，而且其中三種已經達到流利的程度了。

influence
in + flu + ence
▶ 〔ˋɪnfluəns〕 名 影響，作用，影響力，勢力
influence on～「對～的影響力」

influential
in + fluent + ial
▶ 〔͵ɪnfluˋɛnʃəl〕 形 有影響力的，有影響的，
有權勢的

influenza
▶ 〔͵ɪnfluˋɛnzə〕 名 流行性感冒
flu〔flu〕名 influenza的縮寫
（口語說法，較常使用）

As children grow older, they should think more for themselves,
and be less under the influence of their parents' opinions.
當孩子年紀漸增，他們應該要更為自己打算，並較不受到父母意見影響。

affluent
af + fluent
▶ 〔ˋæfluənt〕 形 富裕的，豐富的，富饒的

affluence
affluent + ce
▶ 〔ˋæfluəns〕 名 豐富，富裕，流入，湧入

Even though Japan is in a recession, it is still a relatively affluent
country.
雖然現在景氣衰退，但日本仍然是個相當富裕的國家。

⓴ ceed　cess　ced(e)　行走

020

proceed
pro + ceed
▶ 〔prəˋsid〕 動 繼續進行，前進，開始，進行
proceed to～「繼續下去～，開始～」

process
pro + cess
▶ 〔ˋprɑsɛs〕 名 過程，進程，步驟，程序
動 加工，處理，用電腦處理

procedure
proceed + ure
▶ 〔prəˋsidʒə〕 名 程序，手續，步驟

procession
process + ion
▶ 〔prəˋsɛʃən〕 名 行列，隊伍，行進

This operation is a routine procedure, so the probability of
complications is low.
這項手術是例行程序，所以術後併發症的可能性較低。

succeed
suc + ceed
▶ 〔səkˋsid〕 動　成功，接替，繼任，接連

recede
re + cede
▶ 〔rɪˋsid〕 動　後退，遠去，撤回，變模糊

re**ced**ing hairline

He tried to draw attention away from his receding hairline by growing his hair to amazing lengths.
他把頭髮留得超長，企圖藉此轉移眾人對他日漸後退的髮線的注意力。

recess
re + cess
▶ 〔rɪˋsɛs〕 名　休息，休會，休庭，（牆壁等的）凹處，隱蔽處

recession
recess + ion
▶ 〔rɪˋsɛʃən〕 名　後退，退場，撤退，衰退，凹處

The country has been in an economic recession for over ten years.
該國陷入經濟衰退期已超過十年。

The judge ordered a twenty-minute recess.
法官下令休庭二十分鐘。

precede
pre + cede
▶ 〔priˋsid〕 動　處在…之前，高於，領先
precede（人）into～「帶領（人）進入～」

preceding
precede + ing
▶ 〔priˋsidɪŋ〕 形　在前的，在先的，前面的

precedent
precede + ent
▶ 〔ˋprɛsədnt〕 名　先例，慣例，判例
形　在前的，在先的

precedence
precede + ence
▶ 〔ˋprɛsədəns〕 名　居前，領先，優先權
take precedence over～「優先於～，地位高於～」

He later regretted letting parties take precedence over studying.
他後來很後悔自己把派對看得比讀書重要。

The waiter gestured for the guest to precede him into the room.
那位侍者做出手勢帶領客人進入房間。

concede
con + cede
▶ 〔kənˋsid〕動 （勉強）承認，讓步，容許，承認失敗

concession
concede + ion
▶ 〔kənˋsɛʃən〕名 讓步，讓予，承認，特許

Trevor finally conceded that he was wrong.
崔佛最後終於承認自己錯了。

exceed
ex + ceed
▶ 〔ɪkˋsid〕動 超過，勝過，超出

exceedingly
exceed + ing + ly
▶ 〔ɪkˋsidɪŋlɪ〕副 非常地，極度地

excess
ex + cess
▶ 〔ɪkˋsɛs〕名 超過，過量，無節制，過分的行為
形 過量的

Diana's performance exceeded her boss's expectations.
黛安娜的表現超過了上司對她的期待。

Donna's mother was exceedingly happy when Donna was accepted at the university.
唐娜考上大學的時候，她的母親感到非常高興。

 21 **tele** 距離，遠方
021

telegram
tele + gram
▶ 〔ˋtɛləˏgræm〕名 電報

telephone
tele + phone
▶ 〔ˋtɛləˏfon〕名 電話

*tele*phone

television
tele + vision
▶ 〔ˋtɛləˏvɪʒən〕名 電視，電視業

telepathy
tele + pathy
▶ 〔təˋlɛpəθɪ〕名 心靈感應，傳心術

telescope
tele + scope
▶ 〔ˋtɛləˏskop〕名 望遠鏡

telescopic
telescope + ic

▶ 〔ˌtɛləˋskɑpɪk〕 形　望遠鏡的，有先見之明的，伸縮自如的，眼力好的

She stared in disbelief at the telegram informing her she had been caught cheating on her taxes.
她不敢置信地瞪著那份電報，上頭通知她被查出逃漏稅。

 syn　sym　相同
022

sympathy
sym + pathy

▶ 〔ˋsɪmpəθɪ〕 名　同情，同情心，共鳴
（反義）antipathy〔ænˋtɪpəθɪ〕 名　反感，厭惡

sympathize
sympathy + ize

▶ 〔ˋsɪmpəˌθaɪz〕 動　同情，體諒，贊成
sympathize with（人）about～「因～而同情（人）」

sympathetic
sympathy + tic

▶ 〔ˌsɪmpəˋθɛtɪk〕 形　同情的，贊同的

Lawrence has done little to deserve sympathy for the situation he is now in.
勞倫斯現在所處的狀況並不值得同情。
Lucinda wouldn't stop mentioning her antipathy towards her boss.
露辛達不斷提到她對老板的反感。

syndrome
syn + drome

▶ 〔ˋsɪnˌdrom〕 名　併發症，症候群
AIDS＝acquired immune deficiency syndrome
「後天性免疫不全症候群」
Down syndrome「唐氏症」

An irregularity on the 21st chromosome causes Down syndrome.
第21對染色體的變異是引起唐氏症的原因。

symphony
sym + phone + y

▶ 〔ˋsɪmfənɪ〕 名　交響樂，交響樂團，和諧

symbol
sym + bol
▶ 〔ˋsɪmbl〕 名 象徵，標誌，記號，符號

*sym*bol

symbolize
symbol + ize
▶ 〔ˋsɪmbl͵aɪz〕 動 象徵，用符號表示

symbolic
symbol + ic
▶ 〔sɪmˋbɑlɪk〕 形 象徵的，象徵性的，符號的

symptom
sym + ptom
▶ 〔ˋsɪmptəm〕 名 症狀，徵兆，表徵

I think I'll stay home today because I have flu-like symptoms.
我想我今天會待在家裡，因為我出現類似流感的症狀。

In a Christian marriage, wedding rings symbolize a promise of fidelity between a husband and wife.
在基督教的婚姻中，婚戒象徵的是夫妻之間彼此忠實的諾言。

23 **log(ue)**   語言，言詞
023

logic
log + ic
▶ 〔ˋlɑdʒɪk〕 名 邏輯，邏輯學

logical
logic + al
▶ 〔ˋlɑdʒɪkl〕 形 邏輯學的，合邏輯的，合理的

logician
logic + ian
▶ 〔loˋdʒɪʃən〕 名 邏輯學家

She didn't seem to realize that people didn't take her seriously because there was no logic in her complaint.
她似乎不瞭解，大家不把她當一回事是因為她的抱怨毫無邏輯可言。

apologize
apo + log + ize
▶ 〔əˋpɑlə͵dʒaɪz〕 動 道歉，認錯
apologize for V-ing 「為了～道歉」
apologize to（人）for～ 「為了～向（人）道歉」

apology
apo + log + y

▶　〔əˋpɑlədʒɪ〕名　道歉，賠罪

It is customary to accept an apology when one is given.
一般習慣在受到致歉時接受道歉。

 24　## mono　一個，單獨　
024

monotone
mono + tone

▶　〔ˋmɑnə͵ton〕名　單調，單音調

monotonous
monotone + ous

▶　〔məˋnɑtənəs〕形　單調的，無變化的

monotony
monotone + y

▶　〔məˋnɑtənɪ〕名　單調，無變化

Working on an assembly line can be monotonous work.
裝配線上的作業可能是項單調無聊的工作。

To break the monotony of the week, Mitch went out for dinner on Wednesday.
為了排解一週的單調生活，米契在禮拜三晚上外出用餐。

monologue
mono + logue

▶　〔ˋmɑnḷ͵ɔg〕名　獨白，
獨角戲，
長篇大論

No one wants to talk to Peter, because he often lapses into lengthy monologues.
沒人想跟彼得說話，因為他常逕自陷入長篇大論。

monopoly
mono + poly

▶　〔məˋnɑplɪ〕名　獨佔，專賣，壟斷
= exclusive sale
the monopoly prohibition law「獨佔禁止法」

monopolize
monopoly + ize

▶　〔məˋnɑpḷ͵aɪz〕動　壟斷，擁有…的專賣權，獨佔

It is not fair that one student monopolizes the teacher's time when there are 30 other students in the class.
一個學生獨佔老師的時間，對班上其他30個學生是不公平的。

 dia 穿過，兩者之間的
025

dialogue dia + logue	▶	〔ˋdaɪəˌlɔg〕 图 對話，交談
diagonal dia + gon + al	▶	〔daɪˋægən̩〕 形 對角線的，斜的，斜紋的 图 對角線，斜線
diachronic dia + chron + ic	▶	〔ˌdaɪəˋkrɑnɪk〕 形 歷經時間的，歷時的

One of the most difficult things about writing a story is writing realistic yet interesting dialogue.
寫故事最難的事之一，就是在創作實際對話的同時也要使其有趣。

 meter **metr** 測量，距離
026

meter	▶	〔ˋmitə〕 图 公尺
barometer baro + meter	▶	〔bəˋrɑmətə〕 图 氣壓計
thermometer thermo + meter	▶	〔θəˋmɑmətə〕 图 溫度計
diameter dia + meter	▶	〔daɪˋæmətə〕 图 直徑

The helicopter landing circle is 20 feet in diameter.
直昇機降落圈的直徑為20英尺。

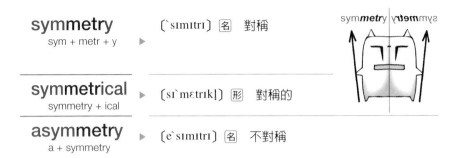

symmetry
sym + metr + y ▶　〔`sɪmɪtrɪ〕名　對稱

symmetrical ▶
symmetry + ical　〔sɪ`mɛtrɪk]〕形　對稱的

asymmetry ▶
a + symmetry　〔e`sɪmɪtrɪ〕名　不對稱

Although each snowflake is unique, they are all similarly symmetrical.
儘管每片雪花都是獨一無二的，但它們在形狀上卻同樣地對稱。

27　care　cur(e)　注意，照料
027

care ▶
〔kɛr〕名　看護，照料，憂慮
　　　動　關心，擔心，關懷，照顧，在乎
take care of～「照顧～，處理～」
care for～「照料～，計較～，
（用於疑問句・否定句）喜歡～」

careful ▶
care + ful　〔`kɛrfəl〕形　仔細的，小心的，徹底的

careless ▶
care + less　〔`kɛrlɪs〕形　粗心的，草率的，隨便的，
　　　　　　漫不經心的

carefully ▶
careful + ly　〔`kɛrfəlɪ〕副　小心謹慎地，仔細地

carelessly ▶
careless + ly　〔`kɛrlɪslɪ〕副　粗心大意地，草率地

The shop assistant carefully wrapped the glasses so they wouldn't break.
店員小心翼翼地將玻璃杯包裝起來以防破裂。

curious ▶
cur + ous　〔`kjʊrɪəs〕形　好奇的
be curious to V「對～感到好奇、有興趣」

curiosity
curious + ity

▶ 〔ˌkjʊrɪˋɑsətɪ〕 名　好奇心，
古玩

Monkeys are naturally curious animals.
猴子是天性好奇的動物。

Just out of curiosity, how long have you been a member of the American Bonsai Club?
純粹好奇問一下，你加入美國盆栽俱樂部有多久了？

accurate
ac + cur + ate

▶ 〔ˋækjərɪt〕 形　準確的，精確的

accurately
accurate + ly

▶ 〔ˋækjərɪtlɪ〕 副　準確地，精確地

accuracy
accurate + cy

▶ 〔ˋækjərəsɪ〕 名　正確性，準確性

inaccurate
in + accurate

▶ 〔ɪnˋækjərɪt〕 形　不正確的，不精確的

inaccurately
inaccurate + ly

▶ 〔ɪnˋækjərɪtlɪ〕 副　不正確地，不精確地

inaccuracy
inaccurate + cy

▶ 〔ɪnˋækjərəsɪ〕 名　不正確，不精確

In order to improve your typing skills, you need to work on both speed and accuracy.
為了提升打字技巧，你必須同時加強速度和準確度。

cure

▶ 〔kjʊr〕 名　治療，療法
動　治癒，糾正，治療

There is still no cure for the common cold.
目前仍然沒有治療感冒的良方。

secure
se + cure

▶ 〔sɪˋkjʊr〕 形　安全的，穩當的，被妥善保管的

security
secure + ity

▶ 〔sɪˋkjʊrətɪ〕 名 安全，防護，保證，保障，證券

insecure
in + secure

▶ 〔ˏɪnsɪˋkjʊr〕 形 不安全的，有危險的，不穩定的

The bank tightened security after the attempted robbery.
銀行在搶劫未遂案件發生後加強了保安。

 man   main   手
028

manual
man + al

▶ 〔ˋmænjʊəl〕 形 用手操作的，手工的
名 手冊，簡介

manually
manual + ly

▶ 〔ˋmænjʊəlɪ〕 副 用手地，手工地

The reason it isn't working is because you didn't read the instruction manual. 沒辦法運作的原因是因為你沒有先讀過使用說明書。
Because Lilly learned to drive using a car with an automatic transmission, she has trouble driving cars with manual transmissions.
莉莉學的是自排車，因此開手排車對她來說有困難。

manage
man + age

▶ 〔ˋmænɪdʒ〕 動 管理，經營，處理
manage to V「設法做到～，努力完成～」

manager
manage + er

▶ 〔ˋmænɪdʒɚ〕 名 經理，負責人，經紀人

management
manage + ment

▶ 〔ˋmænɪdʒmənt〕 名 管理，經營，處理

How did you manage to eat a liter of ice cream?
你怎麼有辦法吃掉一公升的冰淇淋？

manifest
man + fest

▶ 〔ˋmænəˏfɛst〕 形 顯示的，明白的
動 表明，顯示，表露

manifesto
man + fest

▶ 〔ˏmænəˋfɛsto〕 名 宣言，告示

Her joy at finally being set free manifested itself in her vivid paintings.
終於得到自由的喜悅呈現在她生動的畫作裡。

manipulate
man + pulate
▶ 〔məˋnɪpjəˏlet〕 動 操作，運用，操縱

manipulative
manipulate + ive
▶ 〔məˋnɪpjəˏletɪv〕 形 操作的，巧妙處理的

manipulation
manipulate + ion
▶ 〔məˏnɪpjuˋleʃən〕 名 操作，運用，竄改

manicure
man + cure
▶ 〔ˋmænɪˏkjʊr〕 名 動 修指甲

Exciting new technology makes it possible to manipulate your computer with your voice.
令人振奮的新科技使人們得以用聲音操作電腦。

manufacture
man + facture
▶ 〔ˏmænjəˋfæktʃə〕 名 製造，製造業，產品
動 製造，捏造

manufacturer
manufacture + er
▶ 〔ˏmænjəˋfæktʃərə〕 名 製造業者，廠商

The manufacturer had to recall all the defective products.
廠商必須回收所有的瑕疵商品。

maintain
main + tain
▶ 〔menˋten〕 動 維持，保持，維修，保養

maintenance
maintain + ance
▶ 〔ˋmentənəns〕 名 維持，保持，維修，保養

Donna and Denise have maintained their friendship for over 30 years.
唐娜和丹妮絲的友誼已經維持超過30年了。
The owner of the apartment building, not the tenants, is responsible for maintenance.
公寓的所有人，並非房客，有責任負責公寓的維修。

29 ped　腳，足
029

pedal
ped + al
▶ 〔ˋpɛdl〕 名 踏板 形 足的，踏板的，腳踏的
動 騎腳踏車

| **pedestrian**
ped + ian | ▶ | 〔pə`dɛstrɪən〕 名　行人，步行者 |

| **pedicure**
ped + cure | ▶ | 〔`pɛdɪˌkjʊr〕 名　足部治療，修趾甲 |

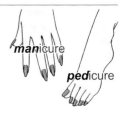

| **pedigree**
ped + degree | ▶ | 〔`pɛdəˌgri〕 名　家譜，血統，出身 |

She pedaled her bike as hard as she could, and was panting by the time she reached the top of the hill.
她使盡全力踩腳踏車，等她到了山頂時，已經氣喘吁吁。

 30 cent　百
030

| **century**
cent + ry | ▶ | 〔`sɛntʃʊrɪ〕 名　世紀，一百年 |

| **centimeter**
cent + meter | ▶ | 〔`sɛntəˌmitɚ〕 名　公分 |

| **percent**
per + cent | ▶ | 〔pɚ`sɛnt〕 名　百分之一，百分比 |

| **percentage**
percent + age | ▶ | 〔pɚ`sɛntɪdʒ〕 名　百分比，比例 |

| **centipede**
cent + ped | ▶ | 〔`sɛntəˌpid〕 名　蜈蚣 |

"Would I like to go out with you?" said Lucy incredulously. "Not in this century!"
露西不敢相信地說：「我願不願意跟你出去約會？絕對不可能！」
【註】not in this century＝「這個世紀都不可能」＝「絕對不可能」

31 mile　mill　千
031

mile	▶ 〔maɪl〕名 英里，哩（約1609公尺）
mileage mile + age	▶ 〔`maɪlɪdʒ〕名 總英里數，行駛哩數
millennium mill + ennium	▶ 〔mɪ`lɛnɪəm〕名 千年期，千禧年
millimeter mill + meter	▶ 〔`mɪləˌmitə〕名 公釐，毫米
million mill + ion	▶ 〔`mɪljən〕名 百萬，百萬元，無數 millions of ～s「無數的～，很多的～」
millionaire million + aire	▶ 〔ˌmɪljən`ɛr〕名 百萬富翁

There are millions of species of insects.
世上有無數種昆蟲。

32 onym　名字，言詞
032

synonym syn + onym	▶ 〔`sɪnəˌnɪm〕名 同義字，類義字
antonym ant + onym	▶ 〔`æntəˌnɪm〕名 反義字
pseudonym pseudo + onym	▶ 〔`sudn̩ˌɪm〕名 假名，筆名
anonym an + onym	▶ 〔`ænəˌnɪm〕名 假名，匿名者，無名氏
anonymous anonym + ous	▶ 〔ə`nɑnəməs〕形 匿名的，作者不明的， 來源不明的
homonym homo + onym	▶ 〔`hɑməˌnɪm〕名 同音異義字，同形異義字， 同形同音異義字

Emily Bronte published her first stories under a pseudonym.
愛蜜莉‧勃朗特使用筆名發表她早期的作品。

"Two," "too," and "to" are homonyms.
"two"、"too"，還有"to"都是同音異義字。

33 acro　頂端，高的位置

033

acronym
acro + onym

▶ 〔ˋækrənɪm〕名 首字母縮略字，頭字語（每個字第一個字母的縮寫，如北大西洋公約組織NATO，以及聯合國教育科學與文化組織UNESCO）

acrobat
acro + bat

▶ 〔ˋækrəbæt〕名 雜技演員，特技演員

acrobatic
acrobat + ic

▶ 〔͵ækrəˋbætɪk〕形 雜技的，特技的

NATO is an acronym for North Atlantic Treaty Organization.
NATO是北大西洋公約組織的縮略字。

34 reg(ul)　規則，法律

034

regular
regul + ar

▶ 〔ˋrɛgjələ〕形 規則的，固定的，定期的

regularly
regular + ly

▶ 〔ˋrɛgjələlɪ〕副 規則地，有規律地，定期地

irregular
ir + regular

▶ 〔ɪˋrɛgjələ〕形 不規則的，無規律的，非定期的

irregularly
irregular + ly

▶ 〔ɪˋrɛgjələlɪ〕副 不規則地

They've been meeting for coffee regularly for over five years.
他們定期的咖啡聚會已經持續超過5年了。

She has become a regular visitor to the art museum.
她成了美術館的常客。

---

regulate
regul + ate

▶ 〔ˋrɛgjəˏlet〕 動　管理，控制，調整

regulation
regulate + ion

▶ 〔ˏrɛgjəˋleʃən〕 名　規章，規則，管理，調整

It's against regulations, but if you promise not to tell anyone, I'll
let you give the monkey a banana.
雖然這違反規則，但如果你答應不告訴別人，我就讓你餵猴子吃香蕉。

The temperature in the computer room must be carefully regulated.
電腦室的溫度必須小心控管。

---

region
reg + ion

▶ 〔ˋridʒən〕 名　地區，領域，範圍

regional
region + al

▶ 〔ˋridʒənl〕 形　地區的，局部的

He comes from a mountainous region of the country, and does
not like the flatness of the plains.
他來自該國的山區地帶，所以不喜歡平原的單調平坦。

35 clos(e)　clud(e)　clus　　關閉　035

---

close

▶ 〔kloz〕 動　關閉，封閉，結束

---

enclose
en + close

▶ 〔ɪnˋkloz〕 動　圈住，圈起，關閉，封入

---

enclosure
enclose + ure

▶ 〔ɪnˋkloʒɚ〕 名　圍住，封入，圈地

---

disclose
dis + close

▶ 〔dɪsˋkloz〕 動　顯露，揭發，透露，公開

Sharon doesn't like going to the zoo because she thinks the animals' enclosures are much too small and cruel.
雪倫不喜歡去動物園，因為她覺得圍欄太小，對動物來說太殘忍了。

The counselor was fired on grounds of disclosing his patients' confidential information.
那名顧問因洩露病人的機密資訊而遭解雇。

include in + clude	▶	〔ɪn`klud〕 動　包括，包含，包含至⋯裡面
inclusive include + ive	▶	〔ɪn`klusɪv〕 形　包含的，包括的
inclusion include + ion	▶	〔ɪn`kluʒən〕 名　包括，包含，包含物
exclude ex + clude	▶	〔ɪk`sklud〕 動　拒絕接納，把⋯排除在外，逐出
exclusive exclude + ive	▶	〔ɪk`sklusɪv〕 形　排外的，除外的，獨有的， 專用的，高級的
exclusion exclude + ion	▶	〔ɪk`skluʒən〕 名　排斥，排除在外， 被排除在外的事物

The prices listed are inclusive of sales tax.
列舉的價格包括營業稅。

This is an exclusive club, so only people of high social standing may join.
這是一間高級俱樂部，只有社會地位高的人士才能加入。

36　circ　circul　circum　圓，環　036

circle circ + le	▶	〔`sɝkl〕 名　圓，圓圈，環狀物
circuit circ + it	▶	〔`sɝkɪt〕 名　一圈，巡迴路線，電路 short circuit「短路」
circular circul + ar	▶	〔`sɝkjələ〕 形　圓形的，環形的，循環的

circulate
circul + ate

▶ 〔`sɜkjəˌlet〕 動　循環，環行，流通，發行

circulation
circulate + ion

▶ 〔ˌsɜkjəˋleʃən〕 名　循環，流通，發行量

This magazine has been in circulation for half a century.
這本雜誌發行已經半個世紀了。
It's important to have a good circle of friends.
擁有良好的交友圈很重要。

circumstance
circum + stance

▶ 〔`sɜkəmˌstæns〕 名　情況，環境，情勢

*circum*stance

circumstantial
circumstance + ial

▶ 〔ˌsɜkəmˋstænʃəl〕 形　視情況而定的

He was innocent, but the circumstantial evidence made him look guilty.
他是無罪的，但是旁證讓他看來有罪。

 37 cri(t)　cern　cret　區別 ⭐ 037

crisis
cri + sis

▶ 〔`kraɪsɪs〕 名　危機，緊急關頭，轉折點

critic
crit + ic

▶ 〔`krɪtɪk〕 名　批評家，評論家

critical
critic + al

▶ 〔`krɪtɪk!〕 形　緊要的，關鍵性的，批判的，不可或缺的

criticize
critic + ize

▶ 〔`krɪtɪˌsaɪz〕 動　批評，批判，評論

criticism
critic + ism

▶ 〔`krɪtəˌsɪzəm〕 名　批評，評論

In the mid-1970's energy crisis, automobile makers started to develop more fuel-efficient car engines.
在1970年代中期的能源危機時期，汽車廠商開始研發省燃料的汽車引擎。

The critic gave the movie two thumbs up.
該影評給予這部電影高度評價。（翹姆指有讚賞的意思）

---

criterion
crit + ion

▶ 〔kraɪ`tɪrɪən〕 名 標準，準則
（名詞複數）criteria 〔kraɪ`tɪrɪə〕

One of the criteria for the job is having good computer skills.
這份工作的徵人標準之一就是要有良好的電腦技能。

---

concern
con + cern

▶ 〔kən`sɝn〕 動 關於，涉及，關係到，關心
be concerned with～「關係到～」
be concerned about～「擔心～」
To whom it may concern「敬啟者」（正式信件的開頭）
concerning～「關於～」

---

discern
dis + cern

▶ 〔dɪ`zɝn〕 動 分辨，識別，看出

---

discernible
discern + ible

▶ 〔dɪ`sɝnəbl〕 形 可識別的

Jodi, the class brain, discerned that the only reason Barney befriended her was so that he could copy her homework.
在班上身為佼佼者的喬蒂，發現巴尼和她當朋友只是為了抄她的作業。

If you look closely, you can just discern the top of the castle in the mist.
如果你仔細看，就能在霧中看到城堡的頂端。

---

discriminate
dis + cri + ate

▶ 〔dɪ`skrɪməˏnet〕 動 區別，辨別，有差別地對待

---

discrimination
discriminate + ion

▶ 〔dɪˏskrɪmə`neʃən〕 名 區別，不公平待遇，歧視

---

indiscriminate
in + dis + cri + ate

▶ 〔ˏɪndɪ`skrɪmənɪt〕 形 無差別的，任意的

The company has a hiring policy that does not discriminate against age, gender, race or religion.
這間公司的雇用政策為平等對待任何年齡、性別、種族或宗教的人。

hypocrisy
hypo + cri + sy

▶ 〔hɪˋpɑkrəsɪ〕 名　偽善，虛偽

hypocrite
hypo + cri + te

▶ 〔ˋhɪpəkrɪt〕 名　偽善者，偽君子

The main grievance of the workers was their boss's hypocrisy in being habitually late for work when he docked workers pay for being even a minute late.
員工的主要不滿是針對他們老板的虛偽行徑，明明自己有遲到惡習，但員工遲到就算只有一分鐘，也會被扣薪水。

secret
se + cret

▶ 〔ˋsikrɪt〕 形　祕密的，機密的
名　祕密，機密，內情

secretary
secret + ary

▶ 〔ˋsɛkrəˏtɛrɪ〕 名　祕書，書記官

The secretary typed up the report.
那位祕書打了了報告書。

38 cult　col　耕作

038

cultivate
cult + ate

▶ 〔ˋkʌltəˏvet〕 動　耕種，栽培，培育

cultivated
cultivate + ed

▶ 〔ˋkʌltəˏvetɪd〕 形　耕種的，栽培的，有教養的

cultivation
cultivate + ion

▶ 〔ˏkʌltəˋveʃən〕 名　耕種，栽培，養殖

Cultivating friendships takes time and energy.
友情的培養需要時間和精力。

culture
cult + ure

▶ 〔ˋkʌltʃə〕 名　文化，教養

cultural
culture + al
▶ 〔ˋkʌltʃərəl〕 形　文化的，人文的，修養的

cultured
culture + ed
▶ 〔ˋkʌltʃəd〕 形　有教養的，有知識的，文雅的

The school festival was a cultural event with food from many countries.
那間學校的校慶是各國美食的文化盛事。

colony
col + ony
▶ 〔ˋkɑlənɪ〕 名　殖民地

colonial
colony + al
▶ 〔kəˋlonjəl〕 形　殖民地的，殖民的
colonial period 殖民時期

colonize
colony +ize
▶ 〔ˋkɑlə͵naɪz〕 動　殖民，開拓殖民地

colonization
colonize + tion
▶ 〔͵kɑlənɪˋzeʃən〕 名　殖民，殖民地化

The US was once a colony of England.
美國曾經是英國的殖民地。

39 **di** **二，兩個**
039

dioxide
di + oxide
▶ 〔daɪˋɑksaɪd〕 名　二氧化物
carbon dioxide「二氧化碳」

Green plants take in carbon dioxide and give off oxygen.
綠色植物吸收二氧化碳，然後排出氧氣。

diploma
di + plo + ma
▶ 〔dɪˋplomə〕 名　畢業文憑，學位證書

diplomat
di + plo + mat
▶ 〔ˋdɪpləmæt〕 名　外交官

diplomacy
diplomat + cy
▶ 〔dɪˋploməsɪ〕 名　外交，外交手腕

diplomatic
diplomat + ic

▶ 〔͵dɪpləˋmætɪk〕 形　外交的，外交人員的
diplomatic relations「外交關係」
diplomatic skill「外交手腕」

The diplomatic relations between Japan and China improved dramatically in 1980's.
中日外交關係在1980年代有戲劇性的改善。

40 bi　二，雙

040

bilingual
bi + lingual

▶ 〔baɪˋlɪŋwəl〕 形　能說兩種語言的，雙語的
名　通雙語的人
be bilingual in French and German
「能說法語和德語」

binocular
bi + ocular

▶ 〔bɪˋnɑkjələ〕 名　雙筒望遠鏡，雙目顯微鏡
形　雙眼的，雙眼用的
binocular telescope「雙筒望遠鏡」

bicycle
bi + cycle

▶ 〔ˋbaɪsɪkl̩〕 名　腳踏車，自行車
口語中經常使用bike。

biweekly
bi + weekly

▶ 〔baɪˋwiklɪ〕 形　每兩週的，隔週的
副　每兩月一次地，隔月地

bimonthly
bi + monthyly

▶ 〔ˋbaɪˋmʌnθlɪ〕 形　每兩月的，隔月的
副　每兩月一次地，隔月地

In Singapore, everyone grows up bilingual, speaking both his or her mother tongue and English.
在新加坡，每個人長大都能說兩種語言，包含他們自己的母語和英語。

41 co　con　com　共同，一起

041

cooperate
co + operate

▶ 〔koˋɑpəͺret〕 動　合作，配合
cooperate with～「與～合作」

cooperation ►
cooperate + ion
〔koˌɑpəˋreʃən〕图　合作，協力，配合

cooperative ►
cooperate + ive
〔koˋɑpəˌretɪv〕形　合作的，願意合作的，合作社的

With everyone's cooperation, we should be able to finish the job in about two hours.
有了大家的合作，我們應該能在兩小時內完成工作。

combine ►
com + bi
〔kəmˋbaɪn〕動　結合，聯合，兼有
图　聯合收割打穀機（具備收割和脫殼兩種機能），企業聯合
combine～with...「結合～與…」
combine～and...「混合～和…」

combination ►
combine + tion
〔ˌkɑmbəˋneʃən〕图　結合，聯合

If you combine acid and water, be sure to add the acid to the water, or you may have a small explosion.
混合酸類跟水時，務必要把酸類加到水中，不然有可能會發生小型爆炸。

common ►
com + mon
〔ˋkɑmən〕形　普通的，常見的，共同的，公共的
common sense「常識，共通感覺（盜竊是不好的，這一類的大眾共通感覺）」
common knowledge「常識（如不鏽鋼不易生鏽這類一般大眾都知道的知識）」

The fact that Mt. Everest is the highest mountain in the world is not common sense but common knowledge.
聖母峰是世界最高峰這個事實並不是共通感覺，而是一般人都知道的知識。

compromise ►
com + promise
〔ˋkɑmprəˌmaɪz〕图　妥協，折衷
動　妥協，讓步

Compromise is the main ingredient of a good friendship.
妥協是構成穩固友情的重要因素。

conclude ►
con + clud
〔kənˋklud〕動　結束，推斷出，締結（條約）

conclusion
conclude + ion
▶ 〔kən`kluʒən〕 名　結論，結尾，結束

conclusive
conclude + ive
▶ 〔kən`klusɪv〕 形　決定性的，最終的，確實的

After only three weeks away from home, Fred came to the conclusion that he was not cut out for travel.
離家才三週，佛烈德得到一個結論，就是自己並不適合旅行。

 42　sens(e)　sent　感覺，知覺
042

sense
▶ 〔sɛns〕 名　感官，感覺，意識，意義，知覺
　　　　　動　感覺到，意識到，了解
sense of humor「幽默感」
make sense「有意義」
make sense of～「理解～」

sensor
sense + or
▶ 〔`sɛnsɚ〕 名　感應器

sensory
sense + ory
▶ 〔`sɛnsərɪ〕 形　知覺的，感覺的
sensory nerve「感覺神經」

It makes sense to do your homework on the day that you get it instead of leaving it until it's too late.
在出作業的當天就寫功課是應該的，而不是拖到來不及才開始寫。

If you can't make sense of the instructions, you should seek help from your teacher.
如果你無法理解教學內容，你應該向老師尋求幫助。

Marcy sensed that she'd better not say another word, or her mother might get angry.
瑪西覺得她最好別再說話，免得惹她媽媽生氣。

The dog, with its keen sense of smell, knew the visitors were coming before they came into sight.
那隻狗憑著敏銳的嗅覺，在訪客現身之前就知道他們來了。

sensitive
sense + ive

▶ 〔`sɛnsətɪv〕 形　敏感的，易受傷害的
be sensitive to～「對～感到敏感」
be sensitive about～「對～介意」

sensitivity
sensitive + ity

▶ 〔ˌsɛnsə`tɪvətɪ〕 名　敏感性，感受性，感光度

She was very sensitive about her large nose.
她很介意她的大鼻子。

He was always sensitive to his friends' feelings.
他對於朋友的情緒變化總是很敏感。

sensible
sense + ible

▶ 〔`sɛnsəbl〕 形　明智的，合情理的，意識到的

It is not sensible to leave the house when the wind is blowing and
the temperature is -20 degrees.
在風大且氣溫零下20度的天候出門是不明智的。

sensuous
sense + ous

▶ 〔`sɛnʃʊəs〕 形　感覺上的，依照感官的，
訴諸美感的

A massage accompanied by aromatherapy is a sensuous experience.
搭配芳香療法的按摩是美好的感官體驗。

sensual
sense + ual

▶ 〔`sɛnʃʊəl〕 形　官能的，肉體上的，肉慾的

This movie is really too sensual for children.
這部電影對小朋友來說實在是太色情了。

consent
con + sent

▶ 〔kən`sɛnt〕 動　同意，贊成，答應
名　同意，贊成，答應

consensus
con + sense + us

▶ 〔kən`sɛnsəs〕 名　一致，輿論

There is a general consensus in the community that it is time to
clean up the rubbish from the streets.
社區一致認為現在該是時候清理街道上的垃圾了。

sensation
sense + tion

▶ 〔sɛn`seʃən〕 名　感覺，知覺，
轟動的事件（或人物）

sensational
sensation + al

▶ 〔sɛn`seʃənl〕 形　引起轟動的，感覺的

I felt a strange sensation in my stomach when I went on the roller coaster.
坐雲霄飛車的時候，我覺得胃有種怪怪的感覺。

There was a sensational story in the newspaper this morning about David Beckham.
今天早上的報紙有一則關於貝克漢的話題新聞。

---

sentiment
sent + ment
▶ 〔ˋsɛntəmənt〕 名　感情，心情，情緒，意見

sentimental
sentiment + al
▶ 〔͵sɛntəˋmɛntl〕 形　多愁善感的，感傷的，
情感上的

I think my husband is getting quite sentimental in his old age.
我覺得我丈夫年紀大了，人變得很多愁善感。

---

resent
re + sent
▶ 〔rɪˋzɛnt〕 動　怨恨，憤慨

resentful
resent + ful
▶ 〔rɪˋzɛntfəl〕 形　忿恨的，怨恨的

resentment
resent + ment
▶ 〔rɪˋzɛntmənt〕 名　憤慨，憤怒，怨恨

When he was a teenager, he resented his parents for being so strict, but he later thanked them.
在他青少年時期，他很氣父母的嚴格管教，但他後來很感謝他們。

Although they have had arguments, there is no resentment between them.
雖然他們有過爭吵，但是他們之間並沒有任何怨恨存在。

---

43 multi　多

043

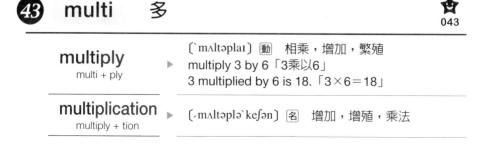

multiply
multi + ply
▶ 〔ˋmʌltəplaɪ〕 動　相乘，增加，繁殖
multiply 3 by 6「3乘以6」
3 multiplied by 6 is 18.「3×6＝18」

multiplication
multiply + tion
▶ 〔͵mʌltəpləˋkeʃən〕 名　增加，增殖，乘法

The rabbits seemed to multiply quickly.
兔子好像繁殖得很快。

Peggy multiplied her efforts in order to get done on time.
為了能按時完成，佩姬加倍努力地工作。

| multitude
multi + itude | ▶ | 〔`mʌltə⸴tjud〕 名　許多，一大群人，大眾
a multitude of cars「許多車」
the multitude「廣大民眾」 |

The movie star was surrounded by a multitude of screaming fans.
那位電影明星被一大群尖叫的影迷包圍。

 44　sider　sir(e)　星
044

consider con + sider	▶	〔kən`sɪdə〕 動　考慮，認為，視為 consider～as...「視～為…」
consider ate consider + ate	▶	〔kən`sɪdərɪt〕 形　體貼的，考慮周到的，小心的
consideration consider + tion	▶	〔kənsɪdə`reʃən〕 名　考慮，體貼
considerable consider + able	▶	〔kən`sɪdərəbl〕 形　相當大的，相當多的， 重要的，值得考慮的
considerably considerable + ly	▶	〔kən`sɪdərəblɪ〕 副　相當，非常，頗

Before making a decision, you need to consider as many factors as possible.
在下決定之前，你應該考慮越多的因素越好。

Heidi is a very considerate person, which may be why she has so many friends.
海蒂是個體貼的人，或許這就是為什麼她有那麼多朋友。

| desire
de + sire | ▶ | 〔dɪ`zaɪr〕 動　渴望，要求
名　慾望，渴望，想要的東西 |

desirable desire + able	▶	〔dɪˋzaɪrəbl〕 [形]　值得擁有的，令人滿意的， 　引起慾望的
desirous desire + ous	▶	〔dɪˋzaɪrəs〕 [形]　渴望的，想要的 be desirous of～「渴望～」

A score of 90 is desirable, but I'll settle for 80.
雖然希望能得到90分，但是80分還算可以接受。

The object of his desire was a very expensive motorcycle.
他想要的東西是一輛非常昂貴的摩托車。

45　spher(e)　球

045

sphere	▶	〔sfɪr〕 [名]　球，球體，行星
hemisphere hemi + sphere	▶	〔ˋhɛməsˏfɪr〕 [名]　（地球的）半球，半球體 the Northern/Southern Hemisphere 「北／南半球」
spherical sphere + ical	▶	〔ˋsfɛrəkl〕 [形]　球的，球面的

Some constellations seen in the Southern Hemisphere are different from those seen in the Northern Hemisphere.
有些在南半球看到的星座和北半球看到的不大相同。

atmosphere atmos + sphere	▶	〔ˋætməsˏfɪr〕 [名]　大氣，氣氛
atmospheric atmosphere + ic	▶	〔ˏætməsˋfɛrɪk〕 [形]　大氣的，氛圍的 atmospheric music「氣氛音樂」

Idling cars send a lot of harmful gases into the atmosphere.
空轉的汽車會排放許多有害氣體到大氣中。

As soon as she walked into the room, the atmosphere changed, and everyone became sullen.
當她一走進房間，氣氛頓時轉變，每個人都變得鬱悶安靜。

46 equ(i) 相同，一致
046

equal equ + al	▶	〔`ikwəl〕 形 相等的，平等的 動 等於
equally equal + ly	▶	〔`ikwəlɪ〕 副 相等地，同樣地，公平地
equality equal + ity	▶	〔ɪ`kwɑlətɪ〕 名 相等，平等
unequal un + equal	▶	〔ʌn`ikwəl〕 形 不相等的，不同的，不平等的 an unequal trade「不公平交易」
equate equ + ate	▶	〔ɪ`kwet〕 動 等同，相等 equate〜with...「使〜等同於…」
equator equate + or	▶	〔ɪ`kwetɚ〕 名 （the equator）赤道
equinox equi + nox	▶	〔`ikwəˌnɑks〕 名 晝夜平分時（春分或秋分） vernal equinox「春分」，autumnal equinox「秋分」

Racial equality is an admirable ideal, but in reality it seems to be difficult to achieve.
種族平等是一崇高的理想，但現實上似乎很難達成。

equivalent equi + val + ent	▶	〔ɪ`kwɪvələnt〕 形 相等的，相同的，等量的 名 相等物，同義字
equivalence equivalent + ce	▶	〔ɪ`kwɪvələns〕 名 相等，等值

2.54 centimeters is the equivalent of one inch.
2.54公分等於一英吋。

adequate ad + equ + ate	▶	〔`ædəkwɪt〕 形 足夠的，適當的，勝任的， 尚可的
adequately adequate + ly	▶	〔`ædəkwɪtlɪ〕 副 適當地，足夠地
adequacy adequate + cy	▶	〔`ædəkwəsɪ〕 名 適當，恰當，足夠
inadequate in + adequate	▶	〔ɪn`ædəkwɪt〕 形 不充分的，不適當的， 不能勝任的

inadequately
inadequate + ly

▶ 〔ɪnˋædəkwɪtlɪ〕 副　不適當地

His work was not great, but it was adequate.
他的作品不是很棒，但還算差強人意。

 47　tend　tens(e)　tent　朝向，擴展
047

tend	▶ 〔tɛnd〕 動　傾向，趨向，易於 tend to～「有～的傾向」
tendency tend + cy	▶ 〔ˋtɛndənsɪ〕 名　傾向，癖性，天分

I tend to get very tired after 10:00 PM.
晚上10點過後我容易變得很累。

There was a period in his life when he had suicidal tendencies, but he is doing much better now.
他曾經有一段時間有自殺的傾向，但是現在他已經好多了。

extend ex + tend	▶ 〔ɪkˋstɛnd〕 動　延長，延伸，擴大，擴展
extent ex + tent	▶ 〔ɪkˋstɛnt〕 名　廣度，寬度，長度，程度，範圍 to some extent「某種程度上來說」
extensive ex + tens + ive	▶ 〔ɪkˋstɛnsɪv〕 形　廣大的，廣闊的，廣泛的， 大量的
extensively extensive + ly	▶ 〔ɪkˋstɛnsɪvlɪ〕 副　廣大地，廣泛地
extension ex + tens + ion	▶ 〔ɪkˋstɛnʃən〕 名　伸展，擴大，延長，電話分機

Doug extended his hand in greeting to his client.
道格伸出手向他的客戶致意。

The situation has improved to some extent, but we are still fighting against archaic prejudice and backward thinking.
雖然在某種程度上情況已有改善，但我們仍在對抗老舊的偏見及落後的思想。

pretend pre + tend	▶ 〔prɪˋtɛnd〕 動　假裝，佯裝，假扮 pretend to V「假裝～」

pretense
pre + tense

▶ 〔prɪˋtɛns〕名　假裝，虛偽，做作

The child thought that if she pretended to be asleep, she would not have to get up and go to school.
那個小孩以為只要她假裝睡著就不用起床上學。

He went back to the store on the pretense of leaving his umbrella behind, but he really wanted to talk to the pretty owner.
他假裝忘了拿傘回去店裡，其實是想跟那位漂亮老闆說話。

---

intend
in + tend

▶ 〔ɪnˋtɛnd〕動　想要，打算

intent
in + tent

▶ 〔ɪnˋtɛnt〕名　意圖，目的，意思，含義

intention
intend + tion

▶ 〔ɪnˋtɛnʃən〕名　意圖，意向，目的，意思

intentional
intention + al

▶ 〔ɪnˋtɛnʃənl̩〕形　故意的，有意的

intentionally
intentional + ly

▶ 〔ɪnˋtɛnʃənl̩ɪ〕副　有意地，故意地

Although his intentions were good, Jody ended up destroying the children's snow fort instead of helping them make it bigger.
雖然喬迪是出於好意，但他卻毀了孩子們的雪堡，而不是幫忙堆得更大。

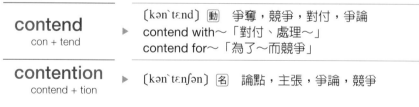

contend
con + tend

▶ 〔kənˋtɛnd〕動　爭奪，競爭，對付，爭論
contend with～「對付、處理～」
contend for～「為了～而競爭」

contention
contend + tion

▶ 〔kənˋtɛnʃən〕名　論點，主張，爭論，競爭

He had to contend with a lot of resistance before he was eventually elected.
在他最終當選之前，他必須對抗許多阻力。

---

attend
at + tend

▶ 〔əˋtɛnd〕動　出席，參加，照料，上（學）

attendance
attend + ance

▶ 〔əˋtɛndəns〕名　到場，出席

attention
attend + tion
▶ 〔əˋtɛnʃən〕 名 注意，注意力，專心

attentive
attend + ive
▶ 〔əˋtɛntɪv〕 形 注意的，留意的，體貼的

The devoted daughter was very attentive to her aging parents.
那位忠心奉獻的女兒對她年邁的雙親體貼入微。

tense
▶ 〔tɛns〕 形 繃緊的，緊張的

tensely
tense + ly
▶ 〔ˋtɛnslɪ〕 副 繃緊地，緊張地

It was a very tense situation in the hospital while the family waited for the outcome of the operation.
在家屬等候手術結果的同時，醫院的氣氛非常緊張。

intense
in + tense
▶ 〔ɪnˋtɛns〕 形 強烈的，劇烈的，極度的

intensely
intense + ly
▶ 〔ɪnˋtɛnslɪ〕 副 強烈地，極度地

intensity
intense + ity
▶ 〔ɪnˋtɛnsətɪ〕 名 強烈，極度

intensive
intense + ive
▶ 〔ɪnˋtɛnsɪv〕 形 加強的，密集的，特別護理的

intensively
intensive + ly
▶ 〔ɪnˋtɛnsɪvlɪ〕 副 強烈地，集中地

intensify
intense + ify
▶ 〔ɪnˋtɛnsəˏfaɪ〕 動 加強，增強，使變激烈

She stared at him with such intensity that he immediately looked away.
她是以那麼熱烈的眼神注視著他，所以他隨即看向他處。

 48 **form** 形，形式
048

form
▶ 〔fɔrm〕 名 形狀，外形，形式，表格
動 形成，塑造，成形

formation
form + tion
▶ 〔fɔrˋmeʃən〕 名 形成，組成，構成

formal fom + al	▶	〔`fɔrml〕 形 正式的，拘束的，正規的
formality formal + ity	▶	〔fɔr`mælətɪ〕 名 拘泥形式，拘謹，正式手續
informal in + formal	▶	〔ɪn`fɔrml〕 形 非正式的，不拘禮節的， 非正規的，通俗的
informality informal + ity	▶	〔ɪnfɔr`mælətɪ〕 名 非正式

As it is a formal event, you should dress appropriately.
因為這是正式活動，所以你應該要穿著得宜。

He already had the job, so the interview with personnel was just a formality.
他已經得到那份工作了，所以與人事部門的面試只是形式一場。

formula form + ula	▶	〔`fɔrmjələ〕 名 公式，配方，慣用語句
formulate formula + ate	▶	〔`fɔrmjə‚let〕 動 公式化，有系統地說明， 想出計劃
formulation formulate + ion	▶	〔‚fɔrmjə`leʃən〕 名 公式化，規劃，構想

They put their heads together and formulated a plan to smuggle food into the karaoke booth.
他們商量後想出辦法把食物偷偷帶進卡拉OK包廂。

inform in + form	▶	〔ɪn`fɔrm〕 動 通知，告知，告發 inform（人）of～「通知（人）～」
information inform + tion	▶	〔‚ɪnfɚ`meʃən〕 名 消息，情報，資訊 a piece of information「一則情報」（情報的量詞 為piece）

The doctor will inform you as soon as the test results are in.
檢查結果一出來，醫生會立即通知你。

reform re + form	▶	〔‚rɪ`fɔrm〕 名 改革，改良 動 改善，改革，改良

The citizens are calling for all kinds of political reforms.
市民要求全面的政治改革。

---

perform
per + form

▶ 〔pəˋfɔrm〕 動　履行，執行，演出，表演

---

performance
perform + ance

▶ 〔pəˋfɔrməns〕 名　演出，表演，履行，實行

Each of the students performed three pieces at the piano recital.
每位學生都在鋼琴獨奏會上演奏三首曲子。

---

49 **vade**　**vas**　**行走**

049

---

evade
e + vade

▶ 〔ɪˋved〕 動　躲避，逃避，迴避

---

evasion
evade + ion

▶ 〔ɪˋveʒən〕 名　逃避，迴避，藉口
tax evasion「逃稅，逃漏稅」

---

evasive
evade + ive

▶ 〔ɪˋvesɪv〕 形　逃避的，託辭的

I felt her question was rude, so I gave her an evasive answer.
我覺得她的問題很失禮，所以我不正面回答她。

---

invade
in + vade

▶ 〔ɪnˋved〕 動　侵略，侵襲

---

invasion
invade + ion

▶ 〔ɪnˋveʒən〕 名　入侵，侵略，侵襲

---

invader
invade + er

▶ 〔ɪnˋvedɚ〕 名　入侵者，侵略者

Because of all the dirty dishes in his sink, and half-eaten food on the table, Jeff's house was invaded by hungry mice.
因為水槽裡的髒碗盤和桌上吃剩的食物，傑夫家被飢餓的老鼠入侵了。

50　graph(y)　gram　文書記錄　 050

graph	▶ 〔græf〕名　圖表，圖解

graphic graph + ic	▶ 〔`græfɪk〕形　生動的，寫實的，圖解的，繪畫的

Another name for a very long comic book is a graphic novel.
很長的漫畫書又叫做圖像小說。

The movie was given an R rating because of the graphic violence.
那部電影因為寫實的暴力影像而被列為R級。

autograph auto + graph	▶ 〔`ɔtə͵græf〕名　簽名，親筆簽名

autography auto + graphy	▶ 〔ɔ`tɑgrəfɪ〕名　筆跡，親筆

diagram dia + gram	▶ 〔`daɪə͵græm〕名　圖表，圖示，時刻表

telegraph tele + graph	▶ 〔`tɛlə͵græm〕名　電報

He tried to learn Morse code because he wanted to be a telegraph operator.
他想成為電報操作員所以努力學習摩斯密碼。

51　bio　生命，活　 051

biography bio + graphy	▶ 〔baɪ`ɑgrəfɪ〕名　傳記

autobiography auto + biography	▶ 〔͵ɔtəbaɪ`ɑgrəfɪ〕名　自傳

biographer biography + er	▶ 〔baɪ`ɑgrəfə〕名　傳記作者

It was her dream to see her autobiography on the bestseller list.
她的夢想是見到她的自傳名列暢銷排行榜上。

52 logy　logi　學問，知識

052

biology bio + logy	▶ 〔baɪˋɑlədʒɪ〕名　生物學
biological biology + ical	▶ 〔͵baɪəˋlɑdʒɪkl̩〕形　生物學的，生物的
psychology psycho + logy	▶ 〔saɪˋkɑlədʒɪ〕名　心理學，心理
psychological psychology + ical	▶ 〔͵saɪkəˋlɑdʒɪkl̩〕形　心理學的，心理的，精神的
psychologist psychology + ist	▶ 〔saɪˋkɑlədʒɪst〕名　心理學家
zoology zoo + logy	▶ 〔zoˋɑlədʒɪ〕名　動物學
zoological zoology + ical	▶ 〔͵zoəˋlɑdʒɪkl̩〕形 動物學的，關於動物的

zoo*logy*

The country was invaded because the UN suspected they were harboring biological weapons.
該國被入侵是因為聯合國懷疑他們藏有生物武器。

The psychologist is doing a study on the effects of stress on children.
那名心理學家正在進行一份關於壓力對孩童影響的研究。

53 pas(s)　通過，前進

053

pass	▶ 〔pæs〕動　通過，經過，（考試）及格，傳遞，（時間）流逝

passable
pass + able

▶ 〔ˋpæsəb!ʃ〕 形　可通行的，尚可的，過得去的

impassable
im + passable

▶ 〔ɪmˋpæsəb!〕 形　不能通行的

passport
pass + port

▶ 〔ˋpæs͵port〕 名　護照

His work is not great, but it is definitely passable.
他的作品不是很優秀，但肯定還算過得去。

passage
pass + age

▶ 〔ˋpæsɪdʒ〕 名　通行，通路，（文章、樂曲等的）
一段、一節

passenger
pass + er

▶ 〔ˋpæsṇdʒɚ〕 名　乘客，旅客

pastime
pas + time

▶ 〔ˋpæs͵taɪm〕 名　消遣，娛樂

Due to a power outage, the train was stopped for several hours
with the passengers inside.
因為停電的關係，火車被迫停下來好幾個小時，裡面還載著乘客。

surpass
sur + pass

▶ 〔səˋpæs〕 動　勝過，優於，多於

surpassing
surpass + ing

▶ 〔səˋpæsɪŋ〕 形　非凡的，卓越的，出眾的

No matter how hard he tried, Tom could not surpass his old
record of eating three large pizzas in one sitting.
無論湯姆多麼努力，他還是無法超越以前一次吃掉三個大比薩的紀錄。

54 order　ordin　秩序

054

order

▶ 〔ˋɔrdɚ〕 名　順序，命令，訂購，秩序
動　命令，指揮，點菜，訂購

orderly order + ly	▶	〔ˋɔrdɚlɪ〕 形 整齊的，有條理的，守秩序的 副 按順序地，整齊地

ordinal ordin + al	▶	〔ˋɔrdɪnl〕 形 序數的，順序的 名 序數 ordinal number(s)「序數（first, second, fifth等表順序的數字）」 cardinal〔ˋkɑrdnəl〕number(s)「基數（one, two, five等一般數字）」

Did you order your food yet?
你點餐了嗎？

Please proceed to the exit in an orderly fashion.
請依序向出口移動。

ordinary ordin + ary	▶	〔ˋɔrdṇˏɛrɪ〕 形 通常的，平常的，普通的
ordinarily ordinary + ly	▶	〔ˋɔrdṇˏɛrɪlɪ〕 副 通常地，慣常地，一般地，平常地
extraordinary extra + ordinary	▶	〔ɪkˋstrɔrdṇˏɛrɪ〕 形 異常的，特別的，非凡的
extraordinarily extraordinary + ly	▶	〔ɪkˋstrɔrdṇˏɛrɪlɪ〕 副 非常，格外地，異常地

The young boy looked very ordinary, but in actuality, he was a famous singer.
那位年輕人看起來非常普通，但實際上，他是一位有名的歌手。

It seems extraordinary that we have managed to get so many stupid people in the same place at the same time.
我們同時間在同樣的地方雇用那麼多愚蠢的人似乎是件離奇的事。

55 know　gn　gnor(e)　知道，領悟　☆ 055

know	▶	〔no〕 動 知道，了解，認識
knowledge know + ledge	▶	〔ˋnɑlɪdʒ〕 名 知識，學問

knowledgeable
knowledge + able
▶ 〔`nɑlɪdʒəbl〕 形 有知識的，博學的，有見識的

Sally is not very knowledgeable on the subject of baseball.
莎莉不是非常了解棒球這項運動。

acknowledge
ac + knowledge
▶ 〔ək`nɑlɪdʒ〕 動 承認，致謝

acknowledgment
acknowledge + ment
▶ 〔ək`nɑlɪdʒmənt〕 名 承認，致謝

If you use the ideas or words of another person, you must make the proper acknowledgment.
如果你要借用他人的想法或話語，你一定得適當地表示引用。

cognize
co + gn + ize
▶ 〔`kɑɡˏnaɪz〕 動 認知

cognition
cognize + tion
▶ 〔kɑɡ`nɪʃən〕 名 認知，知識

recognize
re + cognize
▶ 〔`rɛkəɡˏnaɪz〕 動 認出，認可，承認

recognition
recognize + tion
▶ 〔ˏrɛkəɡ`nɪʃən〕 名 認出，認識，承認

recognizable
recognize + able
▶ 〔`rɛkəɡˏnaɪzəbl〕 形 可辨認的，可識別的，可承認的

Your driver's license might not be recognized in other countries.
你的駕照在其他國家有可能不被認可。

His height makes him easily recognizable.
他的身高讓他很容易被認出。

ignore
i + gnore
▶ 〔ɪg`nor〕 動 忽視，不理會

ignorant
ignore + ant
▶ 〔`ɪgnərənt〕 形 無知的，不學無術的
be ingnorant of～「不知道～，對～無知」

ignorance
ignore + ce
▶ 〔ˋɪgnərəns〕名 無知，不學無術，愚昧

Unfortunately, no matter how much you try to ignore it, the problem will not go away.
很不幸地，無論你多努力想要忽視問題，問題還是不會消失。

If you are ignorant of current events, you might have trouble engaging in daily conversation.
如果你不了解時事，要融入日常對話當中可能會有困難。

 56 gen(e)　　gn　　種族，世系
056

gene
▶ 〔dʒin〕名 基因

genetic
gene + tic
▶ 〔dʒəˋnɛtɪk〕形 起源的，基因的，遺傳學的

genetically
genetic + al + ly
▶ 〔dʒəˋnɛtɪklɪ〕副 從基因方面，從遺傳學角度

They are working on genetically enhancing the plant so that it can grow in very dry conditions.
他們正在研究從基因學角度改良植物，讓它能在非常乾燥的環境下生長。

genius
gen + us
▶ 〔ˋdʒinjəs〕名 天才，天賦，才能
with a stroke of genius「靈光乍現，靈機一動」

ingenious
in + genius
▶ 〔ɪnˋdʒinjəs〕形 足智多謀的，巧妙的，製作精巧的

It was with a stroke of genius that he found a solution to the difficult problem.
他靈機一動發現了解決那個難題的方法。

Larry came up with a simple, yet ingenious design for a machine to sharpen scissors.
賴瑞設計出一個簡單但巧妙的磨剪刀機器。

generate
gene + ate
▶ 〔ˋdʒɛnəˌret〕動 產生，造成，發（熱、電、光等）
generate electricity「發電」

generator
generate + or

▶ 〔`dʒɛnəˌretə〕 图 發電機

The motor of a refrigerator generates a lot of heat, so it should be placed at least ten cm away from the wall.
冰箱的馬達會產生高熱，所以應該放在離牆最少十公分的地方。

generation
generate + ion

▶ 〔ˌdʒɛnəˋreʃən〕 图 世代，產生

Each generation has its own music and fashion.
每個世代都有它們各自的音樂和流行。

general
gene + al

▶ 〔`dʒɛnərəl〕 形 一般的，普遍的，全體的

generally
general + ly

▶ 〔`dʒɛnərəlɪ〕 副 通常，一般地，普遍地
generally speaking「一般而言，整體來說」

Generally speaking, the travel plans are moving forward, but we still have some details to take care of.
整體來說，旅行計劃進展得很順利，只是我們還有些細節需要處理。

oxygen
oxy + gen

▶ 〔`ɑksədʒən〕 图 氧氣

hydrogen
hydro + gen

▶ 〔`haɪdrədʒən〕 图 氫

In the case of an emergency please place the oxygen mask over your face.
緊急的時候，請戴上氧氣面罩。

generous
gene + ous

▶ 〔`dʒɛnərəs〕 形 慷慨的，大方的，寬宏大量的

generosity
generous + ity

▶ 〔ˌdʒɛnəˋrɑsətɪ〕 图 寬宏大量，慷慨

Thank you for your generous offer, but I can take care of the bill.
謝謝你願意慷慨解囊，但我可以付這筆帳的。

pregnant
pre + gn + ant

▶ 〔`prɛgnənt〕 形 懷孕的

pregnancy
pregnant + cy

▶ 〔`prɛgnənsɪ〕 名 懷孕

Clara stopped smoking as soon as she found out she was pregnant.
克萊拉一發現懷孕就停止抽菸。

57 cide　　cis(e)　　sciss　　殺，切割

057

homicide
homi + cide

▶ 〔`hɑmə͵saɪd〕 名 殺人，殺人犯

suicide
sui + cide

▶ 〔`suə͵saɪd〕 名 自殺
commit a suicide「自殺」這裡用commit〔kə`mɪt〕
（犯罪）是因為基督教認為自殺是種罪惡。
love suicide「殉情」（＝double suicide）
family suicide「全家自殺」
mass suicide「集體自殺」

pesticide
pest + cide

▶ 〔`pɛstɪ͵saɪd〕 名 殺蟲劑（農業用）
＝insecticide〔ɪn`sɛktə͵saɪd〕
insect〔`ɪnsɛkt〕（昆蟲）＋cide

genocide
gen + cide

▶ 〔`dʒɛnə͵saɪd〕 名 種族滅絕，集體屠殺

The police were not sure if the death was caused by murder or suicide.
警察不確定這起死亡案件是他殺還是自殺。

Mabel sprayed pesticide all over her vegetable garden.
瑪貝爾在她的蔬菜園裡灑殺蟲劑。

scissors
sciss + or + s

▶ 〔`sɪzəz〕 名 剪刀
a pair of scissors「一把剪刀」（因為有兩片刀片）
【註】不指定時可使用some

Would you get me some scissors, please?
請幫我拿把剪刀好嗎？

decide de + cide	▶	〔dɪˋsaɪd〕 動　決定，決意，下決心
decision decide + ion	▶	〔dɪˋsɪʒən〕 名　決定，決心，結論
decisive decide + ive	▶	〔dɪˋsaɪsɪv〕 形　決定性的，決定的，明確的， 堅決的，果斷的
decisively decisive + ly	▶	〔dɪˋsaɪsɪvlɪ〕 副　決然地，果斷地
decidedly decide + ed + ly	▶	〔dɪˋsaɪdɪdlɪ〕 副　斷然地，明確地

Tess deliberated a long time, but she finally decided that she would have a banana for dessert.
考慮了很久，黛絲最後終於決定甜點要吃香蕉。

precise pre + cise	▶	〔prɪˋsaɪs〕 形　精確的，準確的，嚴格的
precisely precise + ly	▶	〔prɪˋsaɪslɪ〕 副　精確地，準確地，嚴格地
precision precise + ion	▶	〔prɪˋsɪʒən〕 名　精密度，準確性，嚴格

Pam can remember precisely what she was doing the moment she found out that John Lennon died.
潘確切記得當她得知約翰藍儂的死訊時在做什麼。

| concise
con + cise | ▶ | 〔kənˋsaɪs〕 形　簡明的，簡潔的 |
| concisely
concise + ly | ▶ | 〔kənˋsaɪslɪ〕 副　簡潔地 |

Be sure that your writing is clear and concise.
請注意保持文章的清楚簡潔。

 **organ**　組織　
058

| organ | ▶ | 〔ˋɔrgən〕 名　器官，機構，機關，風琴 |

organic organ + ic	▶ ［ɔrˋgænɪk］ 形　有機的，器官的，生物的
organism organ + ism	▶ ［ˋɔrgənˏɪzəm］ 名　生物，有機體

Do you have an organ donor card?
請問你有器官捐贈卡嗎？
Hannah eats only organic vegetables.
漢娜只吃有機蔬菜。

organize organ + ize	▶ ［ˋɔrgəˏnaɪz］ 動　組織，安排，成立組織
organization organize + tion	▶ ［ˏɔrgənəˋzeʃən］ 名　組織，機構，團體

The books are organized in alphabetical order.
這些書依照字母順序歸類整理。
Morris is a member of an organization that does fund raising for charity.
莫里斯是慈善募款組織的成員。

59　ori　開始，起源

059

orient ori + ent	▶ ［ˋorɪənt］ 名　the Orient 東方，東方國家 ［ˋorɪˏɛnt］ 動　朝東，定位，適應 orient（人）to～「使（人）適應～」
orientation orient + tion	▶ ［ˏorɪɛnˋteʃən］ 名　適應，熟悉，方向，定位
oriental orient + al	▶ ［ˏorɪˋɛntl］ 形　東方的，亞洲的，東方文化的

The school designed an orientation program for the new students.
學校為新生策劃了新生訓練。

origin ori + gin	▶ ［ˋɔrədʒɪn］ 名　起源，由來，起因 The Origin of Species《物種起源》（1859年達爾文著作）

original origin + al	▶	〔əˋrɪdʒən〕 形 最初的，原本的，原始的， 有獨創性的
originality original + ity	▶	〔əˏrɪdʒəˋnælətɪ〕 名 獨創性，創造力，創舉
originate origin + ate	▶	〔əˋrɪdʒəˏnet〕 動 發源，產生，發明，創作，引起 originate in/from～「起源自～，始於～」

What is the origin of this word?
這個字的語源是什麼？

Is this your original work, or did you copy it from someone?
這是你自己的創作，還是抄襲別人的作品？

Kanji characters originated in China.
日文漢字起源於中國。

 60 spond spons(e) 答覆
060

| **respond**
re + spond | ▶ | 〔rɪˋspɑnd〕 動 回答，作出反應，回應
respond to～「回答～，對～作出反應」 |
| **response**
re + sponse | ▶ | 〔rɪˋspɑns〕 名 回答，答覆，反應 |

The dog was sleeping so soundly that she did not respond to her master's call.
那隻狗睡得好熟，以至於沒有回應主人的呼喚。

responsible response + ible	▶	〔rɪˋspɑnsəbḷ〕 形 需負責任的，負責的 be responsible for～「對～負責」
responsibility responsible + ity	▶	〔rɪˏspɑnsəˋbɪlətɪ〕 名 責任，責任感，義務
irresponsible ir + responsible	▶	〔ˏɪrɪˋspɑnsəbḷ〕 形 不需承擔責任的，無責任感的， 不可靠的，不負責任的
responsibly responsible + ly	▶	〔rɪˋspɑnsəbḷɪ〕 副 負責地，有責任感地
irresponsibly irresponsible + ly	▶	〔ˏɪrɪˋspɑnsəbḷɪ〕 副 不負責任地，不可靠地

Marcia quickly got used to her new responsibilities.
瑪西亞很快就習慣了新的職務。

After she irresponsibly called in sick to work five or six times, she was fired.
在她不負責任請了五、六次病假後，她就被解雇了。

correspond co + respond	〔͵kɔrɪˋspɑnd〕 動　符合，一致，相當，通信 correspond with～「符合～，和～通信」
correspondence correspond + ence	〔͵kɔrəˋspɑndəns〕 名　一致，符合，相當，通信
correspondent correspond + ent	〔͵kɔrəˋspɑndənt〕 名　對應物，通信者，特派員

She has been corresponding with the same pen pal for over ten years.
她和同一個筆友通信已經超過十年了。

 geo　地球
061

geography geo + graphy	〔ˋdʒɪˋɑgrəfɪ〕 名　地理學，地形，地勢，地理
geographical geography + ical	〔dʒɪəˋgræfɪkḷ〕 形　地理的，地理學的

The unusual geographical formations of the Dakota Badlands were caused by wind erosion.
達科塔惡地獨特的地形是經由風蝕形成的。

geology geo + logy	〔dʒɪˋɑlədʒɪ〕 名　地質學
geological geology + ical	〔dʒɪəˋlɑdʒɪkḷ〕 形　地質的，地質學上的

The rovers on Mars are sending back pictures of the geological features of the surface of the planet.
火星上的探測車正在傳回該星球表面上地質特徵的照片。

geometry
geo + meter + y

▶ 〔dʒɪˋɑmətrɪ〕 名 幾何學

geometric
geometry + ic

▶ 〔dʒɪəˋmɛtrɪk〕 形 幾何學的，幾何圖案的

He always uses unusual geometric patterns in his designs.
他總是在他的設計當中使用獨特的幾何圖案。

 62 grad(e) 階梯，階段
062

grade
▶ 〔gred〕 名 等級，級別，階段，年級

gradual
grade + ual

▶ 〔ˋgrædʒʊəl〕 形 逐漸的，逐步的，平緩的

gradually
gradual + ly

▶ 〔ˋgrædʒʊəlɪ〕 副 逐步地，逐漸地

gradation
grade + tion

▶ 〔ˏgreˋdeʃən〕 名 漸層的變化，（變化的）階段，
（顏色的）層次

Although Chris and Sarah didn't like each other when they first met, they gradually got to know each other and became best friends.
克里斯和莎拉初次見面時並不喜歡對方，但他們逐漸認識彼此成為摯友。

graduate
grad + ate

▶ 〔ˋgrædʒʊˏet〕 動 畢業
〔ˋgrædʒʊɪt〕 名 畢業生
形 研究生的
graduate from～「畢業於～」

graduation
graduate + ion

▶ 〔ˏgrædʒʊˋeʃən〕 名 畢業，畢業典禮

Kelly entered nursing school as soon as she graduated from high school.
凱莉高中一畢業就進入護理學校就讀。

degrade
de + grade

▶ 〔dɪˋgred〕 動 降級，降低，降低地位，
降低品格（或價值等）

Feminist groups are opposed to pornography because it is degrading to women.
女權團體反對色情電影，因為那貶低了女性。

63 **grav** **griev(e)** **grief** 重的
063

gravity grav + ity	▶	〔ˋgrævətɪ〕名 重力，引力，地心引力
gravitate grav + ate	▶	〔ˋgrævəˏtet〕動 受引力作用而運動，被吸引 gravitate toward～「被～強烈地吸引」
gravitation gravitate + ion	▶	〔ˏgrævəˋteʃən〕名 重力，地心引力，受吸引

At parties he tends to gravitate toward the snack table.
在派對上，他總是被吸引到點心桌去。

grieve	▶	〔griv〕動 悲傷，哀悼 grieve at / over / for～「為了～而悲傷」
grievous grieve + ous	▶	〔ˋgrivəs〕形 令人悲痛的，悲傷的，表示悲痛的
grief	▶	〔grif〕名 悲痛，悲傷

Jessica grieved for weeks over the loss of her pet.
潔西卡為她死去的寵物悲傷了好幾週。

grievance grieve + ance	▶	〔ˋgrivəns〕名 不滿，不平，抱怨，牢騷

His main grievance was that there was clearly a double standard in payment policy.
他的不滿主要是因為給薪政策明顯有雙重標準。

64 **scribe** **script** 寫
064

describe de + scribe	▶	〔dɪˋskraɪb〕動 描寫，描繪，敘述，形容
description describe + ion	▶	〔dɪˋskrɪpʃən〕名 描寫，敘述，形容，說明
descriptive describe + ive	▶	〔dɪˋskrɪptɪv〕形 描寫的，記述的

inscribe
in + scribe
▶ 〔ɪn`skraɪb〕動 雕，刻，牢記，（把名字）登記入冊

script
▶ 〔skrɪpt〕名 手跡，筆跡，底稿，腳本

The woman went to the police and gave a description of the man who stole her purse.
那位女性去報警，並向警察描述偷她錢包的男性的特徵。

prescribe
pre + scribe
▶ 〔prɪ`skraɪb〕動 規定，指定，開藥方

prescription
prescribe + ion
▶ 〔prɪ`skrɪpʃən〕名 命令，規定，處方，藥方

The doctor prescribed some medication for my sore throat.
醫生替我的喉嚨痛開了一些藥。

ascribe
a + scribe
▶ 〔ə`skraɪb〕動 把…歸因（於）

This drawing has been ascribed to Marc Chagall.
這幅畫被認定為夏卡爾所作。

I don't think it is fair for you to ascribe your poor work to lack of time.
我認為你把工作做不好歸咎於缺乏時間是不對的。

65 brace 腕

065

bracelet
brace + let
▶ 〔`breslɪt〕名 手鐲

embrace
em + brace
▶ 〔ɪm`bres〕動 擁抱，懷抱，抓住（機會等），欣然接受（提議等）

Jen ran up to her son and embraced him as soon as he stepped off the train.
珍跑向她的兒子，在他步下火車時一把抱住了他。

66　ab　離開，偏離

066

abnormal
ab + normal

▶ 〔æbˋnɔrml〕 形　不正常的，反常的，異常的

There are sometimes unclear lines dividing normal and abnormal behavior.
有時候，正常行為和不正常行為的界線是模糊的。

---

abuse
ab + use

▶ 〔əˋbjuz〕 動　濫用，虐待，傷害
〔əˋbjus〕 名　濫用，虐待，傷害，陋習

---

abusive
abuse + ive

▶ 〔əˋbjusɪv〕 形　虐待的，濫用的

In this school, students are allowed to dress as they please, but if they abuse the privilege, it will be taken away.
在這間學校，學生可以隨他們的喜好打扮，但是如果他們濫用這項權利的話，它就會被取消。

There should be a law protecting pets from abusive owners.
應該要有法律保護寵物免於飼主的虐待。

67　ject　投，擲

067

project
pro + ject

▶ 〔ˋprɑdʒɛkt〕 名　方案，計劃，企劃
〔prəˋdʒɛkt〕 動　企劃，投射，放映，突出，闡述，表明，預計

The population of the Earth is projected to increase even more in the next century.
地球的人口預計在下個世紀還會增加得更多。

reject
re + ject

▶ 〔rɪˋdʒɛkt〕 動　拒絕，抵制，去除，排斥

rejection
reject + ion

▶ 〔rɪˋdʒɛkʃən〕 名　拒絕，退回，摒棄

The manuscript for Harry Potter was rejected by several publishers before it was finally accepted.
哈利波特的小說原稿在出版前曾被一些出版商拒絕過。

---

 sub　下面　

068

subscribe
sub + scribe

▶ 〔səbˋskraɪb〕 動　認捐，捐助，訂閱，訂購，同意，簽名
subscribe to～「訂購～，訂閱～，同意～」

subscription
subscribe + tion

▶ 〔səbˋskrɪpʃən〕 名　捐款，同意，訂閱，署名

submarine
sub + marine

▶ 〔ˋsʌbməˏrin〕 名　潛水艇

subway
sub + way

▶ 〔ˋsʌbˏwe〕 名　地下鐵

I don't think I can work there, because I don't subscribe to their philosophy.
我不認為我可以在那裡工作，因為我並不認同他們的工作方針。

My subscription runs out at the end of the month, so I'll have to renew it soon.
我的訂購這個月底到期，所有我必須快點續購。

---

subject
sub + ject

▶ 〔ˋsʌbdʒɪkt〕 名　科目，主題，題材
▶ 〔səbˋdʒɛkt〕 動　隸屬，服從，遭受
subject～to…「使～服從於…」

subjective
subject + ive

▶ 〔səb`dʒɛktɪv〕 形　主觀的
（反義）objective

subjectively
sujective + ly

▶ 〔səb`dʒɛktɪvlɪ〕 副　主觀地，個人地

Children should never be subjected to such abuse.
孩童從來都不應該受到這樣的虐待。

 ob　往前，反　
069

object
ob + ject

▶ 〔`ɑbdʒɪkt〕 名　物體，對象，目標，目的
〔əb`dʒɛkt〕 動　反對
object to～「反對～」

objection
object + ion

▶ 〔əb`dʒɛkʃən〕 名　反對，異議

objective
object + ive

▶ 〔əb`dʒɛktɪv〕 形　客觀的（反義）subjective
名　目的，目標

objectively
objective + ly

▶ 〔əb`dʒɛktɪvlɪ〕 副　客觀地

Many people object to the new law.
許多人反對新法。

Being objective is not an easy thing to do.
保持客觀並不是件容易的事。

His only objection was that the meeting was scheduled for a Saturday.
他唯一的異議就是會議定在禮拜六。

obstacle
ob + stacle

▶ 〔`ɑbstəkl〕 名　障礙物，妨礙

You will encounter obstacles in your life. The important thing is not to surrender your dreams.
人生中總是會遇到困難，重要的是不要因此放棄自己的夢想。

oblige
ob + lige

▶ 〔ə`blaɪdʒ〕 動　迫使，使不得不，施恩惠，
答應…的請求，幫忙
oblige（人）to V「迫使（人）～，使（人）不得已～」
oblige（人）by V-ing「替（人）～，幫（人）～」

obligatory
oblige + ory

▶ 〔ə`blɪgə͵torɪ〕 形　義不容辭的，有義務的，必須的，必修的

obligation
oblige + tion

▶ 〔͵ɑblə`geʃən〕 名　義務，責任

Could you oblige me by opening the door?
可以麻煩你幫我開門嗎？

Although it is not obligatory, it is highly recommended that you have the annual health check.
雖然那並不是義務，但我們強烈建議您每年作健康檢查。

He felt a strong obligation to take care of his parents in their old age.
他感到有強烈的義務要在父母年老時照顧他們。

obsess
ob + sess

▶ 〔əb`sɛs〕 動　迷住，著迷，纏擾
be obsessed by / with～「被～迷住」

obsession
obsess + ion

▶ 〔əb`sɛʃən〕 名　著迷，擺脫不了的思想，著魔

Alfred is obsessed with watches, and his entire salary is usually spent indulging his obsession.
亞佛列德很迷手錶，他的薪水大多花在滿足自己的慾望上。

---

 70 stru(ct)　stroy　建造，建立
070

structure
struct + ure

▶ 〔`strʌktʃɚ〕 名　結構，構造，建築物

structural
structure + al

▶ 〔`strʌktʃərəl〕 形　建築上的，結構的，構造上的

This structure could be made into a nice house.
這建築物可以蓋成一棟不錯的房子。

The company has decided to make some structural changes.
這間公司決定作一些結構上的改變。

---

construct
con + struct

▶ 〔kən`strʌkt〕 動　建造，構成，創立

constructive construct + ive	▶	〔kən`strʌktɪv〕 形　建設性的，有益的， 結構上的，構造上的
construction construct + ion	▶	〔kən`strʌkʃən〕 名　建造，建設，建築物
destruction de + struct + ion	▶	〔dɪ`strʌkʃən〕 名　破壞，毀滅，消滅
destructive de + struct + ive	▶	〔dɪ`strʌktɪv〕 形　破壞的，毀滅性的，消極的， 無幫助的
destroy de + stroy	▶	〔dɪ`strɔɪ〕 動　毀壞，破壞，消滅，失敗

The schoolchildren constructed paper airplanes.
那些學童造了些紙飛機。

The construction site was off limits to pedestrians.
工地現場禁止行人進入。

Simply complaining about something is not very constructive;
you should suggest alternative ideas.
單純抱怨某件事並不怎麼有建設性，你應該提出替代方案才對。

The UN forces searched for weapons of mass destruction.
聯合國軍隊搜尋了大規模的殺傷性武器。

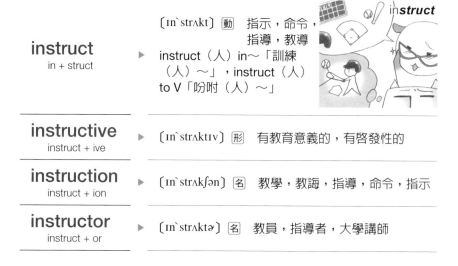

instruct in + struct	▶	〔ɪn`strʌkt〕 動　指示，命令， 　　　　　　　　指導，教導 instruct（人）in～「訓練 （人）～」，instruct（人） to V「吩咐（人）～」
instructive instruct + ive	▶	〔ɪn`strʌktɪv〕 形　有教育意義的，有啓發性的
instruction instruct + ion	▶	〔ɪn`strʌkʃən〕 名　教學，教誨，指導，命令，指示
instructor instruct + or	▶	〔ɪn`strʌktɚ〕 名　教員，指導者，大學講師

Be sure to read the instruction manual before you try to assemble the model.
在組合模型之前，你務必要先讀過說明書。

---

obstruct
ob + struct

▶ 〔əbˋstrʌkt〕 [動]　阻塞，堵塞，妨礙，阻擾

---

obstruction
obstruct + ion

▶ 〔əbˋstrʌkʃn〕 [名]　阻礙，妨礙，阻塞，障礙

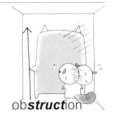

ob***struct***ion

The large vehicle in front obstructed my view.
前面的大型交通工具阻礙了我的視線。

The man was charged with obstruction of justice when he withheld important information.
那個男人因為隱瞞了重要資訊而被控妨礙司法。

---

instrument
in + stru + ment

▶ 〔ˋɪnstrəmənt〕 [名]　儀器，器具，樂器，工具

instrumental
instrument + al

▶ 〔ˌɪnstrəˋmɛntḷ〕 [形]　儀器的，有幫助的，用樂器演奏的

Joyce has been instrumental in the success of this advertising campaign.
喬伊絲的幫忙對廣告活動的成功起了相當作用。

There was soft instrumental music playing in the lobby.
在大廳裡播放著輕柔的樂曲。

---

⑦ part　部分

071

---

part

▶ 〔pɑrt〕 [名]　部分，零件，本分，角色
　　　　　 [動]　分開，分離，告別，分手
take part in～「參加～」

partial
part + ial
▶ 〔`parʃəl〕 形　部分的，局部的，不完全的
be partial to～「偏好～，偏袒～」

partially
patial + ly
▶ 〔`parʃəlɪ〕 副　部分地

partition
part + tion
▶ 〔par`tɪʃən〕 名　分開，分割，隔間，隔板

party
part + y
▶ 〔`partɪ〕 名　聚會，派對，一夥人，當事人，
（契約等的）一方

partly
part + ly
▶ 〔`partlɪ〕 副　部分地，不完全地，在一定程度上

Sharell is partial to the color pink; even her car is pink.
雪瑞偏好粉紅色，甚至連她的車都是粉紅的。
The weather today will be partly cloudy with a small chance of rain.
今天的天氣是部分多雲，降雨機率低。
There is no wall between the rooms, just a flimsy partition.
房間之間沒有牆壁，只有一片薄薄的隔板阻隔。

apart
a + part
▶ 〔ə`part〕 副　分開地，拆散地，單獨地，個別地

apartment
apart + ment
▶ 〔ə`partmənt〕 名　公寓大樓，公寓房間

Joshua took the car completely apart, but he couldn't put it back together again.
約書亞把車子整個給拆了，但卻沒辦法再組合回去。

depart
de + part
▶ 〔dɪ`part〕 動　啟程，出發，離開

departure
depart + ure
▶ 〔dɪ`partʃə〕 名　離開，出發，啟程

department
depart + ment
▶ 〔dɪ`partmənt〕 名　部門，（大學等的）系
department store「百貨公司」

The train will depart from track five.
列車將從五號軌道出發。

This book is a departure from the author's usual style.
這本書偏離了作者慣常的風格。

---

participate
part + cip + ate

▶ 〔pɑrˋtɪsəˌpet〕 動　參加，參與
participate in～「參加～」

---

participation
participate + ion

▶ 〔pɑrˌtɪsəˋpeʃən〕 名　參加，參與

---

participant
participate + ant

▶ 〔pɑrˋtɪsəpənt〕 名　參加者，關係者

All students are expected to participate in the entrance ceremony.
所有的學生都應該參加入學典禮。

All participants will receive a T-shirt.
所有參加者都會收到一件T恤。

---

particular
part + cular

▶ 〔pəˋtɪkjələ〕 形　特定的，特別的
in particular「特別地，尤其」

---

particularly
particular + ly

▶ 〔pəˋtɪkjələlɪ〕 副　特別，尤其

---

particularity
particular + ity

▶ 〔pəˌtɪkjəˋlærətɪ〕 名　特質，個性

Is there anything in particular that you are looking for?
你有特別在找什麼東西嗎？

Your office, particularly your desk, is a mess!
你的辦公室，特別是你的桌子，真是一團亂！

---

particle
part + icle

▶ 〔ˋpɑrtɪk!〕 名　微粒，顆粒，粒子

Tom howled and cursed in pain when he stepped on a particle of broken glass.
當湯姆踩到一粒碎玻璃的時候，他痛苦地號叫並且咒罵。

72 serv(e)　服務，保持　
072

serve	▶	〔sɝv〕 動 服務，供應，任職，服刑，招待，伺候 serve at〜「服務於〜」 serve as〜「任〜（職），當〜」
service serve + ice	▶	〔`sɝvɪs〕 名 服務，效勞，幫助
servant serve + ant	▶	〔`sɝvənt〕 名 僕人，傭人，雇工

This old bottle will serve as a vase for the wildflowers Sadie picked.
這只舊瓶會被拿來當作花瓶插放莎蒂摘的野花。

Could you help me to serve out the food?
你可以幫我出菜嗎？

observe ob + serve	▶	〔əb`zɝv〕 動 注意，觀察，看到，遵守
observer observe + er	▶	〔əb`zɝvɚ〕 名 觀察者，觀察員
observation observe + tion	▶	〔ˌɑbzɝ`veʃən〕 名 觀察，觀測
observance observe + ance	▶	〔əb`zɝvəns〕 名 遵守，奉行
observatory observe + ory	▶	〔əb`zɝvəˌtorɪ〕 名 天文台，氣象台，觀測所

You can observe many types of birds from this watch tower.
你可以在這個觀測塔觀察許多種類的鳥。

The astronomy students took a field trip to the observatory.
這些天文學的學生到天文台作實地考察。

conserve con + serve	▶	〔kən`sɝv〕 動 保存，保護
conservation conserve + tion	▶	〔ˌkɑnsɚ`veʃən〕 名 保存
conservative conserve + ive	▶	〔kən`sɝvətɪv〕 形 保守的，守舊的，傳統的

conservationist
conservation + ist

▶ 〔͵kɑnsə`veʃənɪst〕 名　天然資源保護論者

It is important to conserve our natural resources, because one day they will all be used up.
保護我們的天然資源很重要，因為總有一天這些資源會用盡。

preserve pre + serve	▶ 〔prɪ`zɝv〕 動　保存，防腐，維護 名　蜜餞，果醬，保護區
preservation preserve + tion	▶ 〔͵prɛzə`veʃən〕 名　保護，保存，維持
preservative preserve + ive	▶ 〔prɪ`zɝvətɪv〕 形　保存的，保護的，防腐的 名　保護劑，防腐劑

This forest of ancient trees needs to be preserved for posterity.
這片古代樹林應該要為了後代子孫而好好保護。

She spent the afternoon making strawberry preserves.
她花了一個下午作草莓果醬。

reserve re + serve	▶ 〔rɪ`zɝv〕 動　儲備，保存，保留，預約
reservation reserve + tion	▶ 〔͵rɛzə`veʃən〕 名　保留，預約

We can't sit here, because the table is reserved.
我們不能坐這，因為這桌子已被預約保留了。

---

73  heir　her　繼承
073

heir	▶ 〔ɛr〕 名　繼承人，繼承者
heredity her + edit + ity	▶ 〔hə`rɛdətɪ〕 名　遺傳
hereditary heredity + ary	▶ 〔hə`rɛdə͵tɛrɪ〕 形　世襲的，遺傳的

Male pattern baldness is hereditary, so if your mother's father is bald, you might be too.
雄性禿是遺傳性的落髮，所以如果你外祖父是禿頭，你也可能會禿。

inherit
in + her + it

▶ 〔ɪn`hɛrɪt〕 動 繼承

inheritance
inherit + ance

▶ 〔ɪn`hɛrɪtəns〕 名 繼承，繼承權，遺產，遺傳

Mary went on holiday to Europe, using the $25,000 she inherited from her aunt.
瑪莉用她從阿姨那裡繼承來的兩萬五千元去歐洲度假。

heritage
her + it + age

▶ 〔`hɛrətɪdʒ〕 名 遺產，繼承物，遺留物，傳統
World Heritage「世界遺產」

UNESCO inscribed Horyu-ji Temple on the World Heritage List in 1993. 聯合國教科文組織在1993年將法隆寺列入世界遺產名單中。

 74 just　jur(e)　法律，公正
074

justice
just + ice

▶ 〔`dʒʌstɪs〕 名 正義，公平

injustice
in + justice

▶ 〔ɪn`dʒʌstɪs〕 名 非正義，不公正，不公平

jury
jur + y

▶ 〔`dʒʊrɪ〕 名 陪審團，陪審員，評審委員會

The police are sure to find the person who did this, and justice will be served.
警察一定會找出犯下這件事的犯人，這樣正義將得以伸張。

injure
in + jur

▶ 〔`ɪndʒə〕 動 傷害，損壞，毀壞

injury
injure + y

▶ 〔`ɪndʒərɪ〕 名 傷害，損壞，損害

Although the injury looked serious, it was actually not too bad.
雖然傷害看起來很嚴重，但事實上並沒有那麼糟糕。

justify
just + ify

▶ 〔`dʒʌstəˌfaɪ〕 動 證明…是正當的，證明…無罪，證明合法，辯解

justification
justify + tion

▶ 〔ˌdʒʌstəfə`keʃən〕 名 證明為正當，辯護，辯解，正當的理由

A true pacifist believes that there is never any justification for war.
一個真正的和平主義者相信戰爭是沒有任何正當理由的。

---

adjust
ad + just

▶ 〔ə`dʒʌst〕 動　調節，調整，適應，校正

---

adjustment
adjust + ment

▶ 〔ə`dʒʌstmənt〕 名　調節，調整，校正

The volume on the telephone can be adjusted so that users can still hear in a noisy environment.
電話的音量可以調整，這樣使用者就算在吵雜的環境中仍然可以聽得見。

 (i)um　區域，場所
075

---

museum
muse + um

▶ 〔mju`zɪəm〕 名　博物館，美術館

---

aquarium
aqua + ium

▶ 〔ə`kwɛrɪəm〕 名　魚缸，水族館

---

stadium
stad + ium

▶ 〔`stedɪəm〕 名　體育場，運動場，競技場

---

gymnasium
gym + ium

▶ 〔dʒɪm`nezɪəm〕 名　體育館，健身房

76　muse　思考
076

---

muse

▶ 〔mjuz〕 動　沈思，冥想
　　 名　沈思，冥想
the Muses 希臘神話中的女神繆思

---

amuse
a + muse

▶ 〔ə`mjuz〕 動　使歡樂，逗…開心，娛樂

amusement
amuse + ment

▶ 〔ə`mjuzmənt〕 名　樂趣，娛樂，消遣

The words "museum" and "music" are from the Muses in Greek mythology, the goddesses who were the inspirers of learning and art.
博物館（museum）和音樂（music）兩個字源於希臘神話的謬思，啟發學識和藝術的女神。

 77 leg　loy　法律，規則
077

legal
leg + al

▶ 〔`ligl〕 形　法律上的，合法的，法定的

illegal
il + legal

▶ 〔ɪ`ligl〕 形　不合法的，非法的

Some people think that smoking should be made illegal in all public places.　有些人認為應該要立法禁止在所有的公共場所抽菸。

legislate
leg + ate

▶ 〔`lɛdʒɪsˏlet〕 動　立方，制定(或通過)法律
legislate against～「立法禁止～」

legislation
legislate + ion

▶ 〔ˏlɛdʒɪs`leʃən〕 名　制定法律，立法

legislative
legislate + ive

▶ 〔`lɛdʒɪsˏletɪv〕 形　立法，有立法權的，由法律規定的，立法機構的

legitimate
leg + ate

▶ 〔lɪ`dʒɪtəmɪt〕 形　合法的，正統的

legitimacy
legitimate + cy

▶ 〔lɪ`dʒɪtəməsɪ〕 名　合法性，正統性，合理

The citizen wrote a letter calling for legislation to protect the rights of animals.　市民寫了一份請願書呼籲立法保護動物的權利。

loyal
loy + al

▶ 〔`lɔɪəl〕 形　忠誠的，忠心的

loyalty
loyal + ty

▶ 〔`lɔɪəltɪ〕 名　忠誠，忠心，忠誠的行為

Ed remained a loyal friend even through Ray's period of psychosis.
即便在瑞精神病的期間，艾德仍是一位忠實的朋友。

act　扮演，行動

act	▶	〔ækt〕 名　行為，行動 動　扮演，演戲，行動，起作用
action act + ion	▶	〔`ækʃən〕 名　行動，行為，活動
active act + ive	▶	〔`æktɪv〕 形　活潑的，積極的 （反義）passive
inactive in + active	▶	〔ɪn`æktɪv〕 形　不活動的，無生氣的，怠惰的， 行動緩慢的
activate active + ate	▶	〔`æktə‚vet〕 動　使活潑，使活動起來，使活化
activity active + ity	▶	〔æk`tɪvətɪ〕 名　活動，活動力，活躍，敏捷

To activate the software, you need to register the serial number with the manufacturer.
要啟動軟體，你必須登錄製造商的序號。

Students who get involved in extracurricular activities often get more satisfaction out of their university lives.
參加課外活動的學生往往能在他們的大學生活中得到更多樂趣。

exact ex + act	▶	〔ɪg`zækt〕 形　正確的，精確的
exactly exact + ly	▶	〔ɪg`zæktlɪ〕 副　確切地，精確地，完全地

You must have exact change for the bus fare, or the driver will not let you ride.
你必須要準備剛好的零錢當公車費，不然司機可能不會讓你乘車。

She looks exactly like her aunt Sylvia.
她和她的阿姨施薇亞看起來一模一樣。

react re + act	▶	〔rɪ`ækt〕 動　作出反應，反應，影響，起作用， 使起（化學）反應
reactive react + ive	▶	〔rɪ`æktɪv〕 形　反應性的，易反應的，反作用的， 反動的

reaction
react + ion

▶　〔rɪ`ækʃən〕名　反應，反動，反作用

I could never have predicted that she would react in such a dramatic way to the news that the flight was cancelled.
我從沒料想過她在知道班機取消的消息時會有如此劇烈的反應。

---

 ess　女性
079

由於男女平等的觀念崛起，此類字尾的使用正快速消失中。例如，空服員（flight attendant）已取代空中小姐（stewardess）和空中少爺（steward）兩個字。其他男性意味濃厚的字眼如消防隊員（fireman）也由於女性就業率的增加，已傾向使用不強調性別的firefighter。

---

actress
act + ess

▶　〔`æktrɪs〕名　女演員
actor〔`æktɚ〕名　男演員，
　　　　　　　　演員（亦可指女演員）

hostess
host + ess

▶　〔`hostɪs〕名　女主人，女主持人
host〔host〕名　主人，節目主持人，宿主

Flight attendants used to be called air hostesses.
空服員（flight attendants）以前被稱作空中小姐（air hostesses）。

---

 wait　照料
080

---

wait

▶　〔wet〕動　等待，耽擱，服侍，伺候
wait on～「伺候～，照顧～」

waiter
wait + er

▶　〔`wetɚ〕名　服務生，侍者

wait**er**　wait**ress**

waitress
waiter + ess

▶　〔`wetrɪs〕名　女服務生

Cinderella had to wait on her stepmother hand and foot.
仙度瑞拉必須從頭到腳伺候她的繼母。

 not(e) 　　**寫下來，記錄**
081

note	▶	〔not〕 图　筆記，記錄，注釋，音符 動　注意，提到，記下 take a note of～「把～記下來」 note～down「記下～」
notable note + able	▶	〔`notəbl〕图　值得注意的，顯著的
notion note + ion	▶	〔`noʃən〕图　概念，想法，打算，意圖
noteworthy note + worthy	▶	〔`notˏwɝðɪ〕图　顯著的，值得注意的

If I don't write myself a note, I'll never remember to buy milk on my way home.
如果我不給自己寫張便條的話，我一定不會記得在回家的路上買牛奶的。

No, nothing noteworthy has happened in your two-week absence.
沒有，在你休息的兩個星期內沒有發生什麼值得注意的事情。

notice note + ice	▶	〔`notɪs〕图　公告，通知，預先通知 動　注意，通知
noticeable notice + able	▶	〔`notɪsəbl〕图　顯而易見的，顯著的，值得注意的
noticeably noticeable + ly	▶	〔`notɪsəblɪ〕副　顯著地，明顯地

She was noticeably upset, but she would not say what was bothering her.
她很明顯地心情不好，但是她不肯說到底是什麼讓她煩惱。

| **notify**
note + ify | ▶ | 〔`notəˏfaɪ〕動　通知，告知
notify（人）of～「將～通知（人）」 |
| **notification**
notify + tion | ▶ | 〔ˏnotəfə`keʃən〕图　通知，告知 |

You need to notify the office if you will be away in the afternoon.
如果下午要外出的話，你必須跟辦公室的人說一聲。

---

notorious
note + ous

▶ 〔noˋtorɪəs〕 彤 惡名昭彰的，聲名狼藉的

---

notoriety
note + ety

▶ 〔ˌnotəˋraɪətɪ〕 名 惡名昭彰，聲名狼藉

She gained notoriety in the convent for her preference for colorful fashion.
她對鮮豔色彩服裝的偏好讓她在修道院得到惡名。

Detroit was notorious for high incidence of violent crimes.
底特律過去因為暴力犯罪的高發生率而聲名狼藉。

---

 82 **wake**　睡醒，覺醒　
082

---

wake

▶ 〔wek〕 動　醒來，覺醒，喚醒，使覺悟
wake up「醒來」
wake up from〜「從〜醒過來，從〜覺醒」
wake〜up「喚醒〜」

---

waken
wake + en

▶ 〔ˋwekŋ〕 動　醒來，覺醒，喚醒，使覺醒

---

awake
a + wake

▶ 〔əˋwek〕 彤　醒著的，清醒的，意識到的
動　醒來，覺醒，喚醒，使覺醒

Allen woke up unwillingly from a lovely dream.
亞倫不情願地從甜美的夢中醒來。

Wake me up before you leave.
你出門前叫我起床。

The noise of the alarm clock wakened Wilma from her nap.
鬧鐘的聲響將薇瑪從午睡中吵醒。

The baby had been awake for hours, and the parents were exhausted.
小嬰兒好幾個小時都不睡，搞得他的父母精疲力竭。

vit(e)　vio　viv(e)　生命

083

vitamin
vit + amine

▶ 〔`vaɪtəmɪn〕名 維他命，維生素

Taking vitamin supplements is good, but it will not replace a healthy, balanced diet.
攝取維他命補給品很好，但是那並不能取代健康均衡的飲食。

invite
in + vite

▶ 〔ɪn`vaɪt〕動 邀請，招待，招致，誘惑

invitation
invite + tion

▶ 〔͵ɪnvə`teʃən〕名 邀請，請帖，引誘，招致

inviting
invite + ing

▶ 〔ɪn`vaɪtɪŋ〕形 吸引人的，誘人的

The warm candlelight and the fire in the fireplace were so inviting, that Damien could not refuse his uncle Ned's invitation to stay the night.
溫暖的燭光和壁爐的火是如此吸引人，讓達米安沒辦法拒絕他叔叔奈德留下來過夜的邀請。

vital
vit + al

▶ 〔`vaɪtl〕形 生命的，維持生命必需的，充滿活力的，極其重要的，致命的

vitality
vital + ity

▶ 〔vaɪ`tælətɪ〕名 活力，生氣，生命力

vitally
vital + ly

▶ 〔`vaɪtəlɪ〕副 充滿活力地，極其，十分

It is vital that you put your seat belt on when you drive.
在開車的時候繫上安全帶非常重要。

It is vitally important that you take this medicine every day at the same time.
每天同一時間服用此藥物是非常重要的。

violate
vio + ate

▶ 〔`vaɪə͵let〕動 違反，違背，侵犯，妨礙，褻瀆

violation
violate + ion

▶ 〔͵vaɪə`leʃən〕名 違反，違背，違反行為，侵犯，妨害

violent
vio + ent
▶ 〔`vaɪələnt〕 形 激烈的，猛烈的，暴力的

violently
violent + ly
▶ 〔`vaɪələntlɪ〕 副 激烈地，猛烈地，暴力地

violence
violent + ce
▶ 〔`vaɪələns〕 名 暴力，暴力行為，激烈，猛烈
DV＝domestic violence「家庭暴力，家暴」

The protesters say that allowing the government to tap phone lines is a violation of human rights.
抗議者指出，允許政府竊聽電話是一違反人權的行為。

He becomes violent if he drinks too much alcohol.
他如果喝太多酒，就會變得暴力。

vivid
viv + id
▶ 〔`vɪvɪd〕 形 鮮豔的，鮮明的，有生氣的，活潑的

vividly
vivid + ly
▶ 〔`vɪvɪdlɪ〕 副 生動地，逼真地，鮮明地，活潑地

His memory of meeting her was so vivid that he could describe exactly what she had been wearing.
和她見面的記憶是如此鮮明，以致於他能確切形容出她當時的衣著。

survive
sur + vive
▶ 〔sə`vaɪv〕 動 從…逃生，在…之後仍然生存，活下來，倖存
survive the war「從戰爭中倖存下來」

survival
survive + al
▶ 〔sə`vaɪvl〕 名 倖存，殘存，倖存者
the survival of the fittest「適者生存」

It is possible to survive for a few weeks without food as long as you have water to drink.
只要有水可喝，幾個禮拜不進食是有可能生存下來的。

revive
re + vive
▶ 〔rɪ`vaɪv〕 動 甦醒，復甦，恢復生機，恢復精力，復元

revival
revive + al
▶ 〔rɪ`vaɪvl〕 名 甦醒，復活，再生

After a 20-minute nap, he felt revived and ready to go again.
小睡20分鐘後，他感覺精力恢復可以繼續工作。

an　ant　anc　先

084

ancestor an + cestor	▶ 〔`ænsɛstə〕 名　祖宗，祖先
ancestral ancestor + al	▶ 〔æn`sɛstrəl〕 形　祖先的，祖傳的
ancestry ancestor + y	▶ 〔`ænsɛstrɪ〕 名　祖先，世系，血統

Susan is American, but has French ancestry.
蘇珊是美國人，但她有法國血統。

anticipate ant + cipate	▶ 〔æn`tɪsə,pet〕 動　預期，期望，預料， 預先考慮到，預先做準備
anticipation anticipate + ion	▶ 〔æn,tɪsə`peʃən〕 名　預期，期望，預料， 預期的事物

There was no way we could have anticipated just how well everything would turn out.
我們不可能預料到事情的結果會有多好。

It was with a great sense of anticipation that Japan prepared to host the world cup soccer.
日本準備舉辦世界杯足球賽讓人很期待。

ancient anc + ent	▶ 〔`enʃənt〕 形　古代的，古老的

The ancient city that had been preserved for centuries was destroyed in an earthquake.
保存了幾世紀的古城在地震中被破壞了。

antique ant + ique	▶ 〔æn`tik〕 形　古代的，古老的，年代久遠的， 古董的，古風的 名　古物，古董，古玩，古風
antiquity antique + ity	▶ 〔æn`tɪkwətɪ〕 名　古代，古老，古代的遺物

In antiquity, this area was famous for its handicrafts.
在古代，這個地區以手工藝品聞名。

mem(o) 記憶
085

memo ▶ 〔ˋmɛmo〕图 備忘錄，記錄，聯絡便條
memorandum〔ˏmɛməˋrændəm〕的縮寫

Please draft a memorandum regarding personnel cutbacks, then circulate it to all the section managers.
請起草一份關於人事削減的備忘錄，然後將該份備忘錄送至各部門經理。

memory ▶ 〔ˋmɛmərɪ〕图 記憶，記憶力，回憶
memo + ry

memorize ▶ 〔ˋmɛməˏraɪz〕動 記住，背熟
memory + ize

memorization ▶ 〔ˏmɛmərɪˋzeʃən〕图 記住，熟記
momorize + tion

memorial ▶ 〔məˋmorɪəl〕形 紀念的，記憶的，追悼的
memory + ial

Alice was a good piano player, but she hated memorizing pieces for recitals.
艾莉絲鋼琴彈得好，但是她非常討厭為了發表會背誦琴譜。
Roland returned to his country with no money, but with many wonderful memories.
羅蘭身無分文但滿懷美好的回憶回到他的國家。

remember ▶ 〔rɪˋmɛmbə〕動 記得，想起，記住，牢記
re + mem + ber

remembrance ▶ 〔rɪˋmɛmbrəns〕图 記憶，回想起的往事，紀念
remember + ance in remembrance of～「紀念～」

The city erected a memorial in remembrance of all the citizens who had died in war.
那座城市為所有在戰爭中喪生的市民立碑紀念。

86 vac void vit 空

086

vacuum
vac + um

〔`vækjuəm〕 名 真空，真空吸塵器
形 真空狀態的
動 用真空吸塵器打掃

vacuum my room「用吸塵器打掃我的房間」

Jim's mother told him he couldn't go out until he had finished vacuuming his room.
吉姆的媽媽告訴他除非用吸塵器打掃完房間，不然他也不能出門。

vacant
vac + ant

〔`vekənt〕 形 空的，空白的，空著的，空缺的

vacancy
vacant + cy

〔`vekənsɪ〕 名 空，空白，空間，空處，空缺

vacate
vac + ate

〔`veket〕 動 空出，搬出，使撤退，取消，辭職

vacation
vacate + ion

〔ve`keʃən〕 名 休假，假期，休假日

vacation

There were no vacant spaces in the car park.
停車場沒有任何空位。

The sign at the motel was blinking "vacancy."
汽車旅館的招牌閃爍著「尚有空房」。

evacuate
e + vac + ate

〔ɪ`vækjuˌet〕 動 撤空，撤離，撤退，使避難，使疏散，排空，排泄

evacuation
evacuate + ion

〔ɪˌvækju`eʃən〕 名 撤空，撤離，撤退，疏散，排泄

When the hospital received a bomb threat, the administration immediately called for an evacuation of the entire building.
醫院受到炸彈威脅的時候，行政部門馬上要求全體人員疏散避難。

avoid
a + void

▶ 〔əˋvɔɪd〕 動　避開，躲開，避免

avoidance
avoid + ance

▶ 〔əˋvɔɪdəns〕 名　躲避，迴避，躲避

avoidable
avoid + able

▶ 〔əˋvɔɪdəbl〕 形　能避免的，可迴避的

unavoidable
un + avoidable

▶ 〔ˏʌnəˋvɔɪdəbl〕 形　不可避免的，不能廢除的

If proper precautions had been taken, the accident would have been avoidable.
如果當初有採取適當的預防措施，就能避免這起意外了。

inevitable
in + vit + able

▶ 〔ɪnˋɛvətəbl〕 形　不可避免的，必然發生的

If you drive long enough, it's almost inevitable that you will be involved in an accident.
如果開車時間很長，意外事故幾乎是不可避免會發生。

 test　證明

087

test

▶ 〔tɛst〕 名　試驗，化驗，測驗，小考
　　　　 動　試驗，檢驗，測驗，化驗，分析

Everyone will be required to take a written test and a driving test before they are issued their driver's liscense.
在核發駕照前，每個人都要參加筆試和路考。

testify
test + ify

▶ 〔ˋtɛstəˏfaɪ〕 動　作證，表明，證明，證實

testimony
test + mony

▶ 〔ˋtɛstəˏmonɪ〕 名　證詞，證言，證據，證明

She will have to testify in court against her friend.
她必須出庭作出對她朋友不利的證詞。
His testimony was enough to convict the killer.
他的證詞足以證明兇手有罪。

protest
pro + test

▶ 〔`protɛst〕 名 抗議，異議，反對
〔prə`tɛst〕 動 抗議，反對，對…提出異議
protest against~「抗議~，反對~」

protestant
protest + ant

▶ 〔`protɪstənt〕 名 新教徒
形 新教的

Although I protested paying citizenship tax when I do not have the right to vote, I still had to pay.
雖然我反對在沒有投票權之前繳納公民稅，但是我還是得付錢。

There are many different protestant sects of Christianity.
基督教有許多不同的新教教派。

detest
de + test

▶ 〔dɪ`tɛst〕 動 厭惡，憎惡

I wanted to take the stray puppy home, but my mother detests having animals in the house.
我想要帶那隻流浪狗回家，但是我媽媽討厭家裡養寵物。

contest
con + test

▶ 〔`kontɛst〕 名 爭奪，競爭，比賽
〔kən`tɛst〕 動 爭奪，與…競賽，競爭，角逐
contest a seat in Congress「角逐美國國會席次」

contestation
contest + tion

▶ 〔ˌkontɛs`teʃən〕 名 爭論

Although the peasants felt the taxes were unfair, they knew that the king's decision was beyond contestation.
雖然農民們認為課稅不公，但是他們知道國王的決定是沒有爭論空間的。

88 ven(t) 來，產生

⭐
088

event
e + vent

▶ 〔ɪ`vɛnt〕 名 事件，大事，比賽項目，後果，結果

eventual
event + ual

▶ 〔ɪˋvɛntʃuəl〕 彫 最終發生的，最後的，結果的

eventually
eventual + ly

▶ 〔ɪˋvɛntʃuəlɪ〕 副 最後，終於

If you keep eating chocolate all the time without brushing your teeth regularly, eventually your teeth will rot.
如果你一直繼續吃巧克力不刷牙，最後你的牙齒都會爛光。

prevent
pre + vent

▶ 〔prɪˋvɛnt〕 動 防止，預防，妨礙，阻止
prevent（人）from V-ing「阻止（人）～」

preventive
prevent + ive

▶ 〔prɪˋvɛntɪv〕 彫 預防的，防止的

prevention
prevent + ion

▶ 〔prɪˋvɛnʃən〕 名 預防，防止，阻止，妨礙

She closed the shutters as a preventive measure against the typhoon that had been predicted.
預報颱風即將來襲，她將百葉窗關上作為預防。
A flock of sheep prevented me from getting to work on time.
一群羊阻礙我準時上班。

invent
in + vent

▶ 〔ɪnˋvɛnt〕 動 發明，創造

inventive
invent + ive

▶ 〔ɪnˋvɛntɪv〕 彫 發明的，創造的，有發明才能的，善於創造的

invention
invent + ion

▶ 〔ɪnˋvɛnʃən〕 名 發明，創造，發明物，創作品，捏造，虛構

inventor
invent + or

▶ 〔ɪnˋvɛntɚ〕 名 發明家，發明者，創作者

advent
ad + vent

▶ 〔ˋædvɛnt〕 名 出現，到來
Advent「基督降臨，降臨節」

adventure
advent + ure

▶ 〔əd`vɛntʃə〕 名　冒險，冒險精神，冒險活動

venture
vent + ure

▶ 〔`vɛntʃə〕 名　冒險，投機活動，企業
動　冒險

venturesome
venture + some

▶ 〔`vɛntʃəsəm〕 形　冒險的，投機的，危險的

The advent of the internet has hugely affected international communication.
網際網路的出現大大影響了國際間的交流模式。

"It'll be an adventure," he said, as he dove into the shark-nfested waters.
「這是場冒險。」他一邊說著，一邊潛入鯊魚肆虐的水域。

It was a cold and windy day, but she still decided to venture outside.
那是個寒冷風大的日子，但是她還是決定要冒險出門。

convent
con + vent

▶ 〔`kɑnvɛnt〕 名　修女團，女修道院

convention
convent + ion

▶ 〔kən`vɛnʃən〕 名　會議，集合，公約，協定，慣例，習俗，常規

conventional
convention + al

▶ 〔kən`vɛnʃənl〕 形　習慣的，慣例的，普通的，傳統的，符合習俗的

His teaching style is not conventional, but it is effective.
他的授課方式和一般不同，但是很有效。

convenient
con + ven + ent

▶ 〔kən`vinjənt〕 形　合宜的，方便的，便利的

conveniently
convenient + ly

▶ 〔kən`vinjəntlɪ〕 副　方便地，便利地，合宜地

convenience
convenient + ce

▶ 〔kən`vinjəns〕 名　方便，合宜

inconvenient
in + convenient

▶ 〔ˌɪnkən`vinjənt〕 形　不方便的，打擾的，令人為難的

inconveniently
inconvenient + ly

▶ 〔ˌɪnkən`vinjəntlɪ〕 副　不方便地

inconvenience
inconvenient + ce

▶ 〔ˌɪnkən`vinjəns〕 名　不便，麻煩，打擾

The train bound for Birmingham will be arriving 35 minutes late;
we apologize for the inconvenience.
前往伯明罕的火車將會誤點35分鐘，很抱歉造成您的不便。

 89 publ　popul　人，人民
089

public publ + ic	▶ 〔ˌpʌblɪk〕 彤　公眾的，公共的，政府的，眾所周知的 in public「公開地，當眾」
republic re + public	▶ 〔rɪˋpʌblɪk〕 名　共和國，共和政體
republican republic + an	▶ 〔rɪˋpʌblɪkən〕 彤　共和國的，共和政體的， 　　　　　　　　　（美國）共和黨的 　　　　　　 名　擁護共和政體者，共和主義者， 　　　　　　　　　（美國）共和黨人士
publicly public + ly	▶ 〔ˋpʌblɪklɪ〕 副　公開地，公然地
publicity public + ity	▶ 〔pʌbˋlɪsətɪ〕 名　名聲，宣傳，宣揚，宣傳品， 　　　　　　　　　公開場合

The politician got good publicity when he rescued a drowning child.
那位政治人物因為救了一個溺水的孩子而得到好名聲。

All visitors to the People's Republic of China need to have a proper
visa.　所有前往中華人民共和國的旅客都必須取得符合來訪目的的簽證。

publish publ + ish	▶ 〔ˋpʌblɪʃ〕 動　出版，發行，發表
publisher publish + er	▶ 〔ˋpʌblɪʃɚ〕 名　出版者，出版社，發表者
publication public + tion	▶ 〔ˌpʌblɪˋkeʃən〕 名　出版，發行，出版物，發表

He has published several children's picture books, but this is his
first novel.　他已經出版了幾本兒童繪本，但這是他第一本小說。
This magazine is a monthly publication.　這本雜誌是月刊。

popular popul + ar	▶ 〔ˋpɑpjələ〕 彤　民眾的，大眾的，受歡迎的， 　　　　　　　　　流行的，廣為流傳的 be popular among～「受～歡迎，受～好評」

popularity
popular + ity

▶ 〔ˌpɑpjəˋlærətɪ〕名　普及，流行，大眾化，聲望

I don't think squid flavored ice cream would ever gain much popularity.
我不覺得烏賊口味的冰淇淋會受歡迎。

populate
popul + ate

▶ 〔ˋpɑpjəˌlet〕動　居住於

population
populate + ion

▶ 〔ˌpɑpjəˋleʃən〕名　人口，全部居民

Tokyo has a large foreign population.
東京的外籍人口眾多。

 90　noun　nun　通知，告知
090

noun

▶ 〔naʊn〕名　名詞

pronoun
pro + noun

▶ 〔ˋpronaʊn〕名　代名詞

pronounce
pro + noun + ce

▶ 〔prəˋnaʊns〕動　發…的音，發音，宣稱，斷言，表示，發表意見

pronunciation
pronounce + tion

▶ 〔prəˌnʌnsɪˋeʃən〕名　發音，發音法，讀法

One of the difficulties in learning a foreign language is the differences in pronunciation.
學習外語的困難之一在於發音的不同。

The psychiatrist pronounced him insane.
精神科醫師判斷他患有精神病。

announce
an + noun + ce

▶ 〔əˋnaʊns〕動　宣佈，發佈，通知，聲稱，播報

announcer
announce + er

▶ 〔əˋnaʊnsə〕名　宣告者，廣播員，播音員

announcement
announce + ment

▶ 〔əˋnaʊnsmənt〕名　通告，佈告，預告，宣告，宣佈

I didn't realize I had left my car lights on until I heard the announcement on the loud speaker.
我沒有發現車頭燈是開著的，直到我聽見喇叭通知才知道。

The teacher will announce the start time of the test.
老師會宣佈考試開始的時間。

renounce re + noun + ce	▶	〔rɪˋnauns〕 動　聲明放棄，拋棄，宣佈中止，退出，與⋯斷絕關係，拒絕承認
renouncement renounce + ment	▶	〔rɪˋnaunsmənt〕 名　放棄，否認，拒絕，絕交
renunciation renounce + tion	▶	〔rɪˏnʌnsɪˋeʃən〕 名　宣告放棄，拋棄，宣佈脫離關係，拒絕承認

He renounced his claim as president of his grandfather's company.
他宣佈放棄擔任他祖父公司的董事長的權利。

91　cit　civ　城市，市民

091

city cit + y	▶	〔ˋsɪtɪ〕 名　城市，都市，全體市民
citizen cit + izen	▶	〔ˋsɪtəzn̩〕 名　市民，居民，公民
citizenship citizen + ship	▶	〔ˋsɪtəzn̩ˏʃɪp〕 名　公民權，市民權，公民（或市民）身分

After living in Britain for 40 years, she finally decided to apply for citizenship.
在英國住了40年後，她終於決定申請公民身分。

civil civ + il	▶	〔ˋsɪvl̩〕 形　市民的，公民的，客氣的，文明的 the Civil War「南北戰爭」（1861-65） be civil to～「對～有禮貌」
civilian civil + ian	▶	〔sɪˋvɪljən〕 名　平民，百姓
civilize civil + ize	▶	〔ˋsɪvəˏlaɪz〕 動　使文明，使開化，教化，使文雅

| **civilized**
civilize + ed | ▶ | 〔ˋsɪvəˌlaɪzd〕形 文明的，開化的，有教養的，
有禮貌的 |
| **civilization**
civilize + tion | ▶ | 〔ˌsɪvḷəˋzeʃən〕名 文明，文化，開化（過程） |

Alice's parents managed to be civil even though they strongly disliked her new boyfriend.
雖然艾莉絲的父母很不喜歡她的新男友，他們還是勉強維持客氣的態度。

 92 migr 移動，離開
092

migrate migr + ate	▶	〔ˋmaɪˌgret〕動 遷移，移居，（候鳥等的）定期遷移 migrate from～to...「從～移居至…」
migration migrate + ion	▶	〔maɪˋgreʃən〕名 遷移，（候鳥等的）遷徙
migratory mirate + ory	▶	〔ˋmaɪgrəˌtorɪ〕形 遷移的，有遷居習慣的， 流浪的
immigrate im + migrate	▶	〔ˋɪməˌgret〕動 遷移，遷入，使遷移 immigrate to～「移居至～，移民至～」
immigration immigrate + ion	▶	〔ˌɪməˋgreʃən〕名 移居，移民，入境審查
immigrant immigrate + ant	▶	〔ˋɪməgrənt〕名 移民，僑民

You will need to go through immigration upon entering the country.
入境前你必須經過入境審查。

emigrate e + migrate	▶	〔ˋɛməˌgret〕動 移居外國（或外地），使移居 emigrate from～to…「從～移居至…」
emigration emigrate + ion	▶	〔ˌɛməˋgreʃən〕名 移居，移民出境，移民
emigrant emigrate + ant	▶	〔ˋɛməgrənt〕名 移民，移出者

After World War II, many Japanese people emigrated to Brazil.
第二次世界大戰後，許多日本人移民到巴西。

93 pan （吃）麵包

093

company com + pan + y	▶ 〔`kʌmpənɪ〕 名　公司，陪伴，同伴 （一起吃麵包的人，有捧同樣飯碗的意思）
companion company + ion	▶ 〔kəm`pænjən〕 名 同伴，伴侶，朋友， （受雇照顧病人等的） 看護
accompany ac + company	▶ 〔ə`kʌmpənɪ〕 動 陪同，伴隨，伴奏， 伴唱
accompanist accompany + ist	▶ 〔ə`kʌmpənɪst〕 名　伴隨者，伴奏者，伴唱者
accompaniment accompany + ment	▶ 〔ə`kʌmpənɪmənt〕 名　伴隨物，附加物，伴奏， 伴唱

accom**pan**y

The violinist played a solo with a piano accompaniment.
那位小提琴家在鋼琴的伴奏下演奏了一曲獨奏曲。

94 ache 疼痛

094

ache	▶ 〔ek〕 名　疼痛，同情，憐憫 動　疼痛，同情，憐憫，感到痛苦
headache head + ache	▶ 〔`hɛd͵ek〕 名　頭痛
toothache tooth + ache	▶ 〔`tuθ͵ek〕 名　牙痛

After spending the day moving to a new apartment, Joe had
muscle aches all over his body.
在搬家一整天後，喬全身的肌肉痠痛。

95 **cel(er)**　快的，迅速的　
095

accelerate ac + celer + ate	▶	〔æk`sɛlə.ret〕[動]　使增速，促進，促使，加快， 增長，增加
accelerator accelerate + or	▶	〔æk`sɛlə.retə〕[名]　加速裝置，油門，催化劑
acceleration accelerate + ion	▶	〔æk.sɛlə`reʃən〕[名]　加速，促進

There is no magic potion for developing language skills at an accelerated pace.
沒有什麼神奇魔藥能迅速加強語言的能力。

excel ex + cel	▶	〔ɪk`sɛl〕[動]　勝過，優於，突出 excel in/at～「擅長～」 excel～in/at...「擅長…而勝過～」
excellent excel + ent	▶	〔`ɛkslənt〕[形]　出色的，傑出的
excellence excel + ence	▶	〔`ɛksləns〕[名]　優秀，傑出，卓越，長處，優點

Although her language skills are low, Mary excels in math and science.
雖然瑪莉的語言能力不好，但是她擅長數學和自然科學。

96 **pet(e)**　**peat**　渴望，要求　
096

appetite a + pet + ite	▶	〔`æpə.taɪt〕[名]　食慾，胃口，慾望，愛好
appetizer appetite + ize + er	▶	〔`æpə.taɪzə〕[名]　開胃菜

Blair has a real appetite for violence, so his friends don't let him drink alcohol.
布萊爾有強烈的暴力傾向，所以他的朋友不讓他喝酒。

compete com + pete	▶ 〔kəm`pit〕動　競爭，對抗，比賽 compete for～「為了～而競爭（或比賽）」 compete in～「比賽～」
competition compete + tion	▶ 〔ˌkɑmpə`tɪʃən〕名　競爭，角逐，比賽
competitive compete + ive	▶ 〔kəm`pɛtətɪv〕形　競爭的，競爭性的，好競爭的

Barney won the writing competition with a story about his favorite pet.
巴尼以一篇他最愛的寵物的文章贏得寫作比賽。

competent compete + ent	▶ 〔`kɑmpətənt〕形　有能力的，能幹的，能勝任的， 稱職的
competence competent + ce	▶ 〔`kɑmpətəns〕名　能力，勝任，稱職

Tracy's brother is very competent at using a computer, so she always asks him for help.
崔西她哥哥的電腦能力很強，所以她總是向他尋求電腦方面的幫助。

repeat re + peat	▶ 〔rɪ`pit〕動　重複，複述
repeatedly repeat + ed + ly	▶ 〔rɪ`pitɪdlɪ〕副　一再，再三，多次
repetition repeat + tion	▶ 〔ˌrɛpɪ`tɪʃən〕名　重複，反覆

The shampoo bottle said I should "wash, rinse and repeat if necessary."
洗髮精瓶子上寫著我應該要「搓揉髮絲，沖洗乾淨，必要的話再重複動作」。

97　san(e)　健康

097

sane	▶ 〔sen〕形　神智正常的，頭腦清楚的，健全的， 明智的
sanity sane + ity	▶ 〔`sænətɪ〕名　精神健全，精神正常，清醒，明智

insane
in + sane

▶ 〔ɪn`sen〕 形　患有精神病的，精神錯亂的，
　　　　　　　　精神異常的

insanity
insane + ity

▶ 〔ɪn`sænətɪ〕 名　瘋狂，精神錯亂，精神失常

People who go swimming in the ice-cold river must be insane.
在冰冷的河水裡游泳的人一定是瘋了。

The defendant was found not guilty by reason of insanity.
被告由於精神異常的原因被判無罪。

sanitary
sanity + ary

▶ 〔`sænəˌtɛrɪ〕 形　公共衛生的，衛生上的，衛生的

sanatorium
san + ium

▶ 〔ˌsænə`torɪəm〕 名　療養院

There are strict regulations for keeping hospitals sanitary.
醫院衛生的保持有著嚴格的規定。

98　fess　說，坦白

098

confess
con + fess

▶ 〔kən`fɛs〕 動　坦白，承認，
　　　　　　　　告解，懺悔
confess to a crime「認罪」

confession
confess + ion

▶ 〔kən`fɛʃən〕 名　承認，坦白

con**fess**

The priest fell asleep while listening to a devotee's confession.
神父在聽信徒告解的時候睡著了。

Since the police threatened the suspect, the confession was ruled inadmissible in court.
由於警察威脅嫌疑犯，該份自白在法庭上不被採用。

profess
pro + fess

▶ 〔prə`fɛs〕 動　公開宣稱，表白，聲稱，承認

profession
profess + ion

▶ 〔prə`fɛʃən〕 名　職業

professional
profession + al
▶ ﹝prəˋfɛʃnl﹞ 形　職業的，很內行的

professor
profess + or
▶ ﹝prəˋfɛsə﹞ 名　教授

He was a banker by profession, but his real passion was for gardening.
他的正職是銀行行員，但是他真正熱愛的是園藝。

99　neg　ny　ni　**否定**　
099

negate
neg + ate
▶ ﹝nɪˋget﹞ 動　否定，取消，無效，使無效

negation
negate + ion
▶ ﹝nɪˋgeʃən﹞ 名　否定，反對，反駁

negative
negate + ive
▶ ﹝ˋnɛgətɪv﹞ 形　否定的，否認的，反面的
名　否定，拒絕，底片
（反義）positive

negatively
negative + ly
▶ ﹝ˋnɛgətɪvlɪ﹞ 副　否定地，消極地

I had the photos developed, but I lost the negatives, so I can't make copies.
我已經洗好照片了，但是我弄丟了底片，所以沒辦法加洗。

The bad weather had a negative effect on the turnout at the school festival.
惡劣的天候替校慶的出席人數帶來負面影響。

---

neglect
neg + lect
▶ ﹝nɪgˋlɛkt﹞ 動　忽視，忽略，疏忽
名　忽略，疏忽，疏漏

negligent
neg + lig + ent
▶ ﹝ˋnɛglɪdʒənt﹞ 形　疏忽的，粗心的，隨便的，不在意的

negligence
negligent + ce
▶ ﹝ˋnɛglɪdʒəns﹞ 名　疏忽，粗心，隨便，不修邊幅

negligible
neg + lig + ible
▶ ﹝ˋnɛglɪdʒəbl﹞ 形　可以忽略的，無關緊要的，微不足道的

The plants in the corner were yellow and drooping from neglect.
角落的植物由於疏於照顧而發黃枯萎。

The differences between version one and version two are negligible.
第一版跟第二版的差異很小。

---

deny
de + ny
▶ 〔dɪˋnaɪ〕 動　否定，否認
deny V-ing「否定～，否認～」

denial
deny + al
▶ 〔dɪˋnaɪəl〕 名　否定，否認，拒絕承認

He denied stealing the car, but no one believed him.
他否認偷了那輛車，但是沒有人相信他。

 100　nav(i)　船
100

---

navigate
navi + gate
▶ 〔ˋnævəˏget〕 動　航行於，飛行於，駕駛，操縱，導航，航行，航空

navigator
navigate + or
▶ 〔ˋnævəˏgetə〕 名　領航員，導航裝置，航海者，航海探險家

navigation
navigate + ion
▶ 〔ˏnævəˋgeʃən〕 名　航海，航空，航行，領航，導航，航運

She navigated the icy streets expertly.
她熟練地在薄冰覆蓋的街道上駕駛。

---

navy
nav + y
▶ 〔ˋnevɪ〕 名　海軍，海軍艦隊

naval
nav + al
▶ 〔ˋnevl̩〕 形　海軍的，軍艦的，船的

He came home to live with his parents after getting a medical discharge from the navy.
他由於健康理由自海軍除役後，回家和他的父母住在一起。

101 **chem** 煉金術
101

---

alchemy
al(=the) + chem + y

▶ 〔ˋælkəmɪ〕名 煉金術
【註】"al" 為阿拉伯語的定冠詞。新聞上的「蓋達（Al Qaeda）」組織即為一例。

---

alchemist
alchemy + ist

▶ 〔ˋælkəmɪst〕名 煉金術士

The alchemist tried his whole life to turn iron into gold.
那位煉金術士花了一輩子的時間嘗試煉鐵成金。

---

chemist
chem + ist

▶ 〔ˋkɛmɪst〕名 化學家，藥劑師

chemistry
chemist + ry

▶ 〔ˋkɛmɪstrɪ〕名 化學，化學性質，化學作用

chemical
chem + ical

▶ 〔ˋkɛmɪkl〕形 化學的，化學上的，化學用的
名 化學製品，化學藥品

Julie got a chemistry set for Christmas, and promptly burned a hole in the tablecloth.
茱莉聖誕節的時候得到一組化學設備，結果馬上就把桌布燒了一個洞。

The factory disposed of harmful chemicals by dumping them in the river.
那間工廠將有害的化學物質排放到河川中。

---

 102 **nov** 新的
102

---

novel
nov + el

▶ 〔ˋnɑvl〕名 （長篇）小說

novelist
novel + ist

▶ 〔ˋnɑvlɪst〕名 小說家

Gene's first novel was a best-seller, but the second was a commercial failure.
吉恩的小說處女作是本暢銷作，但是他的第二本小說卻賣得很差。

---

innovate
in + nov + ate

▶ 〔ˋɪnəˏvet〕動 創立，創始，革新，改革，創新

innovation
innovate + ion
▶ 〔͵ɪnəˋveʃən〕 名 革新，改革，創新，新方法，新制度，新事物

innovative
innovate + ive
▶ 〔ˋɪnə͵vetɪv〕 形 創新的

If you want to inspire innovation in your workers, you have to give them some room for creativity.
如果你想要鼓勵員工創新，你必須要給他們一些發揮創造力的空間。

renovate
re + nov + ate
▶ 〔ˋrɛnə͵vet〕 動 更新，重做，修理，改善，恢復

renovation
renovate + ion
▶ 〔͵rɛnəˋveʃən〕 名 更新，修理，恢復活力

The hotel is being renovated, so it might be noisy during the day.
飯店正在裝修中，所以白天的時候可能會很吵。

 gress 前進
103

progress
pro + gress
▶ 〔ˋprɑgrɛs〕 名 前進，進步，發展，進展
〔prəˋgrɛs〕 動 前進，上進，提高，進步

progressive
progress + ive
▶ 〔prəˋgrɛsɪv〕 形 進步的，先進的，發展中的

progression
progress + ion
▶ 〔prəˋgrɛʃən〕 名 前進，連續，發展，改進

Although his ideas were progressive, he had to fight against prejudice and complacency.
雖然他的觀念先進，他還是得對抗偏見與自滿。

Alice is making great progress in her piano lessons.
艾莉絲在鋼琴課表現進步很多。

congress
con + gress
▶ 〔ˋkɑŋgrəs〕 名 會議，代表大會，立法機關，美國國會，議會
〔kənˋgrɛs〕 動 集合
the Diet 〔ˋdaɪət〕 名 「（丹麥，日本等的）國會」
the Parliament 〔ˋpɑrləmənt〕 名 「議會，（英國）國會」

The meeting will congress at precisely 14:00.
會議在下午兩點整準時開始。

aggress ag + gress	▶ 〔əˋgrɛs〕 動 侵略，挑釁，攻擊 aggress to/against～「挑戰～，攻擊～」
aggressive aggress + ive	▶ 〔əˋgrɛsɪv〕 形 侵略的，好鬥的，挑釁的， 有進取精神的，積極的
aggression aggress + ion	▶ 〔əˋgrɛʃən〕 名 侵略，侵略行動，侵犯行為

Dogs that are too aggressive don't make good pets for people with small children.
太具攻擊性的狗並不適合作為有小孩的人的寵物。

 ## apt　適當的
104

apt	▶ 〔æpt〕 形 易於…的，有…傾向的，恰當的， 貼切的 be apt to V「傾向～，易於～」
aptitude apt + itude	▶ 〔ˋæptəˏtjud〕 名 傾向，習性，天資，才能， 恰當，適宜

Before being accepted into the army, applicants must take a series of aptitude tests.
在加入陸軍之前，申請人必須要接受一連串的適性測驗。

adapt ad + apt	▶ 〔əˋdæpt〕 動 使適應，使適合，改編，改寫，適應 adapt～to...「使～適應…」 adapt to～「適應～」
adaptable adapt + able	▶ 〔əˋdæptəbl〕 形 能適應新環境的，適應性強的， 適合的，可改編（或改寫）的
adaptation adapt + tion	▶ 〔əˋdæpʃən〕 名 適應，適合，改寫

If you move to another country, you will need to adapt to a new culture.
如果你移居到外國，你將需要適應新的文化。

fac(e)　fic　臉，表面
105　　　　　　　　　　　　　　　　　　　　　　　　　105

| **face** | ▶ | 〔fes〕 名　臉，面孔，表情，表面，正面，面子 |

| **facial**
face + ial | ▶ | 〔ˋfeʃəl〕 形　臉的，面部的，表面的 |

| **surface**
sur + face | ▶ | 〔ˋsɝfɪs〕 名　面，表面，水面，外觀，外表 |

The part of an iceberg that can be seen above the surface of the ocean is only about 1/8 of the entire mass of the iceberg.
海面上可見的冰山僅僅只是實際體積的八分之一左右。

| **superficial**
super + fic + ial | ▶ | 〔͵supɚˋfɪʃəl〕 形　表面的，外表的，膚淺的，
草率的，粗略的 |

| **superficially**
superficial + ly | ▶ | 〔͵supɚˋfɪʃəlɪ〕 副　淺薄地，膚淺地 |

Although the wound bled a lot, it was superficial, and not serious.
雖然傷口出血很多，但是只傷到表皮，並不嚴重。
Possibly the reason he and his roommate get along so well is because they have kept their relationship on a superficial level.
他和室友能處得那麼好，有可能是因為他們維持著表面關係。

 port　運送，港口
106　　　　　　　　　　　　　　　　　　　　　　　　　106

| **port** | ▶ | 〔port〕 名　港，港口 |

| **portable**
port + able | ▶ | 〔ˋportəbl〕 形　便於攜帶的，手提式的，輕便的 |

| **porter**
port + er | ▶ | 〔ˋportɚ〕 名　搬運工人，服務員 |

import
im + port

〔ɪm`port〕 動　進口，輸入
〔`ɪmport〕 名　進口，輸入，進口商品
import～from...「從…進口～」

export
ex + port

〔ɪks`port〕 動　輸出，出口
〔`ɛksport〕 名　輸出，出口，輸出品，輸出額
export～to...「輸出～至…」

He is in the business of importing hats from Spain.
他從事將帽子自西班牙輸入的生意。

Japan is famous for exporting high-quality electronic goods.
日本以輸出高品質的電子產品聞名。

important
im + port + ant

〔ɪm`portnt〕 形　重要的，重大的，地位高的，
有權力的

importance
important + ce

〔ɪm`portns〕 名　重要，重大，重要性，
重要的地位（或身分）

The importance of his discovery was not recognized at first.
他的發現的重要性在一開始並不被認同。

107　trans　轉移，越過

107

transport
trans + port

〔træns`port〕 動　運送，運輸，搬運
〔`trænsˏport〕 名　運輸，交通工具，交通運輸系統

transportation
transport + tion

〔ˏtrænspɚ`teʃən〕 名　運輸，輸送，運輸工具，
運輸業

What type of transport do you use to get to work?
你是搭乘什麼樣的交通工具上班？

---

transform
trans + form

〔træns`form〕 動　改造，改變，改觀，變換，轉換
transform～into/to...「將～改成…」
transform into～「變成～」

transformation
transform + tion

〔ˏtrænsfɚ`meʃən〕 名　變化，轉變，變形，變質

The ugly duckling transformed into a beautiful swan.
那隻醜小鴨變成一隻美麗的天鵝。

Alchemists tried to transform other metals into gold.
煉金術士試著將其他種類的金屬轉變成黃金。

Clark Kent needed a phone booth to make the transformation into Superman.
克拉克‧肯特需要利用電話亭來變身成為超人。

translate trans + late	▶ 〔træns`let〕 動　翻譯，轉譯，轉化，變化 translate～into...「將～翻譯成…」
translation translate + ion	▶ 〔træns`leʃən〕 名　翻譯，譯本，譯文，轉變，轉化

Could you translate this poem from Japanese into English for me?
你可以幫我把這首詩從日文翻譯成英文嗎？

transfer trans + fer	▶ 〔træns`fɝ〕 動　搬，轉換，調動，轉移，改變， 　　　　　　轉變，調任，轉學 transfer～from A to B「將～從 A 轉移至 B」 transfer from～to...「從～轉移至…，從～調任至…」
transferable transfer + able	▶ 〔træns`fɝəbl̩〕 形　可轉移的，可轉讓的
transference transfer + ence	▶ 〔træns`fɝəns〕 名　轉移，傳遞，調任，轉讓

She decided to transfer to a different department because she did not like the people in her office.
她決定轉調至別的部門，因為她不喜歡她辦公室的同事。

 per(i)　試驗，嘗試　
108

experiment ex + peri + ment	▶ 〔ɪk`spɛrəmənt〕 名　實驗，試驗
experimental experiment + al	▶ 〔ɪkˏspɛrə`mɛntl̩〕 形　實驗性的，試驗性的， 　　　　　　實驗用的

The treatment is experimental, so there is a risk involved.
這個治療法尚在試驗階段，所以有風險。

I did a small experiment to find out if my wet laundry would dry faster inside the house or outside.
我作了一個小實驗，看看濕衣服在屋內和屋外哪邊會比較快乾。

experience
ex + peri + ence
▶ 〔ɪkˋspɪrɪəns〕 名 經驗，體驗，經歷，閱歷
動 經歷，體驗，感受，遭受

experienced
experience + ed
▶ 〔ɪkˋspɪrɪənst〕 形 有經驗的，老練的，熟練的

Although she is an experienced doctor, she is not licensed to practice in this country.
雖然她是經驗豐富的醫生，但是她在這個國家並沒有執業執照。

expert
ex + per
▶ 〔ˋɛkspɚt〕 名 專家，能手，熟練者

expertise
expert + ise
▶ 〔͵ɛkspɚˋtiz〕 名 專門知識，專門技術，專家鑑定

A team of experts determined that the fire was caused by someone smoking in bed. 一隊專家鑑定起火原因是由於有人在床上抽菸。

peril
peri + il
▶ 〔ˋpɛrəl〕 名 危險，危險的事物，冒險
（同義）danger〔ˋdendʒɚ〕
名 危險，危險（物），威脅

perilous
peril + ous
▶ 〔ˋpɛrələs〕 形 危險的，冒險的
（同義）dangerous〔ˋdendʒərəs〕
形 危險的，不安全的，招致危險的

They realized they were in great peril when they felt the back tires of the car slip over the edge of the cliff. 當他們感覺到車子的後輪滑落懸崖邊緣時，他們瞭解自己正身處巨大的危機當中。

109 liber liver 自由
109

liberty
liber + ty
▶ 〔ˋlɪbɚtɪ〕 名 自由，自由權

liberal
liber + al
▶ 〔ˋlɪbərəl〕 形 心胸開闊的，開明的，不守舊的，
自由的，大方的，慷慨的

liberate liber + ate	▶	〔`lıbə‚ret〕 動　解放，使獲自由 liberate（人‧物）from...「將（人‧物）自…中解放」
liberation liberate + ion	▶	〔‚lıbə`reʃən〕 名　解放，解放運動

Some therapists believe that talking about your problems can be the first step in liberating yourself from them.
一些心理治療師相信，談論自己的煩惱是自這些煩惱解放的第一步。

deliver de + liver	▶	〔dɪ`lıvə〕 動　投遞，傳送，運送，給…接生，生（孩子），履行，實現
delivery deliver + y	▶	〔dɪ`lıvərɪ〕 名　投遞，傳送，交付，交貨，交付的物件，分娩

The package was delivered at 6:00 PM.
包裹在下午六點投遞。

 110　libr　liber　測量

Libra libr + a	▶	〔`laıbrə〕 名　天秤座
deliberate de + liber + ate	▶	〔dɪ`lıbərɪt〕 形　深思熟慮的，慎重的，謹慎的 動　仔細考慮，思考，商議
deliberately deliberate + ly	▶	〔dɪ`lıbərɪtlı〕 副　慎重地，謹慎地，從容不迫地，故意地
deliberation deliberate + ion	▶	〔dɪ‚lıbə`reʃən〕 名　深思熟慮，研究，審議，商議，慎重，從容

The jury was in deliberation for over 12 hours before they reached a verdict.
陪審團在達成裁定前商議了超過十二個小時。
He deliberately ignored her remarks.
他故意忽視她的話。

111　caus(e)　cus(e)　原因，歸因

cause
▶ 〔kɔz〕名　原因，起因，理由，動機，目標
　　　　動　導致，使發生，引起
（反義）effect
cause and effect「有因果關係的」

causal
cause + al
▶ 〔`kɔzḷ〕形　原因的，因果的

because
be(=by) + cause
▶ 〔bɪ`kɔz〕連　因為

Contrary to popular opinion, there is no causal relationship between going outside with wet hair and catching a cold.
和一般的看法相反，頂著濕頭髮出門和感冒並沒有什麼因果關係存在。

accuse
ac + cuse
▶ 〔ə`kjuz〕動　指控，控告，譴責，指責，
　　　　　　　　把…歸咎於
accuse（人）of～「指控（人）～，譴責（人）～」

accusation
accuse + tion
▶ 〔ˌækjə`zeʃən〕名　指控，控告，指責，
　　　　　　　　（被控告的）罪名

excuse
ex + cuse
▶ 〔ɪk`skjuz〕動　原諒，辯解，准許…離開
excuse（人）for～「原諒（人）～」

Before you make accusations against someone, you should make sure that your information is correct.
在你指責他人之前，你應該要確定自己的資訊正確。

112　prim(e)　prin　第一的，主要的

prime
▶ 〔praɪm〕形　最初的，原始的，基本的，主要的，
　　　　　　　首位的
prime time「（廣播電視）黃金時段」
prime minister「首相」

primary
prime + ary

▶ 〔ˋpraɪ⋅mɛrɪ〕形 首要的，主要的，初級的，原始的，最初的，基本的

primarily
primary + ly

▶ 〔praɪˋmɛrəlɪ〕副 首先，起初，原來，首要地，主要地，根本上

There are some things that cannot be shown on prime time television.
有些東西不能在電視的黃金時段播出。

She said that lack of financial resources is her primary reason for deciding not to take the trip.
她說資金短缺是她決定不參加旅行的主要原因。

primitive
prim + ive

▶ 〔ˋprɪmətɪv〕形 原始的，遠古的，早期的

Even though they had several television sets and personal computers, all the other facilities in their house were quite primitive.
雖然他們有好幾台電視和個人電腦，但是他們家裡的其他設備都頗為原始。

Technology that was cutting edge even a few years ago is now considered primitive.
幾年前最先進的科技在現在已經被認為是落伍了。

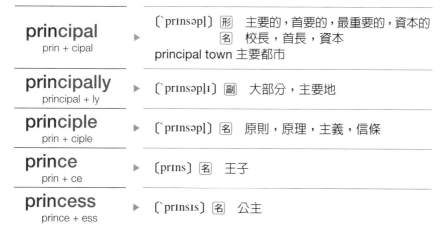

principal
prin + cipal

▶ 〔ˋprɪnsəpl〕形 主要的，首要的，最重要的，資本的
名 校長，首長，資本
principal town 主要都市

principally
principal + ly

▶ 〔ˋprɪnsəplɪ〕副 大部分，主要地

principle
prin + ciple

▶ 〔ˋprɪnsəpl〕名 原則，原理，主義，信條

prince
prin + ce

▶ 〔prɪns〕名 王子

princess
prince + ess

▶ 〔ˋprɪnsɪs〕名 公主

He never let the outside pressure cause him to do anything against his principles.
他從來不因為外來的壓力而做任何違反他的原則的事情。

clea(r)　　clar(e)　　明亮的

113

clear	▶ 〔klɪr〕 形 清澈的，明亮的，清楚的，晴朗的 動 使乾淨，收拾，放晴
clearly clear + ly	▶ 〔`klɪrlɪ〕 副 明亮地，清楚地，顯然地
clearance clear + ance	▶ 〔`klɪrəns〕 名 清除，出清，清倉大拍賣
clarity clar + ity	▶ 〔`klærətɪ〕 名 清楚，明晰，清澈
clean	▶ 〔klin〕 形 清潔的，清白的，整齊的，徹底的

He is clearly not suited for this job.
很顯然地他並不適合這份工作。

The store is having a huge clearance sale; everything is 50%off.
那間店正在清倉大拍賣，所有的東西都打五折。

Clarity is one quality that makes a diamond more expensive.
淨度是鑽石價格增加的特質之一。

clarify clar + ify	▶ 〔`klærəˌfaɪ〕 動 澄清，闡明，淨化
clarification clarify + tion	▶ 〔ˌklærəfəˋkeʃən〕 名 澄清，淨化，說明

Paul was asked to clarify his point of view, as no one understood what he meant.
保羅被要求說明他的觀點，因為沒有任何人瞭解他的意思。

declare de + clare	▶ 〔dɪˋklɛr〕 動 宣佈，宣告，聲明，宣稱，表示
declaration declare + tion	▶ 〔ˌdɛkləˋreʃən〕 名 宣佈，宣告，宣言，聲明 declaration of war「宣戰」 the Declaration of Independence「（1776年）獨立宣言」

She declared that she would never smoke again, but she was caught with a cigarette two days later.
她宣佈不再抽菸，但兩天後被人發現她在吸菸。

114　murd　mort　死亡
114

murder murd + er	▶	〔`mɝdə〕 名　謀殺，兇殺，謀殺罪 動　謀殺，兇殺，扼殺
murderer murder + er	▶	〔`mɝdərə〕 名　謀殺犯，兇手

The murderer was apprehended and locked away, much to the relief of the family of the victim.
兇手被逮捕入監對受害者家屬來說實在是一大寬慰。

mortal mort + al	▶	〔`mɔrtl〕 形　會死的，凡人的，致死的，極大的
mortality mortal + ity	▶	〔mɔr`tæləti〕 名　必死性，死亡率，失敗率，人類
immortal im + mortal	▶	〔ɪ`mɔrtl〕 形　不朽的，流芳百世的，長久的， 不死的，神仙的
immortality immortal + ity	▶	〔ˌɪmɔr`tæləti〕 名　不死，不朽，不滅， 不朽的聲名

No matter how much you wish for immortality, it is impossible to achieve.
無論你多麼希望能長生不死，那都是不可能實現的。

115　voice　voc　說話，聲音
115

voice	▶	〔vɔɪs〕 名　聲音，表達的意見 動　用言語表達，說出
vocal voc + al	▶	〔`vokl〕 形　聲音的，口頭的，歌唱的 名　聲樂
vocabulary voc + abulary	▶	〔və`kæbjəˌlɛrɪ〕 名　字彙，語彙

After she had voiced her opinion, she left and never came back.
她在說出自己的意見後就離開了，而且再也沒有回來。

sor(e)　　疼痛的，痛苦的　　
116

sore ▶	〔sor〕形　痛的，惹人生氣的，惱火的，痛心的，極度的
sorrow sor + row ▶	〔`saro〕名　悲痛，悲傷，憂傷，傷心事，悲傷的原因，懊悔，遺憾
sorrowful sorrow + ful ▶	〔`sarəfəl〕形　悲傷的，傷心的，令人傷心的

I felt a great deal of sorrow when I heard that my grandmother had died.
聽說祖母過世的消息時，我感到非常悲傷。

 loc(o)　　場所，位置　　
117

local loc + al ▶	〔`lokl〕形　地方性的，當地的，本地的，鄉土的，局部的
locate loc + ate ▶	〔lo`ket〕動　確定…的地點（或範圍），把…設置在，探出，找出，定居
location locate + ion ▶	〔lo`keʃən〕名　位置，場所，所在地，（電影的）外景拍攝地
locomotion loco + motion ▶	〔͵lokə`moʃən〕名　運動，移動
locomotive loco + motive ▶	〔͵lokə`motɪv〕名　機車，火車頭

After doing very well, the owners of the small restaurant decided to move to a new, larger location.
因為生意非常順利，那間小餐廳的負責人決定搬遷到一個較大的新地點。

 fus(e)　　注入，融合　　
118

fuse ▶	〔fjuz〕名　保險絲 動　把保險絲接入（電路），熔化，熔接

fusion fuse + ion	▶	〔`fjuʒən〕 名　熔化，熔解，融合，聯合
fusible fuse + ible	▶	〔`fjuzəbl〕 形　易熔的，可熔化的
refuse re + fuse	▶	〔rɪ`fjuz〕 動　拒絕，拒受，不准，不肯
refusal refuse + al	▶	〔rɪ`fjuzl〕 名　拒絕，優先購買權

In the end she refused the job offer because she didn't want to move to a different city.
最後她拒絕了那份工作，因為她不想要搬到別的城市。

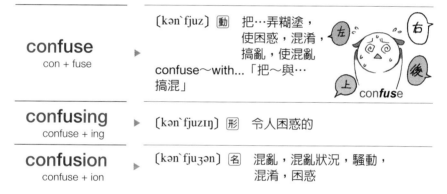

confuse con + fuse	▶	〔kən`fjuz〕 動　把…弄糊塗， 使困惑，混淆， 搞亂，使混亂 confuse～with...「把～與… 搞混」
confusing confuse + ing	▶	〔kən`fjuzɪŋ〕 形　令人困惑的
confusion confuse + ion	▶	〔kən`fjuʒən〕 名　混亂，混亂狀況，騷動， 混淆，困惑

Someone yelled, "Everything in the store is 75% off !" and mass confusion ensued at the department store.
有人大叫：「全店25折！」然後百貨公司就陷入了一陣大混亂。

Be careful not to confuse the gas pedal for the brakes, or you might be in big trouble.
小心不要錯把油門當成煞車，不然你可能會有大麻煩。

119 **duc(e)　duct**　引導

| **introduce**
intro + duce | ▶ | 〔ˌɪntrə`djus〕 動　介紹，引見，引進，採用
introduce～to...「介紹～給…」 |

introduction
introduce + ion
▶ 〔͵ɪntrə`dʌkʃən〕 图　介紹，正式引見，引進，
　　　　　　　　　　　　 引言，序言

introductory
introduce + ory
▶ 〔͵ɪntrə`dʌktərɪ〕 图　介紹的，前言的，開頭的

The introductory paragraph should explain what will be discussed in the main body of the text.
開頭的段落應該解釋正文內要討論的東西。

produce
pro + duce
▶ 〔prə`djus〕 動　生產，出產，製造，生育

producer
produce + er
▶ 〔prə`djusə〕 图　生產者，製造者，製作人

production
produce + ion
▶ 〔prə`dʌkʃən〕 图　生產，製作，作品，產物

product
pro + duct
▶ 〔`prɑdəkt〕 图　產品，產物，產量，結果，成果，
　　　　　　　　　　 作品，創作

productive
product + ive
▶ 〔prə`dʌktɪv〕 图　生產的，生產性的，豐饒的，
　　　　　　　　　　 肥沃的，生產…的

productivity
productive + ity
▶ 〔͵prodʌk`tɪvətɪ〕 图　生產力，生產率，豐饒，多產

This company produces disposable chopsticks.
這間公司生產免洗筷。

I've been at work for three hours, but I've done nothing productive; I think I'll go home.
我已經工作了三小時，但是沒什麼成效，我想我還是回家好了。

reduce
re + duce
▶ 〔rɪ`djus〕 動　減少，縮小，降低

reduction
reduce + ion
▶ 〔rɪ`dʌkʃən〕 图　減少，削減，縮小，下降

Mandy lost five kilograms by simply reducing the amount of sugar she put in her coffee.
曼蒂單憑減少放進咖啡的糖量就減了五公斤。

All the stores are reducing prices of the old models now that the new models are here.
既然新的模型已經到貨，所有的商店都將舊款模型降低價格。

deduce
de + duce

▶ 〔dɪˋdjus〕 動 演繹，推論，追溯

deduction
deduce + ion

▶ 〔dɪˋdʌkʃən〕 名 扣除，減除，扣除額，減除額，推論，演繹

deductive
deduce + ive

▶ 〔dɪˋdʌktɪv〕 形 推論的，演繹的

Bob deduced that Ally was his secret admirer when he saw her spraying perfume on a letter.
當鮑伯看見艾莉將香水灑在信紙上時，他推測艾莉就是偷偷仰慕他的人。

conduct
con + duct

▶ 〔ˋkɑndʌkt〕 名 行為，品行，舉動，指導，引導
〔kənˋdʌkt〕 動 引導，帶領，指揮，實施，處理，管理

conductor
conduct + or

▶ 〔kənˋdʌktɚ〕 名 領導者，管理人，指揮，車掌

In his excitement, the conductor lost his footing and landed in the violin section.
由於太過興奮，指揮家失足落入小提琴區。

The conductor walked through the train car checking the validity of passenger tickets.
車掌走過車廂，檢查乘客的車票是否有效。

 ## cit(e)　呼叫，叫喚
120

cite

▶ 〔saɪt〕 動 引用，引…為證，舉出，（法庭）傳喚

citation
cite + tion

▶ 〔saɪˋteʃən〕 名 引用，印證，（法庭）傳票

recite
re + cite

▶ 〔rɪˋsaɪt〕 動 背誦，朗誦，敘述

recital
recite + al

▶ 〔rɪˋsaɪt!〕 名 背誦，朗誦，詳述，獨奏會

recitation
recite + tion

▶ 〔͵rɛsəˋteʃən〕 名 背誦，朗誦，背誦的詩（或文章），詳述

The waiter recited the menu flawlessly.
那位侍者完美地背誦出菜單。

121　mand　mend　命令，要求

121

command com + mand	▶	〔kə`mænd〕 動 命令，指揮，統率 名 命令，控制，指揮
demand de + mand	▶	〔dɪ`mænd〕 動 要求，請求，需要 名 要求，請求，需要，需求
demanding demand + ing	▶	〔dɪ`mændɪŋ〕 形 苛求的，使人吃力的，高要求的

The dog obediently followed all his owner's commands.
那隻狗忠順地服從主人的命令。

The course is very demanding, but students learn a lot.
這門課要求高，但是學生可以學到很多。

recommend re + com + mend	▶	〔ˌrɛkə`mɛnd〕 動 推薦，介紹，建議，提出建議 recommend〜to...「推薦〜給…」
recommendation recommend + tion	▶	〔ˌrɛkəmɛn`deʃən〕 名 推薦，推薦信，介紹信， 建議

Bethany asked her teacher to write a letter of recommendation for her.
貝瑟妮拜託她的老師為她寫一份推薦函。

Can you recommend a good place to spend a Sunday afternoon?
你可以推薦一個適合消磨週日下午的好地方嗎？

122　sec　sequ　跟隨，後續

122

second sec + ond	▶	〔`sɛkənd〕 形 第二的，次要的 名 秒，瞬間

secondary
second + ary

▶ 〔ˋsɛkənˌdɛrɪ〕 形 第二的，第二位的，次要的，從屬的

secondary school「中等學校」
secondary education「中等教育」
tertiary〔ˋtɝʃɪˌɛrɪ〕school/education「高等教育，大學教育」

Although the car was totally destroyed in the crash, her parents said it was only of secondary importance as long as Sarah was not injured.
雖然車子在衝撞中全毀，但是莎拉的父母說那是其次，只要她沒受傷就好。

sequent
sequ + ent

▶ 〔ˋsikwənt〕 形 連續的，繼起的，其次的
名 收場，結果

sequential
sequent + ial

▶ 〔sɪˋkwɛnʃəl〕 形 連續的，相繼的，隨結果而來的

sequentially
sequential + ly

▶ 〔sɪˋkwɛnʃəlɪ〕 副 相繼地，連續地，結果地

sequence
sequent + ce

▶ 〔ˋsikwəns〕 名 連續，接續，一連串，次序，順序，後果，結果
a/the sequence of 〜s（名詞複數）接二連三的〜，連續的〜

In her mind Julianna tried to remember the sequence of events that led up to her living on the streets of Amsterdam.
在心裡，茱莉安娜試著回想導致她住在阿姆斯特丹街頭的一連串事件。

If the pages aren't numbered sequentially, it will be difficult to find the page you need.
如果沒有書頁沒有照順序編號，你會很難找到你要的那一頁。

consequent
con + sequent

▶ 〔ˋkɑnsəˌkwɛnt〕 形 因⋯而起的，隨之發生的

consequently
consequent + ly

▶ 〔ˋkɑnsəˌkwɛntlɪ〕 副 結果，因此，必然地

consequence
consequent + ce

▶ 〔ˋkɑnsəˌkwɛns〕 名 結果，後果，重大，重要性

Alan was late for work every day; consequently, he got fired.
亞倫每天都上班遲到，想當然爾，他被開除了。

subsequent sub + sequ + ent	▶ 〔`sʌbsɪˌkwɛnt〕 形	後來的，其後的，隨後的， 接著發生的，繼…之後的
subsequently subsequent + ly	▶ 〔`sʌbsɪˌkwɛntlɪ〕 副	其後，隨後，接著
subsequence subsequent + ce	▶ 〔`sʌbsɪˌkwɛns〕 名	後繼，繼起的事件，後果

Jonas witnessed a crime, and was subsequently asked to appear in court.
強納斯目擊了一宗犯罪，隨後他被要求出庭作證。

 vict   vinc(e)   勝利

victory vict + ory	▶ 〔`vɪktərɪ〕 名	勝利，戰勝，成功
victorious victory + ous	▶ 〔vɪk`torɪəs〕 形	勝利的，戰勝的，凱旋的
victor vict + or	▶ 〔`vɪktə〕 名	勝利者，戰勝者，得勝者

The athletes did a victory dance after they won the match.
選手們在贏得比賽後跳了一支勝利的舞。

convict con + vict	▶	〔kən`vɪkt〕 動　證明…有罪，判…有罪，判決， 　　　　　　使認罪，使悔悟 〔`kɑnvɪkt〕 名　（服刑的）囚犯，已決犯 convict（人）of～「判（人）～罪，使（人）悔悟～」 be convicted of～「被判犯～罪」
conviction convict + ion	▶	〔kən`vɪkʃən〕 名　定罪，證明有罪，確信，信念， 　　　　　　說服力

She promised she would never be late for class again, but her promise was without conviction.
她答應再也不會上課遲到，但是她的承諾無法令人信服。

convince
con + vince

▶ 〔kən`vɪns〕 動　使確信，使信服，說服
convince（人）of～「使（人）確信～，說服（人）相信～」　be convinced of～「確信～」

convincing
convince + ing

▶ 〔kən`vɪnsɪŋ〕 形　有說服力的，令人信服的，有論據證實的

As the evidence was not very convincing, the jury handed down a verdict of "not guilty."
由於證據不夠具說服力，陪審團作出「無罪」的判決。

 sign　象徵，標誌

124

sign

▶ 〔saɪn〕 名　記號，符號，標誌，招牌，手勢，暗號，前兆
動　簽署，簽名，做手勢，預示

signal
sign + al

▶ 〔`sɪgnl〕 名　信號，暗號，信號器，標誌，表示，導因，近因

signature
sign + ture

▶ 〔`sɪgnətʃə〕 名　簽名，簽署
autograph〔`ɔtə͵græf〕 名　（名人的）親筆簽名，親筆稿，手跡

signify
sign + ify

▶ 〔`sɪgnə͵faɪ〕 名　表示…的意思，表明，示意，意味著

significant
signify + ant

▶ 〔sɪg`nɪfəkənt〕 形　有意義的，意義深長的，重要的，重大的，顯著的

significance
significant + ce

▶ 〔sɪg`nɪfəkəns〕 名　重要性，意義，含義，意思

This check is not valid without a signature.
如果沒有簽名，這張支票就無效。

What does this flag signify?
這面旗子有什麼含義？

A significant amount of your time will be spent talking to potential customers.
你將花費相當大的時間和潛在客戶交談。

She didn't realize the significance of their initial encounter until much later.
她直到後來才瞭解他們初次見面的重要性。

assign
a + sign

▶ 〔ə`saɪn〕 動　分配，分派，派定，指定，把…歸於

assignment
assign + ment

▶ 〔ə`saɪnmənt〕 名　（分派的）任務，工作，作業，分配，指派

The new detective was nervous about being assigned to such an important case. 新來的刑警對於被發配到這麼重要的案件大感緊張。

resign
re + sign

▶ 〔rɪ`zaɪn〕 動　放棄，辭去，辭職
resign from～「辭去～（職位）」

resignation
resign + tion

▶ 〔ˌrɛzɪg`neʃən〕 名　辭職，放棄，辭呈

The president resigned as soon as the news was out that he had faked his degree.
總統在他學歷造假的新聞出來後立即就辭去他的職位。

She turned in her resignation and left without looking back.
她交出辭呈然後頭也不回地走了。

125 med(i)　治療

125

medicine
medi + cine

▶ 〔`mɛdəsṇ〕 名　藥，內服藥，醫學，藥學

medicinal
medicine + al

▶ 〔mə`dɪsṇl〕 形　藥的，藥用的，有藥效的

medical
medi + cal

▶ 〔`mɛdɪkḷ〕 形　醫學的，醫療的

medicate
medi + ate

▶ 〔`mɛdɪˌket〕 動　用藥治療

medication
medicate + ion

▶ 〔ˌmɛdɪ`keʃən〕 名　藥物治療，藥物

remedy
re + med + y

▶ 〔`rɛmədɪ〕 名　治療，治療法，補救，補償

Frank says he drinks vodka for purely medicinal purposes.
法蘭克說他喝伏特加單純只是為了藥用目的。

Sue refused to take any medicine, and her cold got worse and worse.
蘇拒絕服用任何藥物，所以她的感冒越來越嚴重。

Everyone has a different remedy for curing hiccups, but none of them work.
每個人都有自己治療打嗝的方法，但是沒一個方法有效。

meditate medi + ate	▶	〔`mɛdə,tet〕 動　沈思，冥想，深思熟慮，計劃，打算
meditation meditate + ion	▶	〔,mɛdə`teʃən〕 名　沈思，默想，冥想

The monk was so lost in meditation that he didn't notice the two cats that were fighting right next to him.
那位僧侶完全沈浸在冥想中，所以他沒有注意到身旁的兩隻貓在打架。

 126　fam(e)　fan(t)　說，談論　
126

fame	▶	〔fem〕 名　聲譽，名望，名聲
famous fame + ous	▶	〔`feməs〕 形　著名的，出名的 be famous for～「以～聞名」
infamous in + famous	▶	〔`Infəməs〕 形　聲名狼藉的，臭名昭彰的，不名譽的

The politician was infamous for completely ignoring minority concerns.
那位政治人物由於完全忽視弱勢族群的問題而臭名昭彰。

infant in + fant	▶	〔`Infənt〕 名　嬰兒，幼兒 形　嬰兒的，供嬰兒用的，初期的，未成年的
infancy infant + cy	▶	〔`InfənsI〕 名　嬰兒期，幼年，初期
infantile infant + ile	▶	〔`Infən,taIl〕 形　幼稚的，嬰兒的

The law dictates that babies should ride in infant seats in the back seat of a car.
法律規定，幼兒搭車時應坐在汽車後座的嬰兒座椅。

var　變化

127

vary ▶	〔`vɛrɪ〕動　使不同，變更，修改，使多樣化，變化，呈多樣化
varied vary + ed ▶	〔`vɛrɪd〕形　各種各樣的，不相同的，多變的，多彩的
variable vary + able ▶	〔`vɛrɪəbl〕形　易變的，多變的，可變的
variety vary + ety ▶	〔və`raɪətɪ〕名　多樣化，變化，種類，種種 a variety of 〜s（名詞複數）「各式各樣的〜」
variation vary + tion ▶	〔ˌvɛrɪ`eʃən〕名　變化，變動，差別，差異，變奏曲
variant vary + ant ▶	〔`vɛrɪənt〕名　變形，轉化，變形，變體 形　有差異的，不同的，易變的
various vary + ous ▶	〔`vɛrɪəs〕形　不同的，各種各樣的，許多的

The answers to this question may vary.
這個問題的答案並不一定。

The wind is blowing at velocities varying from 30-40 miles per hour.
風正以每小時30到40哩的速度刮著。

There are many variations of this type of disease.
這類疾病有許多變種。

For his recital piece, Steve played a Mozart theme and variations.
獨奏曲的部分，史帝夫演奏了一首莫札特主旋律和變奏曲。

128　mov(e)　mob　移動，動作

128

move ▶	〔muv〕動　移動，搬開，使感到，推動，前進，搬家
movement move + ment ▶	〔`muvmənt〕名　運動，活動，動作，行動，移動，移居
remove re + move ▶	〔rɪ`muv〕動　移動，搬開，移除，遷移

removable
remove + able

▶ 〔rɪ`muvəbl〕 形　可移動的，可解職的

removal
remove + al

▶ 〔rɪ`muvl〕 名　移動，調動，搬遷，移除，排除

Even the slightest movement will trigger the alarm.
就算是極小的動作也會觸發警鈴。

Bob went to the doctor to have a mole removed from his forehead.
鮑伯去找醫生把他額頭上的痣點掉。

mobile
mob + ile

▶ 〔`mobɪl〕 形　可動的，移動式的，活動的，
　　　　　　多變的，機動的
mobile phone 「行動電話」＝cell 〔sɛl〕 phone

mobilize
mobile + ize

▶ 〔`mobḷˌaɪz〕 動　動員，調動，使流通，使鬆動

immobilize
im + mobilize

▶ 〔ɪ`mobɪˌlaɪz〕 動　使不動，使不能移動
immobilizer 〔ɪ`mobɪˌlaɪzɚ〕 名　汽車防盜系統

Jason knew he should be running away, but he was immobilized with fear.
傑森知道他應該要逃走，但是恐懼使他動彈不得。

 mot(e) 　**動作**
129

motion
mot + ion

▶ 〔`moʃən〕 名　移動，運動，動作

motionless
motion + less

▶ 〔`moʃənlɪs〕 形　不動的，靜止的

emotion
e + motion

▶ 〔ɪ`moʃən〕 名　感情，情感，激動

emotional
emotion + al

▶ 〔ɪ`moʃənḷ〕 形　感情（上）的，易動情的，
　　　　　　訴諸感情的，激起情感的

emotionally
emotional + ly

▶ 〔ɪ`moʃənlɪ〕 副　感情上，情緒上，衝動地

It was with great emotion that the family was re-united after five years apart.
分開五年後的家人重聚非常感人。

motive mot + ive	▶	〔ˋmotɪv〕形　成為原動力的，起動的，推動的 名　動機，主旨，目的
motivate motive + ate	▶	〔ˋmotə͵vet〕動　給…動機，刺激，激發 motivate（人）to V「激發（人）～」
motivation motivate + ion	▶	〔͵motəˋveʃən〕名　刺激，推動，積極性

The thought of having to clean his room again, after his mother inspected his work, motivated him to do a very thorough job the first time.
想到在媽媽檢查過後可能得再打掃一次，激發他在一開始就非常徹底地打掃他的房間。

Even if the motive is to bring an end to suffering, many people still maintain that mercy killing is immoral.
雖然動機是為了結束痛苦，許多人還是認為安樂死是不道德的。

| **remote**
re + mote | ▶ | 〔rɪˋmot〕形　相隔很遠的，遙遠的，偏僻的，
久遠的，關係疏遠的，遙控的 |
| **remotely**
remote + ly | ▶ | 〔rɪˋmotlɪ〕副　遠距離地，遙遠地，間接地，
極少地，出神地 |

By lunchtime, the students weren't remotely interested in the lecture any more.
到了午餐時間，學生們不再有興趣專心上課。

| **promote**
pro + mote | ▶ | 〔prəˋmot〕動　晉升，升級，促進，發揚，發起，
創立 |
| **promotion**
promote + ion | ▶ | 〔prəˋmoʃən〕名　晉升，促進，增進，發起，
推銷，促銷 |

Organizations like "Greenpeace" try to promote awareness of environmental issues.
一些像是「綠色和平」的組織，皆致力於提升對環境問題的認知。

130　divid(e)　divis　分開

| **divide** | ▶ | 〔dəˋvaɪd〕動　劃分，分發，分配，使對立，
分開，分裂 |

| **divisible**
 divide + ible | ▶ | 〔də`vɪzəbl〕形　可分的，可分隔的，可除盡的 |
| **division**
 divide + ion | ▶ | 〔də`vɪʒən〕名　分開，分割，分配，分裂，部分，
 部門，片段 |

All even numbers are divisible by two.
所有的偶數皆可用2整除。

They divided the pie into eight equal pieces.
他們把派分成八等分。

individual in + divid + ual	▶	〔͵ɪndə`vɪdʒʊəl〕形　個人的，個體的，個別的， 單獨的，特有的，獨特的
individually individual + ly	▶	〔͵ɪndə`vɪdʒʊəlɪ〕副　單獨地，分別地，獨特地， 與眾不同地
individualist individual + ist	▶	〔ɪndə`vɪdʒʊəlɪst〕名　個人主義者，利己主義者
individualistic individualist + ic	▶	〔͵ɪndə͵vɪdʒʊəl`ɪstɪk〕形　個人主義的，利己主義的
individualism individual + ism	▶	〔ɪndə`vɪdʒʊəl͵ɪzəm〕名　個人主義，利己主義

These cookies are individually wrapped.
這些餅乾都一個一個包好。

Although he lives in a group-centered society, he is very individualistic.
雖然他住在一個集體中心的社會，他卻是非常個人主義。

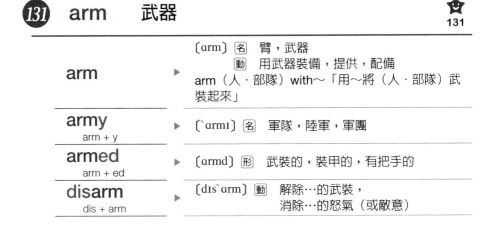

131　arm　武器

★131

arm	▶	〔ɑrm〕名　臂，武器 動　用武器裝備，提供，配備 arm（人‧部隊）with～「用～將（人‧部隊）武 裝起來」
army arm + y	▶	〔`ɑrmɪ〕名　軍隊，陸軍，軍團
armed arm + ed	▶	〔ɑrmd〕形　武裝的，裝甲的，有把手的
disarm dis + arm	▶	〔dɪs`ɑrm〕動　解除⋯的武裝， 消除⋯的怒氣（或敵意）

disarmed
disarm + ed

▶ 〔dɪsˋɑrmd〕 形　解除武裝的

Using the skills she learned in self-defense class, Rebecca was able to disarm her attacker and run to safety.
藉著防身課上學到的技巧，瑞貝卡得以解除攻擊者的武裝並安全逃走。

alarm
al + arm

▶ 〔əˋlɑrm〕 名　警報，警報器，鬧鐘，驚慌，恐懼，擔憂
動　向…報警，使驚慌不安，使恐懼，打擾

alarming
alarm + ing

▶ 〔əˋlɑrmɪŋ〕 形　驚人的，令人擔憂的，告急的

When the fire alarm goes off, be sure to leave the building in an orderly manner.
火警警鈴響起時，請務必依序離開大樓。

The virus spread at an alarming rate.
病毒以驚人的速度擴散。

---

132 ## bas(e)　基礎，低處

132

bass	▶ 〔bes〕 名　男低音，貝斯，低音樂器，低音音程
base	▶ 〔bes〕 名　基礎，基地，總部，基本部分 動　以… 為基礎
basis bas + is	▶ 〔ˋbesɪs〕 名　基礎，根據，原則，主要部分，基本成分
basic base + ic	▶ 〔ˋbesɪk〕 形　基礎的，基本的，初步的
basically basic + al + ly	▶ 〔ˋbesɪk]ɪ〕 副　基本上，根本上
basement base + ment	▶ 〔ˋbesmənt〕 名　地下室，地下層

She meets her friend on Friday nights on a regular basis.
她固定每個禮拜五晚上和朋友見面。

debase
de + base
▶ 〔dɪˋbes〕 動 降低（品質、價值等），貶低（人格），使（貨幣）貶值

The artistic image of geisha has been debased by the popular opinion that there is no skill involved.
大眾認為藝妓不具任何技藝，這樣的看法貶低了其藝術形象。

 ann 年，每年的
133

annual
ann + ual
▶ 〔ˋænjʊəl〕 形 一年的，一年一次的，每年的，全年的

annually
annual + ly
▶ 〔ˋænjʊəlɪ〕 副 每年，每年一次

anniversary
ann + vers + ary
▶ 〔͵ænəˋvɝsərɪ〕 形 週年的，週年紀念的
名 週年紀念，週年紀念日，結婚週年，結婚紀念日

An annual flower lives and dies within one year.
一年生的花在一年間歷經生長與枯萎。

In the annual report, the school claimed that truancy had declined by 40%.
在學年報告中，學校指出學生曠課率降低了40%。

 cracy crat 統治，權勢
134

aristocracy
aristo + cracy
▶ 〔͵ærəsˋtɑkrəsɪ〕 名 貴族，上層社會，貴族統治，精英統治

aristocrat
aristo + crat
▶ 〔æˋrɪstə͵kræt〕 名 貴族，主張貴族統治者，佼佼者

aristocratic
aristocrat + ic
▶ 〔͵ærɪstəˋkrætɪk〕 形 貴族的，儀態高貴的，勢利的，贊成貴族的，愛挑剔的

democracy
demo + cracy
▶ 〔dɪˋmɑkrəsɪ〕 名 民主，民主主義，民主制度，民主政體，民主國家

democrat demo + crat	▶ 〔ˋdɛməˌkræt〕 名 民主主義者，（美國）民主黨人
democratic democrat + ic	▶ 〔ˌdɛməˋkrætɪk〕 形 民主的，民主主義的， 民主政體的， （美國）民主黨的

Only members of the aristocracy are allowed beyond this point.
只有貴族成員允許進入。

---

135 cred 相信，信賴

credit cred + it	▶ 〔ˋkrɛdɪt〕 名 信譽，信用，信賴 credit card 名 信用卡
creditable credit + able	▶ 〔ˋkrɛdɪtəbl〕 形 值得稱讚的，可給予信用貸款的， 可歸功於…的，可信的
credible cred + ible	▶ 〔ˋkrɛdəbl〕 形 可信的，可靠的
incredible in + credible	▶ 〔ɪnˋkrɛdəbl〕 形 不能相信的，不可信的， 難以置信的

With her history of telling tall tales, it's impossible for anyone to find her a credible source of information.
由於她有唬爛的前科，幾乎沒有人會把她當作可靠的消息來源。

---

136 val vail 有價值的

value val + ue	▶ 〔ˋvælju〕 名 重要性，益處，價值，價格，價值觀
valuable value + able	▶ 〔ˋvæljuəbl〕 形 值錢的，貴重的，有用的， 有價值的
valid val + id	▶ 〔ˋvælɪd〕 形 有根據的，確鑿的，令人信服的， 合法的，有效的

invalid in + valid	▶	〔ɪn`vælɪd〕 形　無效的，無價值的
validity valid + ity	▶	〔və`lɪdətɪ〕 名　正當，正確，有效性，效力， 合法性
valueless value + less	▶	〔`væljulɪs〕 形　無價值的，沒有用處的
invaluable in + valuable	▶	〔ɪn`væljəbl〕 形　非常貴重的，無價的， 無法估價的
evaluate e + val + ate	▶	〔ɪ`væljuˏet〕 動　估…的價，對…評價
evaluation evaluate + ion	▶	〔ɪˏvælju`eʃən〕 名　估價，評價，估算

This membership card is invalid without another form of identification.
沒有其他身分證明文件的話，這張會員卡是無效的。

This leather bag is excellent value for the money.
這個皮包以這個價錢來說可是非常划算。

He has been an invaluable asset to our team.
他一直是我們團隊不可或缺的重要一員。

She made a quick evaluation of the situation, and decided it was
best to run away.　她迅速地衡量了狀況，然後決定逃跑為上策。

avail a + vail	▶	〔ə`vel〕 動　有用，有益，有幫助，有助於 　　　　　名　效用，利益，幫助 to no avail=without avail「徒勞地，完全無用」
available avail + able	▶	〔ə`veləbl〕 形　可用的，在手邊，可利用的， 可得到的，有空的，有效的
availability available + ity	▶	〔əˏvelə`bɪlətɪ〕 名　有效，有益，可利用性， 可得到的東西（或人），可得性

He tried and tried to open the jar, but to no avail, it remained
tightly sealed.
他一直試著要打開瓶子，但是徒勞無功，蓋子還是蓋得緊緊的。

 urb　城市

urban urb + an	▶	〔`ɝbən〕 形　城市的，居住在城市的

urbane urb + an	▶ 〔ɝˋben〕 形　都市化的，彬彬有禮的，高雅的
urbanize urban + ize	▶ 〔ˋɜbənˏaɪz〕 動　使都市化，使文雅
urbanization urbanize + tion	▶ 〔ˏɜbənɪˋzeʃən〕 名　都市化

The expanding urban population has made some new demands on the local government.
城市人口增加替本地政府帶來了一些新問題。

suburb sub + urb	▶ 〔ˋsʌbɝb〕 名　（城市周圍的）近郊住宅區， 　　　　　郊區，邊緣，外圍 the suburbs 郊區
suburban suburb + an	▶ 〔səˋbɝbən〕 形　郊區的，近郊的

I live just out of town in the suburbs.
我住在城鎮外的郊區。

---

138 cil(e)　呼喊，呼叫

138

council coun + cil	▶ 〔ˋkaʊnsl̩〕 名　會議，政務會，議事，商討
councilor council + or	▶ 〔ˋkaʊnsl̩ə〕 名　議會議員，顧問
reconcile re + con + cile	▶ 〔ˋrɛkənsaɪl〕 動　使和解，使和好，調停，調解， 　　　　　使一致 reconcile～with... 「使～與…一致，使～與…和 解」

After their huge fight, Janet didn't know if she and Shawn would be reconciled.
大吵過後，珍妮特不確定她和尚恩能不能夠和好。

Some people have no trouble reconciling the demands of having a career with raising a family.
有些人毫不費力就能在事業與家庭兩難中取得平衡。

139 calc　小石頭
139

calculate calc + ate	▶ 〔ˋkælkjə͵let〕 動　計算，估計，推測，作打算 〔古代人用數石頭計算〕
calculating calculate + ing	▶ 〔ˋkælkjə͵letɪŋ〕 形　計算的，有算計的，慎重的
calculation calculate + ion	▶ 〔͵kælkjəˋleʃən〕 名　計算，計算結果，估計， 推測，預測
calculator calculate + or	▶ 〔ˋkælkjə͵letɚ〕 名　計算者，計算表，計算機
calcium calc + ium	▶ 〔ˋkælsɪəm〕 名　鈣

He was accused of being calculating and manipulative, but he was only doing what he thought was best.
他被批評愛算計和操控欲強，但他只是在做他認為最好的。

When you calculate the cost, don't forget to include the 12% consumption tax.
你計算費用的時候，不要忘記加上12%的消費稅。

 140 guar(d)　gard　注意，注視
140

guard	▶ 〔gɑrd〕 動　保衛，守衛，警衛，看守，監視， 防範，警惕
regard re + guard	▶ 〔rɪˋgɑrd〕 動　把…看作，把…認為，注重， 注意，看待 regard～as...「把～視為…」 in regard to～「關於～」 regards「致意」
regardless regard + less	▶ 〔rɪˋgɑrdlɪs〕 形　不注意的，不留心的，不關心的 regardless of～「不管～，不顧～」
disregard dis + regard	▶ 〔͵dɪsrɪˋgɑrd〕 動　不理會，不顧，漠視，不尊重

guarantee
guar + antee

〔͵gærən`ti〕 名　保證，保證書，擔保品，抵押品
動　保證，擔保

Please give my regards to your family.
請替我向你的家人致意。

Please disregard the last announcement, the keys have been found.
請不用在意先前的通知，鑰匙已經找到了。

The guarentee that you will lose wieght is only valid so long as you follow the program to the letter.
減重的保證只有在你遵守減重計劃的規則時才會成立。

 term　結束，最後
141

term	〔tɜm〕名　期，期限，學期，任期，術語，條件，條款 the terms of the contract「契約條款」
terminology term + logy	〔͵tɜmə`nɑlədʒɪ〕名　術語，專門用語
terminal term + al	〔`tɜmən̩〕形　末端的，終點的，極限的，末期的，晚期的 名　終點，末端，極限
terminate term + ate	〔`tɜmə͵net〕動　使停止，使終止，使結束
terminator terminate + or	〔`tɜmə͵netə〕名　終止者，終止物，終結者

These are the terms of the contract; if you agree, please sign here.
這些是合約條款，如果你同意的話，請在這裡簽名。

I don't understand the terminology in this computer guidebook.
我不懂這本電腦指南的專門術語。

Cancer is often a terminal illness.
癌症通常是致命的絕症。

Her tactless remark terminated the pleasant conversation.
她笨拙的話結束了這場愉快的談話。

determine
de + term + ine

▶ 〔dɪˋtɝmɪn〕 動　決定，下決心，判決，裁定

determination
determine + tion

▶ 〔dɪˌtɝməˋneʃən〕 名　堅定，決心，果斷，決斷力

After watching the replay, the umpire determined that the runner was safe.
看過重播後，裁判判定跑者安全上壘。

Jessie started her diet with great determination, but by the second day, she was eating ice cream for breakfast.
潔西抱著堅定的決心開始節食，但是到了第二天，她早餐就開始吃冰淇淋。

142　prob　prov(e)　proof　測驗，證明
142

probable
prob + able

▶ 〔ˋprɑbəb!〕 形　很可能發生的，很可能成為事實的，有充分根據的，可信的

improbable
im + probable

▶ 〔ɪmˋprɑbəb!〕 形　不大可能的，未必會發生的，未必確實的

probably
probable + ly

▶ 〔ˋprɑbəblɪ〕 副　大概，或許，很可能

probability
probable + ity

▶ 〔ˌprɑbəˋbɪlətɪ〕 名　可能性，或然性，可能的結果

The probability of getting all 50 family members in the same place at the same time is quite low.
50名家庭成員同時齊聚一堂的可能性很低。

The firemen said that faulty electric wiring was the probable cause of the fire.　消防員說火災的可能原因是有缺陷的電路配線。

prove

▶ 〔pruv〕 動　證明，證實，查驗，證明是

proof

▶ 〔pruf〕 名　證據，物證，檢驗，考驗，證明

He tried to prove his innocence by taking a polygraph test.
他試著藉由接受測謊檢查來證明他是無辜的。

Although Doug suspected Claire of eating his donut, he had no proof.
雖然道格懷疑克萊兒吃了他的甜甜圈，但是他沒有證據。

improve im + prove	▶	〔ɪm`pruv〕 動 改進，改善，增進，提高…價值，增加
improvement improve + ment	▶	〔ɪm`pruvmənt〕 名 改進，改善，增進，改進處，進步

There have been great improvements in public transportation in the last few years. 近年公共交通已大幅改善。

approve a + prove	▶	〔ə`pruv〕 動 贊成，同意，批准，認可
approval approve + al	▶	〔ə`pruvḷ〕 名 批准，認可，贊成，同意

You need to have the proposal approved by the committee before you can go ahead with the plan.
在進行計劃之前，提案必須要得到委員會的認同。

The hamburgers are made with government-approved beef.
漢堡皆由政府核可的牛肉製成。

---

143 mod(e)　測量，尺寸

143

mode	▶	〔mod〕 名 方法，做法，方式，形式，種類
model mod + el	▶	〔`madḷ〕 名 模型，雛形，原型，模範，模特兒，型號，樣式
modify mode + ify	▶	〔`madə͵faɪ〕 動 更改，修改
modification modify + tion	▶	〔͵madəfə`keʃən〕 名 修改，改變，修正

After evaluating the performance of the car, they made some modifications in the design.
評估過汽車性能後，他們將設計作了些修改。

modern mod + ern	▶	〔`madən〕 形 現代的，近代的，現代化的，時髦的，最新的 名 現代人，現代化的人
modernize modern + ize	▶	〔`madən͵aɪz〕 動 使現代化，現代化
modernization modernize + tion	▶	〔͵madənə`zeʃən〕 名 現代化，現代化的事物

When Trent suddenly recovered from a 10-year coma, he was amazed at all the advances in modern technology.
崔倫特忽然從10年的昏迷中清醒，對現代科技的進步感到非常驚訝。

This architect prefers traditional design to modern.
這位建築師偏好傳統的設計更甚於現代風格。

---

moderate
mod + ate

▶ 〔`madərɪt〕 形　中等的，適度的，有節制的，溫和的，一般的，平庸的
moderato 〔‚madə`rato〕 形副 〔音〕中板

---

moderation
moderate + ion

▶ 〔‚madə`reʃən〕 名　溫和，穩健，緩和，降低，適度，節制

Regular, moderate exercise is essential for good health.
規律、適度的運動對擁有良好健康是不可或缺的。

It's okay to eat junk food as long as you do so in moderation.
只要適量，吃垃圾食物是可以的。

---

modest
mod + est

▶ 〔`madɪst〕 形　謙虛的，審慎的，適度的，有節制的

---

modesty
modest + y

▶ 〔`madɪstɪ〕 名　謙虛，虛心，節制，樸素

---

modestly
modest + ly

▶ 〔`madɪstlɪ〕 副　謙虛地，審慎地，適度地

The football hero modestly declined to talk about his many accomplishments.
那位足球員謙虛地拒絕談論自己眾多的成就。

---

accommodate
ac + com + mod + ate

▶ 〔ə`kamə‚det〕 動　能容納，能提供…膳宿，可搭載，使適應
accommodate～to... 「使～適應…」

---

accommodation
accommodate + ion

▶ 〔ə‚kamə`deʃən〕 名　適應，調節，住處，膳宿

All doors should be wide enough to accommodate the width of wheelchairs.
所有的門都應該要寬得足以讓輪椅通過。

The accommodations were reasonably priced, and very comfortable.
住宿的價格合理，而且環境非常舒適。

imag(e)　imit　圖像
144

image	▶ 〔ˋɪmɪdʒ〕 图　肖像，形象，印象，映像，影像
imagine imag + ine	▶ 〔ɪˋmædʒɪn〕 動　想像，臆斷，猜想，料想
imagination imagine + tion	▶ 〔ɪˌmædʒəˋneʃən〕 图　想像力，創造力，空想， 想像出來的東西
imaginary imagine + ary	▶ 〔ɪˋmædʒəˌnɛrɪ〕 形　想像中的，虛構的，幻想的
imaginative imagine + ive	▶ 〔ɪˋmædʒəˌnetɪv〕 形　虛構的，幻想的，有想像力的， 富於想像力的
imaginable imagine + able	▶ 〔ɪˋmædʒɪnəbl〕 形　能想像的，想像得到的

She had an imaginary friend until she was six years old.
她一直到六歲還有一位想像的朋友。

If you use your imagination, you can see pictures in the clouds.
如果你運用想像力，你能在雲裡看見圖畫。

imitate imit + ate	▶ 〔ˋɪməˌtet〕 動　模仿，以⋯做為範例，仿效， 仿製，偽造
imitation imitate + ion	▶ 〔ˌɪməˋteʃən〕 图　模仿，模擬，仿造，偽造， 仿製品

The chairs are covered with imitation leather.
椅子上覆蓋著人造皮革。

145 **cap(it)　頭，首要** ⭐
145

cap	▶ 〔kæp〕 图　帽子，蓋，罩 the cap of fools「超級大傻瓜（笨到極點）」
captain cap + tain	▶ 〔ˋkæptɪn〕 图　陸軍上尉，海軍上校，空軍上尉， 船長，艦長，機長，隊長，領隊

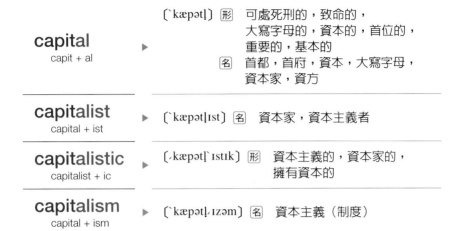

capital
capit + al

〔ˋkæpətḷ〕 形 可處死刑的，致命的，大寫字母的，資本的，首位的，重要的，基本的
名 首都，首府，資本，大寫字母，資本家，資方

capitalist
capital + ist

〔ˋkæpətḷɪst〕 名 資本家，資本主義者

capitalistic
capitalist + ic

〔ˌkæpətḷˋɪstɪk〕 形 資本主義的，資本家的，擁有資本的

capitalism
capital + ism

〔ˋkæpətḷˌɪzəm〕 名 資本主義（制度）

The capital city of Japan is Tokyo.
日本的首都是東京。
I don't have the capital to start my own business.
我沒有資金好開始自己的事業。

146 lav 洗

146

lava

〔ˋlɑvə〕 名 熔岩，火山岩

lava

lavatory
lava + ory

〔ˋlævəˌtorɪ〕 名 廁所，盥洗室，洗手間

lavatory

lavender
lav + ender

〔ˋlævəndə〕 名 薰衣草，淡紫色

The lavatory is down the hall on the left.
洗手間就在走廊底左手邊。
In aromatherapy, essential oils of lavender are used for relaxation.
在芳香療法中，薰衣草精油用來讓人舒緩放鬆。

147　(l)lect　lig　leg　集合，選出

| collect
co + llect | ▶ | 〔kə`lɛkt〕 動 | 收集，採集，使集合，
領取（信件等），聚集，堆積，收款 |

| collector
collect + or | ▶ | 〔kə`lɛktə〕 名 | 收集者，採集者，收藏家，
收取款項（或東西）的人，收稅員 |

| collection
collect + ion | ▶ | 〔kə`lɛkʃən〕 名 | 收集，採集，收取，收藏品，
募捐，聚集，積聚 |

| recollect
re + collect | ▶ | 〔ˌrɛkə`lɛkt〕 動 | 回憶，追憶，記起，使記起 |

| recollection
recollect + ion | ▶ | 〔ˌrɛkə`lɛkʃən〕 名 | 回憶，記憶，記憶力，
回憶起的事物，往事 |

She still has vivid recollections of her youth.
她還清楚地記得年輕時候的事。

| elect
e + lect | ▶ | 〔ɪ`lɛkt〕 動 | 選舉，推選，選擇，決定 |

| election
elect + ion | ▶ | 〔ɪ`lɛkʃən〕 名 | 選舉，當選 |

| elective
elect + ive | ▶ | 〔ɪ`lɛktɪv〕 形 | 選舉的，選修的 |

| elector
elect + or | ▶ | 〔ɪ`lɛktə〕 名 | 選舉人 |

All the politicians awaited election day with anticipation.
所有的政治人物熱切地期待選舉日的到來。

| select
se + lect | ▶ | 〔sə`lɛkt〕 動 | 選擇，挑選，選拔，作出選擇 |

| selection
select + ion | ▶ | 〔sə`lɛkʃən〕 名 | 選擇，被挑選出的人（或物），
選集，文選 |

| selective
select + ive | ▶ | 〔sə`lɛktɪv〕 形 | 有選擇性的，有選擇能力的，
淘汰的 |

The buffet had a selection of fresh fruits and vegetables as well as a variety of main courses.
那間自助餐廳有新鮮水果和蔬菜以及多種主菜可供選擇。

intellect intel + lect	▶	〔ˋɪntḷ͵ɛkt〕 名 智力，理解力，思維能力
intellectual intellect + ual	▶	〔͵ɪntḷ ˋɛktʃuəl〕 形 智力的，理智的，需智力的，聰明的 名 知識分子
intelligent intel + lig + ent	▶	〔ɪnˋtɛlədʒənt〕 形 有才智的，聰明的，明智的，有理性的
intelligence intelligent + ce	▶	〔ɪnˋtɛlədʒəns〕 名 智能，智慧，理解力，情報，情報機關 CIA=Central Intelligence Agency「（美國）中央情報局」

Exposure to chemical fumes can affect a child's intellectual development. 曝露在化學煙霧中可能影響孩童的智能發展。
Although he is not enormously intelligent, Norm is good-hearted, and loved by everyone.
雖然諾姆不是極為聰明，但他的心腸好，而且受到大家的愛戴。

lecture lect + ure	▶	〔ˋlɛktʃɚ〕 名 授課，演講
lecturer lecture + er	▶	〔ˋlɛktʃərɚ〕 名 演講者，大學講師

The students all seemed to enjoy their sociology lectures.
學生們似乎都很喜愛他們的社會學課程。

legend leg + end	▶	〔ˋlɛdʒənd〕 名 傳說，傳奇故事，傳奇人物，（地圖、圖片等的）說明，圖例
legendary legend + ary	▶	〔ˋlɛdʒənd͵ɛrɪ〕 形 傳說的，傳奇的，著名的

If you look at the map legend, you'll find that the dotted red line indicates a train line.
如果你看地圖的說明，你會發現紅色虛線代表的是火車路線。
Within the confines of the small school, his ability to sleep in class without getting caught was legendary.
在那所小學校內，他上課睡覺不被發現的能力已經成為傳說。

148 **solve** **solut(e)** 解開，分解
148

solve ▶	〔sɑlv〕 動　解決，闡明，解答（題目）

solution solute + ion ▶	〔sə`luʃən〕 名　解答，解決辦法，解釋， 　　　　　　　　（題目的）解法

There is an easy solution to this problem if you just sit down and think about it.
只要你好好坐下來思考，這個問題有一個簡單的解決方案。

resolve re + solve ▶	〔rɪ`zɑlv〕 動　解決，解答，消除（疑惑等）， 　　　　　　　使分解，決心，決議 resolve to V 「決心～」

resolute re + solute ▶	〔`rɛzə͵lut〕 形　堅決的，堅定的，果敢的

resolution resolute + ion ▶	〔͵rɛzə`luʃən〕 名　決心，決定，分解，解析

resolutely resolute + ly ▶	〔`rɛzə͵lutlɪ〕 副　堅決地，毅然地

He chained himself to the giant tree and resolutely refused to move when the logging crew came in.
他用鏈子把自己綁在大樹上，並在伐木隊抵達時堅決拒絕離開。

absolute ab + solute ▶	〔`æbsə͵lut〕 形　絕對的，完全的，專制的， 　　　　　　　不容置疑的 an absolute fool「一個絕對的傻瓜」 the absolute darkness「完全的黑暗」

absolutely absolute + ly ▶	〔`æbsə͵lutlɪ〕 副　絕對地，完全地， 　　　　　　　（口語）沒錯/一點也沒錯

I don't care how much you want it, you are absolutely not getting another piece of chocolate.
我不管你多想要，你絕對不能再吃一片巧克力。

fer　　運送，攜帶

fertile fer + tile	▶ 〔`fɜtl〕 形　多產的，繁殖力強的，肥沃的，能生育的，（創造力或想像力）豐富的
fertility fertile + ity	▶ 〔fɜ`tɪlətɪ〕 名　肥沃，繁殖力，（思想等的）豐富
fertilize fertile + ize	▶ 〔`fɜtl͵aɪz〕 動　使肥沃，施肥
fertilizer fertilize + er	▶ 〔`fɜtl͵aɪzɚ〕 名　肥料

Houseplants need to be fertilized regularly, or the leaves might turn yellow.
室內盆栽需要定期施肥，不然葉子可能會枯黃。

prefer pre + fer	▶ 〔prɪ`fɜ〕 動　寧可，寧願，更喜歡 prefer～to... 「喜歡～更甚於…」
preferable prefer + able	▶ 〔`prɛfərəbl〕 形　更好的，更可取的，更合意的
preference prefer + ence	▶ 〔`prɛfərəns〕 名　偏愛，偏愛的事物（或人），偏袒，優先權

If you don't have a preference, I'll take the green T-shirt, and you take the yellow one.
如果你沒有特別的偏好，那我拿綠色的T恤，你拿黃的。

confer con + fer	▶ 〔kən`fɜ〕 動　授予（學位等），給予，商談，協商 confer with（人‧團體）on～「就～與（人‧團體）協商」
conference confer + ence	▶ 〔`kɑnfərəns〕 名　會議，討論會，協商會

Rachael conferred with her business partner before going ahead with her plan.
瑞秋在開始她的計劃之前，先與她的生意夥伴商量過了。

infer
in + fer

▶ 〔ɪnˋfɝ〕 動 推斷，推論，猜想，意味著，暗示，作出推論
infer～from... 「依據…推論出～」

inference
infer + ence

▶ 〔ˋɪnfərəns〕 名 推論，推斷，推斷的結果

I inferred from her comments that she was quite pleased with how things turned out.
從她的發言，我猜想她對於事情的結果相當滿意。

refer
re + fer

▶ 〔rɪˋfɝ〕 動 把…歸因於，論及，談到，有關，涉及，參考
refer to～ 「談到～，與～有關，參考～」

reference
refer + ence

▶ 〔ˋrɛfərəns〕 名 提及，涉及，參考，參考文獻，出處

In his best-selling book, Sean made reference to the writings of J.D.Salinger.
在尚恩的暢銷書中，他參考了沙林傑的作品。

differ
dif + fer

▶ 〔ˋdɪfɚ〕 動 不同，相異，意見不同
differ from～ 「與～不同，與～意見不同」

different
differ + ent

▶ 〔ˋdɪfərənt〕 形 不同的

difference
differ + ence

▶ 〔ˋdɪfərəns〕 名 差別，差異，差距

Although their political views differ, they are still great friends.
雖然他們的政治觀點不同，但他們仍是好朋友。

suffer
suf + fer

▶ 〔sʌfɝ〕 動 遭受，經歷，忍受，受苦
suffer from～ 「因 ～（疾病）而痛或不舒服，受～之苦」

sufferable
suffer + able

▶ 〔ˋsʌfərəbl̩〕 形 可容許的，可忍受得了的

sufferance
suffer + ance

▶ 〔ˋsʌfərəns〕 名 忍受，忍耐，忍耐力，容忍
beyond sufferance 「超過忍受的限度」

In the spring time I often suffer from hay fever.
春天時節，我常受花粉症之苦。

150 ton(e) 聲音，響聲

★150

tone ▶ 〔ton〕名 音，音色，音調，腔調，語氣，色調

Even though he was tone deaf, he still insisted on singing in the choir, and because he was president of the company, no one could refuse.
雖然他是音痴，他還是堅持要參加合唱團，而且由於他是公司的董事長，沒有人能拒絕他的加入。

astonish
as + ton + ish
▶ 〔əˋstɑnɪʃ〕動 使吃驚，使驚訝
be astonished at～「由於～而震驚」

astonishment
astonish + ment
▶ 〔əˋstɑnɪʃmənt〕名 驚訝，驚愕，令人驚訝的事物

astonishing
astonish + ing
▶ 〔əˋstɑnɪʃɪŋ〕形 令人驚訝的，驚人的

astonishingly
astonishing + ly
▶ 〔əˋstɑnɪʃɪŋlɪ〕副 令人驚訝地

Ron managed to escape from some astonishingly difficult situations.
榮恩設法從一些困難得令人驚訝的處境中逃出。

151 tact tast(e) tach tag 接觸

★151

tactics
tact + ics
▶ 〔ˋtæktɪks〕名 戰術，用兵學，策略，手段

When the child realized that begging his mother for ice cream was not effective, he decided to change his tactics: he held his breath until his face turned blue.
那孩子了解到央求媽媽買冰淇淋給他是沒用的，於是決定改變策略：他摒住呼吸直到臉色發青。

contact
con + tact

> ［ˋkɑntækt］ 名　接觸，觸碰，交往，聯繫，聯絡，隱形眼鏡
>
> ［kənˋtækt］ 動　與…接觸，與…聯繫
> contact lens（es）「隱形眼鏡」
> a contact phone number「聯絡電話號碼」
> be in contact with～「與～聯絡」

Have you been in contact with Elly?
你和艾莉有聯絡嗎？

---

taste

> ［test］ 動　嚐，吃起來，有…的味道
> 名　味覺，味道，滋味，愛好

tasty
taste + y

> ［ˋtestɪ］ 形　美味的，可口的

tasteful
taste + ful

> ［ˋtestfəl］ 形　有鑑賞力的，有審美力的

tastefully
tasteful + ly

> ［ˋtestfəlɪ］ 副　風流地，高雅地，雅緻地

tasteless
taste + less

> ［ˋtestlɪs］ 形　沒味道的，味道差的，乏味的，無鑑賞力的

tastelessly
tasteless + ly

> ［ˋtestlɪslɪ］ 副　無味地，乏味地，無鑑賞力地，無品味地

The interior of the restaurant is tastefully decorated in a French café theme.
這間餐廳的內部高雅地裝潢成法式咖啡廳風格。

---

attach
at + tach

> ［əˋtætʃ］ 動　裝上，貼上，使附著，附加，附屬，伴隨，使喜愛
> attach～to...「把～附加到…」
> be attached to～「喜愛～」

attachment
attach + ment

> ［əˋtætʃmənt］ 名　連接，安裝，附著，附屬物，連接物，情感

The Peanuts character Linus is very attached to his blanket.
史努比裡面的角色奈勒斯對他的毛毯非常依戀。

When you are finished with the document, please attach it to an e-mail and send it to me.
當你完成這份文件後，請將檔案附加到電子郵件然後寄給我。

detach
de + tach

▶ 〔dɪˋtætʃ〕 [動]　分開，拆卸，使分離，派遣，分遣
detach～from...「將～從…拆下」

detached
detach + ed

▶ 〔dɪˋtætʃt〕 [形]　分離的，不連接的，不帶感情的，公平的，超然的
a detached house「獨立式的房屋」

After Steve returned from hiking in the Himalayas for six months, he felt very detached from society.
史帝夫在喜馬拉雅山徒步旅行六個月回來後，他強烈感到與社會脫節。

contagious
con + tag + ous

▶ 〔kənˋtedʒəs〕 [形]　接觸傳染的，感染性的，會蔓延的

The disease was highly contagious, so all the victims had to be kept in quarantine.
此疾病具高度傳染性，因此所有的病患都需要被隔離。

 152　fact　fect　feat　fic(e)　影響，造成
152

fact

▶ 〔fækt〕 [名]　事實，實際，實情，真相

factor
fact + or

▶ 〔ˋfæktɚ〕 [名]　因素，要素

The fact that the temperature was -15 did not bother him. He went out skiing anyway.
零下15度這件事對他來說不算什麼，他還是出門滑雪了。

affect
af + fect

▶ 〔əˋfɛkt〕 [動]　影響，對…發生作用，使感動，使震動

affection
affect + ion

▶ 〔əˋfɛkʃən〕 [名]　影響，感染，愛慕，感情

affectionate
affection + ate

▶ 〔əˋfɛkʃənɪt〕 形　充滿深情的，溫柔親切的

He displayed his affection for his grandchildren by making them all kinds of toys.
他藉著幫孫子們做各種玩具表現對他們的愛。

---

infect
in + fect

▶ 〔ɪnˋfɛkt〕 動　傳染，感染，使受影響，污染，腐蝕
be infected with～「受到～感染」

---

infection
infect + ion

▶ 〔ɪnˋfɛkʃən〕 名　傳染，侵染，感染，傳染病

---

infectious
infect + ous

▶ 〔ɪnˋfɛkʃəs〕 形　傳染的，傳染性的，有感染力的

Natalie has such an infectious laugh, that when you hear her, you can't help laughing yourself.
娜塔莉的笑是這麼具感染力，所以當你聽見她的笑聲時，你不由自主地也會跟著笑。

---

effect
ef + fect

▶ 〔ɪˋfɛkt〕 名　結果，效果，效力，作用，影響
cause and effect「因果關係」

---

effective
effect + ive

▶ 〔ɪˋfɛktɪv〕 形　有效的

---

effectively
effective + ly

▶ 〔ɪˋfɛktɪvlɪ〕 副　有效地，生效地

---

effectiveness
effective + ness

▶ 〔əˋfɛktɪvnɪs〕 名　有效，有力

The sleeping pills Ron took were so effective that even after the plane landed, he continued to sleep until the flight attendant woke him up.
榮恩吃的安眠藥非常有效，連飛機著陸他還繼續睡到空服員叫他起床。

---

defeat
de + feat

▶ 〔dɪˋfit〕 動　戰勝，擊敗，使失敗，挫敗

---

defect
de + fect

▶ 〔dɪˋfɛkt〕 名　缺點，缺陷，不足之處

---

defective
defect + ive

▶ 〔dɪˋfɛktɪv〕 形　有缺陷的，不完美的

The electronic dog he got for his birthday was defective, and it meowed like a cat.
他生日收到的電子狗有瑕疵，它會像貓一樣喵喵叫。

| feat | ▶ | 〔fit〕名　功績，業績，英勇事跡 |

| feature
feat + ure | ▶ | 〔ˋfitʃə〕名　特徵，特色，面貌，相貌
動　以⋯為特色，（電影）由⋯主演，起重要作用，作為主要角色 |

An interesting feature of this building is the Roman columns.
羅馬圓柱是這棟建築物的一個有趣特色。

| efficient
ef + fic + ent | ▶ | 〔ɪˋfɪʃənt〕形　效率高的，有能力的，能勝任的 |

| efficiently
efficient + ly | ▶ | 〔ɪˋfɪʃəntlɪ〕副　效率高地，有效地 |

| efficiency
efficient + cy | ▶ | 〔ɪˋfɪʃənsɪ〕名　效率，效能，功效 |

Maggie is able to work efficiently when she has no distractions, but when the television is on, she can't get anything done.
瑪姬不分心的時候工作效率很好，但是電視開著的時候，她沒辦法完成任何事。

| sufficient
suf + fic + ent | ▶ | 〔səˋfɪʃənt〕形　足夠的，充分的，能勝任的 |

| sufficiently
sufficient + ly | ▶ | 〔səˋfɪʃətlɪ〕副　足夠地，充分地 |

| sufficiency
sufficient + cy | ▶ | 〔səˋfɪʃənsɪ〕名　充分，足量 |

| insufficient
in + sufficient | ▶ | 〔ˏɪnsəˋfɪʃənt〕形　不充分的，不足的，不適合的，不勝任的 |

This case was dismissed due to insufficient evidence.
本案件由於證據不足而被駁回。

| office
of + fice | ▶ | 〔ˋɔfɪs〕名　辦公室，營業處，政府機關 |

| officer
office + er | ▶ | 〔ˋɔfəsə〕名　軍官，公務員，警官，警察 |

official
office + ial

▶ 〔əˋfɪʃəl〕 形 官員的，公務上的，官方的，
法定的，正式的

It's not official yet, but I think Trish and Don got engaged.
雖然還沒正式公開，但是我想翠許和唐訂婚了。

(153) magni maj mast max 巨大的

153

magnificent magni + fic + ent ▶	〔mægˋnɪfəsənt〕 形	壯麗的，宏偉的，豪華的， 華麗的
magnificently magnificent + ly ▶	〔mægˋnɪfɪsntlɪ〕 副	壯麗地，宏偉地，壯觀地
magnificence magnificent + ce ▶	〔mægˋnɪfəsn̩s〕 名	壯麗，輝煌，華貴，高尚， 莊嚴
magnify magni + fy ▶	〔ˋmægnə͵faɪ〕 動 放大，擴大，誇張，誇大 a magnifying glass「放大鏡」	
magnifier magnify + er ▶	〔ˋmægnə͵faɪə〕 名 擴大者，誇大者，放大鏡	
magnitude magni + itude ▶	〔ˋmægnə͵tjud〕 名	巨大，廣大，重大，重要， 強度

This microscope magnifies things by one hundred.
這個顯微鏡能放大物體百倍。

The story started out magnificently, but the ending was a disappointment.
故事一開始氣勢宏偉，但是結局很令人失望。

majesty maj + esty ▶	〔ˋmædʒɪstɪ〕 名	雄偉，壯麗，莊嚴， （帝王的）威嚴，權威，君權， （大寫）陛下
majestic majesty + ic ▶	〔məˋdʒɛstɪk〕 形 雄偉的，威嚴的，崇高的	

The majestic outline of Mt. Everest could be seen from the cabin window.
從機艙的窗戶可以看到聖母峰壯麗的輪廓。

master
mast + er

〔`mæstə〕 图　主人，雇主，
能控制掌握某事物的人
動　精通，掌握

mastery
master + y

〔`mæstərɪ〕 图　支配，統治，熟練，精通

masterly
master + ly

〔`mæstəlɪ〕 形　熟練的，精湛的，巧妙的
副　熟練地，精湛地，巧妙地

masterpiece
master + piece

〔`mæstəˏpis〕 图　傑作，名作

This sculpture is the masterpiece of a local artist.
這件雕塑是本地一位藝術家的傑作。

major
maj + or

〔`medʒə〕 形　較大的，較多的，主要的，
重要的，主修的
（反義）minor

majority
major + ity

〔məˋdʒɔrətɪ〕 图　多數，過半數，大多數

Although there are a few who don't like the idea, the majority of the family members support donating the family fortune to charity.
雖然有少數人不贊同，但是大多數的家庭成員都支持將家族財產捐給慈善機構。

maxim
max + im

〔`mæksɪm〕 图　格言，箴言，座右銘

maximum
max + imum

〔`mæksəməm〕 图　最大量，最大數，最大限度
形　最大的，最多的，最高的
（反義）minimum

maximal
maxim + al

〔`mæksəḷ〕 形　最大的，最高的，最全面的
（反義）minimal

maximize
maxim + ize

〔`mæksəˏmaɪz〕 動　增加至最大限度，
達到最大值
（反義）minimize

The maximum setting for this heater is 28 degrees Celsius.
這台暖氣機的最高設定溫是攝氏28度。

154　min(i)　微小的

154

mince min + ce	▶ 〔mɪns〕 動　切碎，剁碎，細分， 　　　　　矯揉造作地說（或作） minced meat「碎肉」
minor min + or	▶ 〔ˋmaɪnɚ〕 形　較小的，較少的，不重要的， 　　　　　次要的，副修的 （反義）major
minority minor + ity	▶ 〔maɪˋnɔrətɪ〕 名　少數，少數派，少數民族 （反義）majority
minimum mini + mum	▶ 〔ˋmɪnəməm〕 名　最少量，最少數，最低極限 　　　　　形　最小的，最少的，最低的 （反義）maximum
minimal mini + al	▶ 〔ˋmɪnəml〕 形　最小的，極微的 （反義）maximal
minimize mini + ize	▶ 〔ˋmɪnəˏmaɪz〕 動　減到最少，縮到最小 （反義）maximize
miniature mini + ture	▶ 〔ˋmɪnɪətʃɚ〕 名　縮樣，縮圖，縮小模型，微型畫

Before her first big Hollywood film, she had only a few minor roles.　在她拍攝第一部好萊塢大片之前，她只演過幾個小角色。

People who have never traveled abroad are in the minority these days.　現在沒有出國旅行過的人只佔少數。

Beth put minimal effort into her project, but the results were satisfactory.
貝絲只花了最小限度的努力在她的企劃上，但是結果卻很令人滿意。

diminish di + min + ish	▶ 〔dəˋmɪnɪʃ〕 動　減少，縮小，縮減，失勢，被貶低

The good fortune of others does not diminish your own accomplishments.
其他人的好運並不減損你自身的成就。

minister mini + ster	▶ 〔ˋmɪnɪstɚ〕 名　部長，大臣，牧師
ministry mini + stry	▶ 〔ˋmɪnɪstrɪ〕 名　部門，內閣，牧師的職務 the Ministry「（英）部，（日）省」

The Ministry of Finance approved budget cuts for defense spending.
財政部通過減少軍事防禦預算。

administer ad + minister	▶	〔əd`mɪnəstə〕 動　管理，掌管，執行，給予，提供
administration administer + tion	▶	〔əd͵mɪnə`streʃən〕 名　管理，經營，行政，施政，施行，（藥的）用法
administrative administer + ive	▶	〔əd`mɪnə͵stretɪv〕 形　管理的，行政的

Some people have been successful at kicking their smoking habit by using patches that administer nicotine through the skin.
有些人藉由使用讓尼古丁經由皮膚進入體內的貼片成功戒除菸癮。

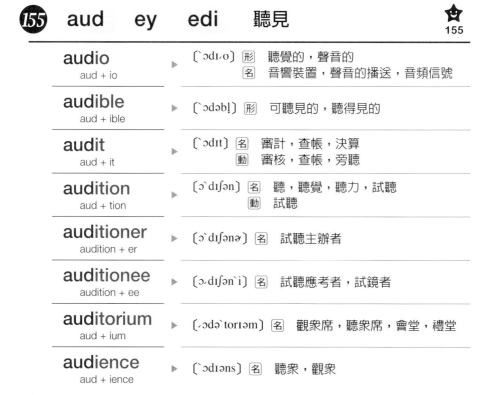

155　aud　ey　edi　聽見

★ 155

audio aud + io	▶	〔`ɔdɪ͵o〕 形　聽覺的，聲音的 名　音響裝置，聲音的播送，音頻信號
audible aud + ible	▶	〔`ɔdəbl〕 形　可聽見的，聽得見的
audit aud + it	▶	〔`ɔdɪt〕 名　審計，查帳，決算 動　審核，查帳，旁聽
audition aud + tion	▶	〔ɔ`dɪʃən〕 名　聽，聽覺，聽力，試聽 動　試聽
auditioner audition + er	▶	〔ɔ`dɪʃənɚ〕 名　試聽主辦者
auditionee audition + ee	▶	〔ɔ͵dɪʃən`i〕 名　試聽應考者，試鏡者
auditorium aud + ium	▶	〔͵ɔdə`torɪəm〕 名　觀眾席，聽眾席，會堂，禮堂
audience aud + ience	▶	〔`ɔdɪəns〕 名　聽眾，觀眾

Auditions for the play will be held on December 3rd in the auditorium.
那齣戲的試鏡將於12月3日在禮堂進行。

obey ob + ey	▶	〔ə`be〕 動　服從，聽從，執行，遵守，按照…行動
obedient ob + edi + ent	▶	〔ə`bidjənt〕 形　服從的，順從的，恭順的
obedience obedient + ce	▶	〔ə`bidjəns〕 名　服從，順從
obediently obedient + ly	▶	〔ə`bidɪəntlɪ〕 副　服從地，順從地，忠順地
disobedient dis + obedient	▶	〔͵dɪsə`bidɪnet〕 形　不服從的，違抗命令的， 違反（規則等）的
disobedience disobedient + ce	▶	〔͵dɪsə`bidɪəns〕 名　不服從，違抗，違反
disobediently disobedient + ly	▶	〔͵dɪsə`bidɪəntlɪ〕 副　不服從地，不守規則地

My dog is very clever and obeys my every command.
我的狗非常聰明，而且聽從我的每一個命令。

He raised his children to be obedient.
他將孩子養育得服從恭順。

 156　war(e)　ward　警告，提醒
156

warn war + n	▶	〔wɔrn〕 動　警告，告誡，提醒
warning warn + ing	▶	〔`wɔrnɪŋ〕 名　警告，告誡，警報，徵候，前兆

The dog gave a low warning growl when the mailman came to the door.
郵差來到門前時，那隻狗低吼出聲警告。

aware a + ware	▶	〔ə`wɛr〕 形　知道的，察覺的 be aware of～「意識到～，知道～」
unaware un + aware	▶	〔͵ʌnə`wɛr〕 形　不知道的，未察覺到的

awareness
aware + ness

▶ 〔ə`wɛrnɪs〕 名　察覺，覺悟，體認

Raising people's awareness of a problem is the first step in making changes.
提高人們對於問題的體認是改變的第一步。

reward re + ward	▶ 〔rɪ`wɔrd〕 名　報答，報償，報應，獎賞，酬金，獎品 動　報答，報償，酬謝，獎勵，報應，懲罰
rewarding reward + ing	▶ 〔rɪ`wɔrdɪŋ〕 形　有益的，有報酬的
award a + ward	▶ 〔ə`wɔrd〕 名　獎，獎品，獎狀，獎學金 動　授予，給予

There is a 50,000 NTD reward for any information that will lead to the capture of the criminal.
提供協助逮捕犯人的消息將會得到5萬元的獎賞。

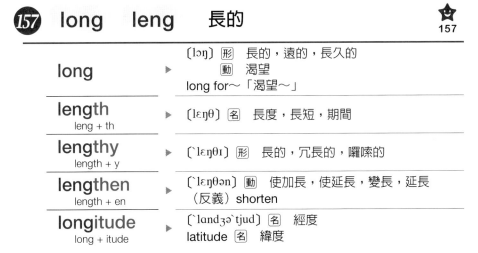

157 long　leng　長的
157

long	▶ 〔lɔŋ〕 形　長的，遠的，長久的 動　渴望 long for～「渴望～」
length leng + th	▶ 〔lɛŋθ〕 名　長度，長短，期間
lengthy length + y	▶ 〔`lɛŋθɪ〕 形　長的，冗長的，囉嗦的
lengthen length + en	▶ 〔`lɛŋθən〕 動　使加長，使延長，變長，延長 （反義）shorten
longitude long + itude	▶ 〔`lɑndʒə`tjud〕 名　經度 latitude 名　緯度

She came to dread the lengthy Wednesday meetings.
她變得害怕參加每週三冗長的會議。

It is possible to shorten jeans, but very difficult to lengthen them.
把牛仔褲改短是有可能的，但是要加長就非常困難。

wild(er) 野生的，荒野的
158

wild ▶	〔waɪld〕形 野生的，荒涼的，難駕馭的， 猛烈的，瘋狂的，荒唐的 名 荒野，荒地，未開發的地方
wilderness wilder + ness ▶	〔`wɪldənɪs〕名 荒野，荒漠，不受控制的狀態， 使人困惑的狀況

The criminals were exiled to the wilderness of Siberia.
罪犯被流放至西伯利亞的荒野。

bewilder be + wilder ▶	〔bɪ`wɪldə〕動 使迷惑，使糊塗，使迷路
bewilderment bewilder + ment ▶	〔bɪ`wɪldəmənt〕名 迷惑，昏亂，混亂，雜亂

On his first trip to Tokyo, Tim was bewildered by the bright lights,
crowds of people, and neon signs he could not read.
第一次到東京旅行，提姆被閃爍的燈光、擁擠的人群和他看不懂的霓虹招
牌給搞糊塗了。

 blo(o) 破裂
159

blow blo + w ▶	〔blo〕動 吹，刮，吹動，吹響，吹奏，爆炸
bloom bloo + m ▶	〔blum〕名 花，開花，開花期，最佳時期 動 開花，生長茂盛，青春煥發，繁榮
blossom blo + som ▶	〔`blasəm〕名 花，開花，開花期，生長期， 興旺期

When the cherry blossoms are in full bloom, you will see many
people in the park, enjoying the view.
櫻花開滿時，你會看見許多人在公園欣賞那片景象。

bureau 櫃子，書桌

160

bureau ▶	〔`bjuro〕 图 事務處，聯絡處，社，分社， （政府機構的）局，司署，處 a travel bureau「旅行社」 FBI=Federal Bureau of Investigation「聯邦調查局」
bureaucracy ▶ bureau + cracy	〔bju`rɑkrəsɪ〕 图 官僚政治，官僚，繁文縟節， 形式主義
bureaucrat ▶ bureau + crat	〔`bjurəˌkræt〕 图 官僚，官僚主義者

The bureaucrat in charge of the organization made it difficult for any constructive change to take place.
負責管理組織的官僚讓任何具有建設性的改變都很難發生。

mon 警告

161

monitor ▶ mon + or	〔`mɑnətə〕 图 班長，級長，監聽員，監控器 動 監控，監測

The company monitors all of its phone calls to make sure employees are being polite to customers.
那間公司監聽內部所有的電話，以確保員工與客戶談話時有禮貌。

monument ▶ mon + ment	〔`mɑnjəmənt〕 图 紀念碑，紀念塔，紀念館， 遺址
monumental ▶ monument + al	〔ˌmɑnjə`mɛntḷ〕 形 紀念建築物的，紀念性的， 巨大的，重要的，不朽的

The young artist's first art exhibit was a monumental success.
那位年輕藝術家的首次展覽大大成功。

Mount Rushmore in South Dakota, USA, is a huge monument carved into the side of a mountain.
美國南達科他州的羅斯摩爾山是一座雕刻在山側的巨大紀念碑。

admonish
ad + mon + ish

〔əd`mɑnɪʃ〕[動] 告誡，警告，提醒，勸告，責備
admonish（人）to V「勸（人）〜」

Parents should admonish their children when they misbehave.
父母應該要在孩子行為不端時勸告他們。

---

summon
sum + mon

〔`sʌmən〕[動] 召喚，傳喚，請求，召集，鼓起
（勇氣），振作（精神）

Since she has been summoned to jury duty, Barbara will have to take a week off work.
芭芭拉因為被召集為陪審團一員，將要請一個禮拜的假。

---

162 adul adol 成人
★ 162

adult
adul + t

〔ə`dʌlt〕[形] 成年的，成年人的
[名] 成年人

adolescent
adol + ent

〔͵ædḷ`ɛsn̩t〕[形] 青春期的，
青少年的，
未成熟的
[名] 青少年

*adul*t

*adol*escent

adolescence
adolescent + ce

〔͵ædḷ`ɛsn̩s〕[名] 青春期，青少年時期，
發育成形階段

Adolescence can be a very difficult time of life.
青春期可能是人生中非常難熬的階段。

---

163 like 像〜一樣的
★ 163

like

〔laɪk〕[形] 相像的，有相同性質的，類似的
[動] 喜歡，願意，希望

likely
like + ly

〔`laɪklɪ〕[形] 很可能的，適當的，正合要求的
[副] 很可能

likeliness likely + ness	▶ 〔`laɪklɪnɪs〕 名 可能，可能性
unlikely un + likely	▶ 〔ʌn`laɪklɪ〕 形 不太可能的，靠不住的， 不可能發生的
unlikeliness unlikely + ness	▶ 〔ˌʌn`laɪklɪnɪs〕 名 未必，不太可能

If you don't like the first book in this series, it is not likely that you will enjoy the other five.
如果你不喜歡這系列的第一集，你不太可能會喜歡其他的五本。

 ## hood 狀態，集團
164

childhood child + hood	▶ 〔`tʃaɪldˌhʊd〕 名 幼年時期，童年時期
adulthood adult + hood	▶ 〔ə`dʌlthʊd〕 名 成年
neighborhood neighbor + hood	▶ 〔`nebɚˌhʊd〕 名 鄰近地區，近鄰，整個街坊
likelihood likely + hood	▶ 〔`laɪklɪˌhʊd〕 名 可能，可能性 in all likelihood「十之八九，極有可能」
unlikelihood unlikely + hood	▶ 〔ʌn`laɪklɪhʊd〕 名 不太可能（的事）

With your excellent qualifications, you will, in all likelihood, get the job.
以你優秀的條件，你將很有可能得到那份工作。

 ## forc(e) fort 力量，強烈
165

force	▶ 〔fors〕 名 力量，力氣，武力，軍事力量 動 強迫，迫使，強行攻佔 force（人）to V = force（人）into V-ing「強迫 （人）～」

forcible force + ible	▶	〔`forsəbl〕 形 強迫的，強制的，有說服力的
forcibly forcible + ly	▶	〔`forsəblɪ〕 副 強迫地，強制地，有說服力地
enforce en + force	▶	〔ɪn`fors〕 動 實施，執行，強制，強迫，堅持

It is not a good idea to make rules and laws that will be difficult or impossible to enforce.
制定不容易或者不可能實行的規章和法律並不是個好主意。

Deanna was afraid of the water, but her parents forced her to take swimming lessons anyway.
狄安娜怕水，但是她的父母還是強迫她上游泳課。

reinforce re + in + force	▶	〔ˌriɪn`fors〕 動 增援，加強，增加，補充，加固 reinforce～with... 「以…強化～」
reinforcement reinforce + ment	▶	〔ˌriɪn`forsmənt〕 名 增援，加強，加固，強化， 增強材料，援軍

The wind can get so strong in this region, that all wooden doors are reinforced with metal bars.
這個地區有時候風力強勁，因此所有的木門都用鐵條強化。

fort	▶	〔fort〕 名 堡壘，要塞
effort ef + fort	▶	〔`ɛfət〕 名 努力，盡力，努力的成果，成就
effortless effort + less	▶	〔`ɛfətlɪs〕 形 不出力的，容易的
effortlessly effortless + ly	▶	〔`ɛfətlɪslɪ〕 副 輕鬆地，毫不費勁地

The bodybuilder effortlessly ripped the door off its hinges.
健美先生毫不費力地就將門從鉸鏈拆下。

comfort
com + fort

〔`kʌmfət〕 動 安慰，慰問，使安逸舒適
名 安逸，舒適，安慰，慰問，
給予安慰的東西

comfortable
comfort + able

〔`kʌmfətəbl〕 形 使人舒服的，舒適的，寬裕的，
豐富的，自在的

comfortably
comfortable + ly

〔`kʌmfətəblɪ〕 副 舒服地，舒適地，安逸地，
寬裕地

uncomfortable
un + comfortable

〔ʌn`kʌmfətəbl〕 形 不舒服的，不安的，
不自在的，令人不舒服的

uncomfortably
uncomfortable + ly

〔ˌʌn`kʌmfətəblɪ〕 副 不舒適地，不自在地，
令人不舒服地

Kevin wears the same shoes every day because he says they are comfortable.
凱文每天都穿同一雙鞋，因為他說那雙鞋很舒服。

166 mark merc(e) merch 買賣 166

market
mark + et

〔`markɪt〕 名 市場，股票市場，市集，銷路，
需求
動 （在市場上）銷售，
購買（或賣出）

marketing
market + ing

〔`markɪtɪŋ〕 名 （市場的）交易，銷售，運銷，
行銷學

The flea market was cancelled due to bad weather.
跳蚤市場因為天候惡劣而取消了。

merchandise
merch + andise

〔`mɝtʃənˌdaɪz〕 名 商品，貨物

merchant
merch + ant

〔`mɝtʃənt〕 名 商人，零售商

All merchandise must be declared at customs after going through immigration.
所有的商品必須在通關後向海關申報。

| **commerce**
com + merce | ▶ | 〔`kɑmɝs〕 名 商業，貿易，交易 |

| **commercial**
commerce + ial | ▶ | 〔kəˋmɝʃəl〕 形 商業的，商務的，營利本位的，
商業廣告性的 |

Commercial airlines are often in financial trouble.
商業性的航空公司經常陷入財務困難。

| **mercy**
merc + y | ▶ | 〔`mɝsɪ〕 名 慈悲，憐憫，仁慈，寬容，
仁慈行為，善行
at the mercy of～「受～所支配，任～處置，在～
掌握中」 |

| **merciful**
mercy + ful | ▶ | 〔`mɝsɪfəl〕 形 仁慈的，慈悲的，寬容的 |

| **merciless**
mercy + less | ▶ | 〔`mɝsɪlɪs〕 形 無情的，殘酷的，毫無慈悲心的 |

| **mercilessly**
merciless + ly | ▶ | 〔`mɝsɪlɪslɪ〕 副 無情地，殘忍地 |

Gina was tired of being at the mercy of her stingy uncle, so she moved away. 吉娜厭倦了受她吝嗇的叔父擺佈，所以她搬走了。
The sun beat down mercilessly on the plantation workers.
太陽毒辣地照在農場工人身上。

 puls(e) **pel** 擠出
167

| **pulse** | ▶ | 〔pʌls〕 名 脈搏，有節奏的跳動，意向，心態，
活力
動 搏動，跳動，拍打，振動 |

| **pulsate**
pulse + ate | ▶ | 〔`pʌlˏset〕 動 搏動，悸動，脈動 |

| **pulsation**
pulsate + ion | ▶ | 〔pʌlˋseʃən〕 名 脈搏，悸動，脈動 |

The doctor carefully took John's pulse.
醫生仔細地測量約翰的脈搏。

| **compulsory**
com + puls + ory | ▶ | 〔kəmˋpʌlsərɪ〕 形 必須做的，義務的，必修的，
強制，強迫的 |

compulsion
compulsory + ion

〔kəmˋpʌlʃən〕名　（被）強迫，（被）強制，
強制力，強迫力

It is compulsory for Korean men to do two years of military service.
韓國男性需服義務兵役兩年。

compel
com + pel

〔kəmˋpɛl〕動　強迫，使不得不，強求
compel（人）to V「強迫（人）～」

compelling
compel + ing

〔kəmˋpɛlɪŋ〕形　強制的，令人注目的，
令人感嘆的，令人信服的

He presented a compelling argument for improving public transportation.
他提出一個極具說服力的改善公共交通的論點。

---

 plex　複雜　
168

complex
com + plex

〔ˋkɑmplɛks〕形　複雜的，錯綜複雜的，難懂的，
複合的，合成的
　　　　　　名　複合物，綜合體，集團，情結
housing complex「複合式住宅區」
complex highway system「立體高速公路」

complexity
complex + ity

〔kəmˋplɛksəti〕名　複雜（性），錯綜（性），
錯綜複雜的事物

There is a very complex system of tunnels under the castle.
城堡下有非常複雜的地道系統。

He went to counseling to try to get over his inferiority complex.
他去諮詢想治療他的自卑感。

perplex
per + plex

〔pɚˋplɛks〕動　使困惑，使費解，使複雜化

perplexity
perplex + ity

〔pɚˋplɛksəti〕名　困惑，茫然，使人困惑的事情，
雜亂狀態，糾纏

She had a perplexed look on her face when she opened her safe and found it empty.
當她打開金庫發現裡面是空的時，她露出困惑的表情。

169　center　centr　中心

169

center ▶	〔`sɛntə〕名　中心，中央，人口集中地區，中樞，核心 動　集中，居中
central center + al ▶	〔`sɛntrəl〕形　中心的，中央的，便利的，主要的，核心的，重要的

Be sure to drill that hole in the exact center of the piece of wood.
請務必將那個洞鑽在木板的正中央。

concentrate con + centr + ate ▶	〔`kɑnsɛnˌtret〕動　集中，聚集，集結，濃縮，全神貫注，全力以赴 concentrate～on...「集中～在…」 concentrate on～「全神貫注於～」
concentration concentrate + ion ▶	〔ˌkɑnsɛn`treʃən〕名　集中，專心，專注，濃縮，濃度

The noise of the construction made it difficult for the test-takers to concentrate.
工地的噪音讓考生難以專心。

Balancing on a tightrope takes considerable concentration.
在繩索上保持平衡需要相當的集中力。

eccentric ec + centr + ic ▶	〔ɪk`sɛntrɪk〕形　古怪的，反常的
eccentricity eccentric + ity ▶	〔ˌɛksɛn`trɪsəti〕名　古怪，怪癖，古怪的行為或習慣

The eccentric old man carried a bird on his shoulder wherever he went.
那個古怪的老人不論去哪裡，總帶著一隻鳥在他肩膀上。

170　tempo　時間

170

tempo ▶	〔`tɛmpo〕名　速度，拍子，發展進行速度

temporal
tempo + al

▶ 〔`tɛmpərəl〕 形　時間的，暫存的，短暫的，非永恆的，世間的，世俗的

temporary
tempo + ary

▶ 〔`tɛmpə͵rɛrɪ〕 形　臨時的，暫時的，一時的

temporarily
temporary + ly

▶ 〔͵tɛmpə`rɛrəlɪ〕 副　暫時地，臨時地

This is only a temporary home until your house is completed.
在你家蓋好之前，這裡只是一個暫居處。

contemporary
con + temporary

▶ 〔kən`tɛmpə͵rɛrɪ〕 形　當代的，同時代，同年齡的
名　同時代的人，同年齡的人，同時期的東西，當代人

Bartok is a contemporary composer.
巴爾托克是現代的作曲家。

Some authors who are now famous were not respected by their contemporaries.
現在有名的一些作家在他們活著的時代並未受到重視。

vers(e)　vert　轉變

171

verse

▶ 〔vɝs〕 名　詩，韻文，詩句，詩行，詩節

converse
con + verse

▶ 〔kən`vɝs〕 動　交談，談話

conversation
converse + tion

▶ 〔͵kɑnvɚ`seʃən〕 名　會話，談話，非正式會談，談話技巧，談吐

conversational
conversation + al

▶ 〔͵kɑnvɚ`seʃənl〕 形　會話的，健談的

conversationalist
conversational + ist

▶ 〔͵kɑnvɚ`seʃənlɪst〕 名　交談者，口才好的人

Good conversationalists listen as much as they talk.
好的談話者不只懂得說話也懂得傾聽。

adverse
ad + verse

▶ 〔ædˋvɝs〕 形　逆向的，相反的，反對的
be adverse to～「與～相反，反對～」

adversity
adverse + ity

▶ 〔ədˋvɝsətɪ〕 名　逆境，厄運

The drug has been known to be very effective while causing few adverse effects.
眾所皆知那種藥非常有效而且副作用很小。

advertise
ad + vert + ise

▶ 〔ˋædvɚ͵taɪz〕 動　為…做廣告，為…宣傳

advertisement
advertise + ment

▶ 〔͵ædvɚˋtaɪzmənt〕 名　廣告，宣傳，公告，啟事

advertising
advertise + ing

▶ 〔ˋædvɚ͵taɪzɪŋ〕 名　廣告業，廣告，登廣告

The advent of TV gave rise to an entirely new type of advertising.
電視的出現帶來一種全新的廣告方式。

You might be able to sell your sofa if you advertise it in the classified section of the newspaper.
如果你在報紙的廣告欄登廣告，你可能有辦法賣掉你的沙發。

convert
con + vert

▶ 〔kənˋvɝt〕 動　轉變，變換
convert～into/to...「將～轉變成…」

conversion
convert + ion

▶ 〔kənˋvɝʃən〕 名　改變，轉變，變換，改變信仰

Do you know the formula for converting Fahrenheit to Celsius?
你知道將華氏溫度轉換成攝氏的公式嗎？

diverse
di + verse

▶ 〔daɪˋvɝs〕 形　不同的，互異的，多變化的

diversion
diverse + ion

▶ 〔daɪˋvɝʒən〕 名　轉移，轉換，分散注意力，娛樂，消遣

diversity
diverse + ity

▶ 〔daɪˋvɝsətɪ〕 名　差異，不同點，多樣性

divert
di + vert

▶ 〔daɪˋvɝt〕 動　使轉向，使分心，轉移，娛樂
divert oneself with～「用～轉移自己的心情」

Because of the immigrants from many different countries, Vancouver is a diverse city.
溫哥華有來自各國的移民人口，是一座多樣化的城市。

reverse re + verse	▶	〔rɪ`vɝs〕 動 顛倒，翻轉，倒退，倒轉 形 顛倒的，相反的，反面的
reversible reverse + ible	▶	〔rɪ`vɝsəbl̩〕 形 可反轉的，可調換的，雙面可用的

This jacket is reversible, so it's like having two jackets.
這件夾克兩面都可以穿，所以就好像是有兩件夾克一樣。

universe uni + verse	▶	〔`junəˌvɝs〕 名 宇宙，天地萬物，全世界，全人類
universal universe + al	▶	〔ˌjunə`vɝsl̩〕 形 普遍的，宇宙的，全世界的， 萬能的，完整的
universally universal + ly	▶	〔ˌjunə`vɝslɪ〕 副 普遍地，一般地，到處， 通用地，萬能地
university universe + ity	▶	〔ˌjunə`vɝsətɪ〕 名 大學，綜合性大學，大學校園， 大學全體人員

You can't assume that your point of view will be universally accepted.
你不能假設你的看法會被所有人接受。

 vey vi 道路，途徑
172

convey con + vey	▶	〔kən`ve〕 動 運送，傳達，表達，轉讓
conveyor convey + or	▶	〔kən`veɚ〕 名 搬運者，運輸裝置 conveyor belt「傳送帶，輸送帶」
conveyance convey + ance	▶	〔kən`veəns〕 名 運送，運輸，表達，傳達， 交通工具

The suitcases were put onto the conveyor belt, and delivered to the luggage handlers.
行李箱被放在傳送帶上，然後運送至行李處理機。

obvious ob + vi + ous	▶	〔`ɑbvɪəs〕 形 明顯的，顯著的

obviously
obvious + ly

▶ 〔`ɑbvɪəslɪ〕 副　明顯地，顯然地

It was very obvious that the young couple was in love.
那對年輕人很明顯彼此相愛。

Kevin was obviously happy about something, but he wouldn't tell anyone his secret.
凱文很明顯地為了某事在開心，但是他不願意告訴任何人他的祕密。

---

 corp　身體　　
173

corpse
corp + se

▶ 〔kɔrps〕 名　屍體，殘骸

The coroner was examining the corpse, trying to find a likely cause of death.
驗屍官正在檢查屍體，試圖發現可能的死亡原因。

corporate
corp + ate

▶ 〔`kɔrpərɪt〕 形　法人（組織）的，團體的，公司的，共同的，全體的

corporation
corporate + ion

▶ 〔ˌkɔrpəˋreʃən〕 名　法人，社團法人，股份（有限）公司

The community supported the corporation because it employed so many people.
社區支持這間公司，因為有許多人皆受其雇用。

---

 dam　demn　傷害，損害　　
174

damage
dam + age

▶ 〔`dæmɪdʒ〕 名　損害，損失，賠償金
動　損害，毀壞

Fortunately, the typhoon did not do any damage.
幸好颱風並沒有造成任何損害。

condemn
con + demn

▶ 〔kənˋdɛm〕 動　責難，責備，譴責，宣告…有罪，判…刑
condemn（人）to death「判決（人）死刑」

The serial killer was condemned to life imprisonment.
那位連續殺人犯被判無期徒刑。

 rect 直
175

correct co + rect	▶	〔kə`rɛkt〕 形 正確的，對的，恰當的，端正的 動 糾正，改正，矯正，校準
correctly correct + ly	▶	〔kə`rɛktlɪ〕 副 正確地，得體地
correctness correct + ness	▶	〔kə`rɛktnɪs〕 名 正確，得當，（言行的）端正
correction correct + ion	▶	〔kə`rɛkʃən〕 名 訂正，修改，校正
incorrect in + correct	▶	〔͵ɪnkə`rɛkt〕 形 不正確的，錯誤的，不真實的， 不適當的

The paper printed a correction to the mistake in reporting that
appeared the previous day's paper.
報紙刊登了一則前一天報導錯誤的更正啟事。

direct di + rect	▶	〔də`rɛkt〕 動 針對，指揮，命令，導演， 指示，指導 形 筆直的，直截了當的，率直的， 恰好的，正好的
directly direct + ly	▶	〔də`rɛktlɪ〕 副 直接地，筆直地，坦率地， 直截了當地，正好地

The police officer was directing traffic.
警察指揮交通。

If you want to know the true answer to that question, you should
ask your boss directly.
如果你想要知道問題的正確答案，你應該要直接問你的上司。

erect e + rect	▶	〔ɪ`rɛkt〕 形 直立的，垂直的，豎起的 動 使豎立，樹立，建立，設立
erection erect + ion	▶	〔ɪ`rɛkʃən〕 名 直立，豎直，建立，建造

The building was erected in 1802.
那棟建築物建造於1802年。

rectangle
rect + angle

▶ 〔rɛk`tæŋgl〕名　矩形，長方形，長方形物

rectangular
rectagle + ar

▶ 〔rɛk`tæŋgjələ〕形　矩形的，長方形的

Draw a rectangle with two sides twice as long as the others.
請畫一個兩邊為另外兩邊的兩倍長的長方形。

176　ply　　pli　　play　　ploy　　彎曲，重疊 ⭐176

apply
ap + ply

▶ 〔ə`plaɪ〕動　塗，敷，應用，實施，申請，請求
apply～to...「將～塗在…，將～實施在…，把～用於…」
apply for～「申請～」

applicable
apply + able

▶ 〔`æplɪkəbl〕形　可應用的，合用的，可實施的，適當的，合適的

applicant
apply + ant

▶ 〔`æpləkənt〕名　申請人

application
apply + tion

▶ 〔͵æplə`keʃən〕名　應用，適用，運用，申請，請求，申請書

Make sure you are dressed well when you go in to apply for a job.
應徵工作的時候，確保你衣著恰當。

display
dis + play

▶ 〔dɪ`sple〕動　陳列，展出，顯示，表現，炫耀
名　展覽，展覽品，顯示，炫耀

The display in the window was very attractive.
櫥窗的陳列非常吸引人。

employ
em + ploy

▶ 〔ɪm`plɔɪ〕動　雇用，使用，利用，使從事於

employment
employ + ment

▶ 〔ɪm`plɔɪmənt〕名　雇用，受雇，職業，工作
employer「雇主」
employee「雇員，員工」

177 tri 三個
177

triangle tri + angle	▶	〔ˋtraɪˏæŋgl〕 名 三角形，三角形之物，三角鐵， 三個一組，三角關係
tricycle tri + cycle	▶	〔ˋtraɪsɪkl〕 名 三輪車，三輪腳踏車
triple tri + ple	▶	〔ˋtrɪpl〕 形 三倍的，三重的，三方的
trilingual tri + lingual	▶	〔traɪˋlɪŋgwəl〕 形 能講三種語言的， 三種語言的

A triangle is made up of three sides.
三角形由三邊組成。

 178 custom 個人習慣
178

custom	▶	〔ˋkʌstəm〕 名 習俗，慣例，習慣，海關，關稅 customs「海關」
customary custom + ary	▶	〔ˋkʌstəmˏɛrɪ〕 形 習慣上的，慣常的，合乎習俗的
customer custom + er	▶	〔ˋkʌstəmɚ〕 名 顧客，買主

In Japan it is customary to take one's shoes off when entering a home.
在日本，一般習慣進入家門前將鞋子脫掉。

accustom ac + custom	▶	〔əˋkʌstəm〕 動 使習慣 be accustomed to～「習慣於～」

As soon as her eyes became accustomed to the dark, Judy saw that she was in a room full of skeletons.
眼睛一習慣黑暗，茱蒂就發現她身在一間滿是骷髏的房間。

dan　domin　　領主的權力
179

danger dan + ger	▶ 〔ˋdendʒɚ〕 名 危險，危險（物），威脅
dangerous danger + ous	▶ 〔ˋdendʒərəs〕 形 危險的，不安全的，招致危險的
endanger en + danger	▶ 〔ɪnˋdendʒɚ〕 動 危及，使遭到危險 endangered species「瀕臨絕種的生物」

The giant panda of China is an endangered species, as much of its natural habitat is being destroyed.
由於天然的棲息地遭受破壞，中國的熊貓正瀕臨絕種。

dominate domin + ate	▶ 〔ˋdɑmə͵net〕 動 支配，統治，控制， 在…中佔主要地位， 處於支配地位
dominant domin + ant	▶ 〔ˋdɑmənənt〕 形 佔優勢的，支配的，統治的， 佔首位的
dominance domin + ance	▶ 〔ˋdɑmənəns〕 名 優勢，支配（地位）， 統治（地位）

The Brazilian team dominated in the last half of the game.
巴西隊在下半場比賽中取得優勢。

 clin(e)　　傾斜
180

incline in + cline	▶ 〔ɪnˋklaɪn〕 動 傾斜，屈身，傾向，有意 be inclined to V「想要～，有～的傾向」 incline one's ear to～「洗耳恭聽～的話」
inclination incline + tion	▶ 〔͵ɪnkləˋneʃən〕 名 傾向，意向，愛好，趨勢， 傾斜，斜坡

I'm inclined to agree with Tom in this case.
我傾向贊同湯姆對這件事的看法。

If you have the time or the inclination, would you make a cake to bring to the party?
如果你有空而且願意的話，能不能請你做一個蛋糕帶來派對？

decline
de + cline

〔dɪˋklaɪn〕 動　下降，下跌，減少，衰落，衰退，婉拒，謝絕

decline to V
「謝絕（或婉拒）～」
on the decline「衰退中的，在下坡位置的」

I'm very sorry, but I will have to decline your kind invitation.
我很抱歉，但我必須拒絕你好意的邀請。

181 dec 合適

decent
dec + ent

〔ˋdisṇt〕 形　正派的，合乎禮儀的，體面的，像樣的，親切的

decently
decent + ly

〔ˋdisṇtlɪ〕 副　合適地，體面地，像樣地，有禮貌地

decency
decent + cy

〔ˋdisṇsɪ〕 名　合宜，得體，寬容，正派，高雅

He didn't even have the decency to tell her why he left her alone with four children.
他不懂情理，連跟她解釋拋下她和四個孩子的原因都沒有。

decorate
dec + ate

〔ˋdɛkəˌret〕 動　裝飾，修飾，佈置
decorate～with...「用…裝飾～」

decoration
decorate + ion

〔ˌdɛkəˋreʃən〕 名　裝飾，裝潢，裝飾品

The café was decorated in an Italian theme.
咖啡廳以義大利風格裝飾。

creas(e)　增加，成長　
182

increase in + crease	▶ 〔ɪnˋkris〕 動　增大，增加，增強，增殖 〔ˋɪnkris〕 名　增大，增加，增強
increasingly increase + ing + ly	▶ 〔ɪnˋkrisɪŋli〕 副　漸增地，越來越多地

He was finding it increasingly difficult not to laugh as the child seriously told the story.
在那孩子認真說故事的同時，他發現越來越難忍住不笑出來。

decrease de + crease	▶ 〔dɪˋkris〕 動　減少，減小 〔ˋdikris〕 名　減少，減小，減少額

The decreasing population of people under 40 is causing concern with regard to the social security system.
未滿40歲的人口減少，引發大眾對社會福利制度的關切。

 light　**lic**　入迷　
183

delight de + light	▶ 〔dɪˋlaɪt〕 名　欣喜，愉快，樂事，樂趣 動　使高興，高興，喜愛，取樂
delightful delight + ful	▶ 〔dɪˋlaɪtfəl〕 形　令人愉快的，令人高興的，可愛的
delighted delight + ed	▶ 〔dɪˋlaɪtɪd〕 形　高興的，快樂的

The cat was delighted to find a ball of yarn to play with.
那隻貓很高興找到一團紗玩。

delicate de + lic + ate	▶ 〔ˋdɛləkət〕 形　易碎的，嬌貴的，纖弱的， 精美的，雅緻的
delicacy delicate + cy	▶ 〔ˋdɛləkəsɪ〕 名　精美，嬌嫩，優雅，微妙， 纖弱，佳餚

Caviar is a delicacy, but I think it tastes terrible.
魚子醬是一道珍饈，但是我覺得很難吃。

pend　pens　吊，懸掛

pendant pend + ant	▶ 〔`pɛndənt〕 名　下垂物，垂飾，掛件，懸吊裝置， 拉線開關
pendulum pend + ulum	▶ 〔`pɛndʒələm〕 名　擺錘，鐘擺， 搖擺不定的事態（或局面等）
append ap + pend	▶ 〔ə`pɛnd〕 動　添附，附加，貼上，掛上
appendix append + ix	▶ 〔ə`pɛndɪks〕 名　附錄，附件，附加物 （名詞複數）appendixes/appendices 〔ə`pɛndəˏsiz〕
appendicitis append + citis	▶ 〔ˏəpɛndəˋsaɪtɪs〕 名　闌尾炎，盲腸炎

Appendicitis, if caught in time, is not serious, but it can be very dangerous if left unattended.
盲腸炎如果早期發現就不會太嚴重，但是放著不管是很危險的。

depend de + pend	▶ 〔dɪ`pɛnd〕 動　相信，信賴，依靠，依賴， 依…而定，懸而未決 depend on～「依靠～，取決於～」
dependable depend + able	▶ 〔dɪ`pɛndəbl〕 形　可靠的，可信任的
dependability dependable + ity	▶ 〔dɪˏpɛndə`bɪlətɪ〕 名　可信任，可靠性
dependent depend + ent	▶ 〔dɪ`pɛndənt〕 形　依靠的，依賴的，取決於…的 be dependent on～「依賴～，取決於～」
dependently dependent + ly	▶ 〔dɪ`pɛndəntlɪ〕 副　依賴地
dependence dependent + ce	▶ 〔dɪ`pɛndəns〕 名　依靠，依賴，視…而定，信任

independent in + dependent	▶	〔͵ɪndɪˋpɛndənt〕形 獨立的，自主的，自立的， 單獨的
independently independent + ly	▶	〔͵ɪndɪˋpɛndəntlɪ〕副 獨立地，自立地，無關地
independence independent + ce	▶	〔͵ɪndɪˋpɛndəns〕名 獨立，自主，自立

Dependability is one quality that you will need to demonstrate if you plan to advance in your career.
如果你想要提升你的事業，可靠性會是你需要展現的一個特質。

suspend sus + pend	▶	〔səˋspɛnd〕動 懸掛，懸浮，中止，延緩
suspender suspend + er	▶	〔səˋspɛndə〕名 懸掛物，（褲子或裙子的）背帶， 吊襪帶
suspension suspend + ion	▶	〔səˋspɛnʃən〕名 懸掛，懸浮，懸置，暫停，中止
suspense suspend + se	▶	〔səˋspɛns〕名 懸念，懸疑，懸而不決，暫時停止
suspensive suspense + ive	▶	〔səˋspɛnsɪv〕形 中止的，暫停的，未決的， 不安的

The largest suspension bridge in the world is the Akashi-Kaikyo bridge, which links Shikoku to Honshu.
世界最長的吊橋是連接四國和本州的明石海峽大橋。

 press 擠壓，擠出
185

press	▶	〔prɛs〕動 按，壓，擠，壓碎，強迫，緊迫 press（人）to V「強迫（人）～」
pressure press + ure	▶	〔ˋprɛʃə〕名 壓，按，擠，壓力，壓迫，緊迫， 催促

The child pressed her nose to the window of the candy store.
小孩把她的鼻子緊貼在糖果店的櫥窗上。

There is not enough air pressure in my bicycle tires, and it's very difficult to ride.　我的腳踏車輪胎氣壓不夠，所以非常難騎。

impress im + press	▶ 〔ɪm`prɛs〕 動　給…極深的印象，使感動， 　　使銘記，印，壓印
impressive impress + ive	▶ 〔ɪm`prɛsɪv〕 形　給人深刻印象的，令人欽佩的， 　　感人的
impression impress + ion	▶ 〔ɪm`prɛʃən〕 名　印象，模糊的觀念，感想， 　　壓印，印記 make an impression on～「對～感動」
impressionist impression + ist	▶ 〔ɪm`prɛʃənɪst〕 名　印象主義者，印象派畫家
impressionism impression + ism	▶ 〔ɪm`prɛʃənˏɪzəm〕 名　印象主義，印象派

Sheila impressed her classmates by her ability to hold her breath for two minutes.
希拉摒息兩分鐘的能力讓她的同學們印象深刻。

Although the president's speech was short, it made an impression on all who were listening.
雖然董事長的演說很短，但還是感動了所有在場的人。

express ex + press	▶ 〔ɪk`sprɛs〕 動　表達，陳述，表示
expression express + ion	▶ 〔ɪk`sprɛʃən〕 名　表達，表示，表情，臉色， 　　表現力，措辭，詞句
expressive express + ive	▶ 〔ɪk`sprɛsɪv〕 形　表現的，表達…的， 　　表情豐富的，意味深長的

The painting was such a beautiful expression of emotions that many of the museum guests were moved to tears.
那幅畫的感情表現是這麼地豐富，許多到美術館參觀的訪客都感動得流下眼淚。

depress de + press	▶ 〔dɪ`prɛs〕 動　使消沉，使沮喪，使心灰意冷， 　　壓低，削弱，抑制
depression depress + ion	▶ 〔dɪ`prɛʃən〕 名　沮喪，意氣消沉，不景氣，蕭條
depressing depress + ing	▶ 〔dɪ`prɛsɪŋ〕 形　沮喪的，消沉的
depressant depress + ant	▶ 〔dɪ`prɛsn̩t〕 形　有鎮靜作用的

The man fell into depression after his pet bird died.
那個男人自從他的寵物鳥死後，整個人變得意志消沈。

She couldn't snap out of her depression on her own, so she saw a counselor who prescribed anti-depressant medication.
她無法自己走出消沈的情緒，所以去找諮詢師接受抗抑鬱藥物的治療。

oppress op + press	▶	〔ə`prɛs〕 動 壓迫，壓制，使（心情）沈重，使煩惱，折磨
oppression oppress + ion	▶	〔ə`prɛʃən〕 名 壓迫，壓制，壓抑，沈悶
oppressive oppress + ive	▶	〔ə`prɛsɪv〕 形 壓迫的，壓制的，不公正的，苛重的，專制的，暴虐的

In the 17th century, many people traveled to the new world to escape political oppression.
十七世紀時，許多人前往新世界躲避政治迫害。

 186 tract   treat   tir(e)   拉，拖
186

attract at + tract	▶	〔ə`trækt〕 動 吸引，引起（注意或興趣等），引誘
attractive attract + ive	▶	〔ə`træktɪv〕 形 有吸引力的，引人注目的
attraction attract + ion	▶	〔ə`trækʃən〕 名 吸引，吸引力，吸引物，名勝

Flowers with strong smells and bright colors attract bees.
香氣強烈且顏色鮮豔的花朵能吸引蜜蜂。

Working long hours for little pay is not an attractive proposition to most people.
工時長而且薪資低廉對大多數人來說並不是個有吸引力的條件。

distract dis + tract	▶	〔dɪ`strækt〕 動 轉移，分散，使分心，困擾，使錯亂，使苦惱 distract（人）from...「使（人）無法專心…」
distractive distract + ive	▶	〔dɪ`stræktɪv〕 形 分散注意力的

distraction
distract + ion

▶ 〔dɪˋstrækʃən〕 名　分心，注意力分散，
分散注意的事物

The parade outside distracted Jake from his homework.
外面的遊行讓傑克無法專心寫作業。

abstract
abs + tract

▶ 〔ˋæbstrækt〕 形　抽象的，難懂的，純理論的
名　摘要，梗概，抽象派藝術作品

abstractive
abstract + ive

▶ 〔æbˋstræktɪv〕 形　抽象的

abstraction
abstract + ion

▶ 〔æbˋstrækʃən〕 名　抽象，抽象概念

A "good attitude" is an abstract idea that is difficult to define in concrete terms, but it is important, nonetheless.
「良好的態度」是一個抽象的概念，很難用具體的語言定義，但是不管如何，這個概念是很重要的。

treat

▶ 〔trit〕 動　看待，對待，把⋯看作，治療，請客
名　請客
treat～as...「把～看作⋯」
treat～with...「用⋯治療～」

treatment
treat + ment

▶ 〔ˋtritmənt〕 名　對待，待遇，處理，治療，治療法

This is my treat; put your money away.
這次我請客，把你的錢收起來。

He's getting treatment for his sore back.
他正接受背痛的治療。

retire
re + tire

▶ 〔rɪˋtaɪr〕 動　退休，退役，退出

retirement
retire + ment

▶ 〔rɪˋtaɪrmənt〕 名　退休，退職，退役，退休生活

retiree
retire + ee

▶ 〔rɪˌtaɪəˋri〕 名　退休人員

He wanted to retire by the time he was forty, but he didn't make it until forty-five.　他想要在40歲時退休，但他一直到45歲才成功。
Ena lived in a retirement home.　艾娜住在一所老人院裡。

cert 確切

certain cert + ain	〔`sɝtən〕 形　確鑿的，無疑的，可靠的，確信的 It is certain（that）～「無疑的是～，一定是～」 be certain（that）～「確信會～」
certainly certain + ly	〔`sɝtənlɪ〕 副　無疑地，必定，確實， （用於回答）當然，可以，沒問題
certainty certain + ty	〔`sɝtəntɪ〕 名　確實，必然
uncertain un + certain	〔ʌn`sɝtṇ〕 形　不明確的，含糊的，不確定的， 不能確信，不穩定的
uncertainly uncertain + ly	〔ʌn`sɝtṇlɪ〕 副　猶豫不決地，沒把握地
uncertainty uncertain + ty	〔ʌn`sɝtṇtɪ〕 名　不確定，不確信，不可靠， 不確定的事物

It was with great uncertainty that Jerry opened the door to the
house that was supposedly haunted.
傑瑞帶著極為猶豫的心情，打開了傳說中鬼屋的大門。
I'm still uncertain as to whether I should go to Guam or Singapore
for my next holiday.
我還是不確定下次度假要去關島還是新加坡。

ascertain as + certain	〔ˌæsɚ`ten〕 動　查明，確定，弄清

Just a moment please, while we ascertain that this passport is
valid.
我們確認這本護照是否有效時，請稍待片刻。

certify cert + ify	〔`sɝtəˌfaɪ〕 動　證明，證實，擔保，保證， 發證書（或執照等）
certificate cert + ificate	〔sɚ`tɪfəkɪt〕 名　證明書，執照，結業證書， 憑證，單據 a birth certificate「出生證明書」 a certificate of death「死亡證明書」 a medical certificate「健康狀況證明書，診斷書」

certification
certificate + ion

▶ 〔͵sɝtɪfəˋkeʃən〕 名　證明，檢定，保證

The priest certified that they were now husband and wife.
牧師證婚宣佈他們現在結為夫婦。

 188 cept　cap　ceiv(e)　ce(i)(p)t　cup　　接受

accept ac + cept	▶ 〔əkˋsɛpt〕 動　接受，同意，承認，認可， 承擔（責任）
acceptable accept + able	▶ 〔əkˋsɛptəbḷ〕 形　可以接受的，值得接受的， 差強人意的
acceptance accept + ance	▶ 〔əkˋsɛptəns〕 名　接受，領受，歡迎，贊同，承認

Sleeping in class is not acceptable behavior.
課堂上睡覺是不被接受的行為。

capable cap + able	▶ 〔ˋkepəbḷ〕 形　有…的能力，能夠做…的， 有能力的，能幹的 be capable of V-ing「能夠～，有～的能力」
capability capable + ity	▶ 〔͵kepəˋbɪlətɪ〕 名　能力，才能，性能，功能， 潛力
capacity cap + ity	▶ 〔kəˋpæsətɪ〕 名　容量，容積，能量，能力， 才能，理解力
incapable in + capable	▶ 〔ɪnˋkepəbḷ〕 形　不能勝任的，不會的，不能的， 無能的 be incapable of V-ing「不能夠～，沒有～的能力」

The school bus has a capacity of 34 passengers.
這輛校車能容納34名乘客。

By the time they are in elementary school, most children are capable of tying their own shoes.
到了上小學的時候，大多數的孩子都能夠自己綁鞋帶。

conceive con + ceive	▶ 〔kənˋsiv〕 動　構想出，想像，設想，懷（胎）， 抱有（想法），認為

conceivable conceive + able	▶	〔kənˋsivəbl〕 形　可想到的，可想像的， 可理解的，可相信的
inconceivable in + conceivable	▶	〔ˌɪnkənˋsivəbl〕 形　不能想像的，不可思議的， 不能相信的
concept con + cept	▶	〔ˋkɑnsɛpt〕 名　概念，觀念，思想
conception concept + ion	▶	〔kənˋsɛpʃən〕 名　概念，觀念，想法， 構想，懷孕，胚胎，開始

People once thought that traveling by air was inconceivable.
人們一度認為坐飛機旅行是不可想像的。

deceive de + ceive	▶	〔dɪˋsiv〕 動　欺騙，蒙蔽，哄騙（某人）做…， 行騙
deceit de + ceit	▶	〔dɪˋsit〕 名　欺騙，欺詐，奸詐，騙局，騙人的話
deceitful deceit + ful	▶	〔dɪˋsitfəl〕 形　騙人的，欺詐的，虛假的，誤導的
deception deceive + ion	▶	〔dɪˋsɛpʃən〕 名　欺騙，欺詐，受騙，騙人的事物， 詭計
deceptive deceive + ive	▶	〔dɪˋsɛptɪv〕 形　迷惑的，騙人的，虛偽的，欺詐的

Through clever lies and very good acting, the man was able to deceive everyone and make them believe he was a real pilot.
利用巧妙的謊言和非常精湛的演技，那個男人成功地欺騙眾人，讓大家相信他真的是個機長。

perceive per + ceive	▶	〔pɚˋsiv〕 動　感覺，感知，意識到，理解
perception perceive + ion	▶	〔pɚˋsɛpʃən〕 名　感知，感覺，察覺，認識， 觀念，看法，感知能力，洞察力
perceptible perceive + ible	▶	〔pɚˋsɛptəbl〕 形　可感知的，可察覺的，可辨的
imperceptible im + perceptible	▶	〔ˌɪmpɚˋsɛptəbl〕 形　察覺不出的，感覺不到的， 極細微的

The librarian gave a barely perceptible smile as the boy returned his books three days late.
男孩歸還逾期三天的借書時，圖書館員給他一個幾乎看不出來的微笑。

except ex + cept	〔ɪk`sɛpt〕 動 把…除外，不計 介 除了…之外
exception except + ion	〔ɪk`sɛpʃən〕 名 例外，例外的人（或事物），除外
exceptional exception + al	〔ɪk`sɛpʃənl〕 形 例外的，異常的，特殊的， 優秀的，卓越的
exceptionally exceptional + ly	〔ɪk`sɛpʃənəlɪ〕 副 例外地，異常地，特殊地

I usually don't accept late papers, but since you were in the hospital, I will make an exception.
我通常是不收遲交的報告的，但因為你當時住院，我會破例收下。

occupy oc + cup + y	〔`ɑkjə͵paɪ〕 動 佔領，佔據，佔用，使忙碌， 使從事，擔任（職務）
occupant occupy + ant	〔`ɑkjəpənt〕 名 佔有人，居住者
occupation occupy + tion	〔͵ɑkjə`peʃən〕 名 工作，職業，佔據，佔用
preoccupy pre + occupy	〔pri`ɑkjə͵paɪ〕 動 使全神貫注，使入神 be preoccupied with～「專注於～」
preoccupation preoccupy + tion	〔pri͵ɑkjə`peʃən〕 名 全神貫注，關注的事物

This house looks empty. Does anyone occupy it?
這房子看起來是空的。有人住在這裡嗎？

He was so preoccupied with his work that he did not feel the earthquake.
他非常專心地工作，所以沒有感覺到地震。

receive re + ceive	〔rɪ`siv〕 動 收到，接到，接受，得到，受到， 接待
reception receive + ion	〔rɪ`sɛpʃən〕 名 接待，接見，接待會，歡迎會， 宴會，接受，接納

receptionist
reception + ist

▶ 〔rɪ`sɛpʃənɪst〕 名 接待員，傳達員

---

receipt
re + ceipt

▶ 〔rɪ`sit〕 名 收到，接到，收據，收條

Be sure to get a receipt for all the purchases you make with the company credit card.
你用公司的信用卡買東西的時候，一定要拿收據。

---

 opt 選擇
189

option
opt + ion

▶ 〔`ɑpʃən〕 名 選擇，選擇權，選擇自由，可選擇的東西，選修科目

optional
option + al

▶ 〔`ɑpʃn̩l〕 形 隨意的，非必須的

You may choose one of three options for your duties today.
你今天的工作可以從三個選擇中挑一個來做。

---

adopt
ad + opt

▶ 〔ə`dɑpt〕 動 採取，採納，過繼，收養

adoption
adopt + ion

▶ 〔ə`dɑpʃən〕 名 採納，採用，正式通過，收養

They have adopted three children already, and are in the process to adopt one more.
他們已經收養三個孩子了，而且正準備再收養一個。

The company adopted a zero-tolerance policy against sexual harassment.
那間公司針對性騷擾採取了絕不寬貸的方針。

---

 or(e) 言，說
190

oral
or + al

▶ 〔`orəl〕 形 口頭的，口述的，口部的
oral communication「談話，會話」

His oral response was more detailed than his written one.
他口頭上的回答比他的書面回覆要來得詳細。

adore
ad + ore

▶ 〔ə`dor〕 動　崇拜，崇敬，敬重，愛慕，熱愛

adorable
adore + able

▶ 〔ə`dorəbl〕 形　值得崇拜的，可敬重的，可愛的

adoration
adore + tion

▶ 〔ˌædə`reʃən〕 名　崇拜，敬愛，傾慕

The couple gazed with adoration into each other's eyes.
那對戀人注視彼此的雙眼，眼裡盡是愛意。

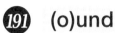 **(o)und**　流動，波動　
191

abound
ab + ound

▶ 〔ə`baʊnd〕 動　大量存在，富足，充足，充滿，多產
　　abound in～「充滿～，富於～」

abundant
ab + und + ant

▶ 〔ə`bʌndənt〕 形　大量的，充足的，豐富的，富裕的

abundantly
abundant + ly

▶ 〔ə`bʌndəntlɪ〕 副　大量地，充足地，豐裕地

There is an abundant supply of people applying for the job, so we should be able to find someone good.
應徵這個工作的人很多，我們應該能找到一個不錯的人選。

surround
sur + ound

▶ 〔sə`raʊnd〕 動　圍繞，圈住，包圍
　　　　　　　 名　圍繞物

surrounding
surround + ing

▶ 〔sə`raʊndɪŋ〕 形　周圍的，附近的
　　（名詞複數）surroundings「環境，周圍的事物，周圍的情況」

I am going to surround my house with trees.
我打算要在我家四周種滿樹。

The cat walked around smelling everything, getting used to her new surroundings.
那隻貓四處走動聞味道，漸漸習慣她的新環境。

192 nect nex 連結
192

connect con + nect	▶	〔kə`nɛkt〕 動 連接，聯想，聯繫，結合， 使有關係
connection connect + ion	▶	〔kə`nɛkʃən〕 名 連接，聯絡，關係，關聯，親屬 in connection with～「與～有關，連接上～」
disconnect dis + connect	▶	〔͵dɪskə`nɛkt〕 動 使分離，分開，斷開， 切斷（電話、電源等）
disconnection disconnect + ion	▶	〔͵dɪskə`nɛkʃən〕 名 分離，切斷，絕緣

I can't connect to the Internet from home, so I can't finish my homework.　因為不能從家裡連線上網，所以我沒辦法完成我的功課。

annex an + nex	▶	〔ə`nɛks〕 動 附加，增添，併吞，合併， 把…作為附錄 〔`ænɛks〕 名 附加物，附件，附錄，（房屋等 的）擴建部分

The building had a small annex on the north end.
這棟建築北側有一間擴建的小別館。

 193 ali alter 別的
193

alien ali + en	▶	〔`elɪən〕 名 外國人，外星人 形 外國的，外國人的，性質不同的， 不相容的
alienate alien + ate	▶	〔`eljən͵et〕 動 使疏遠，離間，使轉移，使轉向
alienation alienate + ion	▶	〔͵eljə`neʃən〕 名 疏遠，離間

He alienated all his business associates by being rude and overly-aggressive.
他粗魯且過於強勢的態度使他疏遠了他的生意夥伴。

alter	▶	〔`ɔltə〕 動 改變，修改，變樣

alteration alter + tion	▶	〔ˌɔltəˋreʃən〕 名 改變，變更，修改，變樣
alternate alter + ate	▶	〔ˋɔltənɪt〕 形 （兩個）交替的，輪流的， 　　　　　　供選擇的，供替換的 〔ˋɔltɚˌnet〕 動 交替，輪流
alternation alternate + ion	▶	〔ˌɔltɚˋneʃən〕 名 交替，輪流
alternative alternate + ive	▶	〔ɔlˋtɜnətɪv〕 形 替代的，供選擇的 名 選擇，供選擇的東西，替代方案
alternatively alternative + ly	▶	〔ɔlˋtɜnəˌtɪvlɪ〕 副 二者擇一地

It takes about eight hours to drive; alternatively, you can take an express train, and be there in less than four hours.
開車花費大約八小時，或者，你可以搭乘特快車，不到四小時就會到那裡。

194　fid(e)　fy　fi　faith　相信　★194

confide con + fide	▶	〔kənˋfaɪd〕 動 透露，吐露，將…委託，信任 confide in～「向～吐露祕密，對～有信心」 confide～to...「向…吐露～，將～託付給…」
confidence confide + ence	▶	〔ˋkɑnfədəns〕 名 自信，信心，把握，信賴，信任
confident confide + ent	▶	〔ˋkɑnfədənt〕 形 確信的，有信心的，自信的， 　　　　　　　　自負的 be confident of～「確信～」
confidential confident + ial	▶	〔ˌkɑnfəˋdɛnʃəl〕 形 機密的，獲信任的， 　　　　　　　　　參與機密的

She confided in her friend that she was thinking of getting a new job.
她向朋友吐露她正在考慮換工作的祕密。

Her confidence was badly shaken by her repeated failures.
她的自信因為一連串的失敗而大為動搖。

This information is confidential, so don't repeat it to anyone.
這是機密情報，所以不要告訴任何人。

defy
de + fy
▶ 〔dɪˋfaɪ〕 動　公然反抗，蔑視，向…挑戰

defiant
defy + ant
▶ 〔dɪˋfaɪənt〕 形　違抗的，挑戰的，蔑視的，大膽的

defiantly
defiant + ly
▶ 〔dɪˋfaɪəntlɪ〕 副　挑戰地，大膽對抗地

defiance
defy + ance
▶ 〔dɪˋfaɪəns〕 名　反抗，蔑視，藐視，挑戰
in defiance of～「無視～，違抗～」

The spinning top seemed to defy the laws of gravity as it hovered over the surface of the table.
當那顆旋轉的陀螺在桌面上方盤旋時，就好像是違反地心引力法則一樣。

faith
▶ 〔feθ〕 名　信念，信任，信仰，信條

faithful
faith + ful
▶ 〔ˋfeθfəl〕 形　忠實的，忠誠的，忠貞的

Sandra placed a lot of faith in her father's wisdom, and always took his advice.
珊卓拉非常信賴她父親的智慧，總是聽取他的建言。

195 gree　grac(e)　grat(e)　高興
195

agree
a + gree
▶ 〔əˋgri〕 動　意見一致，同意，贊同，相符
agree to～「同意，接受～（提案等）」
agree with～「贊成～（人・意見）」

agreeable
agree + able
▶ 〔əˋgriəbl〕 形　令人愉快的，宜人的，欣然贊同的，符合的，一致的

agreement
agree + ment
▶ 〔əˋgrimənt〕 名　同意，一致，協定，協議

disagree
dis + agree
▶ 〔͵dɪsəˋgri〕 動　不一致，不符，意見不合

disagreeable
disagree + able
▶ 〔͵dɪsəˋgriəbl〕 形　不合意的，不愉快的，討厭的，難相處的

Although the smell of the durian fruit is quite disagreeable, the taste is surprisingly good.
雖然榴連的味道很臭，但是味道嚐起來卻是出乎意料地好吃。

They made an agreement to help each other get into shape.
他們協議要幫助彼此減肥。

Although they don't always agree, they are still very good friends.
雖然他們並不總是意見一致，但仍然是很好的朋友。

grace	▶	〔gres〕名 優美，優雅，（神的）恩典，風度，魅力
graceful grace + ful	▶	〔`gresfəl〕形 優美的，雅緻的，典雅的，懂禮貌的，得體的
gracious grace + ous	▶	〔`greʃəs〕形 親切的，和藹的，仁慈的

Even if you don't plan to be a professional dancer, practicing ballet can improve your grace.
就算你不打算成為一個職業舞者，練習芭蕾還是能讓你的姿態更優雅。

The main cause of his problems at work is a lack of social graces.
造成他在工作上問題的主要原因是缺乏社交魅力。

gratify grat + ify	▶	〔`grætə‚faɪ〕動 使高興，使滿意，滿足（慾望等）
gratification gratify + tion	▶	〔‚grætəfə`keʃən〕名 滿足，滿意，喜悅，使人滿意之事，可喜的事物
grateful grate + ful	▶	〔`gretfəl〕形 感謝的，令人愉快的，可喜的 be grateful to（人）for～「因為～而感謝（人）」
gratitude grat + itude	▶	〔`grætə‚tjud〕名 感激之情，感恩，感謝

Kaitie gratified her mother's curiosity by telling all about her new boyfriend.
凱蒂將所有關於她新男友的事告訴她母親，滿足了她的好奇心。

Paying with a credit card and downloading an E-book saves you a trip to the bookstore and provides instant gratification.
信用卡付費和下載電子書的方式節省了你去書店的時間，而且馬上就能欣賞。

| congratulate
con + grat + ate | ▶ | 〔kənˋɡrætʃəˏlet〕 動　祝賀，恭喜
congratulate（人）on～「為了～向（人）祝賀」 |
| congratulation
congratulate + ion | ▶ | 〔kənˏɡrætʃəˋleʃən〕 名　祝賀，慶賀，祝賀詞
Congratulations on～！「恭賀～！」 |

Congratulations on finally finishing your project!
恭喜你終於完成企劃案！

 itude　　**狀態**　　　　　　　　　　　　　　

| latitude
lat + itude | ▶ | 〔ˋlætəˏtjud〕 名　緯度，
　　　　　緯度地區
（反義）longitude 經度 |

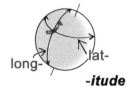

The latitude of Amsterdam is 52 degrees north.
阿姆斯特丹的緯度是北緯52度。

| attitude
att + itude | ▶ | 〔ˋætətjud〕 名　態度，意見，看法，姿勢 |

A positive attitude is a great aid in difficult tasks.
積極的態度在面對困難的工作時有極大的幫助。

 chron　　**時間**　　　　　　　　　　　　　　

chronic chron + ic	▶	〔ˋkrɑnɪk〕 形　（病）慢性的，（人）久病的， 　　　　　長期的，習慣性的
chronically chronic + ly	▶	〔ˋkrɑnɪklɪ〕 副　慢性地，長期地
chronicle chron + icle	▶	〔ˋkrɑnɪkl〕 名　編年史，年代記，歷史，記事

synchronize
syn + chron + ize

〔`sɪŋkrənaɪz〕動 同時發生，影音同步
synchronized swimming「水上芭蕾」

The doctor diagnosed the patient as having chronic alcoholism.
醫生診斷出病人患有慢性酒精中毒。

 front 前部
198 198

front	〔frʌnt〕名 前面，正面，前線 形 前面的，正面的
frontier front + er	〔frʌn`tɪr〕名 國境，邊境，邊疆 frontier spirit「開拓精神，進取精神」
confront con + front	〔kən`frʌnt〕動 面臨，遭遇，勇敢地面對，對抗
confrontation confront + tion	〔ˌkɑnfrən`teʃən〕名 對質，對抗
confrontational confrontation + al	〔ˌkɑnfrən`teʃənəl〕形 對抗的，對抗性的

Japan is known as a non-confrontational society.
日本以非對抗性的社會聞名。

 soci 同伴，同盟
199 199

society soci 0+ ety	〔sə`saɪətɪ〕名 社會，社團，協會，社交界 【參考】Audubon Society 奧杜邦協會（保護自然生態的協會）
social soci + al	〔`soʃəl〕形 社會的，社交的，社會性的， 喜歡交際的
sociable soci + able	〔`soʃəbl〕形 好交際的，善交際的，社交性的， 交際的

sociability
sociable + ity

▶ 〔ˌsoʃəˋbɪlətɪ〕图　社交性，善於交際

socialism
social + ism

▶ 〔ˋsoʃəlˌɪzəm〕图　社會主義

socialist
social + ist

▶ 〔ˋsoʃəlɪst〕图　社會主義者

The society in which children grow up today is very different from when I was young.　現今孩子成長的社會和我年輕時的非常不同。

associate
as + soci + ate

▶ 〔əˋsoʃɪˌet〕動　聯想，使聯合，使結合，結交
〔əˋsoʃɪɪt〕图　夥伴，同事，朋友，合夥人
associate～with...「把～跟…聯想在一起」

association
associate + ion

▶ 〔əˌsosɪˋeʃən〕图　協會，公會，聯盟，聯合，
聯想，夥伴關係
【參考】NBA＝National Basketball Association
全美籃球協會

I'll have to check with my associates before I can give you a definite answer.　在給你確切的答覆之前，我必須先向我的同事確認一下。
Children often associate Christmas with getting lots of presents.
孩子們常常將聖誕節和收到很多禮物聯想在一起。

200　vance　vant　前進

★
200

advance
ad + vance

▶ 〔ədˋvæns〕動　推進，促進，提出，提升，進展，
進步
图　前進，發展
in advance「預先，事前」

advanced
advance + ed

▶ 〔ədˋvænst〕形　在前面的，先進的，開明的，
高級的，高等的，年邁的

advancement
advance + ment

▶ 〔ədˋvænsmənt〕图　前進，進展，促進，晉升，
提高，增加

The line to buy tickets was long, but it was advancing quickly.
排隊買票的人龍很長，但是前進得很快。
Even at her advanced age and failing health, Ena is cheerful and positive.　就算在晚年健康逐漸衰退的時候，艾娜仍保持愉快積極。

advantage ad + vant + age	▶	〔əd`væntɪdʒ〕名　有利條件，優點，優勢，利益， 好處
advantageous advantage + ous	▶	〔ˌædvən`tedʒəs〕形　有利的，有助的，有益的
disadvantage dis + advantage	▶	〔ˌdɪsəd`væntɪdʒ〕名　不利條件，不利，損失， 損害
disadvantageous dis + advantageous	▶	〔dɪsˌædvən`tedʒəs〕形　不利的，情況不好的

People who are bilingual have a great advantage when trying to find a job in international business.
在找國際商業的相關工作時，會說兩種語言的人有非常大的優勢。

Tall people are at a disadvantage when trying to purchase clothing.
身材高大的人衣服不好買。

 fin(e)　結束，終止，限度
201

| **finish**
fin + ish | ▶ | 〔`fɪnɪʃ〕動　結束，完成 |

I will be glad to finally finish this miserable job!
我會很高興終於能完成這份令人痛苦的工作！

final fin + al	▶	〔`faɪnl〕形　最後的，最終的
finale fin + ale	▶	〔fɪ`nɑlɪ〕名　終曲，末樂章，終場，結尾
finally final + ly	▶	〔`faɪnlɪ〕副　最後，終於，決定性地
finalize final + ize	▶	〔`faɪnlˌaɪz〕動　完成，結束

After trying various and strange techniques, Nancy's hiccups finally went away after an hour.
嘗試過各種奇怪的方法後，南西終於在一個小時後停止打嗝。

confine
con + fine
▶ 〔kənˋfaɪn〕 動　限制，局限，禁閉

confinement
confine + ment
▶ 〔kənˋfaɪnmənt〕 名　限制，幽禁，監禁

The rabbit was confined to a small cage.
兔子被關在一只小籠子內。

define
de + fine
▶ 〔dɪˋfaɪn〕 動　解釋，給⋯下定義

definition
define + tion
▶ 〔͵dɛfəˋnɪʃən〕 名　下定義，定義，釋義

definite
define + ite
▶ 〔ˋdɛfənɪt〕 形　明確的，確切的，肯定的，限定的

definitely
definite + ly
▶ 〔ˋdɛfənɪtlɪ〕 副　明確地，明顯地，清楚地，
肯定地，當然

If you want a good definition of a word, you should consult a dictionary.
如果你想要知道一個字完整的定義，你應該要查閱字典。

Ross is definitely going to be in his office at 2:00, so call him then.
羅斯肯定會在2點的時候進辦公室，所以到時候再打電話給他。

I can't give you a definite answer, because I don't have all the
information.
我不能給你一個明確的答案，因為我並沒有全部的資訊。

finance
fin + ance
▶ 〔faɪˋnæns〕 名　財政，金融，財政學，財源，
資金，財務情況

financial
finance + ial
▶ 〔faɪˋnænʃəl〕 形　財政的，金融的，金融界的

We simply don't have the finances to buy another car.
我們完全沒有錢再買另外一輛汽車。

infinite
in + fin + ite
▶ 〔ˋɪnfənɪt〕 形　無限的，無邊的，極大的

infinity
infinite + ty
▶ 〔ɪnˋfɪnətɪ〕 名　無限，無窮

Mrs. Jones has infinite patience with all her grandchildren.
瓊斯太太對她的孫子們有極大的耐心。

fine	▶	〔faɪn〕形　美好的，優秀的，纖細的，晴朗的，健康的，細微的
refine re + fine	▶	〔rɪ`faɪn〕動　精煉，使優雅
refined refine + ed	▶	〔rɪ`faɪnd〕形　精煉的，優雅的，有教養的

He is too refined to respond to the insult.
他為人太有教養，甚至不願回應對他的侮辱。

202　fict　fig　製造，虛構

| **fiction**
fict + ion | ▶ | 〔`fɪkʃən〕名　小說，虛構，虛構的事，謊言 |
| **fictional**
fiction + al | ▶ | 〔`fɪkʃənḷ〕形　虛構的，小說的 |

He is most known for his biographies, but recently he has also tried his hand at fiction.
他以他的傳記作品聞名，但是最近他開始嘗試寫小說。
Santa Claus is a fictional character.
聖誕老人是一個虛構人物。

| **figure**
fig + ure | ▶ | 〔`fɪgjɚ〕名　人影，體態，人物，數字，金額，圖表
動　計算，認為
figure～out「算出～，理解～」 |
| **figurative**
figure + ive | ▶ | 〔`fɪgjərətɪv〕形　比喻的，象徵的 |

I couldn't figure out the problem with my car, so I took it to a mechanic.
我想不出車子的問題出在哪，所以我把車送去修車技工那裡。
His heart skipped a beat as her figure appeared in the doorway.
當她的身影出現在門口時，他的心跳漏了一拍。

it 行走
203 | 203

initiate in + it + ate	▶ 〔ɪˋnɪʃɪˏet〕動 開始，創始 〔ɪˋnɪʃɪɪt〕形 初步的，新加入的
initiative in + it + ive	▶ 〔ɪˋnɪʃətɪv〕名 主動的開始，進取心，主動權 形 開始的，初步的，創始的
initial in + it + ial	▶ 〔ɪˋnɪʃəl〕形 開始的，最初的，字首的 名 首字母

Although Beth's initial reaction was negative, she soon grew to like the efficiency of the new filing system.
雖然貝絲最初的反應是否定的，但她很快就喜歡上新歸檔系統的效率。

Don't wait to be told what to do; you should act on your own initiative.
不要等著別人告訴你該作什麼，你應該要自己主動地行動。

transit trans + it	▶ 〔ˋtrænsɪt〕名 運輸，通過，通路，轉變，過渡
transition transit + ion	▶ 〔trænˋzɪʃən〕名 過渡，過渡時期，轉變，變遷
transitional transition + al	▶ 〔trænˋzɪʃənḷ〕形 轉變的，過渡期的，過渡性的

Change is never easy, but after the initial transitional period, things will be much better.
改變從來就不容易，但是過了最初的過渡期後，事情將會好得多。

 oper 工作
204 | 204

operate oper + ate	▶ 〔ˋɑpəˏret〕動 運作，運轉，營運，動手術， 操作（機器等）
operation operate + ion	▶ 〔ˏɑpəˋreʃən〕名 操作，運轉，經營，手術

operator
operate + or

〔`ɑpə‚retə〕 名　操作者，接線生，經營者，
　　　　　施行手術的醫生
【參考】opera 〔`ɑpərə〕 名　歌劇

Don't operate heavy equipment after taking this medicine.
服用此藥後，請勿操作任何危險器械。

The patient came out of the operation feeling a little weak.
手術結束後，病人感到有些虛弱。

 205 ## pass　path　pati　苦惱，感受
205

passion
pass + ion

〔`pæʃən〕 名　熱情，激情

passionate
passion + ate

〔`pæʃənɪt〕 形　熱情的，激昂的，易怒的

The missionary spoke with great passion about getting medical help to people in need of it.
那位傳教士激昂地談論幫助需要的人們得到醫療援助的事。

He was once very passionate about his job, but years of thankless labor have made him less than enthusiastic.
他曾對他的工作充滿熱情，但幾年來的努力不受重視，讓他熱忱不再。

passive
pass + ive

〔`pæsɪv〕 形　被動的，消極的，順從的
（反義）active

passively
passive + ly

〔`pæsɪvlɪ〕 副　被動地，消極地，順從地

He sat there passively, waiting for someone to speak.
他被動地坐在那裡，等著別人跟他說話。

pathetic
path + tic

〔pə`θɛtɪk〕 形　可憐的，可悲的，微弱的

pathetically
pathetic + ly

〔pə`θɛtɪkəlɪ〕 副　可憐地，可悲地，微弱地

The dog was pathetically thin, but when he wagged his tail, Agatha couldn't resist taking him home with her.
那隻狗瘦得可憐，但是當他搖起尾巴時，愛葛莎忍不住要把他帶回家。

| patient
pati + ent | ▶ | 〔ˋpeʃənt〕 形　有耐心的，能忍受的，能容忍的
名　病人 |

| patiently
patient + ly | ▶ | 〔ˋpeʃəntlɪ〕 副　耐心地，堅韌不拔地 |

| patience
patient + ce | ▶ | 〔ˋpeʃəns〕 名　耐心，忍耐，耐性，毅力 |

| impatient
im + patient | ▶ | 〔ɪmˋpeʃənt〕 形　無耐心的，不耐煩的，
無法忍受的，切盼的 |

| impatiently
im + patiently | ▶ | 〔ɪmˋpeʃəntlɪ〕 副　不耐煩地，性急地，焦急地，
急躁地 |

| impatience
im + patience | ▶ | 〔ɪmˋpeʃəns〕 名　無耐心，不耐煩，性急 |

After he'd been waiting for 15 minutes, he started to grow impatient,
after 30 minutes, he was furious.
在等了15分鐘後，他開始感到不耐煩；30分鐘後，他大發雷霆。

 206　tom　切分
206

| atom
a + tom | ▶ | 〔ˋætəm〕 名　原子，微小物，微量 |

| atomic
atom + ic | ▶ | 〔əˋtamɪk〕 形　原子的，原子能的，極微的 |

They have an atomic clock that keeps time perfectly.
他們有一個完全準時的原子鐘。

| anatomy
ana + tom + y | ▶ | 〔əˋnætəmɪ〕 名　解剖學，解剖，（詳細的）分析，
（動植物的）解剖結構 |

| anatomical
anatomy + ical | ▶ | 〔͵ænəˋtamɪkl〕 形　解剖學上的，解剖的，結構上的 |

| anatomically
anatomical + ly | ▶ | 〔͵ænəˋtamɪklɪ〕 副　解剖學上，結構上 |

The statue of the anatomically correct nude was removed from the park due to protests of the local clergy.
由於地方神職人員的抗議，公園那座展現人體性器官的塑像被撤除了。

 don　dit　給予，提供

donate don + ate	▶ 〔ˋdonet〕 動　捐獻，捐贈
donation donate + ion	▶ 〔doˋneʃən〕 名　捐獻，捐贈，捐款，捐贈物
donor don + or	▶ 〔ˋdonɚ〕 名　贈送人，捐贈者

If you want to make a donation, there is a box by the door.
如果你想要捐款，門邊有一個箱子。

edit e + dit	▶ 〔ˋɛdɪt〕 動　編輯，校訂，剪輯，剪接
editor edit + or	▶ 〔ˋɛdɪtɚ〕 名　編輯，（報刊專欄的）主筆，編者，校訂者，社論撰寫人
editorial editor + al	▶ 〔͵ɛdəˋtorɪəl〕 形　編輯（上）的，編者的，社論的 名　社論，重要評論
edition edit + ion	▶ 〔ɪˋdɪʃən〕 名　（發行物的）版，（某版的）發行數量，版本

The company produces a new edition of its word processing software every year.　這間公司每年都發行新版本的文字處理軟體。

 cour　cord　心

courage cour + age	▶ 〔kˋ ɝɪdʒ〕 名　膽量，勇氣，英勇
courageous courage + ous	▶ 〔kəˋredʒəs〕 形　英勇的，勇敢的

courageously
courageous + ly
▶ 〔kəˋredʒəslɪ〕 副 勇敢地

encourage
en + courage
▶ 〔ɪnˋkɝɪdʒ〕 動 鼓勵，慫恿，促進，助長，激發

encouragement
encourage + ment
▶ 〔ɪnˋkɝɪdʒmənt〕 名 鼓勵，獎勵，促進

discourage
dis + courage
▶ 〔dɪsˋkɝɪdʒ〕 動 使沮喪，勸阻

The evening news reported that one fireman courageously saved the lives of 20 people who were trapped in a burning building.
晚間新聞報導，一位消防員勇敢地救出20位被困在起火大樓裡的人。

Thelma said that the encouragement of her friends pulled her through her illness.
黛瑪說她朋友的鼓勵幫助她克服了她的疾病。

accord
ac + cord
▶ 〔əˋkɔrd〕 動 一致，符合，調和
名 一致，符合，調和，條約
according to～「根據～，取決於～，據～所載，據～所說」

accordingly
accord + ing + ly
▶ 〔əˋkɔrdɪŋlɪ〕 副 照著，相應地，因此，於是

accordance
accord + ance
▶ 〔əˋkɔrdəns〕 名 一致，和諧，符合
in accordance with～「與～一致，依照～」

According to the weather forecaster, it will be snowy and cold all weekend.
依據天氣預報，整個週末將會下雪寒冷。

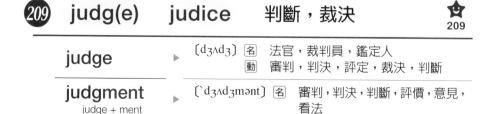

209 **judg(e)** **judice** 判斷，裁決 ⭐ 209

judge
▶ 〔dʒʌdʒ〕 名 法官，裁判員，鑑定人
動 審判，判決，評定，裁決，判斷

judgment
judge + ment
▶ 〔ˋdʒʌdʒmənt〕 名 審判，判決，判斷，評價，意見，看法

You'll have to use your own judgment on this. I don't know what is best for you.
關於這件事情，你必須運用自己的判斷力。我不知道什麼才是對你最好的。

prejudice
pre + judice

▶ 〔`prɛdʒədɪs〕 名　偏見，歧視，偏愛，偏袒

She experienced some prejudice due to her ethnic background.
她由於種族背景的緣故，有過一些受到歧視的經驗。

210　phone　phe　聲音

210

microphone micro + phone	▶ 〔`maɪkrə͵fon〕 名	麥克風，擴音器
prophesy pro + phe + sy	▶ 〔`prɑfə͵saɪ〕 動	預言，預告
prophecy pro + phe + cy	▶ 〔`prɑfəsɪ〕 名	預言，預言能力
prophet pro + phe + t	▶ 〔`prɑfɪt〕 名	先知，預言者，預言家

There were some prophecies that the world would end in 2000, but it did not happen.
有些預言說世界會在2000年滅亡，但是那並沒有發生。

211　amb　四周，周邊

211

ambiguity amb + iguity	▶ 〔͵æmbɪ`gjuətɪ〕 名	意義不明確，模稜兩可的話
ambiguous anb + iguous	▶ 〔æm`bɪgjuəs〕 形	含糊不清的，引起歧義的

The politician gave only ambiguous answers to the questions the reporters asked.
對於記者的問題，那位政治人物只給了模稜兩可的答案。

ambition amb + tion	▶ 〔æm`bɪʃən〕 名	雄心，抱負，野心，追求的目標

ambitious
ambtion + ous

▶ 〔æm`bɪʃəs〕形　有雄心的，有抱負的

Ambition is a good thing, but don't let it cloud your judgment.
有野心是好事，但是不能讓那影響你的判斷力。

 item　ident　相同，相似
212

item
▶ 〔`aɪtəm〕名　項目，品項，（新聞等的）一則

itemize
item + ize

▶ 〔`aɪtəm،aɪz〕動　分條列述，詳細列舉

Alice insisted on getting an itemized list of all the charges at the hotel.
艾莉絲堅持要一份旅館消費明細表。

identify
ident + ify

▶ 〔aɪ`dɛntə،faɪ〕動　確認，識別，視…（與…）為同一事物，感同身受

identification
identify + tion

▶ 〔aɪ،dɛntəfə`keʃən〕名　認出，識別，確認，身分證明

identical
ident + ical

▶ 〔aɪ`dɛntɪkḷ〕形　同一的，完全相同的，（雙胞胎）同卵的

I couldn't identify the spice that the chef had used to give the sauce an unusual flavor.
我吃不出來主廚使用的是什麼香料，讓這道醬汁有一種獨特的風味。

213 anx　ang　不安，苦惱
213

anxious
anx + ous

▶ 〔`æŋkʃəs〕形　焦慮的，掛念的，渴望的
be anxious to V「渴望～」
be anxious for～「為～而焦慮，渴望～」

anxiously
anxious + ly

▶ 〔`æŋkʃəslɪ〕 副 焦急地，擔憂地

anxiety
anx + ety

▶ 〔æŋˋzaɪətɪ〕 名 焦慮，掛念，渴望

Lucy is anxiously waiting for her father to come home and take her out for ice cream.
露西焦急地等待她父親回家之後帶她去吃冰淇淋。

angry
ang + ry

▶ 〔`æŋgrɪ〕 形 發怒的，生氣的

anger
ang + er

▶ 〔`æŋgɚ〕 名 憤怒，生氣

He displayed his anger by jumping up and down and screaming.
他跳上跳下、尖聲叫喊展現出他的憤怒。

 214 real 現實的
214

real

▶ 〔`rɪəl〕 形 真的，真正的，現實的，實際的

realize
real + ize

▶ 〔`rɪəˏlaɪz〕 動 領悟，了解，認識到，實現

realization
realize + tion

▶ 〔ˏrɪələˋzeʃən〕 名 領悟，認識，真實，現實，體現

reality
real + ity

▶ 〔rɪˋælətɪ〕 名 現實，真實，事實

realist
real + ist

▶ 〔`rɪəlɪst〕 名 現實主義者，注重實際的人

realistic
realist + ic

▶ 〔rɪəˋlɪstɪk〕 形 現實的，注重實際的，現實主義的

Do you think that is a real diamond or a fake?
你認為那是真鑽還是假鑽？

main　man　停留
215

remain
re + main

▶ 〔rɪˋmen〕 動　剩下，餘留，繼續存在，留下，保持

remainder
remain + er

▶ 〔rɪˋmendə〕 名　剩餘物，其餘的人

June will have to remain in the hospital for at least a few weeks.
瓊恩至少得住院幾個禮拜。

She thought it best to remain silent.
她覺得她最好保持沈默。

permanent
per + man + ent

▶ 〔ˋpɜmənənt〕 形　永久的，永恆的，永遠的，固定性的，常在的

permanently
permanent + ly

▶ 〔ˋpɜmənəntlɪ〕 副　永久地，長期不變地

permanency
permanent + cy

▶ 〔ˋpəmənənsɪ〕 名　永久，不變耐久性，永久的事物

You should think carefully before you get a tattoo, because they are, for all practical purposes, permanent.
你刺青前應該要考慮清楚，因為實際上，刺青是永久的。

 gest　ger　提示
216

suggest
sug + gest

▶ 〔səˋdʒɛst〕 動　建議，提議，暗示，啓發，使人想起，使人聯想到

suggestion
suggest + ion

▶ 〔səˋdʒɛstʃən〕 名　建議，提議，暗示，示意

suggestive
suggest + ive

▶ 〔səˋdʒɛstɪv〕 形　暗示的，示意的，引起聯想的

suggestible
suggest + ible

▶ 〔səˋdʒɛstəbl〕 形　耳根軟的，容易受暗示影響的，可建議的

After being locked up for several days, the prisoner became highly suggestible, and confessed to a crime he did not commit.
在拘留數日後，囚犯變得非常容易受到影響，於是認了他沒有犯的罪。

exaggerate exag + ger + ate	〔ɪɡˋzædʒəˏret〕 動　誇張，誇大
exaggerration exaggerate + ion	〔ɪɡˏzædʒəˋreʃən〕 名　誇張，誇大，誇張的言語， 誇張的手法

Since he is prone to exaggerate, no one really believes that the situation was so terrible.
因為他有誇大的傾向，沒有人真的相信狀況有那麼糟糕。

 217 **ecut(e)** 　執行　
217

execute ex + ecute	〔ˋɛksɪˏkjut〕 動　實施，實行，執行，履行， 將…處死
execution execute + ion	〔ˏɛksɪˋkjuʃən〕 名　實行，執行，履行，完成， 處死刑
executive execute + ive	〔ɪɡˋzɛkjʊtɪv〕 形　執行的，經營管理的，行政的 名　執行者，行政官，經理， 業務主管

The plan was executed perfectly, and the cat burglar stole the diamond within ten minutes.
計劃執行得非常完美，那名身手敏捷的賊在十分鐘內就將鑽石偷走。

 218 **pleas(e)** 　喜悅　
218

please	〔pliz〕 動　使高興，使滿意，合…的心意，請 be pleased with～「對～感到高興，對～感到滿意」
pleasure please + ure	〔ˋplɛʒə〕 名　愉快，高興，滿足，樂事，樂趣
pleasant please + ant	〔ˋplɛzənt〕 形　令人愉快的，舒適的，討人喜歡的， 和藹可親的

Since her boss was very pleased with her work, Sarah got a huge raise.
莎拉的上司對她的工作表現很滿意，所以她得到大幅加薪。

219 famil 家庭的

219

family famil + y	▶	〔`fæməlɪ〕名 家，家庭，家人，家族
familiar family + ar	▶	〔fə`mɪljə〕形 熟悉的，常見的，普通的，通曉的
unfamiliar un + familiar	▶	〔͵ʌnfə`mɪljə〕形 不熟悉的，不常見的，陌生的
familiarity familiar + ity	▶	〔fə͵mɪlɪ`ærətɪ〕名 熟悉，通曉，親近

She looks familiar, but I don't know where I have met her before.
她看起來很眼熟，但是我記不得先前在哪裡見過她。

220 plain plan 平的

220

plain	▶	〔plen〕名 平原，曠野 形 簡樸的，樸素的，清楚的，明白的，坦白的
plainly plain + ly	▶	〔`plenlɪ〕副 清楚地，明顯地，坦率地，簡樸地
explain ex + plain	▶	〔ɪk`splen〕動 解釋，說明，闡明
explanation explain + tion	▶	〔͵ɛksplə`neʃən〕名 說明，解釋
plan	▶	〔plæn〕名 計劃，方案，打算，方法

Some of the concepts of physics are difficult, but this textbook explains them simply so that they are easier to understand.
物理學的一些概念是困難的，但是這本教科書簡單地說明，所以那些概念比較容易懂。

221 prison　prehen(d)　抓住，約束

221

prison	▶ 〔`prɪzṇ〕 名 監獄，監禁，拘留所 【參考】在美國，短期的拘留所為prison，長期的監獄則稱為jail。
prisoner prison + er	▶ 〔`prɪzṇɚ〕 名 犯人，囚犯，羈押犯，俘虜
imprison im + prison	▶ 〔ɪm`prɪzṇ〕 動 監禁，關押，限制，禁錮
imprisonment imprison + ment	▶ 〔ɪm`prɪzṇmənt〕 名 監禁，關押，禁錮

He was sent to prison for a crime he did not commit.
他因為一件他沒犯的罪而坐牢。
For years he felt imprisoned by his illness.
有好幾年的時間，他覺得自己被疾病所禁錮。

apprehend ap + prehend	▶ 〔͵æprɪ`hɛnd〕 動 逮捕，對…擔憂，理解，領會
apprehension apprehend + ion	▶ 〔͵æprɪ`hɛnʃən〕 名 憂慮，擔心，理解，逮捕
apprehensive apprehend + ive	▶ 〔͵æprɪ`hɛnsɪv〕 形 憂慮的，恐懼的，善於領會的 be apprehensive about～「對～感到憂慮不安」

The suspect was apprehended at 4:00 this morning.
嫌犯於今天凌晨四點遭到逮捕。
Since the plane crashed, people have been a little apprehensive about traveling.
自從飛機失事以來，人們對於旅行這件事感到些許不安。

comprehend com + prehend	▶ 〔͵kɑmprɪ`hɛnd〕 動 理解，了解，領會

comprehensive
comprehend + ive
▶ 〔͵kɑmprɪˋhɛnsɪv〕形　廣泛的，無所不包的，綜合的，有充分理解力的

comprehension
comprehend + ion
▶ 〔͵kɑmprɪˋhɛnʃən〕名　理解，理解力

comprehensible
comprehend + ible
▶ 〔͵kɑmprɪˋhɛnsəbl〕形　可理解的

It was difficult to comprehend why he put his fist through the window.
他用拳頭打穿窗戶的舉動讓人很難理解。

 222 **claim**　**clam**　**呼喊**
222

claim
▶ 〔klem〕動　（依據權利）要求，聲稱，主張
　名　要求，權利

exclaim
ex + claim
▶ 〔ɪksˋklem〕動　（由於興奮、痛苦、憤怒等）呼喊，驚叫，（表示抗議等）大聲叫嚷

exclamation
exclaim + tion
▶ 〔͵ɛkskləˋmeʃən〕名　呼喊，驚叫，感嘆，感嘆句
exclamation point「驚嘆號（！）」

Scientists once claimed that the atom was the smallest unit of matter.
科學家一度主張原子是物質最小的單位。

"Oh, how beautiful!" Vanessa exclaimed as she saw her new home.
「喔，好美！」凡妮莎一看到她的新家就讚嘆地大叫。

Although many people use several, one exclamation point is all that is needed for punctuation.
雖然使用數個驚嘆號的人很多，但根據標點法，其實只需要一個。

proclaim
pro + claim
▶ 〔prəˋklem〕動　宣告，公佈，聲明

This city proudly proclaims that it is the cleanest in Japan.
這個城市驕傲地宣佈他們是日本最乾淨的城市。

223 **meas** **mens(e)** 測量
223

measure
meas + ure
▶ 〔ˋmɛʒɚ〕 名 尺寸，度量單位，措施
動 測量，計量，估量

measurable
measure + able
▶ 〔ˋmɛʒərəbl〕 形 可測量的，可預見的，重大的

immeasurable
im + measurable
▶ 〔ɪˋmɛʒərəbl〕 形 不可計量的，無邊無際的，廣大的

measurement
measure + ment
▶ 〔ˋmɛʒəmənt〕 名 測量法，測量，三圍，尺寸

All the students have made measurable progress since starting the course.
自課程開始，所有的學生都有了大幅的進步。

dimension
di + mens + ion
▶ 〔daɪˋmɛnʃən〕 名 尺寸，面積，大小，重要性，範圍
動 在…上標尺寸

dimensional
dimension + al
▶ 〔daɪˋmɛnʃənl〕 形 尺寸的，（數）因次的
three dimensional「三次元的，3D的」

The three-dimensional movie felt so realistic that Fay screamed when the bloody hand appeared to come straight at her.
三次元電影是那麼的真實，當菲看見血淋淋的手向她伸過來的時候，她驚聲尖叫。

immense
im + mense
▶ 〔ɪˋmɛns〕 形 巨大的，廣大的，無限的，非常好的

immensely
immense + ly
▶ 〔ɪˋmɛnslɪ〕 副 非常，很

Miranda was immensely relieved to find out that she didn't have cancer.
發現自己沒有得癌症的時候，米蘭達大大鬆了一口氣。

224　found　fund　基礎，根基

224

| found | ▶ | 〔faund〕 動　建立，建造，創立，創辦 |

| foundation
found + tion | ▶ | 〔faun`deʃən〕 名　建立，基礎，根據，基金會，
地基，粉底霜（液） |

The little village was founded in the 1700's.
這座小村莊建立於1700年代。

| profound
pro + found | ▶ | 〔prə`faund〕 形　深刻的，深切的，深奧的 |

The advent of e-mail has had a profound effect on international communication.　電子郵件的出現替國際間的交流帶來了深刻的影響。

| fund | ▶ | 〔fʌnd〕 名　資金，基金，（銀行）存款
動　提供（事業、活動等的）資金 |

| fundamental
fund + ment + al | ▶ | 〔ˌfʌndə`mɛntl〕 形　基礎的，根本的
名　基本原理 |

| fundamentally
fundamental + ly | ▶ | 〔ˌfʌndə`mɛntlɪ〕 副　基礎地，根本地 |

The school is funded by tax money.　學校的資金由稅金提供。
Knowing some fundamentals of music will make it easier for you to learn to play the guitar.
知道一些基本樂理會讓你學吉他更容易。

225　price　prize　preci　價值，價格

225

| price | ▶ | 〔praɪs〕 名　價格，價錢，代價
動　給…定價 |

| priceless
price + less | ▶ | 〔`praɪslɪs〕 形　貴重的 |

| prize | ▶ | 〔praɪz〕 名　獎賞，獎品，獎金 |

The old house was filled with priceless antiques.
這間古宅滿是貴重的古董。

precious
preci + ous
▶ 〔`prɛʃəs〕 形 貴重的，珍貴的，寶貝的

preciousness
precious + ness
▶ 〔`prɛʃəsnɪs〕 名 珍貴，貴重

She considers her box of letters from her father more precious than diamonds. 她認為裝著她父親寫的信的盒子比鑽石更珍貴。

appreciate
ap + preci + ate
▶ 〔ə`priʃɪˌet〕 動 欣賞，感謝，體會，增值

appreciative
appreciate + ive
▶ 〔ə`priʃɪˌetɪv〕 形 有欣賞力的，表示讚賞的，感謝的
be appreciative of～「對～表示讚賞，感謝～」

appreciation
appreciate + ion
▶ 〔əˌpriʃɪ`eʃən〕 名 欣賞，鑑賞，感謝，漲價，增值

It is always a good idea to be appreciative of people who help you.
向幫助你的人表達謝意總是個好主意。

One can never fully appreciate other people's problems.
人永遠無法完全體會他人的問題。

 226 cover 掩飾，蓋上
226

cover
▶ 〔`kʌvə〕 動 遮蓋，掩飾，包含，適用於

coverage
cover + age
▶ 〔`kʌvərɪdʒ〕 名 覆蓋，覆蓋範圍，保險項目，新聞報導

discover
dis + cover
▶ 〔dɪs`kʌvə〕 動 發現，發覺，找到

discovery
discover + y
▶ 〔dɪs`kʌvərɪ〕 名 發現，被發現的事物

When she arrived at work, she discovered to her horror that she'd left all her important documents at home.
她到公司時，驚恐地發現她把所有重要的文件都忘在家裡了。

recover
re + cover
▶ 〔rɪ`kʌvə〕 動 重新獲得，重新找到，恢復，康復，挽回，彌補
recover from～「從～恢復」

recovery
recover + y

▶ 〔rɪˋkʌvərɪ〕 [名] 重獲，復得，恢復

Alice took a few days off work to recover from her operation.
艾莉絲為了手術後的復元，向公司請了幾天假。

He was able to recover the data he lost from his computer when the power went out.
他成功將停電時電腦失去的檔案救回。

 227 cas chance cay cid 發生
227

casual
cas + ual

▶ 〔ˋkæʒuəl〕 [形] 偶然的，碰巧的，隨便的，不拘禮節的，非正式的

casually
casual + ly

▶ 〔ˋkæʒjuəlɪ〕 [副] 偶然地，無意地

casualty
casual + ty

▶ 〔ˋkæʒjuəltɪ〕 [名] 傷亡人員，意外事故

The only good thing that could be said about the war is that there were few casualties.
關於這場戰爭，唯一的好事是傷亡者很少。

Everyone was surprised when she casually mentioned that she would be going to live in New Zealand for three years.
她偶然提到她要在紐西蘭住上三年的時候，每個人都很驚訝。

chance

▶ 〔tʃæns〕 [名] 偶然，運氣，可能性，機會
by chance 「偶然地」

Richard, by chance, met an old college friend at a party, and they ended up getting married.
理察偶然在一場派對遇見大學時代的朋友，而且他們最後還結婚了。

decay
de + cay

▶ 〔dɪˋke〕 [動] 腐爛，蛀蝕，衰敗，衰退
[名] 腐爛，蛀牙，衰敗，衰退

The forest floor is covered with leaves in various states of decay.
森林的地面被各種不同腐爛程度的葉子所覆蓋。

occasion
oc + cas + ion
▶ 〔əˋkeʒən〕 名　場合，時刻，時機，機會

occasional
occasion + al
▶ 〔əˋkeʒənl〕 形　偶爾的，特殊場合的，應景的

occasionally
occasional + ly
▶ 〔əˋkeʒənlɪ〕 副　偶爾，間或

I occasionally call my grandmother to have a chat.
我偶爾會打電話跟我的祖母聊天。

incident
in + cid + ent
▶ 〔ˋɪnsədn̩t〕 名　事件，事變，插曲

incidental
incident + al
▶ 〔͵ɪnsəˋdɛntl〕 形　附帶的，非主要的，偶然發生的

incidence
incident + ce
▶ 〔ˋɪnsədn̩s〕 名　發生率，影響範圍

The incident seemed insignificant, but it changed her life forever.
這個事件看起來無足輕重，但卻永遠改變了她的人生。

228　dur(e)　持久

228

endure
en + dure
▶ 〔ɪnˋdjʊr〕 動　忍耐，忍受，容忍，持久

endurance
endure + ance
▶ 〔ɪnˋdjʊrəns〕 名　忍耐，耐久力，持久力

duration
dur + tion
▶ 〔djʊˋreʃən〕 名　（時間的）持續，持久，持續期間

durable
dur + able
▶ 〔ˋdjʊrəbl̩〕 形　經久的，耐用的，持久的

during
dur + ing
▶ 〔ˋdjʊrɪŋ〕 介　在⋯期間

Her boots were so well-made and durable that she was able to wear them every day for five years.
她的靴子做工精良而且很耐用，所以她可以五年來每天都穿。

229　art　技術

229

art	▶ 〔ɑrt〕名　藝術，美術，藝術品，技術，技藝
artificial art + ial	▶ 〔͵ɑrtə`fɪʃəl〕形　人工的，人造的，不自然的
article art + icle	▶ 〔`ɑrtɪk!〕名　物品，商品，文章，條文

This magazine has lots of informative articles.
這本雜誌有許多廣博見聞的文章。

Even though the label says "100% juice", there are some artificial colors and flavors added.
就算這上面標示了「100%純果汁」，裡面還是添加了許多人工色素和香料。

230　flict　攻擊，擊倒

230

inflict in + flict	▶ 〔ɪn`flɪkt〕動　給予（打擊），使遭受（損傷等），強加
infliction inflict + ion	▶ 〔ɪn`flɪkʃən〕名　施加，施加的事物

The school bully inflicted a lot of pain on the new student.
校園惡霸替那名新生帶來莫大的痛苦。

conflict con + flict	▶ 〔kən`flɪkt〕動　矛盾，衝突 〔`kɑnflɪkt〕名　衝突，分歧，鬥爭 conflict with～「與～衝突」
confliction conflict + ion	▶ 〔kən`flɪkʃən〕名　爭執，爭論

I wonder whether the conflict between Israel and Palestine will ever be resolved.
我懷疑以色列和巴勒斯坦的衝突是否有解決的一天。

I couldn't go to the party because it conflicted with an important meeting.
我不能參加那場派對是因為那和一場重要會議時間衝突。

231 **fraid**　**fright**　恐怖，害怕
231

afraid a + fraid	▶ 〔ə`fred〕形　害怕的，恐怕，遺憾，恐懼的，擔心的 be afraid of～「害怕～」 be afraid to V「害怕不敢～」

The three little pigs said that they were not afraid of the Big Bad Wolf, but when he came to their houses, they ran away.
三隻小豬說他們不怕大野狼，但是當他到他們家時，他們逃走了。

frighten fright + en	▶ 〔`fraɪtn̩〕動　使驚恐，嚇唬，害怕
frightful fright + ful	▶ 〔`fraɪtfəl〕形　可怕的，難看的，醜的

The dog was frightened by the sound of the thunder.
打雷的聲音嚇著那隻狗。

232 **chief**　**chieve**　頭，領袖
232

chief	▶ 〔tʃif〕名　首領，長官，領袖 形　等級最高的，為首的，主要的
chiefly chief + ly	▶ 〔`tʃiflɪ〕副　主要地，大部分，首先，第一

He was the chief instigator of the riots, so the police were trying hard to incarcerate him.
他是暴動的主謀，所以警察努力設法要監禁他。

achieve a + chieve	▶ 〔ə`tʃiv〕動　完成，實現，達到
achievement achieve + ment	▶ 〔ə`tʃivmənt〕名　達成，成就，成績

The professor was given an award for lifetime achievement.
那位教授獲頒終身成就獎。

firm 堅決的，穩固的
233

firm	▶ 〔fɜm〕 形 穩固的，堅定的，堅決的 動 使穩固，使牢固，使確定下來
firmly firm + ly	▶ 〔`fɜmlɪ〕 副 堅固地，穩固地，堅決地

A good apple is firm and crisp.
一顆好的蘋果結實又清脆。

affirm af + firm	▶ 〔ə`fɜm〕 動 斷言，堅稱，證實，確認
affirmative affirm + ive	▶ 〔ə`fɜmətɪv〕 形 肯定的，表示贊成的

The child persisted in begging for ice-cream until his parents gave him an affirmative answer.
那個小孩不斷要求要吃冰淇淋，直到他的父母答應為止。

confirm con + firm	▶ 〔kən`fɜm〕 動 證實，確定，堅定，批准，確認
confirmation confirm + tion	▶ 〔ˌkɑnfə`meʃən〕 名 確定，確證，批准

Travelers must call and confirm their reservations 48 hours before the flight.
旅客在班機起飛的48個小時前必須打電話確認機位。

 pater patri 父
234

paternal pater + al	▶ 〔pə`tɜnl〕 形 父親的，父系的，由父親遺傳的 （反義）maternal〔mə`tɜnl〕 形 母親的，母性的，母系的， 母體遺傳的

My paternal grandmother was 98 when she died; my maternal grandmother is 92.
我祖母過世的時候98歲，外婆現在是92歲。

patriot
patri + ot
▶ 〔`petrɪət〕 名　愛國者

patriotic
patriot + ic
▶ 〔͵petrɪ`ɑtɪk〕 形　愛國的

patriotism
patriot + ism
▶ 〔`petrɪətɪzəm〕 名　愛國心，愛國精神，愛國主義

The crowd waved the flag and sang patriotic songs.
群眾揮動旗子高唱愛國歌曲。

 235　mit　miss　寄送，通過

permit
per + mit
▶ 〔pɚ`mɪt〕 動　允許，許可，准許，容許

permission
permit + ion
▶ 〔pɚ`mɪʃən〕 名　允許，許可，同意

permissive
permit + ive
▶ 〔pɚ`mɪsɪv〕 形　許可的，寬容的

You need permission from the management before you can use the multi-purpose room.
在使用多用途活動室之前，你必須先取得管理人的許可。

You will not be permitted to chew bubble gum in class.
課堂上不允許嚼口香糖。

---

admit
ad + mit
▶ 〔əd`mɪt〕 動　承認，准許進入，容許

admittance
admit + ance
▶ 〔əd`mɪtəns〕 名　進入，入場許可

admission
admit + ion
▶ 〔əd`mɪʃən〕 名　進入許可，入場費，入場券

Admission for the theater is $15.00.
劇場的入場費是15美元。

The little boy finally admitted that he had eaten the cookies.
小男孩終於承認是他吃掉餅乾的。

dismiss dis + miss	▶	〔dɪs`mɪs〕 動 讓…離開，解散，遣散，開除
dismissal dismiss + al	▶	〔dɪs`mɪsl〕 名 解散，打發走，解雇，開除

Class was dismissed 25 minutes early on account of the impending storm.　由於暴風雨逼近，所以課程提早25分鐘結束。

commit com + mit	▶	〔kə`mɪt〕 動 犯（罪），做（錯事），使作出保證， 把…交給
commitment commit + ment	▶	〔kə`mɪtmənt〕 名 託付，承諾，保證，信奉，犯罪
committee commit + ee	▶	〔kə`mɪtɪ〕 名 委員會，監護人

Once you make a commitment, you should do everything you possibly can to follow through on your promise.
一旦你作出承諾，你應該要盡你所能實現諾言。

submit sub + mit	▶	〔səb`mɪt〕 動 使服從，使受到，提交
submissive submit + ive	▶	〔sʌb`mɪsɪv〕 形 服從的，柔順的
submission submit + ion	▶	〔sʌb`mɪʃən〕 名 屈從，歸順，順從，提交（物）

The student was asked to submit his report by the end of the week.
學生被要求在週末以前交出他的報告。

He was never able to get married because he expected all his girlfriends to be submissive.
他一直都沒能結婚，因為他要求歷任女友都要順從溫柔。

⓶⓷⓺ habit　hibit　繼續保持

236

habit	▶	〔`hæbɪt〕 名 習慣，習性
habitual habit + ual	▶	〔hə`bɪtʃʊəl〕 形 習慣的，習以為常的

habitat
habit + at

▶ 〔`hæbɚˌtæt〕 名　（動物的）棲息地，（植物的）產地

habitation
habit + tion

▶ 〔ˌhæbəˋteʃən〕 名　居住，住處，住所

He has a habit of scratching his head when he is under pressure.
在他感到壓力的時候，他有抓頭的習慣。

It is difficult to raise some animals outside of their natural habitat.
在自然棲息地外飼養某些動物是困難的。

inhabit
in + habit

▶ 〔ɪnˋhæbɪt〕 動　居住於，棲息於，存在於，佔據

inhabitant
inhabit + ant

▶ 〔ɪnˋhæbətənt〕 名　（某地區的）居民，居住者，（某地區）棲居的動物

The inhabitants of the small town were surprised when a meteorite landed on the library lawn.
當小鎮居民發現一顆隕石墜落在圖書館的草坪上時，他們感到非常驚訝。

prohibit
pro + hibit

▶ 〔prəˋhɪbɪt〕 動　（以法令、規定等）禁止，妨礙，阻止

prohibition
prohibit + ion

▶ 〔ˌproəˋbɪʃən〕 名　禁止，禁令

Smoking is now prohibited in all public places in this city.
這座城市現在禁止在所有公共場所吸菸。

exhibit
ex + hibit

▶ 〔ɪgˋzɪbɪt〕 動　展示，表示，舉辦展示會，展出產品（或作品）
　　　　　名　展示品，展示會

exhibition
exhibit + ion

▶ 〔ˌɛksəˋbɪʃən〕 名　展覽會，展覽品，表現

I want to see the exhibit of local artists at the museum on Saturday.
我禮拜六想去看美術館展覽的本地藝術家作品。

I think you better get some sleep; you are exhibiting signs of exhaustion.
我想你最好睡一下，你看起來累壞了。

237 **fail** **false** **fault** 失敗，錯誤
237

| **fail** | ▶ | 〔fel〕 動 失敗，不及格
fail in～「失敗～，缺少～」，fail to V「未能～」 |
| **failure**
fail + ure | ▶ | 〔`feljə〕 名 失敗，失敗者，失敗的嘗試，
不履行，沒做到 |

The plan was not a total failure, but it still needs some work.
計劃並不是徹底失敗，而是還需要一些努力。

| **false** | ▶ | 〔fɔls〕 形 不正確的，不真實的，假的 |
| **falsely**
false + ly | ▶ | 〔`fɔlslɪ〕 副 錯誤地，不正確地，虛假地 |

He was falsely accused of stealing pencils from the supply room.
他受到不實的指控，說他從供應室裡偷鉛筆。

My grandmother took her false teeth out every night before she went to bed.
我的祖母每天就寢前都會將她的假牙取下。

| **fault** | ▶ | 〔fɔlt〕 名 缺點，毛病，錯誤
find fault with～「挑剔～」 |

The teacher found no fault with Betty's grammar, but the organization of her essay was terrible.
老師找不出任何文法錯誤，但是貝蒂寫的文章結構非常糟糕。

 238 **broad** **bread** 廣泛的
238

broad	▶	〔brɔd〕 形 寬的，闊的，遼闊的，廣泛的，概括的
breadth bread + th	▶	〔brɛdθ〕 名 寬度，幅度，寬宏，廣度 （反義）length
broadcast broad + cast	▶	〔`brɔd͵kæst〕 動 廣播，播送，傳佈

The radio broadcast originated from Russia.
收音機廣播起源於俄羅斯。

She traveled the length and breadth of Asia.
她遊遍亞洲所有地方。

 239　cur　跑　

current cur + ent	▶	〔`kɜənt〕 形　當前的，現行的，通用的，流行的
currently current + ly	▶	〔`kɜəntlɪ〕 副　現在，一般，流暢地
currency current + cy	▶	〔`kɜənsɪ〕 名　貨幣，通用，流通，流傳

There are hundreds of weekly magazines that report on current events.
有數百本的週刊報導時事。

The Euro is now the official currency of the European Union.
歐元現在是歐盟的官方貨幣。

occur oc + cur	▶	〔ə`kɜ〕 動　發生，出現，存在，浮現
occurrence occur + ence	▶	〔ə`kɜəns〕 名　發生，出現，事件

When did the accident occur?
意外是什麼時候發生的？

Earthquakes are an everyday occurrence around here, so no one even seems to take notice of them.
這附近每天都會發生地震，所以好像沒人會去注意。

 240　par(e)　pair　準備　

prepare pre + pare	▶	〔prɪ`pɛr〕 動　準備，籌備，做（飯菜） prepare～＝prepare for～「準備～」

preparation
prepare + tion

▶ 〔͵prɛpəˋreʃən〕 名　準備，預備，準備工作

preparatory
prepare + ory

▶ 〔prɪˋpærə͵torɪ〕 形　準備的，預備的，籌備的

For this cake recipe, preparation time is one hour, and baking time is 25 minutes.
這個蛋糕食譜的準備時間為一個小時，然後烘焙時間為25分鐘。

Fred attends a preparatory school.
佛烈德念的是預備學校。

repair
re + pair

▶ 〔rɪˋpɛr〕 動　修理，修補，補救

repairer
repair + er

▶ 〔rɪˋpɛrə〕 名　修理者，修理工

repairable
repair + able

▶ 〔rɪˋpɛrəbḷ〕 形　可修理的，可補償的，可挽回的

irreparable
ir + repairable

▶ 〔ɪˋrɛpərəbḷ〕 形　不能修補的，不能挽救的

The flood did irreparable damage to the houses near the river.
洪水替河川附近的住家帶來不可補救的損害。

It would cost so much to repair my DVD player, that I might just buy a new one.
修理DVD播放器太花錢了，所以我可能會直接買一台新的。

separate
se + par + ate

▶ 〔ˋsɛpə͵ret〕 動　分隔，區分，分開，分居
　　形　個別的，獨立的，分開的

separation
separate + ion

▶ 〔͵sɛpəˋreʃən〕 名　分開，分離，分隔線，分居

The children did not cope well after the separation of their parents.
在父母分開後，孩子們適應得不太好。

In this youth hostel, men and women have separate rooms.
在這間青年旅舍，男性和女性房間分開。

241 mind　　ment　　心
241

mind	▶	〔maɪnd〕名　頭腦，心智 動　注意，留意，介意
remind re + mind	▶	〔rɪˋmaɪnd〕名　提醒，使想起 remind（人）of～「提醒（人）想起～」
reminder remind + er	▶	〔rɪˋmaɪndə〕動　提醒者，提醒物

Mind your step.
請注意腳邊。

Please send a reminder to everyone about the meeting on Tuesday.
請就星期二的會議發送給大家一份提醒單。

The smell of freshly cut grass reminds me of my childhood.
聞到剛割下的青草味讓我想起童年時光。

mental ment + al	▶	〔ˋmɛntl〕形　精神的，心理的，智力的
mentally mental + ly	▶	〔ˋmɛntlɪ〕副　心理上，精神上，智力上
mentality mental + ity	▶	〔mɛnˋtælətɪ〕名　智力，精神性，心理狀態

Perhaps we should talk about this later when you are in a better mental state.
或許我們應該稍後等你精神狀況好一點時再談這件事。

242 joy　　喜悅
242

joy	▶	〔dʒɔɪ〕名　歡樂，高興，樂事，樂趣
joyful joy + ful	▶	〔ˋdʒɔɪfəl〕形　高興的，充滿喜悅的，使人高興的
enjoy en + joy	▶	〔ɪnˋdʒɔɪ〕動　欣賞，享受，喜愛

enjoyment
enjoy + ment

▶ 〔ɪnˋdʒɔɪmənt〕 名　樂趣，享受，令人愉快的事

Ned was speechless with joy when Cora accepted his proposal.
當柯拉接受奈德的求婚時，奈德高興得說不出話來。

 243　proper　propri　自己的
243

proper	▶	〔ˋprɑpɚ〕 形　適合的，適當的，恰當的，合乎體統的
properly proper + ly	▶	〔ˋprɑpɚlɪ〕 副　恰當地，正確地，有禮貌地，體面地
improper im + proper	▶	〔ɪmˋprɑpɚ〕 形　不適當的，不合標準的，不正確的，不成體統的
improperly improper + ly	▶	〔ɪmˋprɑpɚlɪ〕 副　不正確地，不適當地

Improper use of this medicine could have adverse effects.
不當地服用此藥可能會帶來反效果。
Eating nothing but chocolate bars can not be considered a proper diet.
除了巧克力棒什麼都不吃並不被認為是適當的飲食。

appropriate ap + propri + ate	▶	〔əˋproprɪˌet〕 形　適當的，恰當的，相稱的
appropriately appropriate + ly	▶	〔əˋproprɪˌetlɪ〕 副　適當地，合適地，相稱地
inappropriate in + appropriate	▶	〔ˌɪnəˋproprɪɪt〕 形　不適當的
inappropriately inappropriate + ly	▶	〔ˌɪnəˋproprɪɪtlɪ〕 副　不適當地

Jeans are not appropriate dress for a wedding ceremony.
牛仔褲不是適合參加婚禮的服裝。

⚫244 sembl(e)　simil　simul　相同，一起

assemble
as + semble
▶ 〔ə`sɛmbl̩〕 動　集合，召集，聚集，配裝，集會

assembly
assemble + y
▶ 〔ə`sɛmblɪ〕 名　與會者，集會，集合

disassemble
dis + assemble
▶ 〔ˌdɪsə`sɛmbl̩〕 動　拆開，拆卸

disassembly
dis + assembly
▶ 〔ˌdɪsə`sɛmblɪ〕 名　拆開，拆卸

The entire community assembled to witness the opening of the new library.
整個社區的人聚集在一起見證新圖書館的開幕。

resemble
re + semble
▶ 〔rɪ`zɛmbl̩〕 動　像，類似

resemblance
resemble + ance
▶ 〔rɪ`zɛmbləns〕 名　相似，相似點，相似程度，相似物

There is a very strong resemblance between Dean and his brother.
狄恩和他的弟弟長得非常像。

Although this resembles a poisonous mushroom, it is okay to eat it.
雖然這看起來像一枚毒菇，但其實是可以食用的。

similar
simil + ar
▶ 〔`sɪmələ〕 形　相像的，相仿的，類似的

similarly
similar + ly
▶ 〔`sɪmɪləlɪ〕 副　同樣地，相仿地

similarity
similar + ity
▶ 〔ˌsɪmə`lærətɪ〕 名　類似，相似，相似點，類似點

dissimilar
dis + similar
▶ 〔dɪ`sɪmələ〕 形　不同的，相異的

dissimilarity
dissimilar + ity
▶ 〔dɪsˌsɪmə`lærətɪ〕 名　不同，相異，相異點

These two colors are very similar.
這兩個顏色非常類似。

They are both US American women, but the similarity ends there.
她們兩個都是美國女性，但是她們之間的相似處僅止於此。

| **assimilate**
as + simil + ate | ▶ | 〔əˋsɪmḷˌet〕 動　吸收，使同化，使相似
assimilate oneself to～「使自己變成與～一樣，使自己與～同化」
assimilate into～「被～同化，融入～」 |

| **assimilation**
assimilate + ion | ▶ | 〔əˌsɪmḷ`eʃən〕 名　吸收，同化 |

It did not take Leonardo very long to assimilate into the Canadian culture.
李奧納多沒花多久的時間就融入了加拿大文化。

| **simultaneous**
simul + taneous | ▶ | 〔ˌsaɪməlˋtenɪəs〕 形　同時發生的，同時存在的，同步的，一齊的 |

| **simultaneously**
simultaneous + ly | ▶ | 〔ˌsaɪməlˋtenɪəslɪ〕 副　同時地 |

| **simultaneity**
simultaneous + ity | ▶ | 〔ˌsaɪməltəˋnɪətɪ〕 名　同時發生，同時完成 |

"We didn't do it!" the twins exclaimed simultaneously.
「不是我們做的！」那對雙胞胎同時大叫。

245　noy　noc　仇恨，傷害

| **annoy**
an + noy | ▶ | 〔əˋnɔɪ〕 動　惹惱，使煩惱，困擾，令人討厭（或不快） |

| **annoyance**
annoy + ance | ▶ | 〔əˋnɔɪəns〕 名　惱怒，打擾，使人煩惱的事，討厭的東西（或人） |

Mosquitoes are more than an annoyance; they are responsible for spreading many kinds of deadly diseases.
蚊子不光是討人厭而已，它們還是許多種致命疾病散播的原因。

innocent in + noc + ent	▶	〔`ɪnəsn̩t〕 形　無罪的，清白的，無害的，天真的
innocence innocent + ce	▶	〔`ɪnəsn̩s〕 名　無罪，清白，天真無邪，純真

At last his innocence was proven, and he could get on with his life.
他的清白終於被證明，從此得以繼續他的生活。

 blood　bleed　bless　血　
246　　　　　　　　　　　　　　　　　　　　　　　　246

blood	▶	〔blʌd〕 名　血液，血統，血氣，生命
bloody blood + y	▶	〔`blʌdɪ〕 形　流血的，血淋淋的，殘忍的，血紅的
bleed	▶	〔blid〕 動　出血，流血

The victim was covered in blood.
受害者渾身是血。

bless	▶	〔blɛs〕 動　為⋯祝福，為⋯祈神賜福，保佑 Bless you! 「請保重！」 【註】一般在旁人打噴嚏時會說的話。
blessing bless + ing	▶	〔`blɛsɪŋ〕 名　（上帝的）賜福，祝福

"Bless you!" he said when she sneezed.
她打噴嚏的時候，他對她說：「請保重！」

 int　內側，裡面　
247　　　　　　　　　　　　　　　　　　　　　　　　247

internal int + ernal	▶	〔ɪn`tɜn̩l〕 形　內部的，內在的，內心的，內服的 （反義）external 〔ɪk`stɜnəl〕 　　　　 形　外面的，外部的 an internal remedy「內服藥」 an external remedy「外用藥」

internally
internal + ly

▶ 〔ɪnˋtɜnəlɪ〕 副　內部地，內在地
（反義）externally〔ɪkˋstɜnlɪ〕
副　在（或從）外部，外表上

Vitamin E can be taken internally, or applied externally to the skin.
維他命E可以內服，也可以外用塗敷於皮膚上。

---

intimate
int + ate

▶ 〔ˋɪntəmɪt〕 形　親密的，熟悉的

---

intimately
intimate + ly

▶ 〔ˋɪntəmɪtlɪ〕 副　熟悉地，親密地

---

intimacy
intimate + cy

▶ 〔ˋɪntəməsɪ〕 名　熟悉，親密，親近，
親暱的言語（或行為）

Although Julia had known them for years, she did not feel she
had got to know them intimately.
雖然茱莉亞認識他們好幾年了，但是她不覺得自己跟他們很熟。

---

 fem　女性
248

---

female
fem + ale

▶ 〔ˋfimel〕 名　女人，雌性動（植）物
形　女（性）的，雌性的

---

feminine
fem + inine

▶ 〔ˋfɛmənɪn〕 形　女性的，婦女的，女孩子氣的

---

unfeminine
un + feminine

▶ 〔ʌnˋfɛmənɪn〕 形　不像婦女的，不溫柔的

---

feminist
feminine + ist

▶ 〔ˋfɛmənɪst〕 名　男女平等主義者，女性主義者

Carol is old-fashioned, and thinks that women should not wear
jeans because it is unfeminine.
卡洛兒很老派，她覺得女性不應該穿牛仔褲因為那不夠有女人味。

---

 hon　榮譽，誠實
249

---

honest
hon + est

▶ 〔ˋɑnɪst〕 形　誠實的，正直的，真誠的

dishonest
dis + honest

▶ 〔dɪsˋɑnɪst〕形　不誠實的，不正直的

honesty
honest + y

▶ 〔ˋɑnɪstɪ〕名　正直，誠實

Many people believe that honesty is one of the most important
components of a friendship.
許多人相信誠實是一段友誼中最重要的事。

honor
hon + or

▶ 〔ˋɑnɚ〕名　榮譽，信譽，光榮的事或人
　　　　　　動　使增光，尊敬

dishonor
dis + honor

▶ 〔dɪsˋɑnɚ〕名　不名譽，丟臉，侮辱，
　　　　　　　　　丟臉的事（或人）

honorable
honor + able

▶ 〔ˋɑnərəbl〕形　可敬的，高尚的，光榮的

Michael felt honored when he was asked to make a speech at his
old high school.
麥可收到在他高中母校演講的邀請時感到榮幸。

250　cell　ceal　隱藏

250

cell

▶ 〔sɛl〕名　小囚房，細胞
cell phone 「行動電話，手機」

cellar
cell + ar

▶ 〔ˋsɛlɚ〕名　地下室，地窖
wine cellar 「酒窖」

The thin inner skin of an onion is unique because it is a single
layer of cells.
洋蔥內皮的特別之處在於它是由單層的細胞組成。

conceal
con + ceal

▶ 〔kənˋsil〕動　隱蔽，隱藏，隱瞞

concealment
conceal + ment

▶ 〔kənˋsilmənt〕名　隱藏，隱瞞，隱匿處

The artist's masterpiece was concealed by a white cloth so no
one could see it before the gallery opening.
那位藝術家的傑作被白布蓋住，所有沒有人能在畫廊開張前看見它。

251 **stand** (i)st 立

251

---

outstanding
out + stand + ing

▶ 〔`aut`stændɪŋ〕 形 突出的，顯著的，傑出的，重要的

He gave an outstanding performance on stage.
他在舞台上展現了傑出的表演。

---

standpoint
stand + point

▶ 〔`stænd‚pɔɪnt〕 名 立場，觀點，看法
from the standpoint of～「從～的觀點來看」

From the standpoint of keeping peace, this is not a good idea.
從維護和平的觀點來看，這並不是個好主意。

---

constant
con + st + ant

▶ 〔`kɑnstənt〕 形 固定的，不變的，持續的

---

constantly
constant + ly

▶ 〔`kɑnstəntlɪ〕 副 不斷地，時常地

---

constancy
constant + cy

▶ 〔`kɑnstənsɪ〕 名 堅定，堅決，忠誠，恆久不變

There was a constant stream of people visiting the shrine on New Year's Day.
在元旦當天，不斷有參拜神社的人潮。

---

constitute
con + st + itute

▶ 〔`kɑnstə‚tjut〕 動 構成，設立（機構等），制定，指定

---

constitution
constitute + ion

▶ 〔‚kɑnstə`tjuʃən〕 名 憲法，章程，體質，體格，（事物的）構造
the Constitution「憲法」

Water is constituted of hydrogen and oxygen.
水由氫及氧組成。

---

destine
de + st + ine

▶ 〔`dɛstɪn〕 動 命定，注定
be destined to V「注定要～」

---

destiny
destine + y

▶ 〔`dɛstənɪ〕 名 命運，天命，神意

destination
destine + tion

▶ 〔‚dɛstə`neʃən〕 图　目的地，終點，目標，目的

Mother Theresa felt it was her destiny to devote her life to helping people in need.
德蕾莎修女認為她的命運是奉獻她的生命給需要她幫助的人。

By the time they finally reached their destination, they were too tired to eat a meal before they collapsed into bed.
等他們終於到達目的地，在他們直接倒到床上前，他們早已經累得吃不下飯了。

establish
e + st + ablish

▶ 〔ə`stæblɪʃ〕 動　建立，創辦，確立，制定，規定

established
establish + ed

▶ 〔əs`tæblɪʃt〕 形　已建立的，已確立的，已制定的

establishment
establish + ment

▶ 〔ɪs`tæblɪʃmənt〕 图　建立，設立，創立，
建立的機構

The charitable organization was established in 1809.
這個慈善組織設立於1809年。

exist
ex + ist

▶ 〔ɪg`zɪst〕 動　存在，生存，生活

existence
exist + ence

▶ 〔ɪg`zɪstəns〕 图　存在，生存，生活，存在物，實體

existent
exist + ent

▶ 〔ɪg`zɪstənt〕 形　存在的，實有的

coexist
co + exist

▶ 〔`koɪg`zɪst〕 動　共存

Farming coexists with industry in this area of the country.
在該國的這一區域，農業與工業並存。

He was hospitalized for talking to people who don't exist.
他因為和不存在的人說話而住院治療。

ple(n)　pli　ply　充足，充分

252

plenty ▶	〔`plɛntɪ〕 图　豐富，充足，大量 形　很多的，足夠的 plenty of～「很多的～」
plentiful plenty + ful ▶	〔`plɛntɪfəl〕 形　豐富的，充足的，多的

We have plenty of time before the train leaves, so why don't we get some lunch?　火車開走前還有很多時間，我們要不要先吃午餐？
The weather conditions were ideal for a plentiful apple crop this year.
今年的天氣狀況是蘋果豐收的理想天候。

complete com + ple + te ▶	〔kəm`plit〕 形　完整的，完成的，完全的 動　使完整
completely complete + ly ▶	〔kəm`plitlɪ〕 副　完整地，完全地，徹底地
completion complete + ion ▶	〔kəm`pliʃən〕 图　完成，結束，圓滿，實現
complement complete + ment ▶	〔`kɑmpləmənt〕 图　補充物，補足物，配對物
complementary complement + ary ▶	〔͵kɑmplə`mɛntəri〕 形　互補的，補充的

A 60 degree angle is complementary to a 30 degree angle.
60度和30度互為餘角。

compliment com + pli + ment ▶	〔`kɑmpləmənt〕 图　讚美的話，恭維 動　讚揚
complimentary compliment + ary ▶	〔͵kɑmplə`mɛntəri〕 形　讚賞的，恭維的，贈送的

Passengers in first class compartments will receive a complimentary glass of champagne.
頭等艙的旅客將收到一杯免費贈送的香檳。

Rosa received a lot of compliments on her new painting.
羅莎的新畫作得到許多讚揚。

accomplish
ac + com + pli + sh

▶ 〔əˋkɑmplɪʃ〕 動　完成，實現，達到

accomplishment
accomplish + ment

▶ 〔əˋkɑmplɪʃmənt〕 名　成就，成績，完成

Making it to the Olympics is a great accomplishment for any athlete.
參加奧運對任何運動員來說都是莫大的成就。

supply
sup + ply

▶ 〔səˋplaɪ〕 動　供給，供應，提供
　　 名　供給，供應量，供應品，庫存
supply（人・設施）with～「提供～給（人・設施）」

supplement
supply + ment

▶ 〔ˋsʌpləmənt〕 名　增補，補充，補給品

supplementary
supplement + ary

▶ 〔͵sʌpləˋmɛntəri〕 形　增補的，補充的，追加的

My supply of coffee filters is running low; I'd better get some more.
我的咖啡濾紙庫存快不夠了，我最好再買一些。

The doctor suggested I take vitamin supplements to improve my health.
醫生建議我吃維他命補給品改善我的健康。

 253 frag　破碎
253

fragment
frag + ment

▶ 〔ˋfrægmənt〕 名　碎片，破片，斷片，
　　　　（文藝作品等的）未完成部分

fragmentary
fragment + ary

▶ 〔ˋfrægmən͵tɛrɪ〕 形　碎片的，零碎的，不全的，
　　　　不連續的

fragile
frag + ile

▶ 〔ˋfrædʒəl〕 形　易碎的，易損壞的，脆弱的

Be careful not to step on the fragments of glass from the broken mirror.
小心別踩到破鏡的玻璃碎片。

This package is fragile; please handle it with care.
這個包裹是易碎品，請小心處理。

254 **nat(e)**　誕生　
254

nature _{nat + ure}	▶ 〔`netʃɚ〕 名　自然，自然界，自然狀態，本質
natural _{nature + al}	▶ 〔`nætʃərəl〕 形　自然的，有關自然界的，天然的

Earthquakes, tidal waves, and floods are all examples of natural disasters.
地震、海嘯還有洪水都是自然災害的例子。

nation _{nat + ion}	▶ 〔`neʃən〕 名　國民，國家
national _{nation + al}	▶ 〔`næʃənl̩〕 形　全國性的，國家的，國立的， 國家主義的
nationality _{national + ity}	▶ 〔͵næʃə`nælətɪ〕 名　國籍
nationalist _{national + ist}	▶ 〔`næʃənl̩ɪst〕 名　民族主義者，國家主義者
nationalism _{national + ism}	▶ 〔`næʃənl̩ɪzəm〕 名　民族主義，國家主義
nationalize _{national + ize}	▶ 〔`næʃənl̩͵aɪz〕 動　使國有化，使成為全國性的

Write your full name and nationality on the immigration card.
請在入境卡上填寫你的全名以及國籍。

native _{nat + ive}	▶ 〔`netɪv〕 形　天生的，出生地的，本國的 native American「美國原住民」【印地安人的正式稱呼】

He has not been home to his native country for three years.
他已經三年沒有回到故土了。

innate _{in + nate}	▶ 〔ɪn`et〕 形　與生俱來的，天生的，固有的
innately _{innate + ly}	▶ 〔ɪ`netlɪ〕 副　天賦地，內在地，固有地

His innate sense of fairness has served him well in his position as judge.
他天生的正義感讓他很適合當法官。

 255 mir(e)　mar　驚奇，奇異
255

miracle mir + acle	▶ 〔ˋmɪrək1〕 名 奇蹟，驚人的事例
miraculous miracle + ous	▶ 〔mɪˋrækjələs〕 形 神奇的，奇蹟般的，驚人的

David made a miraculous recovery after his accident.
大衛在事故發生後，奇蹟般地復元了。

admire ad + mire	▶ 〔ədˋmaɪr〕 動 欽佩，欣賞，稱讚，誇獎
admirable admire + able	▶ 〔ˋædmərəb1〕 形 值得讚揚的，令人欽佩的， 絕妙的
admiration admire + tion	▶ 〔͵ædməˋreʃən〕 名 欽佩，讚美，羨慕， 令人讚美的人（或物）
admirer admire + er	▶ 〔ədˋmaɪrə〕 名 讚賞者，欽佩者， （對女性的）愛慕者

John's ability to control the children with a sense of humor won the admiration of all the other kindergarten teachers.
約翰用幽默感控制孩子的能力為他贏得了其他幼稚園老師的敬佩。
Lucy got a dozen roses from a secret admirer.
露西收到神祕愛慕者送的一打玫瑰。

marvel mar + vel	▶ 〔ˋmɑrv1〕 名 令人驚奇的事物（或人） 　　　　動 對…感到驚異，感到好奇 marvel at～「對～感到驚訝」
marvelous marvel + ous	▶ 〔ˋmɑrvələs〕 形 令人驚嘆的，不可思議的， 妙極的，了不起的
marvelously marvelous + ly	▶ 〔ˋmɑrvləslɪ〕 副 令人驚訝地，不可思議地

The audience marveled at the actor's moving monologue.
觀眾對於演員動人的獨白感到驚訝。

ly li 依存
256

rely re + ly	▶ 〔rɪˋlaɪ〕動 依靠，依賴，信賴 rely on～「信賴～」
reliable rely + able	▶ 〔rɪˋlaɪəbl〕形 可信賴的，可靠的，確實的
reliability reliable + ity	▶ 〔rɪ͵laɪəˋbɪlətɪ〕名 可靠，可信賴性，可靠程度
reliance rely + ance	▶ 〔rɪˋlaɪəns〕名 信賴，依靠，可依靠的人（或物）
unreliable un + reliable	▶ 〔͵ʌnrɪˋlaɪəbl〕形 不可信任的，不可靠的

You can't rely on the weather forecast, as it's often wrong.
你不可以依賴天氣預測，因為那常常不準。

Nancy is reliable friend; she always keeps her promises.
南西是個值得信賴的朋友，她總是遵守許下的承諾。

liable li + able	▶ 〔ˋlaɪəbl〕形 易…的，會…的，有義務的 be liable to～「對～應負責的」 be liable to illness「容易生病的」
liability liable + ity	▶ 〔͵laɪəˋbɪlətɪ〕名 傾向，責任，義務

You are liable to run into road construction if you take that route, so you might want to consider alternatives.
如果你走這條路，可能會碰上道路工程，所以你應該要考慮走別條路。

 mount 山
257

mount	▶ 〔maʊnt〕動 登上，爬上，騎上，騎在…上， 固定在…上，上升

The hero mounted his horse, and rode off into the sunset.
英雄騎上馬，然後向落日急馳而去。

Donald had his trophy fish mounted on the wall.
唐納德把他贏得比賽的魚標本固定在牆上。

amount
a + mount

▶　〔ə`maʊnt〕 名　總數，總額，數量

He's retired, but he still does a certain amount of work for his former employer.
雖然他退休了，但他還是幫以前的雇主作一定數量的工作。

 258 is(ol)　島
258

island
is + land

▶　〔`aɪlənd〕 名　島

isolate
isol + ate

▶　〔`aɪsḷˏet〕 動　使孤立，使脫離，隔離，孤立
isolate～from... 「使～自…脫離」

isolation
isolate + ion

▶　〔ˏaɪsḷ`eʃən〕 名　隔離，孤立，脫離

He was hiding out in an isolated little village in Canada.
他隱匿在加拿大一座偏僻的小村莊。

259 erg　urg(e)　力量
259

energy
en + erg + y

▶　〔`ɛnədʒɪ〕 名　活力，幹勁，精力，能量

energetic
energy + tic

▶　〔ˏɛnə`dʒɛtɪk〕 形　精力旺盛的，精神飽滿的，積極的

energetically
energetic + al + ly

▶　〔ˏɛnə`dʒɛtɪkḷɪ〕 副　精力充沛地，積極地

Solar power and wind power are two examples of renewable energy sources.
太陽能和風力是可再生能源的兩個例子。

urge

▶　〔ɝdʒ〕 動　催促，慫恿，極力主張，強烈要求
urge（人）to V 「催促（或慫恿）（人）～」

urgent urge + ent	▶	〔ˋɜdʒənt〕 形 緊急的，急迫的，催逼的
urgently urgent + ly	▶	〔ˋɜdʒəntlɪ〕 副 緊急地，急迫地
urgency urgent + cy	▶	〔ˋɜdʒənsɪ〕 名 緊急，迫切，催促，急事

Tom urged his mother to reconsider, but she decided that he would not be able to get his driver's license this year.
湯姆力勸他的母親重新考慮，但是她決定他今年拿不到他的駕照。

Dr. Barnes, you have a phone call. They said it's urgent.
巴恩斯醫生，有電話找你。聽說非常緊急。

 260 verb 言詞 **260**

verb	▶	〔vɜb〕 名 動詞
verbal verb + al	▶	〔ˋvɜbḷ〕 形 言辭上的，言語的，字句的，口頭的
nonverbal non + verbal	▶	〔ˌnɑnˋvɜbḷ〕 形 不使用語言的
verbally verbal + ly	▶	〔ˋvɜbḷɪ〕 副 言詞上，口頭地，照字面地
proverb pro + verb	▶	〔ˋprɑvɜb〕 名 諺語，俗語，眾所周知的人（事）
proverbial proverb + ial	▶	〔prəˋvɜbɪəl〕 形 諺語的，出名的，眾所周知的
proverbially proverbial + ly	▶	〔prəˋvɜbɪəlɪ〕 副 人盡皆知地

She never signed a contract for her apartment; she just had a verbal agreement.
她的公寓從來都沒有簽訂合約，她只作了口頭協議。

Her answer was "yes," but her nonverbal language said "no."
雖然她回答「是」，但是她的表情說「不」。

261 **number**　**numer**　**數字**　
261

number	▶ 〔`nʌmbɚ〕 名　數字，號碼，數量
numberless number + less	▶ 〔`nʌmbɚlɪs〕 形　無數的，數不盡的，無號碼的
numeral numer + al	▶ 〔`njumərəl〕 形　數的，示數的 　　　　　　　　 名　數字
numerous numer + ous	▶ 〔`njumərəs〕 形　許多的，很多的，為數眾多的

Despite his numerous attempts to get rich quick, he still has an average income.
儘管他多方嘗試想要快速致富，但他的收入只是一般而已。

 262 **tort**　**扭，扭轉**　
262

torture tort + ure	▶ 〔`tɔrtʃɚ〕 名　拷打，折磨，痛苦，歪曲，扭曲
distort dis + tort	▶ 〔dɪs`tɔrt〕 動　扭曲，扭歪，歪曲，曲解
distortion distort + ion	▶ 〔dɪs`tɔrʃən〕 名　扭曲，變形，失真

To avoid identification, Luca distorted his voice when he made the phone call.
為了避免被認出，路卡在打電話的時候改變了他的聲音。

Amusement parks often have mirrors that distort people's images and make them look very funny.
遊樂園裡常有鏡子能使人們的映像變得扭曲好笑。

263 laps(e) lips(e) 滑動，滑行
263

lapse	▶ 〔læps〕 名 （時間）流逝，小失誤，跌落，下降
collapse co + lapse	▶ 〔kəˋlæps〕 動 倒塌，崩潰
collapsible collapse + ible	▶ 〔kəˋlæpsəbl〕 形 可折疊的，可拆卸的
eclipse ec + lipse	▶ 〔ɪˋklɪps〕 名 日蝕，月蝕，被遮蔽 a lunar eclipse「月蝕」 a solar eclipse「日蝕」

The collapsible table is convenient to take camping.
折疊桌帶去露營非常方便。

Lulu collapsed with exhaustion after she completed the marathon.
跑完馬拉松後，露露精疲力竭不支倒地。

 264 (s)pend pens(e) 花費（錢或時間）
264

spend	▶ 〔spɛnd〕 動 花（錢或時間），花費
expend ex + pend	▶ 〔ɪkˋspɛnd〕 動 花費（時間、精力），花錢 expend（時間・錢）on/in～「花（時間・錢）在～」
expenditure expend + ture	▶ 〔ɪkˋspɛndɪtʃə〕 名 消費，支出，經費

Rod expended a lot of money and energy on remodeling his old home.
羅德花費許多金錢和精力在改建他的舊房子上。

expense ex + pense	▶ 〔ɪkˋspɛns〕 名 費用，支出，開銷
expensive expense + ive	▶ 〔ɪkˋspɛnsɪv〕 形 高價的，昂貴的，花錢的

Scott put the cost of the dinner with clients on his work expense account.
史考特把他和客戶吃晚餐的費用算在他的工作支出費用上。

dispense
dis + pense

▶ 〔dɪˋspɛns〕 [動] 分配，分發，執行，施行，免除

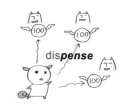
dis**pense**

---

dispensable
dispense + able

▶ 〔dɪˋspɛnsəbl〕 [形] 非必要的，可分配的

indispensable
in + dispensable

▶ 〔ˌɪndɪsˋpɛnsəbl〕 [形] 必不可少的，必需的，責無旁貸的

The cash machine was out of order, and could not dispense money.
那台自動提款機故障了，沒有辦法吐鈔。

This guidebook is indispensable to anyone traveling alone in Japan.
這本旅行指南對在日本獨自旅行的人是不可或缺的。

---

compensate
com + pens + ate

▶ 〔ˋkɑmpənˌset〕 [動] 補償，賠償
compensate（人）for～ with...「用…補償（人）的～」

compensation
compensate + ion

▶ 〔ˌkɑmpənˋseʃən〕 [名] 酬勞，補償，賠償，賠償金

Compensation for presenters will be $50 and a free lunch.
發表人的酬勞是50美元和一頓免費午餐。

---

 pha　phe　顯示，顯露
265

emphasize
em + pha + ize

▶ 〔ˋɛmfəˌsaɪz〕 [動] 強調，著重，加強…的語氣，使顯得突出

emphasis
em + pha + sis

▶ 〔ˋɛmfəsɪs〕 [名] 強調，重視，重點
put emphasis on～「強調～，重視～」

My father, who is never late, always emphasizes the importance of punctuality.
我那從不遲到的父親總是強調守時的重要性。

phenomenon ▶ 〔fə`nɑmə͵nɑn〕 名　現象，稀有的事，傑出的人才
phe + nomenon 　（名詞複數）phenomena 〔fə`nɑmənə〕

The aurora borealis is a natural phenomenon that is not yet completely understood.
北極光是一個尚未被完全瞭解的自然現象。

 fan　　空想，假想
266

fantasy fan + tasy	▶　〔`fæntəsɪ〕 名　空想，幻想，空想的產物
fantastic fantasy + tic	▶　〔fæn`tæstɪk〕 形　想像中的，古怪的，荒唐的， 　　　　　　　　　　　驚人的，極好的

He entertained fantasies of quitting his job and moving to Mexico.
他喜歡幻想辭掉他的工作然後搬到墨西哥居住。

fancy fan + cy	▶　〔`fænsɪ〕 名　迷戀，愛好，想像力，幻想 　　　　　　 動　想像，喜好，想要 　　　　　　 形　別緻的，花俏的，需要高度技巧的
fanciful fancy + ful	▶　〔`fænsɪfəl〕 形　富於幻想的，奇異的，古怪的

His interest in snowboarding is not just a passing fancy; he's been doing it for 10 years.
他對雪地滑板的興趣不只是一時狂熱而已，他從事這項運動已經10年了。

 od　　道路
267

method meth + od	▶　〔`mɛθəd〕 名　方法，辦法，條理，秩序
methodical method + ical	▶　〔mə`θɑdɪkəl〕 形　有條理的，講究方法的
methodically methodical + ly	▶　〔mɪ`θɑdɪkəlɪ〕 副　有條理地，有條不紊地， 　　　　　　　　　　井然地
methodology method + logy	▶　〔͵mɛθəd`ɑlədʒɪ〕 名　方法論，教學法

The police officer methodically went through the contents of the bag, taking pictures of all the contents.
那位警官有條不紊地檢查了包包的內容物，並且替裡面所有的東西拍照。

period peri + od	▶	〔ˋpɪrɪəd〕 名 時期，時間，時代，週期
periodic period + ic	▶	〔͵pɪrɪˋɑdɪk〕 形 週期的，週期性的，定期的
periodical period + ical	▶	〔͵pɪrɪˋɑdɪkl〕 形 週期的，定期的，時而發生的， 期刊的 名 期刊
periodically periodical + ly	▶	〔pɪrɪˋɑdɪklɪ〕 副 週期性地，定期地，偶爾

You should check your balance periodically to make sure you still have enough money in your account.
你應該要定期核對帳戶餘額，以確保你的戶頭裡有足夠的錢。

 268 **sert**　加入　　　　　　　　　　　　
268

insert in + sert	▶	〔ɪnˋsɜt〕 動 插入，嵌入
insertion insert + ion	▶	〔ɪnˋsɜʃən〕 名 插入，嵌入，插入物， （報紙）插入的廣告

She found the tiny key and inserted it into the rusty lock on the chest.
她找到那把小鑰匙，然後把它插入櫃子生鏽的鎖中。

assert as + sert	▶	〔əˋsɜt〕 動 斷言，聲稱，維護，堅持， 主張擁有，確立
assertive assert + ive	▶	〔əˋsɜtɪv〕 形 斷言的，肯定的，武斷的，獨斷的
assertion assert + ion	▶	〔əˋsɜʃən〕 名 斷言，言明，主張，維護，堅持

Being assertive without being aggressive is an important skill to develop.
堅持自信但同時不具有攻擊性是一項需要培養的重要技能。

269　labor　工作，勞動

269

labor	▶ 〔`lebɚ〕 名 勞動，勞工，勞方，工作
laborer labor + er	▶ 〔`lebərɚ〕 名 勞動者，勞工
laborious labor + ous	▶ 〔lə`borɪəs〕 形 費力的，吃力的，牽強的，生硬的

Even though he has a degree in law, he prefers to be a laborer, because he says the work is more satisfying.
即使他有法學學位，他還是比較喜歡當一名勞動者，因為他說這樣的工作更令人滿足。

Keeping the house clean is a laborious task.
維持家庭環境清潔是一份吃力的工作。

elaborate e + labor + ate	▶ 〔ɪ`læbərɪt〕 形 精心製作的，精巧的，詳盡的 〔ɪ`læbə,ret〕 動 精心製作，詳細闡述，詳細說明
elaboration elaborate + ion	▶ 〔ɪ,læbə`reʃən〕 名 精心製作，精巧，詳細闡述
collaborate co + labor + ate	▶ 〔kə`læbə,ret〕 動 共同工作，合作 collaborate with～「與～合作」
collaboration collaborate + ion	▶ 〔kə,læbə`reʃən〕 名 合作

He said that he would be absent, but he refused to elaborate.
他說他會缺席，但是他拒絕說明詳細原因。

laboratory labor + ory	▶ 〔`læbrə,torɪ〕 名 實驗室，研究室

270　proach　proxim　將近，接近

270

approach ap + proach	▶ 〔ə`protʃ〕 動 接近，靠近 名 接近，靠近，通道，入口，方法
approachable approach + able	▶ 〔ə`protʃəbḷ〕 形 可接近的，好親近的

Since people find her very approachable, she often makes new friends.
因為人們覺得她很好親近，所以她常常交到新朋友。

The police were involved in a car chase with speeds approaching 200 km/hr.
警察涉及一場時速將近200公里的飛車追逐。

approximate ap + proxim + ate	▶	〔əˋprɑksəmɪt〕 形　接近的，大約的
approximately approximate + ly	▶	〔əˋprɑksəmɪtlɪ〕 副　大約，近乎

The trip will cost approximately 120,000 yen including hotel costs.
這趟旅行的費用，包含旅館開支大約花費12萬日圓。

271　pear　par　出現，顯露

appear ap + pear	▶	〔əˋpɪr〕 動　出現，顯露，似乎，看來好像
appearance appear + ance	▶	〔əˋpɪrəns〕 名　出現，露面，演出，外貌，外觀
disappear dis + appear	▶	〔͵dɪsəˋpɪr〕 動　消失，不見，突然離開
disappearance disappear + ance	▶	〔͵dɪsəˋpɪrəns〕 名　消失，失蹤

The moon appeared between the clouds.
從雲縫中可看見月亮。

He made a brief appearance at the party, but then went home.
他在派對上短暫露個臉，但之後就回家了。

apparent ap + par + ent	▶	〔əˋpærənt〕 形　表面的，外觀的，明顯的，顯而易見的
apparently apparent + ly	▶	〔əˋpærəntlɪ〕 副　顯然地，表面上，似乎

Joe thinks there is a ghost in his house, because dishes keep
falling off the shelves for no apparent reason.
喬認為他家裡鬧鬼，因為盤子常會無緣無故地從架子上掉下來。

I thought it was going to rain today, but apparently, I was mistaken.
我以為今天會下雨，但是看來我錯了。

transparent trans + par + ent	▶ 〔træns`pɛrənt〕 形	透明的，清澈的，顯而易見的， 一目了然的
transparency transparent + cy	▶ 〔træns`pɛrənsɪ〕 名	透明，透明度，透明的東西

Her skin was so white it was almost transparent.
她的皮膚好白，白到近乎透明。

 fare　旅行　
272

fare	▶ 〔fɛr〕 名	（交通工具的）票價，費用
farewell fare + well	▶ 〔`fɛr`wɛl〕 感 名	再會！別了！ 告別，送別會
welfare well + fare	▶ 〔`wɛl.fɛr〕 名	福利，健康安樂，福利事業， 社會救濟（制度）

Be sure to have the fare ready when you board the train.
上火車的時候，別忘記將車資準備好。

After losing his job, Herman was on welfare for three months.
失業以後，赫爾曼靠救濟金過了三個月。

 sacr　神聖的　
273

sacred sacr + ed	▶ 〔`sekrɪd〕 形	神的，宗教（性）的，神聖的
sacrifice sacr + ice	▶ 〔`sækrə.faɪs〕 名 動	祭品，獻祭，犧牲，犧牲的行為 犧牲，獻出，虧本出售

If you want to study hard and do a good job, it is necessary to sacrifice a lot of your free time for a while.
如果你想要認真念書並且獲得好成績，暫時犧牲自己大量的空閒時間是必要的。

 274 **sci**　知道，理解　

---

science
sci + ence
▶　〔`saɪəns〕 名　科學，自然科學，（一門）科學

conscience
con + science
▶　〔`kanʃəns〕 名　良心，道義心，善惡觀念

conscientious
conscience + ous
▶　〔͵kanʃɪˋɛnʃəs〕 形　憑良心的，誠實的，認真的

Don had a perfect opportunity to cheat on his history exam, but his conscience wouldn't let him.
唐有個大好機會能在考歷史時作弊，但是他的良心不容許他這麼做。

conscious
con + sci + ous
▶　〔`kanʃəs〕 形　神志清醒的，有知覺的，意識到的
be conscious of～「意識到～」

consciously
conscious + ly
▶　〔`kanʃəslɪ〕 副　有意識地，自覺地

consciousness
conscious + ness
▶　〔`kanʃəsnɪs〕 名　有知覺，清醒，
（個人或群體的）意識

unconscious
un + conscious
▶　〔ʌnˋkanʃəs〕 形　失去知覺的，不知道的，
無意識的

unconsciously
unconscious + ly
▶　〔ʌnˋkanʃəslɪ〕 副　未意識到地，無意識地，
失去知覺地

unconsciousness
unconscious + ness
▶　〔ʌnˋkanʃəsnɪs〕 名　無意識，失去知覺，神志不清

Although I couldn't see anyone, I was conscious that I was not the only one in the room.
雖然我看不見任何人，但是我很清楚知道房間裡不只我一個人。

 275 nur(t) nutr nour 養育
275

nurse nur + se	▶	〔nɜs〕 名 護士 動 看護，護理，照料
nursery nurse + ry	▶	〔ˋnɜsərɪ〕 名 幼兒室，育兒室，托兒所

All the children in the nursery were sleeping, for the moment.
那時候托兒所裡面的小孩子全部都在睡覺。

nurture nurt + ure	▶	〔ˋnɜtʃə〕 名 營養物，養育，培育 動 養育，教養
nutrition nutr + tion	▶	〔njuˋtrɪʃən〕 名 營養，滋養，營養物，營養學
nutritious nutrition + ous	▶	〔njuˋtrɪʃəs〕 形 有營養的，滋養的

An avocado may be slightly high in calories, but it is very nutritious.
酪梨的熱量可能有點偏高，但是營養非常豐富。

nourish nour + ish	▶	〔ˋnɜɪʃ〕 動 養育，滋養，培育
nourishment nourish + ment	▶	〔ˋnɜɪʃmənt〕 名 食物，營養品，養育，滋養

She always tried to nourish a sense of creativity in the children in her class.
她總是努力替她班上的孩子們培養創造力。

 276 hum(il) 低
276

humble hum + ble	▶	〔ˋhʌmbl̩〕 形 謙遜的，謙恭的，低下的，卑微的

humbly
humble + ly

▶ 〔ˋhʌmblɪ〕 副　謙遜地，恭順地，卑微地

humbleness
humble + ness

▶ 〔ˋhʌmb!nɪs〕 名　謙遜，卑微

humiliate
humil + ate

▶ 〔hjuˋmɪlɪˏet〕 動　使蒙受恥辱，羞辱，使丟臉

humiliation
humiliate + ion

▶ 〔hjuˏmɪlɪˋeʃən〕 名　丟臉，羞辱，蒙羞

When asked about her recent rise to fame, the actress humbly replied that she had been very lucky.
當被問到最近名聲高漲的事時，女演員謙虛地回答說她只是幸運而已。

---

277 # strain　strict　stress　stretch　緊拉，綁緊
277

---

strain

▶ 〔stren〕 動　緊拉，緊拖，盡力，使勁

Both teams strained and pulled until finally the rope broke.
雙方隊伍使勁拉扯，直到最後繩子斷掉為止。

restrain
re + strain

▶ 〔rɪˋstren〕 動　抑制，控制，限制，阻止

restraint
restrain + t

▶ 〔rɪˋstrent〕 名　克制，阻止，限制

Melinda restrained herself from asking, "Why do you still wear the same clothes you wore 20 years ago?"
瑪琳達克制自己不去問「你為什麼還穿著二十年前穿過的衣服」這個問題。
She gritted her teeth in restraint, and said nothing.
她咬牙忍耐，並且不發一語。

---

strict

▶ 〔strɪkt〕 形　嚴格的，精確的，絕對的，詳細的

strictly
strict + ly

▶ 〔ˋstrɪktlɪ〕 副　嚴厲地，嚴格地，僅僅
strictly speaking「嚴格說來」

strictness
strict + ness

▶ 〔ˋstrɪktnɪs〕 名　嚴格，嚴謹，精確

This rule will be strictly enforced.　這條規定將會嚴格地執行。

restrict re + strict	▶　〔rɪ`strɪkt〕 動　限制，限定，約束
restriction restrict + ion	▶　〔rɪ`strɪkʃən〕 名　限制，約束，限定，限制規定
restrictive restrict + ive	▶　〔rɪ`strɪktɪv〕 形　限制的，約束的

This is a restricted area, and only authorized personnel are allowed in.
這是限制區域，只有經授權的人員才可進入。

stress	▶　〔strɛs〕 名　壓力，緊張，重要性 　　　　動　強調，著重，使緊張
stressful stress + ful	▶　〔`strɛsfəl〕 形　緊張的，壓力重的

We have all been under a great deal of stress lately because we have so many things to do.
最近我們都承受了非常大的壓力，因為我們有太多的事情要處理。

stretch	▶　〔strɛtʃ〕 動　伸直，拉緊，展開，伸縮 　　　　名　伸展，伸長，伸懶腰，伸縮性

I usually have a stretch in the morning as soon as I wake up.
通常早上我一醒來就會伸懶腰。

 count　計算　

count	▶　〔kaʊnt〕 動　計算，數，將…計算在內
countless count + less	▶　〔`kaʊntlɪs〕 形　數不盡的，無數的

Sybil has seen the movie countless times, but never tires of it.
這部電影西碧兒看過無數次了，但是她從未感到厭煩。

account ac + count	▶　〔ə`kaʊnt〕 名　帳目，帳戶，記述，解釋 　　　　動　把…視為，報帳，說明，導致 take~into account「考慮到~」，account for~「說明~」
accountable account + able	▶　〔ə`kaʊntəbl〕 形　（對…）有解釋義務的， 　　　　　　　　　　應負責任的

Adults should be held accountable for their actions.
成年人應該替自己的行為負責。

He has three bank accounts at three different banks.
他在三間銀行分別擁有三個帳戶。

Her account of the story was very different from his.
她對故事的敘述和他的非常不同。

279　bag　budg　袋

bag	▶ 〔bæg〕 名　袋，提袋
baggage bag + age	▶ 〔`bægɪdʒ〕 名　行李
budget budg + et	▶ 〔`bʌdʒɪt〕 名　預算，生活費，經費 動　把…編入預算，按照預算來計劃

The tour group leader budgeted $50 a day for meals for each of the tourists.
旅行團領導人編列預算，每天每位旅客的餐費是50美元。

If you don't budget your time wisely, you may find that you don't have the time to finish the project on time.
如果你不妥善安排時間，你可能會發現時間不夠無法準時完成企劃。

280　flect　flex　彎曲

reflect re + flect	▶ 〔rɪ`flɛkt〕 動　反射，反映，深思，反省
reflection reflect + ion	▶ 〔rɪ`flɛkʃən〕 名　反射，回聲，映像，倒影，反映，容貌酷似的人

The cat growled and hissed at its own reflection in the mirror.
那隻貓對著鏡子裡自己的影像咆哮並發出嘶嘶叫聲。

Students' attitudes in class will be reflected in their grades.
學生的上課態度會反映在成績上。

flexible
flex + ible

▶ 〔`flɛksəbl〕 形　可彎曲的，柔韌的，有彈性的，柔順的，可變通的，靈活的

flexibility
flexible + ity

▶ 〔ˌflɛksə`bɪlətɪ〕 名　易曲性，適應性，靈活性，彈性

Her schedule is quite flexible, but you should give her advanced notice if you want a meeting.
她的時間表頗有彈性，但如果你想要和她會面的話，最好事先給她通知。

 281　plaud　plause　plode　plos　爆發 281

applaud
ap + plaud

▶ 〔ə`plɔd〕 動　向…鼓掌，向…喝采，稱讚，喝采

applause
ap + plause

▶ 〔ə`plɔz〕 名　喝采，稱讚，嘉許

The famous rock group finished their last encore to deafening applause.
那個有名的搖滾樂團在震耳欲聾的喝采聲中結束他們最後一首安可曲。

explode
ex + plode

▶ 〔ɪk`splod〕 動　爆炸，爆破，爆發，突發，激增

explosive
explode + ive

▶ 〔ɪk`splosɪv〕 形　爆炸性的，爆發性的，暴躁的

explosion
explode + ion

▶ 〔ɪk`sploʒən〕 名　爆發，爆炸，炸裂，劇增，劇變

My head is about to explode from thinking too much.
我思考太多，頭快要爆炸了。

 282　astro　aster　星星 282

astronomy
astro + nomy

▶ 〔əs`trɑnəmɪ〕 名　天文學

astronaut
astro + naut

▶ 〔`æstrəˌnɔt〕 名　太空人

asterisk
aster + isk

▶ 〔`æstəˌrɪsk〕 名　星號，星狀物

disaster
dis + aster

▶ 〔dɪ`zæstə〕 名　災害，災難，不幸

Natural disasters like floods and earthquakes claim thousands of lives each year.
洪水和地震等自然災害每年奪走數千條人命。

283　tain　ten　tinu(e)　tin　保有，持有　⭐283

contain
con + tain

▶ 〔kən`ten〕 動　包含，容納，相當於

container
contain + er

▶ 〔kən`tenə〕 名　容器

Common table salt contains sodium and chlorine.
一般的調味鹽含有鈉和氯。

attain
at + tain

▶ 〔ə`ten〕 動　達到，獲得，到達

attainment
attain + ment

▶ 〔ə`tenmənt〕 名　達到，獲得，到達，成就，學識，才能

Sue attained her PhD after five years of hard work and dedication.
蘇在用功苦讀專心致力於學業的五年後，終於獲得博士學位。

obtain
ob + tain

▶ 〔əb`ten〕 動　得到，獲得，得到公認，通用，存在

obtainable
obtain + able

▶ 〔əb`tenəbl〕 形　能得到的

Were you able to obtain a visa to visit the States?
你拿得到美國的短期簽證嗎？

retain
re + tain

▶ 〔rɪ`ten〕 動　保留，保持，留住

retainable
retain + able
▶　〔rɪˋtenəbl〕形　能保持的，可保留的

The president retains the right to exercise veto power over any law passed by congress.
總統有權針對任何國會通過的法律行使否決權。

sustain
sus + tain
▶　〔səˋsten〕動　支撐，承受，維持，支援，支持，遭受

sustainable
sustain + able
▶　〔səˋstenəbl〕形　支撐得住的，能保持的，能維持的

She sustained some serious injuries in the plane crash, but she will be able to recover completely.
她在飛機失事中受了很重的傷，但是她會完全復元的。

continue
con + tinue
▶　〔kənˋtɪnjʊ〕動　繼續，持續

continual
continue + al
▶　〔kənˋtɪnjʊəl〕形　多次重複的，頻頻的，連續的

continuous
continue + ous
▶　〔kənˋtɪnjʊəs〕形　連續的，不斷的

continuation
continue + tion
▶　〔kənˌtɪnjʊˋeʃən〕名　（間斷後的）再開始，繼續不斷，延續，續編

This TV program is a continuation of one from last season, so I don't know what's going on.
這個電視節目是上一季節目的延續，所以我不知道現在是什麼狀況。

continent
con + tin + ent
▶　〔ˋkantənənt〕名　大陸，陸地，大洲

continental
continent + al
▶　〔ˌkantəˋnɛntl〕形　洲的，大陸的，歐洲大陸的，大陸性的

Sometimes hotels will serve a complimentary continental breakfast.
有些旅館會附贈歐式早餐。

284 vag 不穩定的
284

vague
vag + ue

▶ 〔veg〕形　模糊不清的，朦朧的，不明確的

vagueness
vague + ness

▶ 〔`vegnɪs〕名　含糊，茫然

The instructions for this computer are very vague, and hard to understand.
這台電腦的操作指示非常含糊，而且很難懂。

extravagant
extra + vag + ant

▶ 〔ɪk`strævəgənt〕形　奢侈的，浪費的，過度的

extravagance
extravagant + ce

▶ 〔ɪk`strævəgəns〕名　奢侈，浪費，無節制，奢侈品

I can't afford the extravagance of eating out every night of the week.
我負擔不起每個禮拜每天晚上都外出用餐的奢侈浪費。

 285 trem 發抖，震動
285

tremble
trem + ble

▶ 〔`trɛmbl〕動　發抖，震顫，搖晃，搖動

tremendous
trem + endous

▶ 〔trɪ`mɛndəs〕形　巨大的，極大的，極度的，驚人的，很棒的

tremendously
tremendous + ly

▶ 〔trɪ`mɛndəslɪ〕副　極大地，極端地，非常

The child's lips started to tremble, and then she started to cry.
孩子的嘴唇開始顫抖，接著她放聲大哭。

We have already spent a tremendous amount of time on this, I don't think we can afford to spend any more.
我們已經花了很多時間在這上頭，我不認為我們有足夠的時間繼續下去。

286 min 突出

eminent e + min + ent	▶ 〔ˋɛmənənt〕 [形] 出眾的，卓越的，明顯的
eminence eminent + ce	▶ 〔ˋɛmənəns〕 [名] 卓越，顯赫，著名

The scientist was eminent in her field for years, but she finally won the Nobel Prize this year.
那位科學家在她的研究領域聞名多年，但是她直到今年才獲頒諾貝爾獎。

prominent pro + min + ent	▶ 〔ˋprɑmənənt〕 [形] 突起的，突出的，顯著的， 卓越的，重要的
prominently prominent + ly	▶ 〔ˋprɑmənəntlɪ〕 [副] 顯著地，重要地
prominence prominent + ce	▶ 〔ˋprɑmənəns〕 [名] 突起，引人注目的事物， 傑出，卓越，聲望

The doctor's medical diplomas were prominently displayed in the waiting area of the clinic.
那位醫生的醫學執照顯眼地展示在診所的候診區內。

More prominence should be given to the increasing social problems of today's youth.
應該要更加重視現在年輕人與日俱增的社會問題。

 287 trace track 貫穿

trace	▶ 〔tres〕 [名] 痕跡，遺跡 [動] 追蹤，查出，追溯
traceable trace + able	▶ 〔ˋtresəbl̩〕 [形] 可追蹤的，起源於…的

It was not possible to trace the footsteps of the criminal.
追蹤犯人的足跡是不可能的。

This call is not traceable, so you can say whatever you like.
這通電話無法追蹤來源，所以你可以放心說想說的話。

track	▶	〔træk〕名 行蹤，軌道，足跡，小徑
trackless track + less	▶	〔`træklıs〕形 無蹤跡的，無軌道的，無人跡的， 無路的

He went out one winter morning to find deer tracks in the snow in his garden.
他某個冬天早晨外出，發現他院子裡的積雪上有鹿的足跡。

 spir(e)　呼吸

288

spirit spir + it	▶	〔`spırıt〕名 精神，心靈，靈魂
spiritual spirit + ual	▶	〔`spırıtʃuəl〕形 精神（上）的，心靈的，宗教的， 超自然的

Some people believe that your spirit leaves your body when you die.
有些人相信，人死亡的時候靈魂會離開身體。

inspire inv + spire	▶	〔ın`spaır〕動 鼓舞，激勵，賦予…靈感 inspire（人）to V「鼓舞（人）～，給予（人）～ 的靈感」
inspiration inspire + tion	▶	〔ˌınspə`reʃən〕名 靈感，鼓舞人心的人（或事物）

The sun shining on the sparkling snow inspired him to write a poem.
太陽照在發亮的雪上給了他寫詩的靈感。

aspire a + spire	▶	〔ə`spaır〕動 熱望，嚮往，懷有大志 aspire to V「渴求～」
aspiration aspire + tion	▶	〔ˌæspə`reʃən〕名 熱望，志向，抱負， 渴望達到的目的

He aspired to be as successful as his father.
他渴望像他的父親一樣成功。

289 **us(e)** **ut** 使用，利用
289

use	▶ 〔juz〕 動 使用，發揮，行使，耗費
useful use + ful	▶ 〔ˋjusfəl〕 形 有用的，有益的，有幫助的
usefulness useful + ness	▶ 〔ˋjusfəlnɪs〕 名 有用，有益，有效
useless use + less	▶ 〔ˋjuslɪs〕 形 無用的，無價值的，無效的，無益的
usage use + age	▶ 〔ˋjusɪdʒ〕 名 使用，用法，處理

A computer purchased even a few years ago is essentially useless if you want to keep up with all the new technology.
如果你想要跟得上所有的新科技，幾年前才買的電腦基本上已經是毫無用處。

utilize ut + ilize	▶ 〔ˋjutḷͺaɪz〕 動 利用
utilization utilize + tion	▶ 〔ͺjutḷəˋzeʃən〕 名 利用，使用
utility ut + ility	▶ 〔juˋtɪlətɪ〕 名 效用，實用 形 有多種用途的，通用的，實用的

It is the responsibility of each generation to utilize natural resources carefully and responsibly.
小心負責地善用自然資源是每一代人的責任。

 290 **techn(o)** **tect** 技術，技藝
290

technology techno + logy	▶ 〔tɛkˋnɑlədʒɪ〕 名 工藝學，工藝，技術

technological
technology + ical

▶ 〔tɛknəˋlɑdʒɪkl̩〕形　技術（學）的，工藝（學）的

Modern technology these days means that you can be in touch with friends from around the world at the click of a button.
最近的現代科技指的是你按下按鈕就能和全球各地的朋友聯絡。

technique
techn + ique

▶ 〔tɛkˋnik〕名　技巧，技術，技法

technical
techn + ical

▶ 〔ˋtɛknɪkl̩〕形　工藝的，技術的，科技的，技術性的

His technique as a musician is unparalleled, but his playing lacks passion.
他身為音樂家的技巧是無人能比，但是他的演奏缺乏熱情。

architect
archi + tect

▶ 〔ˋɑrkəˌtɛkt〕名　建築師

architecture
architect + ure

▶ 〔ˋɑrkəˌtɛktʃə〕名　建築學，建築風格，建築物

architectural
architecture + al

▶ 〔ˌɑrkəˋtɛktʃərəl〕形　建築學的，有關建築的

Frank Lloyd Wright is a famous architect who had a great affinity for Japan.
法蘭克洛伊萊特一位非常親日的建築家。

 291 **trib(e)**　分配，給予

tribe

▶ 〔traɪb〕名　部落，種族

tribal
tribe + al

▶ 〔ˋtraɪbl̩〕形　部落的，種族的

There are many different types of African tribe.
非洲部落有很多不同的類型。

distribute
dis + trib + ute

▶ 〔dɪˋstrɪbjut〕動　分發，分配，散佈，分佈

distribution
distribute + ion

▶ 〔ˌdɪstrəˋbjuʃən〕名　分發，分配，配給物，分佈，（生物的）分佈區域

A "Bell Curve" depicts a normal distribution.
「鐘型曲線」表示一般正常的分佈區域。

contribute con + trib + ute ▶	〔kənˋtrɪbjut〕 動　捐（款），捐獻，貢獻，投（稿） contribute to～「捐助～，促成～，為～寫稿」
contribution contribute + ion ▶	〔͵kɑntrəˋbjuʃən〕 名　貢獻，捐獻，捐助，投稿， 捐獻的物品（或錢）

When he inherited the money, he made a large contribution to charity.
他繼承那筆財產時，捐了很多錢做慈善事業。

attribute at + trib + ute ▶	〔əˋtrɪbjut〕 動　把…歸因於，認為…是某人所有， 認為…是某人所做 attribute～to...「把～歸因於…，認為～是…所 有，認為～是…所做」

The writer attributes her success to supportive friends and family.
那位作家把她的成功歸功於支持她的朋友和家人。

 ## 292　tect　覆蓋
292

detect de + tect ▶	〔dɪˋtɛkt〕 動　發現，察覺，查出，看穿
detective detect + ive ▶	〔dɪˋtɛktɪv〕 形　偵探的，偵查的，探測用的 名　偵探，私家偵探
detection detect + ion ▶	〔dɪˋtɛkʃən〕 名　發現，發覺，探知
detector detect + or ▶	〔dɪˋtɛktɚ〕 名　發現者，發覺者，探測器，檢驗器

A Geiger counter detects radioactivity.
蓋氏計算器能探測放射線。

protect pro + tect ▶	〔prəˋtɛkt〕 動　保護，防護，為…保險
protective protect + ive ▶	〔prəˋtɛktɪv〕 形　保護的，防護的
protector protect + or ▶	〔prəˋtɛktɚ〕 名　保護者，防禦者，保護裝置， 保護器

protection
protect + ion

▶ 〔prə`tɛkʃən〕 名 保護，防護，警戒，防護物

When working with these chemicals, you should wear protective gloves and goggles.
使用這些化學藥品時，你應該要戴上防護手套和護目鏡。

 293 **quir(e) quis quest quer 要求**
293

acquire
ac + quire

▶ 〔ə`kwaɪr〕 動 取得，獲得，學到，養成

acquisition
ac + quis + tion

▶ 〔͵ækwə`zɪʃən〕 名 獲得，取得，獲得物，增添的人（或物）

He was very proud of his latest acquisition, a valuable antique vase which he bought at a flea market for five hundred yen.
他很自豪他最新的戰利品，就是一只花了五百日圓在跳蚤市場買到的貴重古董花瓶。

inquire
in + quire

▶ 〔ɪn`kwaɪr〕 動 詢問，查問，調查
inquire（人・組織）of～「調查（人・組織）關於～的事」
inquire about～「調查～，詢問～」
inquire（人・組織）as to～「向（人・組織）詢問關於～的事」

inquiry
inquire + y

▶ 〔ɪn`kwaɪrɪ〕 名 詢問，打聽，調查，探究，疑問

The investigator made some inquiries, and found out that Jane Smith had moved away three years ago.
那位調查員展開調查，發現珍・史密斯三年前就已經搬走了。

require
re + quire

▶ 〔rɪ`kwaɪr〕 動 需要，要求，命令

requirement
require + ment

▶ 〔rɪ`kwaɪrmənt〕 名 需要，必需品，要求，必要條件，規定

One of the requirements for the "Iron Man" contest is swimming 4.5 miles.
「鐵人」比賽的條件之一就是必須游泳4.5英里。

quest

▶ 〔kwɛst〕 名　尋找，追求，探索

The knights of King Arthur's round table went on a quest for the Holy Grail.
亞瑟王的圓桌武士繼續追尋聖杯。

conquer
con + quer

▶ 〔`kɑŋkɚ〕 動　攻取，戰勝，克服，征服

conquest
con + quest

▶ 〔`kɑŋkwɛst〕 名　征服，克服，佔領

Napoleon wanted to conquer all of Europe.
拿破崙想要征服全歐洲。

request
re + quest

▶ 〔rɪ`kwɛst〕 名　要求，請求，請求的事
　　　　　　　 動　要求，請求

If you have any special requests for meals, please let the cook know at least a day in advance.
如果你對餐點有任何特別要求，請至少在一天前就預先告知廚師。

 sur(e)　安全

294

sure

▶ 〔ʃʊr〕 形　確信的，有把握的，一定的，確實的

ensure
en + sure

▶ 〔ɪn`ʃʊr〕 動　保證，擔保，使安全，保護

To ensure your safety, be sure to fasten your seatbelt properly.
為了確保你的安全，請務必正確地繫好安全帶。

insure
in + sure

▶ 〔ɪn`ʃʊr〕 動　為⋯投保，接受保險

insurance
insure + ance

▶ 〔ɪn`ʃʊrəns〕 名　保險，保險契約，保險業

It's a good idea to insure your car against hail damage.
為了預防遭到冰雹毀損，幫你的車子保險是個好主意。

assure
as + sure

▶ 〔ə`ʃʊr〕 動　向⋯保證，使確信，使放心，確保

assurance
assure + ance

▶ 〔əˋʃʊrəns〕 名　保證，表示保證的話，把握，信心

The flight attendant assured the passengers that the turbulence was normal and nothing to worry about.
空服員向旅客保證亂流是正常的，不用擔心。

 295 ## vot(e)　誓約 295

vote	〔vot〕 名　選舉，投票，表決，選票 　　　　動　投票，表決，選舉 vote on～「針對～投票」 vote for（人）「投票給（人）」
devote de + vote	〔dɪˋvot〕 動　將…奉獻（給），把…專用（於） devote～to...「將～奉獻給…」 be devoted to～「專心致力於～，深愛～」
devotion devote + ion	〔dɪˋvoʃən〕 名　奉獻，摯愛，熱愛，虔誠

He is devoted to his son.
他深愛他的兒子。

 296 ## suade　suas　勸告，忠告 296

persuade per + suade	〔pɚˋswed〕 動　說服，勸服，使某人相信，被說服 persuade（人）to V「說服（人）～」
persuasion persuade + ion	〔pɚˋsweʒən〕 名　說服，勸說，說服力

If you can persuade your parents to let you go, your Auntie Meg and I will take you to Disneyland.
如果你能說服你爸媽，你梅格阿姨和我就帶你去迪士尼樂園。

dissuade dis + suade	〔dɪˋswed〕 動　勸（某人）勿做某事，勸阻 dissuade（人）to V「勸（人）不要～」

dissuasion
dissuade + ion

▶ 〔dɪˋsweʒən〕 名 勸阻，規勸

She was determined to be a stuntwoman, and although her friends told her it could be dangerous, she would not be dissuaded.
她決心要成為一個特技演員，儘管她的朋友告訴她那可能很危險，但是她不聽勸。

 297　scend　scent　攀登，登上
297

ascend
a + scend

▶ 〔əˋsɛnd〕 動 登高，上升，攀登，登上

ascent
a + scent

▶ 〔əˋsɛnt〕 名 上升，登高，（身分、地位等的）提高，提升，上坡

She ascended the staircase slowly and very quietly, knowing that if her parents woke up she would be in big trouble.
她緩慢且非常安靜地爬上樓梯，因為她知道如果她的父母醒來，她會有大麻煩。

descend
de + scend

▶ 〔dɪˋsɛnd〕 動 下降，下傾

descent
de + scent

▶ 〔dɪˋsɛnt〕 名 下降，下坡，血統，衰落

The passengers were thrown into panic when the plane suddenly started a rapid descent.
當飛機突然急速下降時，乘客們陷入了恐慌。

 298　vol(ve)　轉彎，迴轉
298

involve
in + volve

▶ 〔ɪnˋvɑlv〕 動 使捲入，牽涉，包含，使專注，使忙於
be involved in～「涉入～，專注於～」

involvement
involve + ment

▶ 〔ɪnˋvɑlvmənt〕 名 纏繞，牽連

Alice was given an award of recognition for her involvement in the 'clean-the-streets' project.
艾莉絲由於參與「街頭清掃」計劃而獲得表揚。

evolve e + volve	▶	〔ɪˋvɑlv〕 動　發展，展開，進化，成長
evolution evolve + tion	▶	〔ˌɛvəˋluʃən〕 名　發展，進展，（生物的）進化，進化論

The species has evolved through thousands of years of natural selection.
物種在數千年以來的天擇下逐漸進化。

revolve re + volve	▶	〔rɪˋvɑlv〕 動　旋轉，沿軌道轉，循環往復 a revolving door「旋轉門」
revolution revolve + tion	▶	〔ˌrɛvəˋluʃən〕 名　革命，革命性劇變，公轉，旋轉，循環
revolutionary revolution + ary	▶	〔ˌrɛvəˋluʃənˌɛrɪ〕 形　革命的，革命性的，完全創新的，旋轉的

This revolutionary new product will change the way people brush their teeth!
這項革命性的新產品將會改變人們刷牙的方式！

pain　　pent　　疼痛　

pain	▶	〔pen〕 名　痛，疼痛，痛苦，辛苦，討厭的人（或事）
painful pain + ful	▶	〔ˋpenfəl〕 形　疼痛的，痛苦的
painless pain + less	▶	〔ˋpenlɪs〕 形　不痛的，容易的

I thought that having my wisdom teeth pulled would be very painful, but it wasn't too bad.
我以為拔智齒會很痛，但其實沒有那麼嚴重。

repent re + pent	▶	〔rɪˋpɛnt〕 動　悔悟，悔改，後悔，懊悔
repentance repent + ance	▶	〔rɪˋpɛntəns〕 名　悔改，懺悔

The jury was not sympathetic to the defendant, because he seemed to show no repentance for what he had done.
陪審團並不同情被告，因為他對自己所做的事似乎沒有悔改之意。

 300 **school** **schol** **學校**
300

school	▶ 〔skul〕 名 學校，上學，學業
scholar school + ar	▶ 〔`skɑlə〕 名 學者，人文學者，古典學者
scholarship scholar + ship	▶ 〔`skɑlə.ʃɪp〕 名 學問，學識，學術成就，獎學金

Elizabeth won a scholarship to Harvard.
伊莉莎白獲得去哈佛唸書的獎學金。

301 **par(e)** **pair** **peer** **相等**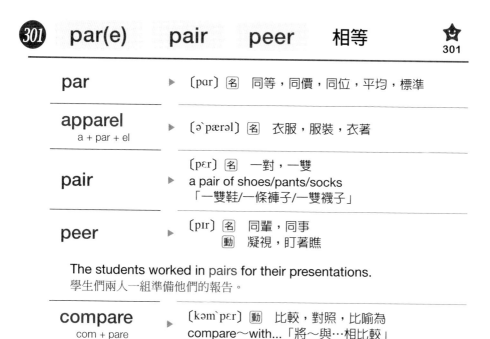
301

par	▶ 〔pɑr〕 名 同等，同價，同位，平均，標準
apparel a + par + el	▶ 〔ə`pærəl〕 名 衣服，服裝，衣著
pair	▶ 〔pɛr〕 名 一對，一雙 a pair of shoes/pants/socks 「一雙鞋/一條褲子/一雙襪子」
peer	▶ 〔pɪr〕 名 同輩，同事 動 凝視，盯著瞧

The students worked in pairs for their presentations.
學生們兩人一組準備他們的報告。

| **compare**
com + pare | ▶ 〔kəm`pɛr〕 動 比較，對照，比喻為
compare～with...「將～與…相比較」 |

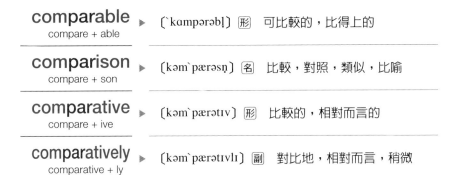

comparable
compare + able

▶ 〔ˋkɑmpərəbḷ〕 厖　可比較的，比得上的

---

comparison
compare + son

▶ 〔kəmˋpærəsṇ〕 匌　比較，對照，類似，比喻

---

comparative
compare + ive

▶ 〔kəmˋpærətɪv〕 厖　比較的，相對而言的

---

comparatively
comparative + ly

▶ 〔kəmˋpærətɪvlɪ〕 副　對比地，相對而言，稍微

Before you make a purchase, it's a good idea to compare a lot of similar products to find the one that most suits your needs.
在你買東西前，最好先比較眾多類似產品，以找到最符合需求的產品。

第 2 章

單字加字首字尾

⭐ 302

abandon ▶ 〔əˋbændən〕動　丟棄，拋棄，遺棄，放棄

abandonment
abandon + ment
▶ 〔əˋbændənmənt〕名　放棄，遺棄，放任

What had once been a thriving village is now nothing but a lot of abandoned buildings.
過去曾繁榮一時的村莊，現在卻只剩下一堆廢棄的建築。

abolish ▶ 〔əˋbɑlɪʃ〕動　廢除，廢止，徹底破壞

abolishment
abolish + ment
▶ 〔əˋbɑlɪʃmənt〕名　廢除，廢止

abolition
abolish + tion
▶ 〔͵æbəˋlɪʃən〕名　廢除，廢止，消滅

The protestors were speaking out for the abolishment of the death penalty.
抗議者正為了廢除死刑而發聲。

abrupt ▶ 〔əˋbrʌptʃ〕形　突然的，意外的，唐突的

abruptly
abrupt + ly
▶ 〔əˋbrʌptlɪ〕副　突然地，意外地，唐突地

The fireworks display in the harbor came to an abrupt end when the boats caught fire.
海港內施放的煙火在船隻著火後突然結束。

absorb ▶ 〔əbˋsɔrb〕動　吸收，汲取，理解（知識等），
　　　　　　　使全神貫注
be absorbed in～「全神貫注於～」

absorption
absorb + tion
▶ 〔əbˋsɔrpʃən〕名　吸收，吸收過程，全神貫注，
　　　　　　　專心致志

He was so absorbed in his studies that he didn't hear the phone ring.
因為他非常專注於課業上，所以沒有聽到電話響起。

absurd ▶ 〔əbˋsɜd〕形　不合理的，荒謬的，可笑的，愚蠢的

absurdity
absurd + ity
▶ 〔əbˋsɜdətɪ〕名　荒謬，荒誕，荒謬的言行

The idea of keeping an elephant for a pet in Tokyo is completely absurd.
在東京養頭大象當寵物的想法根本是荒謬至極。

accumulate ▶ 〔əˋkjumə͵let〕動　累積，積聚，積成堆

accumulation
accumulate + ion
▶ 〔ə͵kjumjəˋleʃən〕名　積累，積聚，堆積，累積物

Under a heavy blanket of dust that had been accumulating for 30 years, was a beautiful grand piano.
在累積了30年的厚重灰塵之下，是一架美麗的大鋼琴。

| acquaint | ▶ | [əˋkwent] 動　使認識，介紹，使了解，使熟悉
acquaint（人）with～「使（人）了解～」
acquaint myself with～「使自己熟悉～」 |
| acquaintance
acquaint + ance | ▶ | [əˋwkentəns] 名　（與人）相識，了解，相識的人 |

Once you become acquainted with the system, it won't be so confusing.
一旦你習慣了系統，就不會這麼混亂了。

actual	▶	[ˋæktʃuəl] 形　實際的，事實上的，現實的
actuality actual + ity	▶	[͵æktʃuˋælətɪ] 名　現實，現實性，事實
actually actual + ly	▶	[ˋæktʃuəlɪ] 副　實際上，真的，竟然

Objects in car mirrors may appear smaller than their actual size.
映在車子後照鏡上的物體看起來可能比實際的尺寸還要小。

303

add	▶	[æd] 動　添加，增加，將…相加
additive add + tive	▶	[ˋædətɪv] 形　附加的 名　添加劑，添加物
addition add + tion	▶	[əˋdɪʃən] 名　加，附加
additional addition + al	▶	[əˋdɪʃənl] 形　添加的，附加的，額外的

She only eats food that have no additives.
她只吃不含食品添加物的食物。

adhere ad + here	▶	[ədˋhɪr] 動　黏附，遵守，堅持，追隨，依附 adhere to～「黏附在～上，遵守～」
adherence adhere + ence	▶	[ədˋhɪrəns] 名　堅持，嚴守，固執，依附，黏附
adhesive adhere + ive	▶	[ədˋhisɪv] 形　黏的，黏著的，有黏性的 名　黏著劑 be adhesive to～「堅持～，黏著～」

He used a cheap adhesive to hang the mirror on the wall, and in the middle of the night, it came crashing down.
他用便宜的黏著劑把鏡子黏在牆上，但到了半夜，鏡子掉下來摔碎了。

If you don't adhere to the rules, you may find your life difficult.
如果你不遵守規則，日子或許會過得很艱難。

aesthetic	▶ 〔ɛsˋθɛtɪk〕 形 美學的，美的，藝術的，審美的
aesthetical aesthetic + al	▶ 〔ɛsˋθɛtɪkḷ〕 形 美學的
aesthetically aesthetical + ly	▶ 〔ɛsˋθɛtɪklɪ〕 副 審美地，美學觀點上地
aesthetics aesthetic + ics	▶ 〔ɛsˋθɛtɪks〕 名 美學，美的哲學

The design of the apartment building is aesthetically appealing, but it is not very practical.
這棟公寓的設計就美學觀點上來說很吸引人，但是並不實用。

afford	▶ 〔əˋford〕 動 買得起，有足夠的…（去做…）
affordable afford + able	▶ 〔əˋfordəbḷ〕 形 負擔得起的

Lana was worried about finding affordable housing in a safe neighborhood.
拉娜擔心無法在治安良好的社區找到一間負擔得起的房子。

agony	▶ 〔ˋægənɪ〕 名 極度痛苦，苦惱，臨死的痛苦
agonize agony + ize	▶ 〔ˋægəˌnaɪz〕 動 感到極度痛苦，十分煩惱，掙扎 agonize over～「對～感到痛苦（或苦惱）」

After agonizing over it for all of three minutes, Hank decided to go to the party instead of finishing his report.
在煩惱整整3分鐘後，漢克決定去參加派對而放棄完成他的報告。

agriculture	▶ 〔ˋægrɪˌkʌltʃə〕 名 農業，農耕，農藝，農學
agricultural agriculture + al	▶ 〔ˌægrɪˋkʌltʃərəl〕 形 農業的，務農的，農用的

Agriculture is the main industry in that area of the country.
農業是該國那個地區的主要產業。

☆
304

aim

〔em〕 動 瞄準，對準
名 瞄準，瞄準的方向，目標，目的
▶ aim（槍・言辭）at～「把（槍・言辭）瞄準（或針
對）～」
aim at～「瞄準～」

aimless
aim + less

▶ 〔`emlɪs〕 形 沒目標的，無目的的

aimlessly
aimless + ly

▶ 〔`emlɪslɪ〕 副 漫無目的地，無目標地

Having a clear picture of your aims and goals is the first step in achieving them. 想清楚你的目的和目標是實現它們的第一步。

allow

〔ə`laʊ〕 動 允許，准許，容許
▶ allow（人）to V「允許（人）～」
allow for～「考慮到～」

allowance
allow + ance

▶ 〔ə`laʊəns〕 名 津貼，補貼，零用錢

Allowing for long lines at security checkpoints, Joseph got to the airport four hours before his flight.
考慮到安全檢察站排隊的人龍，約瑟在班機起飛前4個小時就抵達機場。

amaze

▶ 〔ə`mez〕 動 使大為驚奇，使驚愕

amazing
amaze + ing

▶ 〔ə`mezɪŋ〕 形 驚人的，令人吃驚的

eople take e-mail for granted, but it is truly amazing that you can send data to the other side of the world in a matter of seconds.
人們把電子郵件認為是理所當然的事，但能在短短數秒內將資料寄到地球的另一端其實是很驚人的。

ample

▶ 〔`æmpl〕 形 大量的，豐富的，充裕的，足夠的

amplify
ample + ify

▶ 〔`æmplə͵faɪ〕 動 放大（聲音等），擴大，詳述

We'll have ample time to get some breakfast at our layover in Vienna.
我們在維也納短暫停留時會有足夠的時間吃點早餐。

analogue

〔`ænəlɔg〕 名 相似物，類似情況
▶ 形 模擬指針式的，相似物的，類似的
（反義）digital〔`dɪdʒɪtl〕
形 數字的，指狀的

| analogous
analogue + ous | ▶ | 〔ə`næləgəs〕 形 | 類似的，可比擬的 |

| analogy
analogue + y | ▶ | 〔ə`nælədʒɪ〕 名 | 相似，類似，比擬，類推，類比 |

Often an analogy is drawn between learning a language and driving a car.
學語言和學開車常被放在一起作類比。

| analyze | ▶ | 〔`ænḷˌaɪz〕 動 | 分析，對…進行心理分析，解析 |

| analysis
analyze + sis | ▶ | 〔ə`næləsɪs〕 名 | 分析，分解，解析 |

| analytic
analyze + tic | ▶ | 〔ˌænḷ`ɪtɪk〕 形 | 解析的，分析的，善於分析的 |

The data must be analyzed very carefully before any conclusions can be drawn.
在導出結論之前，數據必須要先非常仔細地分析過。

| anarchy | ▶ | 〔`ænəkɪ〕 名 | 無政府狀態，政治混亂，無法無天 |

| anarchist
anarchy + ist | ▶ | 〔`ænəˌkɪst〕 名 | 無政府主義者，煽動叛亂的人 |

When the government fell, the situation fell into political anarchy.
當政府垮台時，局勢陷入無政府混亂狀態。

☆
305

| animate | ▶ | 〔`ænəˌmet〕 動 | 賦予生命，使栩栩如生地動作，
激勵，使活潑，繪製（卡通片） |

| animation
animate + ion | ▶ | 〔ˌænə`meʃən〕 名 | 活潑，熱烈，激勵，興奮，卡通片 |

The animated movies of Hayao Miyazaki are renowned the world over.
宮崎駿的動畫影片聞名全世界。

| anthropology
anthrop + logy | ▶ | 〔ˌænθrə`palədʒɪ〕 名 | 人類學 |

| anthropologist
anthropology + ist | ▶ | 〔ˌænθrə`palədʒɪst〕 名 | 人類學者 |

Some anthropologists think that studying the behavior of apes will give insight into human behavior.
一些人類學者認為研究猿類的行為能幫助了解人類行為。

arctic	▶	〔`ɑrktɪk〕形　北極的，極寒的 名　北極地帶，北極圈
antarctic ant + arctic	▶	〔æn`tɑrktɪk〕形　南極的，南極地區的

Some air moved down from the arctic, causing freezing temperatures for a week.　空氣自北極向下移動，造成了一週以來的低氣溫。

argue	▶	〔`ɑrgju〕動　爭論，辯論，爭吵，主張 argue with（人）about/on/over～「針對～和（人）爭論（或辯論）」
argu**ment** argue + ment	▶	〔`ɑrgjəmənt〕名　爭執，爭吵，辯論，理由，論點

Barbara and Sam always argue over who will take the garbage out.
芭芭拉和山姆總是為了誰該把垃圾拿出去丟而吵架。

rise	▶	〔raɪz〕動　上升，升起，上漲，升高 名　（數量、程度等）增加，上升，興盛，提升
arise a + rise	▶	〔ə`raɪz〕動　升起，上升，產生，出現，形成

If any problems arise, be sure to consult your doctor immediately.
如果有任何問題，請務必馬上去看醫生。

arrogant	▶	〔`ærəgənt〕形　傲慢的，自大的，自負的
arrogan**ce** arrogant + ce	▶	〔`ærəgəns〕名　傲慢，自大，自負

Generally, he's a nice man, but sometimes his arrogance is a little trying.
整體上來說，他是個不錯的人，但是有時候他的傲慢有點討人厭。

shame	▶	〔ʃem〕名　羞恥心，恥辱，帶來恥辱的人（或事），憾事 Shame on you！「你真丟臉！」
asham**ed** a + shame + ed	▶	〔ə`ʃemd〕形　羞愧的，感到難為情的，恥於…的 be ashamed of～「因為～而感到羞恥」
shame**ful** shame + ful	▶	〔`ʃemfəl〕形　可恥的，丟臉的
shame**less** shame + less	▶	〔`ʃemlɪs〕形　無恥的，不要臉的，傷風敗俗的

"Shame on you, " said the little boy's mother when she found out he had told a lie.
當小男孩的母親發現他說謊時，她責備說：「你真丟臉。」

I was ashamed when my favorite teacher caught me cheating on a test.
我最喜歡的老師抓到我考試作弊時，我感到非常羞愧。

⭐ 306

assume	▶ 〔ə`sjum〕 動	以為，假定為，（想當然地）認為
assumption assume + tion	▶ 〔ə`sʌmpʃən〕 名	假定，設想
assumptive assume + ive	▶ 〔ə`sʌmptɪv〕 形	假設的，傲慢的

It can be dangerous to assume you know what other people are thinking.
以為自己知道別人在想什麼可能會很危險。

athlete	▶ 〔`æθlit〕 名	運動員，體育家
athletic athlete + ic	▶ 〔æθ`lɛtɪk〕 形	運動的，體育的，運動員的，活躍的

Going to the Olympics is a dream of any aspiring athlete.
參加奧運是每個有抱負的運動員的夢想。

author	▶ 〔`ɔθə〕 名	作者，作家
authorize author + ize	▶ 〔`ɔθə,raɪz〕 動	授權給，全權委託，批准，允許
authority author + ity	▶ 〔ə`θɔrətɪ〕 名	權力，當權者，當局，權威

Only authorized personnel are allowed beyond this point.
只有經過授權的員工能進入此處。

She is the leading authority on rehabilitation of trauma victims.
她是創傷病患康復方面的領導權威。

awe	▶ 〔ɔ〕 動 名	敬畏，畏怯
awesome awe + some	▶ 〔`ɔsəm〕 形	可怕的，有威嚴的，很棒的
awful awe + ful	▶ 〔`ɔful〕 形	可怕的，嚇人的，不舒服的，很糟的

banish ▶ 〔`bænɪʃ〕 動 流放，放逐，消除，排除，開除

banishment
banish + ment ▶ 〔`bænɪʃmənt〕 名 放逐，流放，驅逐，開除，排除

Since he lost his money in the stock market, he has banished all thoughts of retiring early.
由於他在股市賠光了所有的錢，他已經放棄提早退休的想法了。

bare ▶ 〔bɛr〕 形 裸的，光禿禿的，空的

barely
bare + ly ▶ 〔`bɛrlɪ〕 副 僅僅，幾乎沒有，光禿禿地

He was barley able to contain his excitement, and almost told the secret.
他幾乎沒法隱藏他的激動，差點就把祕密說出來了。

bear ▶ 〔bɛr〕 動 支持，承擔，忍受，生（小孩）

bearable
bear + able ▶ 〔`bɛrəblʃ〕 形 能耐的，忍得住的

The unjustified criticism was more than she could bear, so she decided to look for another job.
因為那不合理的批評超過了她所能忍耐的極限，所以她決定找別的工作。

behave ▶ 〔bɪ`hev〕 動 表現，舉止，行為檢點

behavior
behave + or ▶ 〔bɪ`hevjɚ〕 名 行為，舉止，態度

The father scolded his child firmly, "If you don't behave, we will go home immediately."
那位父親鄭重地訓斥他的孩子：「如果你不守規矩，我們馬上就回家。」

307

believe ▶ 〔bɪ`liv〕 動 相信，信任，認為

belief ▶ 〔bɪ`lif〕 名 相信，信任，信賴，信念

enny strongly believed that things would turn out all right in the end.
佩妮堅信事情終將好轉。

belong ▶ 〔bə`lɔŋ〕 動 應被放置（在某處），合適，適用，適宜，屬於
belong to～「屬於～，是～的成員」

belonging
belong + ing

▶ 〔bə`lɔŋɪŋ〕 名 所有物，財物（多為複數）

When you leave the room, be sure to take all your belongings with you.
離開房間的時候，務必將你的個人物品全數帶走。

---

benefit

▶ 〔`bɛnəfɪt〕 名 利益，好處，優勢，津貼，義賣
動 對…有益，有益於，得益，受惠
benefit from～「從～得到利益」

beneficial
benefit + ial

▶ 〔͵bɛnə`fɪʃəl〕 形 有益的，有利的，有幫助的

Every year the Moose Club sponsors a benefit dance for various charities.
每年麋鹿俱樂部都會贊助一場為許多慈善團體募款的義賣舞會。

---

betray

▶ 〔bɪ`tre〕 動 背叛，出賣，對…不忠

betrayal
betray + al

▶ 〔bɪ`treəl〕 名 背叛，密告，洩密

Nancy felt betrayed when she found out her best friend had revealed all her secrets to the whole class.
當南西發現自己最要好的朋友在全班面前說出她的祕密時，她覺得自己被背叛了。

---

bold

▶ 〔bold〕 形 英勇的，無畏的，大膽的，放肆的

boldly
bold + ly

▶ 〔`boldlɪ〕 副 勇敢地，大膽地，放肆地，厚顏地

boldness
bold + ness

▶ 〔`boldnɪs〕 名 勇敢，大膽，冒失，放肆，厚臉皮

Jack boldly climbed to the top of the tower, even though he was afraid of heights.
即使傑克怕高，他還是大膽地爬上塔頂。

---

bore

▶ 〔bor〕 動 使厭煩，煩擾
bore（人）with～「～讓（人）感到厭煩（或無聊）」

boredom
bore + dom

▶ 〔`bordəm〕 名 無聊，厭倦

boring
bore + ing

▶ 〔`borɪŋ〕 形 令人生厭的，乏味的，無聊的

Out of boredom, Kate decided to watch the movie even though she knew she wouldn't like it.
出於無聊，凱特決定要看那部電影，即便她知道自己不會喜歡。

botany botan + y	▶	〔`bɑtənɪ〕 名　植物學
botanic botan + ic	▶	〔bo`tænɪk〕 形　植物的，植物學的
botanical botan + ical	▶	〔bo`tænɪkḷ〕 形　植物學的，植物的，來自植物的

Christchurch, New Zealand is famed for its botanical gardens.
紐西蘭基督城以它的植物園而聞名。

⭐ 308　**bother**	▶	〔`bɑðɚ〕 動　煩擾，使惱怒，擔心，費心，麻煩 bother（oneself）V-ing「特地～（常用於否定句）」
bothersome bother + some	▶	〔`bɑðɚsəm〕 形　令人討厭的，麻煩的

on't bother taking your umbrella, because the wind is so strong, you'll get wet anyway.
不用特地帶雨傘了，因為風那麼大，你還是會弄濕的。

bottom	▶	〔`bɑtəm〕 名　底，底部，下端，遠端，盡頭
bottomless bottom + less	▶	〔`bɑtəmlɪs〕 形　無底的，極深的，深不可測的， 不可理解的，無限的

John ate so much that his grandmother said his stomach was like a bottomless pit.
約翰吃超多，他的祖母說他的胃好像是無底洞一樣。

bound	▶	〔baʊnd〕 形　受束縛的，非做不可的，必然的 名　範圍，界限 be bound for～「（準備）前往～」 be bound to V「一定會～」
boundless bound + less	▶	〔`baʊndlɪs〕 形　無窮的，無限的
boundary bound + ary	▶	〔`baʊndrɪ〕 名　邊界，分界線，範圍

He was bound and determined to lose 10 kilograms by New Year's ay .
他決心一定要在元旦前瘦下10公斤。

brave	▶	〔brev〕 形　勇敢的，英勇的
bravery brave + ry	▶	〔`brevərɪ〕 名　勇敢，勇氣
bravo	▶	〔`brɑ`vo〕 名　喝采聲，暴徒 感　好極了

Sometimes telling the truth is a very brave thing to do.
有時候說真話是非常勇敢的行為。

brief	▶	〔brif〕 形　短暫的，簡略的，簡短的，短距離的， 簡潔的，草率的
briefly brief + ly	▶	〔`briflɪ〕 副　簡潔地，簡短地，簡單地說，短暫地

I met the movie star, but only briefly, so I can't really tell you what kind of a person he is.
我見過那位電影明星，但只有一下子，所以我不能告訴你他是怎麼樣的人。

brilliant	▶	〔`brɪljənt〕 形　光輝的，明亮的，色彩豔麗的， 傑出的，優秀的，輝煌的，出色的
brilliance brilliant + ce	▶	〔`brɪljəns〕 名　光輝，光彩，光耀，宏偉，壯麗， （卓越的）才華，才智

According to the critic, the film was "Brilliant, just brilliant."
根據影評所說的，那部電影「精彩絕倫」。

brute	▶	〔brut〕 名　獸，畜生，人面獸心的人，殘暴的人 形　畜生的，殘忍的，蠻橫的，淫蕩的
brutal brute + al	▶	〔`brutl〕 形　殘忍的，冷酷的，野蠻的，粗暴的

With brute strength, the sumo wrestler forced his opponent out of the ring.
憑著野獸般的力量，相撲力士將他的對手逼出土俵（日本相撲競技舞台）。

burden	▶	〔`bɝdn〕 名　重負，重擔，負擔，沉重的責任 動　加重壓於，加負擔於，煩擾，加負荷於 be burdened with～「負擔～」
burdensome burden + some	▶	〔`bɝdnsəm〕 形　累贅的，惱人的，繁重的

bury	▶ 〔`bɛrɪ〕 動　埋葬，掩藏，埋藏，使沈浸，使專心

burial bury + al	▶ 〔`bɛrɪəl〕 名　埋葬，葬禮

The ancient burial grounds that were recently discovered had the archeological world in a frenzy.
最近發現的古代墓葬地在考古學界引起一陣旋風。

309

calm	▶ 〔kɑm〕 形　鎮靜的，沈著的，無風 (浪) 的，平靜的 　　　　 動　使鎮定，使平靜

calmly calm + ly	▶ 〔`kɑmlɪ〕 副　平靜地，寧靜地，冷靜地，沈著地

calmness calm + ness	▶ 〔`kɑmnɪs〕 名　平靜，安寧，冷靜，沈著

The police told everyone to calmly proceed to the emergency exits.
警察要所有人冷靜地走到緊急出口。

cancer	▶ 〔`kænsə〕 名　癌，惡性腫瘤，癌症，（社會等的）弊端，（大寫）巨蟹星座

cancerous cancer + ous	▶ 〔`kænsərəs〕 形　癌的，像癌的，逐步擴散的

More and better treatments for cancer are being developed every year.
每一年都有更多更好的癌症治療方法被開發出來。

category	▶ 〔`kætəˏgorɪ〕 名　種類，部署，類目

categorize category + ize	▶ 〔`kætəgəˏraɪz〕 動　使列入…的範疇，將…分類

categorization categorize + tion	▶ 〔ˏkætəgərɪ`zeʃən〕 名　列入…的範疇，分類

The videos were organized into several different categories.
這些錄影帶被有系統地分成數個不同的類別。

caution	▶ 〔`kɔʃən〕 名　小心，謹慎，警告，告誡

cautious caution + ous	▶ 〔`kɔʃəs〕 形　十分小心的，謹慎的

cautiously cautious + ly	▶ 〔`kɔʃəslɪ〕 副　小心地，謹慎地

The policeman cautiously opened the door and entered the room.
警察小心地打開門然後進入房間。

cease	▶ 〔sis〕 動　停止，終止，停止，結束

ceaseless
cease + less
▶ [`sislɪs] 形　不停的，不間斷的

ceaselessly
ceaseless + ly
▶ [`sislɪslɪ] 副　不停地，持續地

The dinosaur ceased to exist after an asteroid hit the earth.
在一顆小行星撞上地球後，恐龍就滅絕了。

celebrate
▶ [`sɛlə͵bret] 動　慶祝，頌揚

celebration
celebrate + ion
▶ [͵sɛlə`breʃən] 名　慶祝，慶祝活動，慶典

The couple celebrates their wedding anniversary every year by going on a trip.
那對夫婦每年出門都旅行慶祝他們的結婚紀念日。

ceremony
▶ [`sɛrə͵monɪ] 名　儀式，典禮，禮節

ceremonial
ceremony + ial
▶ [͵sɛrə`monɪəl] 形　禮節的，禮儀的，儀式的

The ceremonial changing of the guards occurs every hour on the hour.
衛兵在每個小時整點舉行交接儀式。

★ 310

chaos
▶ [`keas] 名　混亂，雜亂的一團（或一堆等）

chaotic
chaos + tic
▶ [ke`atɪk] 形　混亂的，雜亂無章的，無秩序的

character
▶ [`kærɪktə] 名　性格，性質，特性，特色，角色，（小說、戲劇等的）人物

characteristic
character + tic
▶ [͵kærəktə`rɪstɪk] 形　特有的，獨特的，典型的
　名　特性，特徵，特色

characterize
character + ize
▶ [`kærəktə͵raɪz] 動　描繪…的特性，具有…的特徵，以…為特徵

Honesty is an important characteristic.
誠實是一項重要的特質。

charm
▶ [tʃɑrm] 名　魅力，嫵媚，符咒，咒語，護身符
　動　使陶醉，使高興，吸引

charming
charm + ing
▶ [`tʃɑrmɪŋ] 形　令人高興的，迷人的，有魅力的

Although he is charming, you will soon find that he can't be trusted.
雖然他很有魅力，但是你很快就會發現他不值得信任。

cheer	▶	〔tʃɪr〕 名 喝采，振奮，激勵，鼓勵 動 歡呼，以歡呼聲激勵，使振奮，使高興
cheerful cheer + ful	▶	〔ˋtʃɪrfəl〕 形 興高采烈的，樂意的，愉快的
cheery cheer + y	▶	〔ˋtʃɪrɪ〕 形 興高采烈的，活潑的，令人愉快的，明亮的

The crowd cheered wildly as the team ran onto the field.
當隊伍跑步進場時，觀眾瘋狂地大聲歡呼。

chill	▶	〔tʃɪl〕 名 寒冷，寒氣，風寒，（態度的）冷淡
chilly chill + y	▶	〔ˋtʃɪlɪ〕 形 冷颼颼的，冷淡的，使人寒心的

It's very chilly outside; you'd better take your gloves.
外面非常冷，你最好帶著你的手套。

class	▶	〔klæs〕 名 （社會的）階級，社會等級，等級制度，班級，年級，（一節）課，上課
classy class + y	▶	〔ˋklæsɪ〕 形 優等的，漂亮的，別緻的
classify class + ify	▶	〔ˋklæsəˏfaɪ〕 動 將…分類，將…分等級，將…歸入某類（或某等級）
classification classify + tion	▶	〔ˏklæsəfəˋkeʃən〕 名 分類，分級，類別系統，類別
coast	▶	〔kost〕 名 海岸，沿海地區
coastal coast + al	▶	〔ˋkostl〕 形 海岸的，近（或沿）海的

The coastal regions often have unpredictable weather patterns.
沿海地區往往有令人出乎意料的氣候形態。

code	▶	〔kod〕 名 法規，規則，規範，代號，代碼，電碼，密碼 a dress code「服裝規定」 Morse Code「摩斯電報密碼」
encode en + code	▶	〔ɪnˋkod〕 動 把…譯成電碼（或密碼）

decode
de + code

▶ 〔ˋdiˋkod〕 動 譯解（密碼）

The thief tried to break the bank's security code, but he was caught red-handed.
小偷試著要突破銀行的安全密碼，但是他當場被逮個正著。

☆ 311

coherent

▶ 〔koˋhɪrənt〕 形 一致的，協調的，黏合在一起的，（話語等）條理清楚的，連貫的

coherence
coherent + ce

▶ 〔koˋhɪrəns〕 名 黏著，凝聚，統一，連貫性

incoherent
in + coherent

▶ 〔ˏɪnkoˋhɪrənt〕 形 無條理的，不一貫的

incoherence
incoherent + ce

▶ 〔ˏɪnkoˋhɪrəns〕 名 不連貫，不著邊際，無條理

collide

▶ 〔kəˋlaɪd〕 動 碰撞，相撞，衝突，抵觸
collide with～「與～意見抵觸，與～起衝突」
collide against～「和～激戰」

collision
collide + ion

▶ 〔kəˋlɪʒən〕 名 （意見、利益等的）衝突，抵觸
be in collision with～「和～起衝突」

Surprisingly, there were no casualties in the head-on collision.
令人驚訝的是，那場正面衝突的事故中並未出現任何犧牲者。

---

column

▶ 〔ˋkɑləm〕 名 圓柱，圓柱狀物，（報紙的）欄，專欄，短評論，（士兵的）縱隊，縱列

columnist
column + ist

▶ 〔ˋkɑləmɪst〕 名 專欄作家，專欄編輯

Three great columns held the building up.
三支巨大的圓柱支撐著這棟建築物。

---

communicate

▶ 〔kəˋmjunəˏket〕 動 傳達，傳播，通訊，通話，交流思想（或感情、信息等）
communicate～to...「把～傳達給…」
communicate with（人）「和（人）聯繫」

communication
communicate + ion

▶ 〔kəˏmjunəˋkeʃən〕 名 傳達，交流，通信，訊息，情報，通訊（交通）設施

The main purpose of any language is communication with other speakers of the language.
所有語言存在的目的就是要和使用相同語言的人進行交流。

commune	▶	〔`kɑmjun〕 名 （歐洲一些國家的）最小地方行政區，社區，社區居民
community commune + ity	▶	〔kə`mjunətɪ〕 名 社區，共同社會，共同體，（一般）社會，公眾
communist commune + ist	▶	〔`kɑmjʊˌnɪst〕 名 共產主義者，（常大寫）共產黨員
communism commune + ism	▶	〔`kɑmjʊˌnɪzəm〕 名 共產主義，共產主義社會，（大寫）共產主義政體

Helen's dream was to live in a self-sufficient commune where all food was grown by the members of the community.
海倫的夢想是住在一個自給自足的社區；在那裡，所有的食物皆由社區成員自己栽種。

| commute | ▶ | 〔kə`mjut〕 動 用⋯交換（或代替），（用月票或季票）通勤 |
| commuter
commute + er | ▶ | 〔kə`mjutɚ〕 名 通勤者 |

In the morning, the train is packed with commuters going to work or school.
早晨，火車擠滿了通勤上班或上學的人。

| compatible
com + pat + ible | ▶ | 〔kən`pætəbl〕 形 能共處的，可並立的，適合的，兼用式的，（電腦）相容的 |
| incompatible
in + compatible | ▶ | 〔ˌɪnkən`pætəbl〕 形 不能共處的，不適合的，不相容的 |

This software is incompatible with my operating system.
這套軟體和我的作業系統不相容。

| complain
com + plain | ▶ | 〔kəm`plen〕 動 抱怨，發牢騷，訴說（病痛等），控訴，投訴 |
| complaint
complain + t | ▶ | 〔kəm`plent〕 名 抱怨，抗議，怨言，抱怨的緣由，控告，控訴
file a complaint against～「提出對～的訴訟」 |

If you want to file a complaint against your noisy neighbors, you can do so at the police station.
如果你想要投訴吵鬧的鄰居，你可以在警察局辦理。

★
312

comply ▶ 〔kəm`plaɪ〕 動　（對要求、命令等）依從，遵從
comply with～「遵從～」

compliance ▶ 〔kəm`plaɪəns〕 名　承諾，順從，屈從
comply + ance

uring the dr ought, Sydney residents were told not to use water during the day, but some people did not comply.
在乾季時，雪梨的居民被告知不要在白天用水，但是有些人沒有遵守。

conceit ▶ 〔kən`sit〕 名　自滿，自大，自負，幻想，奇想，
個人意見（或想法），好評

conceited ▶ 〔kən`sitɪd〕 形　自負的，驕傲自滿的，自誇的
conceit + ed

Jasmine refused to go on a date with Chris because she found him too conceited.
潔絲敏拒絕和克里斯約會，因為她覺得他太驕傲自滿了。

concrete ▶ 〔`kɑnkrit〕 形　有形的，實在的，具體的，混凝土的
名　具體物，混凝土，凝結物

concretely ▶ 〔`kɑnkrɪtlɪ〕 副　具體地
concrete + ly

concreteness ▶ 〔`kɑnkritnəs〕 名　具體，確實
concrete + ness

The boss demanded that the team produce a concrete plan for marketing the new products.
上司要求團隊擬出一個銷售新產品的具體方案。

condition ▶ 〔kən`dɪʃən〕 名　情況，（健康等）狀態，環境，
con + dit + ion　　　　　　　　　形勢，條件，疾病，症狀

conditional ▶ 〔kən`dɪʃənl〕 形　附有條件的，以…為條件的
condition + al

The pilot checked the weather conditions before taking off.
機長在起飛前確認了天候狀況。

| console | ▶ | 〔kənˋsol〕 動　安慰，撫慰，慰問 |

| consolation
console + tion | ▶ | 〔ˌkɑnsəˋleʃən〕 名　安慰，慰藉，安慰的人（或事物） |

The child who dropped her ice cream cone cried, and cried, and would not be consoled.
掉了冰淇淋的孩子一直不停地哭，而且不肯接受別人安慰。

| consult
con + sult | ▶ | 〔kənˋsʌlt〕 動　與⋯商量，找（醫生）看病，請教，
　　　　　　查閱（辭典、書籍等），商議，磋商
consult with a doctor「接受醫生的診斷」
consult（人）on～「針對～向（人）尋求意見」 |

| consultation
consult + tion | ▶ | 〔ˌkɑnsəlˋteʃən〕 名　諮詢，商議，診察，會診，參考 |

| consultant
consult + ant | ▶ | 〔kənˋsʌltənt〕 名　顧問，會診醫生，諮詢者 |

Before you put a plan into action, you should consult with the other people involved.
在計劃開始執行之前，你應該要徵求其他相關人士的意見。

⭐
313

| consume | ▶ | 〔kənˋsjum〕 動　消耗，花費，耗盡，吃完，喝光 |

| consumer
consume + er | ▶ | 〔kənˋsjumɚ〕 名　消費者，消耗者 |

| consumption
consume + tion | ▶ | 〔kənˋsʌmpʃən〕 名　消耗，用盡，消費量，消費 |

If you consume more calories than you burn, you will gain weight.
如果你吃下的卡路里比你消耗的要來得多，你會變胖的。

| contemplate
con + template | ▶ | 〔ˋkɑntɛmˌplet〕 動　思量，仔細考慮，注視，打算 |

| contemplation
contemplate + ion | ▶ | 〔ˌkɑntɛmˋpleʃən〕 名　沈思，深思熟慮，凝視，意圖，
　　　　　　期望 |

He sat there contemplating how he would destroy all the evidence.
他坐在那裡思忖他該如何湮滅證據。

| content | ▶ | 〔kənˋtɛnt〕 動　使滿足
　　　　　形　滿足的，滿意的，甘願的
〔ˋkɑntɛnt〕 名　內容，要旨，容量，容納的東西，
　　　　　　具體內容，（書刊等的）目錄
be content with～「滿意～」 |

contented
content + ed

▶ 〔kən`tɛntɪd〕 形　滿足的，知足的，滿意的
be contented with～「滿足於～」

contentment
content + ment

▶ 〔kən`tɛntmənt〕 名　滿足，知足，滿意

Carol was very content with her life.
卡洛兒非常滿意她的生活。

Jimmy was excited to find a large heavy bag on the side of the road, but when he looked inside, he found that the contents were a lot of small stones.
吉米很興奮在路邊發現一個又大又重的手提包，但是當他打開一看，發現裡面裝滿了許多小石子。

contrary
contra + ary

▶ 〔`kɑntrɛrɪ〕 形　相反的，對立的，（天氣）不利的，（風）逆向的
on the contrary「相反地」
contrary to～「與～相反」

Contrary to the popular opinion, eggs are not that unhealthy.
與一般的見解相反，雞蛋並不是那麼不健康的食物。

contrive

▶ 〔kən`traɪv〕 動　發明，設計，策劃，設法做到，謀劃
contrive to V「設法做到～」

contrived
contrive + ed

▶ 〔kən`traɪvd〕 形　人為的，做作的，不自然的

contrivance
contrive + ance

▶ 〔kən`traɪvəns〕 名　發明物，裝置，器械，設計，發明（或設計）才能

He told her that she looked very nice, but the compliment sounded contrived.
他跟她說她看起來很漂亮，但是他的讚美聽起來很做作。

controversy
contro + verse

▶ 〔`kɑntrəˌvɝsɪ〕 名　爭論，辯論，爭議

controversial
controversy + ial

▶ 〔ˌkɑntrə`vɝʃəl〕 形　爭論的，可疑的，好議論的，有爭議的

There was a lot of controversy surrounding the decision to destroy a forest in order to build a new factory.
為了蓋新工廠而破壞森林的決定引起了極大的爭議。

★
314

cost ▶ 〔kɔst〕名　費用，成本，代價，損失
　　　　　　　動　花費，使付出（時間、勞力、代價等）
cost（人）（價錢）〈花了（人）（價錢）〉

costly
cost + ly
▶ 〔ˋkɔstlɪ〕形　貴重的，寶貴的，昂貴的，代價高的

It will cost us a million dollars to fix our library which was damaged by the typhoon.
修復我們被颱風破壞的圖書館將花費100萬美元。

counsel ▶ 〔ˋkaʊnsl̩〕名　商議，審議，忠告
　　　　　　　動　勸告，忠告，提議，商議

counselor
counsel + or
▶ 〔ˋkaʊnsl̩ɚ〕名　顧問，指導老師，諮詢師，輔導員

He is seeing a counselor for anger management.
他為了憤怒管理問題正接受心理諮詢師治療。

court ▶ 〔kort〕名　法庭，法院，（開）庭，場地，庭院，
　　　　　　　　朝廷，宮廷

courteous
court + ous
▶ 〔ˋkɝtjəs〕形　殷勤的，謙恭的，有禮貌的

courtesy
court + sy
▶ 〔ˋkɝtəsɪ〕名　禮貌，殷勤，好意，謙恭有禮的言辭
　　　　　　　　（或舉動）

In Japan, it is common courtesy to take off your shoes when you enter a home.
在日本，進入住家的時候脫鞋是一般人都知道的禮貌。

cow ▶ 〔kaʊ〕名　母牛，乳牛

coward
cow + ard
▶ 〔ˋkaʊəd〕名　懦夫，膽怯者

Tiffany was too much of a coward to let Ted know how much she loved him.　蒂芬妮太過膽怯，不敢讓泰德知道她有多愛他。

craft ▶ 〔kræft〕名　工藝，手藝，同業，行會，行會成員

craftsman
craft + man
▶ 〔ˋkræftsmən〕名　工匠，技工，巧匠，工藝師

craftsmanship
craftsman + ship
▶ 〔ˋkræftsmənˌʃɪp〕名　技巧，技術

Switzerland is known for its high quality craftsmanship.
瑞士以高品質的手工藝技術聞名於世。

create	▶	〔krɪ`et〕動　創造，創作，設計，產生
creative create + ive	▶	〔krɪ`etɪv〕形　創造的，創造性的，啟發想像力的， 有創造力（或想像力）的
creativity creative + ity	▶	〔ˌkrie`tɪvətɪ〕名　創造力
creation create + ion	▶	〔krɪ`eʃən〕名　創造，創作，萬物，創作品，產物
creature create + ure	▶	〔`kritʃɚ〕名　生物，動物，家畜，創造物，產物

Robert loves the creative aspect of painting.
羅伯喜歡繪畫富創造性的那一面。

crime	▶	〔kraɪm〕名　罪，罪行，犯罪，罪過
criminal crime + al	▶	〔`krɪmən̩〕名　罪犯 形　犯罪的，犯法的

Citizens are concerned because the crime rate is increasing in Japan.
日本國民對於日漸提升的犯罪率感到憂心忡忡。

☆ 315 crowd	▶	〔kraʊd〕名　人群，大眾 動　擁擠，聚集 crowd around～「聚集在～周圍」 crowd into～「擠進～」
crowded crowd + ed	▶	〔`kraʊdɪd〕形　擁擠的，擠滿人群的

The children crowded around the baseball hero trying to get autographs.
孩子們為了拿到簽名，圍繞在那位有名的棒球選手身邊。

cruel	▶	〔`kruəl〕形　殘忍的，殘酷的，令人痛苦的
cruelty cruel + ty	▶	〔`kruəltɪ〕名　殘酷，殘忍，殘酷的行為（言語）

There are increasing laws against cruelty to animals.
現在禁止殘忍虐待動物的法律正逐漸增多。

cynical	▶	〔`sɪnɪk̩〕形　憤世嫉俗的，挖苦的，冷嘲的
cynicism cynical + ism	▶	〔`sɪnɪsɪzəm〕名　譏笑，譏諷的言辭

Josie's broken heart has made her cynical about relationships.
喬絲破碎的心讓她對人際關係變得憤世嫉俗。

| deal | ▶ | 〔dil〕名　交易，數量，大量，待遇
動　發（紙牌），分配，經營，交易，處理
deal in～「經營～」
deal with～「應付～，處理～」
make a deal with～「和～交易」 |

| dealer
deal + er | ▶ | 〔`dilə〕名　業者，商人，發牌者，行為者 |

The used car dealer has a reputation for being dishonest.
那位中古車商有做生意不誠實的名聲。

| debt | ▶ | 〔dɛt〕名　債，借款，恩義，負債 |

| indebted
in + debt + ed | ▶ | 〔ɪn`dɛtɪd〕形　受惠的，感激的，負債的
be indebted to（人）「感激（人）」 |

I am indebted to my friend for helping me when I needed it.
我很感激我的朋友在我需要幫忙的時候幫助我。

| dedicate | ▶ | 〔`dɛdəˌket〕動　以…奉獻，把（時間、精力等）
用於，題獻（著作） |

| dedicated
dedicate + ed | ▶ | 〔`dɛdəˌketɪd〕形　專注的，獻身的 |

| dedicatedly
dedicated + ly | ▶ | 〔`dɛdəˌketɪdlɪ〕副　專注地，獻身地 |

| dedication
dedicate + ion | ▶ | 〔ˌdɛdə`keʃən〕名　奉獻，揭幕儀式，專心致力，
獻詞，題詞 |

She promised to dedicate her first book to Jeff.
她答應把她第一本著作獻給傑夫。

| delinquent
de + linqu + ent | ▶ | 〔dɪ`lɪŋkwənt〕形　怠忽職守的，到期末付的，
拖欠的，有過失的，犯法的 |

| delinquently
delinquent + ly | ▶ | 〔dɪ`lɪŋkwəntlɪ〕副　怠慢地 |

| delinquency
delinquent + cy | ▶ | 〔dɪ`lɪŋkwənsɪ〕名　懈怠，違法行為，少年犯罪 |

After robbing three 7-Elevens, Ben was put into a special home for delinquent children.
在搶了三間7-11後，班被送到一座安置少年犯的特別之家。

☆
316

demonstrate ▶　〔`dɛmən,stret〕 動　論證，證明，（用實驗、實例等）
de + monstr + ate　　　　　　　　　　　說明，示範操作（產品），展示，
　　　　　　　　　　　　　　　　　　　遊行示威

demonstration ▶　〔,dɛmən`streʃən〕 名　論證，證明，實地示範，
demonstrate + ion　　　　　　　　　　示威運動，表示

She gave a demonstration on how to make a cheesecake.
她示範起司蛋糕的做法。

dense ▶　〔dɛns〕 形　密集的，稠密的，（煙、霧等）濃厚的，
　　　　　　　　　　　　　　　　愚鈍的

densely ▶　〔`dɛnslɪ〕 副　濃密地，稠密地，密集地
dense + ly

density ▶　〔`dɛnsətɪ〕 名　密集（度），稠密（度），愚鈍
dense + ity

The density of lead is much more than the density of aluminum.
鉛的密度遠遠超過鋁的密度。

She gave him many hints that she didn't like him, but he was a bit
dense, and kept asking her for dates.
她多次暗示不喜歡他，但是他有點遲鈍，還是繼續約她出去約會。

derive ▶　〔dɪ`raɪv〕 動　衍生出，導出，推知，起源，由來
　　　　　　　　　　　　derive from～＝be derived from～「起源於～，來自～」

derivation ▶　〔,dɛrə`veʃən〕 名　起源，由來，起源調查，
derive + tion　　　　　　　　　　　語言的衍生

The Japanese writing system is derived from the Chinese writing
system.
日文的書寫系統源自於中文書寫系統。

desert ▶　〔dɪ`zɝt〕 動　拋棄，遺棄，離棄，逃跑，開小差
　　　　　　　〔`dɛzət〕 名　沙漠，荒野

deserted ▶　〔dɪ`zɝtɪd〕 形　荒蕪的，無人居住的
desert + ed

desertification ▶　〔,dɛzətɪfɪ`keʃən〕 名　沙漠化
desert + tion

The lights and television were on, but the whole house was deserted.
電燈和電視開著，但是家裡沒有半個人在。

despair	▶	〔dɪˋspɛr〕名　絕望，令人絕望的人（或事物）
desperate despair + ate	▶	〔ˋdɛspərɪt〕形　危急的，絕望的，鋌而走險的， 孤注一擲的，極度渴望的
desperately desperate + ly	▶	〔ˋdɛspərɪtlɪ〕副　絕望地，不顧一切地，極度地， 猛烈地
desperation despair + tion	▶	〔͵dɛspəˋreʃən〕名　絕望，不顧一切 in desperation「走投無路」

Helen was so desperate for a bite of chocolate that she braved the typhoon to get to a convenience store.
海倫很渴望能吃上一口巧克力，所以她冒著颱風前去便利商店。

detail	▶	〔ˋditel〕名　細節，詳情，瑣事，枝節 in detail「詳細地」
detailed detail + ed	▶	〔ˋdiˋteld〕形　詳細的，精細的，複雜的

Be sure to give as detailed a description as you can.
請盡可能地描述詳細情形。

★
317

develop	▶	〔dɪˋvɛləp〕動　發展，成長，發達，開發，進步
developer develop + er	▶	〔dɪˋvɛləpɚ〕名　開發者
development develop + ment	▶	〔dɪˋvɛləpmənt〕名　生長，進化，發展，發達，產物

eveloping countries might find it difficult to compete on a world market.
對開發中國家而言，與全球市場競爭是困難的。

diet	▶	〔ˋdaɪət〕名　飲食，食物 be on a diet「節食」 go on a diet「開始節食」
dietary diet + ary	▶	〔ˋdaɪə͵tɛrɪ〕形　飲食的

Too many young women who are not over-weight are going on diets, and compromising their health.
有太多非過重的年輕女性在減肥，而且危及她們的健康。

digit	▶	〔ˋdɪdʒɪt〕名　手指，足趾，數字

digital
digit + al

▶ 〔`dɪdʒɪtḷ〕 形　指的，指狀的，數字的
（反義）analogue〔`ænəlɔg〕
形　模擬指針式的

Some day the digital camera may replace the conventional film camera.
或許有一天數位相機會取代傳統使用軟片的相機。

---

dignify

▶ 〔`dɪgnə‚faɪ〕 動　使有尊嚴，使高貴，抬高…的身價
dignify～by...「藉…抬高～的身價」

dignity
dignify + ty

▶ 〔`dɪgnətɪ〕 名　尊嚴，尊貴

indignity
in + dignity

▶ 〔ɪn`dɪgnətɪ〕 名　輕蔑，屈辱，侮辱言行，無禮舉動

Although the team lost, their show of dignity won the hearts of the audience.
雖然那隊輸了比賽，但是他們不失尊嚴的表現贏得了觀眾的心。

---

disappoint

▶ 〔‚dɪsə`pɔɪnt〕 動　使失望，使（希望等）破滅，挫敗

disappointed
disappoint + ed

▶ 〔‚dɪsə`pɔɪntɪd〕 形　失望的，沮喪的，
（希望等）落空的，受挫折的

disappointment
disappoint + ment

▶ 〔‚dɪsə`pɔɪntmənt〕 名　失望，掃興，沮喪，
令人失望的人（事物）

After all the hype, the viewers found the movie to be a huge disappointment.
在大肆炒作過後，觀眾覺得那部電影令人非常失望。

---

discipline

▶ 〔`dɪsəplɪn〕 名　紀律，教養，懲戒，懲罰，教規，
戒律

disciplinary
discipline + ary

▶ 〔`dɪsəplɪn‚ɛrɪ〕 形　訓練的，紀律的，懲戒的

Christine despised parents using force to discipline their children.
克莉絲汀鄙視使用暴力管教孩子的父母。

---

discreet

▶ 〔dɪ`skrit〕 形　謹慎的，慎重的，考慮周到的，
樸素的，不引人注意的

discretion
discreet + ion

▶ 〔dɪ`skrɛʃən〕 名　謹慎，考慮周到，斟酌（或行動）
的自由，處理權

The committee gave their recommendation, but left the final decision up to the discretion of the president.
委員會提出了他們的建議，但仍把最終決定權留給主席來斟酌裁定。

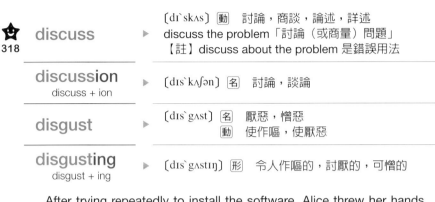

discuss

318

〔dɪˋskʌs〕[動] 討論，商談，論述，詳述
discuss the problem「討論（或商量）問題」
【註】discuss about the problem 是錯誤用法

discussion
discuss + ion

〔dɪˋkʌʃən〕[名] 討論，談論

disgust

〔dɪsˋgʌst〕[名] 厭惡，憎惡
[動] 使作嘔，使厭惡

disgusting
disgust + ing

〔dɪsˋgʌstɪŋ〕[形] 令人作嘔的，討厭的，可憎的

After trying repeatedly to install the software, Alice threw her hands up in disgust and stormed out of the room.
在多次嘗試安裝軟體失敗後，艾莉絲厭惡地攤手放棄，然後衝出房間。

distinct

〔dɪˋstɪŋkt〕[形] 有區別的，明顯的，清楚的

distinctive
distinct + ive

〔dɪˋskɪŋktɪv〕[形] 有特色的，特殊的

distinction
distinct + ion

〔dɪˋstɪŋkʃən〕[名] 區別，差別，不同點，特徵，特性

indistinct
in + distinct

〔͵ɪndɪˋstɪŋkt〕[形] 不清楚，模糊的，微弱的，難以清楚辨識的

Skunks have a distinct smell, you can not mistake them for anything else.
臭鼬有一種獨特的臭味，你不可能把他們誤認為其他東西。

distinguish

〔dɪˋstɪŋgwɪʃ〕[動] 區別，識別，把…區別分類，（憑感官）辨認出，使傑出
distinguish～from...「區別～與…」

distinguished
distinguish + ed

〔dɪˋstɪŋgwɪʃt〕[形] 卓越的，著名的

It was hard to distinguish between Jim and his twin brother Joe.
要區別吉姆和他的雙胞胎兄弟喬很困難。

By winning several awards, Phil distinguished himself as a promising young artist.
獲頒幾個獎項後，費爾以一位前途看好的年輕藝術家而著稱。

| disturb | ▶ | 〔dɪsˋtɝb〕 動　妨礙，打擾，擾亂 |
| disturbance
disturb + ance | ▶ | 〔dɪsˋtɝbəns〕 名　擾亂，打擾，騷擾，混亂，不安 |

If you want to sleep in, you should put the "do not disturb" sign on your door.
如果你想要好好睡覺，你應該要在門上掛著「請勿打擾」的牌子。

| document | ▶ | 〔ˋdɑkjəmənt〕 名　公文，文件，證件，單據 |
| documentary
document + ary | ▶ | 〔͵dɑkjəˋmɛntərɪ〕 形　文件的，記實的，
（電視、電影等）記錄的
名　記錄影片，（電視等的）記錄節目 |

The crew shot a documentary on life in Edo-era Japan.
攝影團隊拍了一部關於日本江戶時代生活的記錄片。

| domestic | ▶ | 〔dəˋmɛstɪk〕 形　家庭的，家事的，國內的，馴養的 |
| domesticate
domestic + ate | ▶ | 〔dəˋmɛstə͵ket〕 動　馴養，使愛家，使適應家庭生活，使（引種的植物）歸化 |

It is impossible to domesticate large wild cats like tigers and lions.
要馴化老虎和獅子之類的大型野生貓科動物是不可能的。

☆ 319　doubt	▶	〔daut〕 動　懷疑，不相信 名　懷疑，不相信，疑問
doubtful doubt + ful	▶	〔ˋdautfəl〕 形　懷疑的，可疑的，不明確的，難以預測的
doubtless doubt + less	▶	〔ˋdautlɪs〕 形　無疑的，肯定的 副　無疑地，必定地
undoubted un + doubt + ed	▶	〔ʌnˋdautɪd〕 形　無容質疑的，肯定的，真正的

It is doubtful that she will come; the weather is bad, and she doesn't have a car.
她會不會來很難說，天氣不好，而且她又沒有車。

| drama | ▶ | 〔ˋdrɑmə〕 名　（一齣）戲，戲劇 |
| dramatic
drama + tic | ▶ | 〔drəˋmætɪk〕 形　戲劇的，劇本的，充滿激情的，令人感動的 |

dramatically
dramatic + al + ly

▶ 〔drə`mætɪk!ɪ〕 副　戲劇性地，引人注目地

The dramatic scenery of the Grand Canyon took oppy's br eath away.
大峽谷那令人感動的風景讓波比嘆為觀止。

---

dread

▶ 〔drɛd〕 動　懼怕，擔心
名　恐怖，可怕的東西（或人）

dreadful
dread + ful

▶ 〔`drɛdfəl〕 形　可怕的，令人恐懼的，糟透的，
非常討厭的

Craig dreaded history class because he could never remember names and dates.
克雷格很怕上歷史課，因為他總是記不得人名和年代。

---

dust

▶ 〔dʌst〕 動　除去灰塵，噴灑農藥
名　灰塵，粉末

dusty
dust + y

▶ 〔`dʌstɪ〕 形　滿是灰塵的，塵狀的，淺灰色的

If you don't dust your furniture every week, it will become very dusty and make you sneeze.
如果不每週擦一次傢俱，它會變得滿是灰塵並讓人打噴嚏。

---

duty

▶ 〔`djutɪ〕 名　責任，義務，本分，稅，職責

dutiful
duty + ful

▶ 〔`djutɪfəl〕 形　盡本分的，恭順的，順從的

Sylvia believes it is the children's duty to take care of aging parents.
西薇亞認為照顧年邁的雙親是孩子的責任。

---

eager

▶ 〔`igɚ〕 形　熱心的，熱切的，渴望的，急切的
be eager for～「渴望～」
be eager to V「渴望～」

eagerly
eager + ly

▶ 〔`igɚlɪ〕 副　渴望地，熱切地

eagerness
eager + ness

▶ 〔`igɚnɪs〕 名　渴望，熱心，熱切

Julia was eager to see her friends at school after the summer holiday.
茱莉亞很渴望暑假過後能在學校見到朋友。

320

ecology ▶ 〔ɪˋkɑlədʒɪ〕名　生態學，生態，環境

ecological
ecology + ical
▶ 〔͵ɛkəˋlɑdʒɪkəl〕形　生態（學）的

ecologist
ecology + ist
▶ 〔ɪˋkɑlədʒɪst〕名　生態學者

After studying ecology, Lana became interested in the relationships between living things and their environments.
學了生態學以後，拉娜開始對生物與其生存環境的關係感興趣。

economy ▶ 〔ɪˋkɑnəmɪ〕名　節約，節省，經濟，經濟狀況
形　廉價的，經濟的

economic
economy + ic
▶ 〔͵ikəˋnɑmɪk〕形　經濟上的，經濟學的

economics
economy + ics
▶ 〔͵ikəˋnɑmɪks〕名　經濟學，（國民的）經濟情況，經濟

economical
economy + ical
▶ 〔͵ikəˋnɑmɪkl〕形　經濟的，節約的，節儉的

economist
economy + ist
▶ 〔ɪˋkɑnəmɪst〕名　經濟學者

The economic situation of the country improved when a new prime minister was elected.
這個國家的經濟狀況在選出新首相時獲得改善。

Instant noodles are an economical meal, but not a very nutritious one.
速食麵是種省錢但不怎麼營養的食物。

educate ▶ 〔ˋɛdʒə͵ket〕動　教育，培養，訓練

education
educate + ion
▶ 〔͵ɛdʒʊˋkeʃən〕名　教育，培養，訓練，受到的教育，教育學

educational
education + al
▶ 〔͵ɛdʒʊˋkeʃənl〕形　教育的，有關教育的，有教育意義的

Kate feels it is important to educate young people on the effects of drugs.
凱特認為教育年輕人毒品的影響很重要。

elder ▶ 〔ˋɛldə〕形　年齡較大的，從前的，資格老的

elderly
elder + ly
▶ 〔ˋɛldəlɪ〕形　年長的，上了年紀的，老式的，過時的

Sonja works in a home for elderly people.
桑雅在一所養老院工作。

electric	▶	〔ɪˋlɛktrɪk〕 形 電的，導電的，發電的，用電的，電動的
electrical electric + al	▶	〔ɪˋlɛktrɪk̩〕 形 與電有關的，電器科學的
electricity electric + ity	▶	〔ˌɪlɛkˋtrɪsətɪ〕 名 電，電流，電力，電學
electron	▶	〔ɪˋlɛktrɑn〕 名 電子
electronic electron + ic	▶	〔ɪlɛkˋtrɑnɪk〕 形 電子的，電子操縱的
electronics electron + ics	▶	〔ɪlɛkˋtrɑnɪks〕 名 電子學

An electric blanket is warm and cozy on a cold winter's night.
在寒冷的冬夜使用電子毛毯是溫暖而且舒適的。

element	▶	〔ˋɛləmənt〕 名 元素，成分
elemental element + al	▶	〔ˌɛləˋmɛntl̩〕 形 自然的，基本的，原始的
elementary element + ary	▶	〔ˌɛləˋmɛntərɪ〕 形 基本的，初級的，基礎的

The movie was classified as drama but it did contain an element of suspense. 這部電影被歸為劇情片，但其中亦帶有懸疑的元素。

★ 321 **eliminate**	▶	〔ɪˋlɪməˌnet〕 動 消除，排除，消滅，不加考慮，（比賽中）淘汰，忽視
elimination eliminate + ion	▶	〔ɪˌlɪməˋneʃən〕 名 排除，除去，根除，淘汰

The doctor told Carol that she would have to eliminate fatty foods from her diet. 醫生告訴卡洛兒，她的飲食應該要避免攝取油膩的食物。

eloquent	▶	〔ˋɛləkwənt〕 形 雄辯的，有說服力的
eloquence eloquent + ce	▶	〔ˋɛləkwəns〕 名 雄辯，（流利的）口才，雄辯術，（語言等的）說服力

He was such an eloquent speaker that he was elected almost unanimously.
由於他辯才無礙，他幾乎是獲得全場一致通過而當選。

embarrass	▶	〔ɪmˋbærəs〕 動 尷尬，使不好意思，使侷促不安
embarrassing embarrass + ing	▶	〔ɪmˋbærəsɪŋ〕 形 使人尷尬的，令人為難的

embarrassment
embarrass + ment
▶ 〔ɪm`bærəsmənt〕名 窘，難堪
in embarrassment「尷尬」

He blushed in embarrassment when he was discovered sleeping at his desk.
他在辦公桌上睡著的事被發現時，他尷尬得臉都紅了。

---

emerge
▶ 〔ɪ`mɝdʒ〕動 浮現，出現，（問題等）發生，顯露，（事實等）暴露

emergence
emerge + ence
▶ 〔ɪ`mɝdʒəns〕名 出現，浮現

emergency
emergence + y
▶ 〔ɪ`mɝdʒənsɪ〕名 緊急情況，突然事件，非常時刻

In the mist they could just discern Nessie's head emerging from the waters of Loch Ness.
薄霧之中，他們只能勉強看到水怪的頭浮出尼斯湖水面。

---

empire
▶ 〔`ɛmpaɪr〕名 帝國，大企業，君權，皇權

emperor
empire + or
▶ 〔`ɛmpərə〕名 皇帝

The Roman leaders, in hopes of expanding the empire, conquered many peoples.
懷著擴展帝國的希望，羅馬的領導人征服了許多民族。

---

enchant
▶ 〔ɪn`tʃænt〕動 使著魔，對…用魔法，使陶醉，使喜悅，使入迷

enchantment
enchant + ment
▶ 〔ɪn`tʃæntmənt〕名 魅力，迷人之處，施魔法，著魔

She was so enchanted by the little cottage in the woods, that she decided to buy it even though it was in need of repair.
她非常著迷於那棟森林小屋，即使需要維修，她還是決定要買下它。

---

engage
▶ 〔ɪn`gedʒ〕動 佔用（時間、精力等），預訂（房間、座位等），訂婚，使從事，使忙於
be engaged in～「從事於～，埋頭致力於～」
be engaged to～「和～訂婚」

engagement
engage + ment
▶ 〔ɪn`gedʒmənt〕名 訂婚，婚約，諾言，約會

Herman and Candice were engaged in a lively conversation when Mildred walked into the room.
蜜德莉走進房間的時候，赫爾曼和坎蒂絲正熱烈地交談著。

322

enlighten ▶ 〔ɪn`laɪtn〕 動 啓發，啓迪，教育，教導

enlightenment ▶ 〔ɪn`laɪtnmənt〕 名 啓蒙，教化，開明
enlighten + ment

At the moment, I have no idea what your goals in this project are; could you please enlighten me?
此刻我並不明白你這項計劃的目標是什麼，能請你提點我嗎？

enormous ▶ 〔ɪ`nɔrməs〕 形 巨大的，龐大的

enormously ▶ 〔ɪ`nɔrməslɪ〕 副 巨大地，龐大地
enormous + ly

University students often eat enormous amounts when they go to all-you-can-eat restaurants.
大學生去吃到飽餐廳時常常吃極大分量的食物。

enrich ▶ 〔ɪn`rɪtʃ〕 動 使富裕，使豐富

enrichment ▶ 〔ɪn`rɪtʃmənt〕 名 致富，豐富
enrich + ment

Composting enriches soil with nutrients that plants need to grow.
堆肥能增加土壤內植物成長所需的養分。

enroll ▶ 〔ɪn`rol〕 動 登記（名字等），註冊，入學，入伍
enroll in〜「入學至〜，登記參加〜」

enrollment ▶ 〔ɪn`rolmənt〕 形 登記，入會，入伍，登記人數
enroll + ment

Tom enrolled in a course to get his driver's license.
為了拿到駕照，湯姆報名參加駕駛課程。

entertain ▶ 〔ˌɛntɚ`ten〕 動 使歡樂，使娛樂

entertaining ▶ 〔ˌɛntɚ`tenɪŋ〕 形 使人得到娛樂的，使人愉快的，有趣的
entertain + ing

entertainer
entertain + er

▶ 〔͵ɛntɚˋtenɚ〕 名 專業演員，表演者

entertainment
entertain + ment

▶ 〔͵ɛntɚˋtenmənt〕 名 演藝，餘興，娛樂，消遣

The movie was not outstanding, but it was entertaining.
那部電影不算傑出，但是很有趣。

enthusiastic

▶ 〔ɪnˏθjuzɪˋæstɪk〕 形 熱情的，熱烈的，熱心的

enthusiasm
enthusiastic + iasm

▶ 〔ɪnˋθjuzɪˏæzəm〕 名 熱心，熱情，熱忱

enthusiast
enthusiastic + iast

▶ 〔ɪnˋθjuzɪˏæst〕 名 對⋯熱衷的人，熱心者

Kay was not very enthusiastic about going to the party at first, but she ended up having a great time.
一開始，凱對於參加派對不怎麼熱衷，但是她最後還是玩得很開心。

Steve is a sports enthusiast, and you can't get him away from the TV on Sundays.
史提夫是運動迷，禮拜天要他離開電視是不可能的。

⭐
323

entire

▶ 〔ɪnˋtaɪr〕 形 全部的，整個的，全然的，完全的，未斷的，連續的

entirely
entire + ly

▶ 〔ɪnˋtaɪrlɪ〕 副 完全地，徹底地

uring Golden Week, it seems the entire population of Japan is traveling somewhere.
在黃金週期間，好像所有日本人都到哪裡去旅行一樣。

Your idea is not entirely without merit, but it needs some refining.
你的想法並非完全一無是處，只是需要一些改進。

title

▶ 〔ˋtaɪtl〕 名 標題，書名，頭銜，稱號，權利，資格

entitle
en + title

▶ 〔ɪnˋtaɪtl〕 動 給⋯權力 (或資格)，給 (書等) 題名，給⋯稱號

I'm reading a book entitled *The Tale of Genji*.
我現在正在讀一本書名為《源氏物語》的書。

entry	▶	〔ˋɛntrɪ〕名　進入，入場，出賽，入口，詞條

entrance entry + ance	▶	〔ˋɛntrəns〕名　入口，進入，入學

Unless you are a member of the golf club, you will not be able to gain entry.
除非你是這個高爾夫球俱樂部的會員，不然你無權進入。

environment	▶	〔ɪnˋvaɪrəmənt〕名　環境，四周狀況，自然環境

environmental environment + al	▶	〔ɪnˏvaɪrənˋmɛntḷ〕形　環境的，有關環境（保護）的

Sometimes environment-friendly goods are not the cheapest.
有時，對環境有利的產品不見得是最便宜的。

equip	▶	〔ɪˋkwɪp〕動　裝備，配備，使有能力，使有資格，賦予 equip～with...「將…裝備於～」

equipment equip + ment	▶	〔ɪˋkwɪpmənt〕名　配備，裝備，設備，器械，用具

If you are going to go camping in ecember , be sure to equip yourself with all the necessary winter survival goods.
如果你12月打算要去露營，別忘記裝備所有冬季求生必需的物品。

erase	▶	〔ɪˋres〕動　擦掉，抹去，消除，清除，忘卻

eraser erase + er	▶	〔ɪˋresə〕名　擦除器（如黑板擦、橡皮擦等）

The blackboard erasers were so full of chalk that they left white streaks on the board.
板擦上滿是粉筆灰，在黑板上留下一道道白色痕跡。

essence	▶	〔ˋɛsṇs〕名　本質，實質，精華，香精

essential essence + ial	▶	〔ɪˋsɛnʃəl〕形　必要的，不可缺的，本質的，基本的

essentially essential + ly	▶	〔ɪˋsɛnʃəlɪ〕副　實質上，本來

It is essential that you get these papers in on time, and not a minute late.
準時交報告是必要的，晚一分鐘都不行。

☆
324

estimate	▶	〔`ɛstə͵met〕 動　估計，估量，評價，判斷
estimation estimate + ion	▶	〔͵ɛstə`meʃən〕 名　評價，判斷，意見，估計，預算

There are an estimated 500 foreigners living in this city.
估計有500名外籍人士住在本市。

ethics	▶	〔`ɛθɪks〕 名　倫理學，道德學，倫理觀，道德標準
ethical ethics + al	▶	〔`ɛθɪkl〕 形　倫理的，道德的
unethical un + ethical	▶	〔ʌn`ɛθɪkl〕 形　不道德的

What you are planning might not be illegal, but it is certainly unethical.
你計劃的事可能不算違法，但一定是違反道德的。

evaporate	▶	〔ɪ`væpə͵ret〕 動　使蒸發，使揮發，使脫水，使消失
evaporation evaporate + ion	▶	〔ɪ͵væpə`reʃən〕 名　蒸發，發散，消失

Sally's anger evaporated quickly when Brit explained he was late because he stopped to help someone fix a flat tire.
在布利特解釋他遲到是因為停下來幫別人修理爆胎後，莎莉的怒氣消失了。

examine	▶	〔ɪg`zæmɪn〕 動　檢察，診察，審問，測驗，調查
examination examine + tion	▶	〔ɪg͵zæmə`neʃən〕 名　檢察，調查，考試，審問

After a basic examination, the doctor concluded that there was nothing wrong with Jane.
在做過基本的檢查後，醫生診斷珍並沒有大礙。

exasperate	▶	〔ɪg`zæspə͵ret〕 動　使惱怒，激怒， 　　　　　　　　　使（疾病、痛苦等）加劇
exasperation exasperate + ion	▶	〔ɪg͵zæspə`reʃən〕 名　惱怒，激怒，惹人惱怒的事

The teacher gave an exasperated sigh when she realized that not one of the students had done their homework.
知道所有的學生都沒作功課，老師惱火地嘆了一口氣。

exert	▶	〔ɪg`zɝt〕 動　盡（力），運用，行使，發揮，施加 exert oneself「努力，盡力」

exertion
exert + ion

▶ 〔ɪgˋzɝʃən〕 名 努力，費力，
（能力、權力等的）運用，行使

You should take it easy and not exert yourself after the operation.
手術過後，你應該要放輕鬆不要太過用力。

exhaust	▶ 〔ɪgˋzɔst〕 動 使精疲力竭，耗盡，排出氣體
exhausted exhaust + ed	▶ 〔ɪgˋzɔstɪd〕 形 耗盡的，用完的，精疲力竭的
exhaustion exhaust + ion	▶ 〔ɪgˋzɔstʃən〕 名 耗盡，枯竭，精疲力竭
exhaustive exhaust + ive	▶ 〔ɪgˋzɔstɪv〕 形 徹底的，消耗（性）的
exhaustible exhaust + ible	▶ 〔ɪgˋzɔstəbḷ〕 形 可被用盡的
inexhaustible in + exhaustible	▶ 〔ˌɪnɪgˋzɔstəbḷ〕 形 用之不竭的，無窮無盡的， 不倦的

Sam was exhausted after running 10 kilometers.
跑完10公里後，山姆精疲力竭。

325

expand	▶ 〔ɪkˋspænd〕 動 展開，使膨脹，擴充，發展
expansion expand + ion	▶ 〔ɪkˋspænʃən〕 名 擴展，擴張，膨脹，擴大物

His business is very small now, but he has plans for expansion.
現在他的事業規模很小，但是他有擴張的計劃。

Water expands as it freezes.
水在結冰的同時會膨脹。

explore	▶ 〔ɪkˋsplor〕 動 探勘，在…探險，探究，探索
explorer explore + er	▶ 〔ɪkˋsplorə〕 名 探險家，探勘者
exploration explore + tion	▶ 〔ˌɛkspləˋreʃən〕 名 勘查，探索，探究，調查
exploratory explore + ory	▶ 〔ɪkˋsplorəˌtorɪ〕 形 探勘的，探究的

Jacob explores a different area of Tokyo every weekend.
雅各每個週末都會去探索東京各地。

The doctors performed an exploratory surgery to find out what was causing the problem.
為了找出病因，醫師團隊做了一項探測手術。

extinct	▶	〔ɪk`stɪŋkt〕形 熄滅了的，滅絕的，絕種的，過時的
extinction extinct + ion	▶	〔ɪk`stɪŋkʃən〕名 滅絕，消滅，熄滅，撲滅，破滅

The giant panda of China is in danger of extinction because it's natural habitat is disappearing.
由於自然棲息地正逐漸消失，中國的大貓熊現在面臨了絕種的危機。

extinguish	▶	〔ɪk`stɪŋgwɪʃ〕動 熄滅，使消失，使破滅
extinguisher extinguish + er	▶	〔ɪk`stɪŋgwɪʃɚ〕名 熄滅者，消滅者，滅火器

lease extinguish that cigarette right now.
請馬上把菸熄掉。

extreme	▶	〔ɪk`strim〕形 盡頭的，極端的，極度的，激烈的，偏激的 名 極端，末端，極度
extremely extreme + ly	▶	〔ɪk`strimlɪ〕副 極端地，極其，非常

He is extremely afraid of snakes and won't even go into the reptile gardens at the zoo.
他超害怕蛇類，甚至連動物園的爬蟲館都不願意去。

fair	▶	〔fɛr〕形 公正的，公平的，尚可的，一般的，相當的，美麗的 名 （定期）集市，商品展覽會，博覽會
fairness fair + ness	▶	〔`fɛrnɪs〕名 公正，公平
unfair un + fair	▶	〔ʌn`fɛr〕形 不公平的，不公正的，不正當的
unfairness unfair + ness	▶	〔ʌn`fɛrnɪs〕名 不公平，不公正

If parents tell their children not to tell lies, it's only fair that they always tell the truth themselves.
如果父母告訴他們的孩子不要說謊，他們自己也應該要說實話才公平。

⭐
326

| farm | ▶ | 〔fɑrm〕 名　農場，農莊住宅，農家 |
| | | 動　耕作，種植，務農 |

| **farmer** farm + er | ▶ | 〔`fɑrmɚ〕 名　農場，農場主，農場經營者 |

| **farming** farm + ing | ▶ | 〔`fɑrmɪŋ〕 名　農業，農場經營，養殖 |

Since Glenda grew up on a farm, she was not used to the crowded, noisy city.
因為葛蘭達在農場長大，她無法適應擁擠嘈雜的城市。

| fascinate | ▶ | 〔`fæsṇ͵et〕 動　迷人，有吸引力，使神魂顛倒 |

| **fascinating** fascinate + ing | ▶ | 〔`fæsṇ͵etɪŋ〕 形　迷人的，極美的，極好的 |

| **fascination** fascinate + ion | ▶ | 〔͵fæsṇ`eʃən〕 名　魅力，有魅力的東西，迷戀 |

eggy, an entomologist, was fascinated by insects even as a child.
昆蟲學家佩姬在她還是孩子的時候就被昆蟲給迷住了。

| fate | ▶ | 〔fet〕 名　命運，天命，天數 |

| **fatal** fate + al | ▶ | 〔`fetḷ〕 形　命運的，毀滅性的，決定命運的，致命的 |

| **fatally** fatal + ly | ▶ | 〔`fetḷɪ〕 副　致命地，不幸地，宿命地 |

| **fateful** fate + ful | ▶ | 〔`fetfəl〕 形　重大的，決定命運的，命中注定的 |

Mary thought it was fate that she and John met at the station one cold, snowy day.
瑪莉認為，她和約翰在一個寒冷下著雪的日子裡在車站相遇是命運的安排。
The injuries are serious, but not fatal.
傷勢很嚴重，但並不會危及生命。

| favor | ▶ | 〔`fevɚ〕 名　贊同，偏愛，偏袒，善意的行為，恩惠 |

| **favorable** favor + able | ▶ | 〔`fevərəbḷ〕 形　贊同的，稱讚的，有利的，適合的，討人喜歡的 |

unfavorable
un + favorable

▶ 〔ʌn`fevrəbl〕 形　不利的，反對的，不適宜的，令人不快的

favorite
favor + ite

▶ 〔`fevərɪt〕 形　特別喜愛的
名　特別喜愛的人（事物）

The mayor fell out of favor with the citizens when he agreed to implement a 9:00 M curfew for all citizens.
當市長同意執行宵禁，禁止市民晚上9點後外出時，他就失去了民心。

fear

▶ 〔fɪr〕 名　害怕，恐懼，（尤指對神的）敬畏
動　害怕，畏懼，擔心，感到憂慮

fearful
fear + ful

▶ 〔`fɪrfəl〕 形　可怕的，害怕的，擔心的
be fearful of～「擔心～」

Fearing the worst, she took a deep breath and walked into her boss's office.
作了最壞的打算，她深吸一口氣然後走進上司的辦公室。

fellow

▶ 〔`fɛlo〕 名　伙伴，同事

fellowship
fellow + ship

▶ 〔`fɛlo͵ʃɪp〕 名　交情，友誼，共同參與，合夥關係

The most productive working teams realize the importance of fellowship and community among the staff.
有效率的工作團隊知道全體工作成員的團隊精神與共同意識的重要性。

feel

▶ 〔fil〕 動　摸，觸，感覺，認為，覺得

feeling
feel + ing

▶ 〔`filɪŋ〕 名　感覺，觸覺，感情

fever

▶ 〔`fivə〕 名　發燒，發熱，熱度，熱病，狂熱
a high fever「發高燒」a slight fever 「有點發燒」
a fever of 38 degrees 「發燒38度」

feverish
fever + ish

▶ 〔`fivərɪʃ〕 形　發熱的，發燒的，狂熱的，興奮的

The baby had a high fever, so we took her to the hospital.
嬰兒發高燒，所以我們帶她去醫院。

fix

▶ 〔fɪks〕 動　固定，修理

fixed
fix + ed

▶ 〔fɪkst〕 形 固定的，不變的

My V player is not working well, and I have no idea how to fix it.
我的DVD播放器不太正常，我不知道要怎麼修理它。

---

flame

▶ 〔flem〕 名 火焰，光輝，光芒，熱情
動 燃燒，（感情）爆發，勃然大怒，點燃

flammable
fame + able

▶ 〔`flæməbl〕 形 易燃的，可燃的，速燃的

This lighter fluid is highly flammable, so keep it away from matches or other open flames.
這種液態打火機非常易燃，所以請遠離火柴或其他火苗貯放。

---

flat

▶ 〔flæt〕 形 平的，平坦的，（輪胎等）洩了氣的，單調的，無聊的

flatter
flat + er

▶ 〔`flætə〕 動 諂媚，奉承，使高興，使感到滿意

flattery
flatter + y

▶ 〔`flætərɪ〕 名 諂媚，奉承，阿諛之辭，諂媚的舉動

Carrie knew his compliments were just flattery, and ignored them.
凱莉知道他的讚美只是奉承之辭，所以並不理會。

---

foresee

▶ 〔for`si〕 動 預見，預知

foreseeable
foresee + able

▶ 〔for`siəbl〕 形 可預見的

foresight
fore + sight

▶ 〔`for͵saɪt〕 名 遠見，先見之明，深謀遠慮，展望

He had the foresight to invest his money to save up for his retirement.
為了替退休生活儲蓄，他有遠見地將錢作投資之用。

---

forgive

▶ 〔fə`gɪv〕 動 原諒，寬恕，豁免

forgiveness
forgive + ness

▶ 〔fə`gɪvnɪs〕 名 寬恕，饒恕

forgiving
forgive + ing

▶ 〔fə`gɪvɪŋ〕 形 寬容的，容許失誤的

fortune

▶ 〔`fɔrtʃən〕 名 財產，財富，好運，命運

fortunate fortune + ate	▶	[ˋfɔrtʃənɪt] 形　幸運的，僥倖的，帶來幸運的
fortunately fortunate + ly	▶	[ˋfɔrtʃənɪtlɪ] 副　幸運地，僥倖地
misfortune mis + fortune	▶	[mɪsˋfɔrtʃən] 名　不幸，惡運，災難

Fortunately, the weather was good so we didn't have to reschedule the picnic.
幸好天氣不錯，我們不需要重新安排野餐的時間。

★
328

frame	▶	[frem] 名　架構，骨架，結構，框架 動　給…裝框子，構築，塑造，制定
framework frame + work	▶	[ˋfremͺwɝk] 名　架構，骨架，構造，機構，組織

Researchers in that field must work within the framework of the scientific method.
那個領域的研究員必須在科學方法的架構之內作研究。

free	▶	[fri] 形　自由的，免費的，空間的，無…的 動　使自由，解放，使解脫 caffeine-free coffee 「不含咖啡因的咖啡」
freedom free + dom	▶	[ˋfridəm] 名　自由，獨立自主，(使用、行動等的) 自由權，免除，解脫

Kendra had a fantasy of going to the zoo and setting all the animals free.
坎德拉幻想去動物園釋放所有動物。

frequent	▶	[ˋfrikwənt] 形　時常發生的，頻繁的，屢次的， 慣常的，習以為常的 [friˋkwɛnt] 動　常到，常去，時常出入於
frequently frequent + ly	▶	[ˋfrikwəntlɪ] 副　頻繁地，屢次地
frequency frequent + cy	▶	[ˋfrikwənsɪ] 名　頻繁，屢次，頻率，次數

He travels to London frequently, so the long flights don't bother him.
他常去倫敦，所以長途飛行對他來說不算什麼。

fresh	▶	〔frɛʃ〕 形 新鮮的，未經加工處理過的，新的，剛發生的
refresh re + fresh	▶	〔rɪˋfrɛʃ〕 動 使清新，使清涼，消除…疲勞，恢復精神
fresh**man** fresh + man	▶	〔ˋfrɛʃmən〕 名 （大學等的）一年級生，新生，新人，新手

The vegetables were not very fresh, but they were still edible.
那些蔬菜不是很新鮮，但還是可以吃。

friend	▶	〔frɛnd〕 名 朋友，友人
friend**ly** friend + ly	▶	〔ˋfrɛndlɪ〕 形 友好的，親切的，朋友關係的
friend**ship** friend + ship	▶	〔ˋfrɛndʃɪp〕 名 友誼，友好，友誼的表現

Zak is a friendly, outgoing man.
柴克是個友善、外向的人。

frustrate	▶	〔ˋfrʌsˏtret〕 動 挫敗，阻撓，使感到灰心
frustrat**ion** frustrate + ion	▶	〔ˏfrʌsˋtreʃən〕 名 挫折，失敗，挫敗

After trying for an hour to get the knot out of the necklace chain, she gave up in frustration.
在花了一個小時試著解開打結的項鍊後，她挫敗地放棄了。

fulfill	▶	〔fʊlˋfɪl〕 動 執行，履行（諾言），實現，達到（目的），滿足（願望）
fulfill**ment** fulfill + ment	▶	〔fʊlˋfɪlmənt〕 名 完成，履行，實現，成（感）

hyllis said her job was fulfilling even though the pay was not so good.
菲麗絲說，雖然薪水不怎麼高，但是她的工作很有成就感。

function	▶	〔ˋfʌŋkʃən〕 名 功能，作用 動 運作，起作用 function as～「起～作用，當作～的功能」
function**al** function + al	▶	〔ˋfʌŋkʃənl〕 形 機能的，職務上的，起作用的

This lawnmower is functional, but it is in need of some repair.
這台割草機還能用，但是它需要修理一下。

⭐ **329** **furnish** ▶ 〔ˋfɜnɪʃ〕 動 給（房間）配置（傢俱等），裝備，供應，提供
furnish～with...「給～裝備…，供應（或提供）…給～」

furnishings
furnish + ing
▶ 〔ˋfɜnɪʃɪŋs〕 名 傢俱，室內陳設

furniture
funish + ture
▶ 〔ˋfɜnɪtʃə〕 名 傢俱，（工廠等的）設備
a piece of furniture「一件傢俱」
a set of furniture「一套傢俱」

The apartment is furnished except for a refrigerator.
除了冰箱，這間公寓一切傢俱都具備齊全。

fury ▶ 〔ˋfjʊrɪ〕 名 暴怒，（天氣、疾病、感情等的）狂暴

furious
fury + ous
▶ 〔ˋfjʊərɪəs〕 形 狂怒的，狂暴的，猛烈的

furiously
furious + ly
▶ 〔ˋfjʊərɪəslɪ〕 副 狂怒地，狂暴地，猛烈地

Lori was furious when she found out that her flight had been cancelled.
當羅莉發現她的班機取消時，她大發雷霆。

fuss ▶ 〔fʌs〕 名 忙亂，大驚小怪，抱怨，緊張不安
make a fuss about～「抱怨～，為～大驚小怪」

fussy
fuss + y
▶ 〔ˋfʌsɪ〕 形 大驚小怪的，難以取悅的，挑剔的
be fussy about～「對～很挑剔，對～大驚小怪」

He is very fussy about his car, and washes it about three times a week.
他對他的車子很講究，一個禮拜就洗三次車。

gift ▶ 〔gɪft〕 名 禮品，天賦，才能

gifted
gift + ed
▶ 〔ˋgɪftɪd〕 形 有天資的，有天賦的
be gifted with～「有～的天賦（才能）」

Because of her unusually advanced mathematic skills, Charlotte is enrolled in a school for gifted children.
夏綠蒂具有不凡的高階數學能力，因此她進入一所專為有天賦的孩童設立的學校就讀。

globe ▶ 〔glob〕 名 球，球狀物，地球儀，地球
the globe「地球」

global globe + al	▶	〔`globl〕 形　球狀的，全世界的

gloom	▶	〔glum〕 名　黑暗，陰暗，昏暗，憂鬱的心情， 沮喪的氣氛 動　變陰暗，感到沮喪，使陰沈 gloom and doom 〔dum〕 前景黯淡無望

gloomy gloom + y	▶	〔`glumɪ〕 形　陰暗的，陰沈的，陰鬱的，憂鬱的

The economists' predictions were all gloom and doom.
所有經濟學者都做出前景黯淡的預測。

glory	▶	〔`glorɪ〕 名　光榮，榮譽，壯麗，壯觀，燦爛，繁榮
glorious glory + ous	▶	〔`glorɪəs〕 形　光榮的，榮耀的，輝煌的，壯觀的， 極好的

We have been having glorious weather lately.
最近的天氣非常好。

330

govern	▶	〔`gʌvən〕 動　統治，管理，控制（感情等）
governor govern + or	▶	〔`gʌvənə〕 名　（美）州長，主管，董事，總裁
government govern + ment	▶	〔`gʌvənmənt〕 名　政府，政體，治理

The country was governed by a dictator, but it is now a democracy.
這個國家曾被獨裁者統治，但現在是一個民主國家。

greet	▶	〔grit〕 動　問候，迎接，招呼
greeting greet + ing	▶	〔`gritɪŋ〕 名　問候，迎接，招呼，賀詞，問候語

Someone from the company will be at the airport to greet the visitors.
公司的人將會在機場迎接客人。

grocer	▶	〔`grosə〕 名　食品雜貨商
grocery grocer + y	▶	〔`grosərɪ〕 名　食品雜貨店，食品雜貨業，食品雜貨 （名詞複數）groceries 〔`grosərɪz〕 名　食品雜貨類

I'll be back in a while; I have to go pick up some groceries.
我過一會兒就回來，我必須要去買一些雜貨。

guilt	▶	〔gɪlt〕名　有罪，犯罪，過失，內疚
guilty guilt + y	▶	〔`gɪltɪ〕形　有罪的，有過失的，內疚的

She felt guilty about having lied to her friend.
她對於跟朋友說謊一事感到內疚。

harass	▶	〔hə`ræs〕動　使煩惱，煩擾，不斷騷擾
harassment harass + ment	▶	〔hə`ræsmənt〕名　煩惱，煩擾，騷擾 sexual harassment「性騷擾」

Recently there have been more women charged with sexually harassing their male employees.
最近有越來越多女性被控性騷擾她們的男性雇員。

harm	▶	〔hɑrm〕名　損傷，傷害，危害
harmful harm + ful	▶	〔`hɑrmfəl〕形　有害的
harmless harm + less	▶	〔`hɑrmlɪs〕形　無害的，無惡意的，無辜的

The emissions from car engines are harmful both to humans and to the environment.　汽車引擎排放的氣體對人體和環境兩者都有害。
Some sharks are harmless to humans.
某些種類的鯊魚對人類無害。

harmony	▶	〔`hɑrmənɪ〕名　和睦，融洽，一致，和諧
harmonious harmony + ous	▶	〔hɑr`monɪəs〕形　和諧的，協調的，和睦的，悅耳的 be harmonious with～「與～調和（或協調、和諧）」

We live in hope that one day all the peoples of the world will be able to exist in harmony.
我們抱有某天世界上所有民族都能和睦相處的希望。

haste	▶	〔hest〕名　急忙，迅速，慌忙，性急 in haste「匆忙中，急忙中」
hasty haste + y	▶	〔`hestɪ〕形　匆忙的，急忙的，倉促的，輕率的

hasten haste + en	▶	〔ˋhesn〕 動　催促，加速，趕緊，趕快，趕緊做 hasten to～「趕緊～」

Greg made a very hasty decision to quit his job when he was having a bad day, but he regretted it later.
因為某天工作不順，葛瑞格非常倉促地決定辭職，但是沒多久就後悔了。

331

hazard	▶	〔ˋhæzəd〕 名　危險，危害物，危險之源
hazardous hazard + ous	▶	〔ˋhæzədəs〕 形　有危險的，冒險的

The radio station announced that there were hazardous driving conditions due to icy roads.
廣播電台宣佈，由於道路結冰，造成有些駕駛路況危險。

heaven	▶	〔ˋhɛvən〕 名　天國，天堂，樂園
heavenly heaven + ly	▶	〔ˋhɛvənlɪ〕 形　天空的，天堂的，神聖的，極好的 （the）heavenly bodies「天體」

"This chocolate cake is just heavenly!" eborah said as she ate her third piece.
在吃下第三塊蛋糕時，黛博拉說：「這個巧克力蛋糕真是太好吃了！」

height	▶	〔haɪt〕 名　高，高度，海拔，身高，高處
heighten height + en	▶	〔ˋhaɪtn〕 動　升高，增高，提高，使更顯著， 使（色彩等）更濃，變強

Mike tried to heighten the mood within his company by having a cocktail hour every Friday evening.
麥克試著透過每個禮拜五晚上的雞尾酒會來升高公司內部的情緒。

hesitate	▶	〔ˋhɛzə͵tet〕 動　躊躇，猶豫
hesitation hesitate + ion	▶	〔͵hɛzəˋteʃən〕 名　躊躇，猶豫
hesitant hesitate + ant	▶	〔ˋhɛzətənt〕 形　遲疑的，躊躇的

 atrick became very anxious when onna hesitated to reply after he asked her to marry him.
在派屈克向唐娜求婚後，他對她遲遲不答覆感到很不安。

hinder	▶	〔ˋhɪndɚ〕 動 妨礙，阻礙，成為障礙
hindrance hinder + ance	▶	〔ˋhɪndrəns〕 名 妨礙，障礙，障礙物，阻礙物

Trevor tried to stay positive and not let his deteriorating eyesight be a hindrance to his business career.
崔佛努力保持積極的態度，不讓他惡化的視力成為他職業生涯的障礙。

horizon	▶	〔həˋraɪzṇ〕 名 地平線，（知識、經驗等的）範圍，眼界，視野
horizontal horizon + al	▶	〔͵harəˋzɑntḷ〕 形 水平的，橫的，地平線的

Every night from her room, Rebecca watched the lights from the fishing boats shining on the horizon.
每天晚上，麗蓓加都會從她的房間眺望地平線那方漁船閃爍的燈光。

horror	▶	〔ˋhɔrɚ〕 名 恐怖，震驚，毛骨悚然
horrible horror + ible	▶	〔ˋhɔrəbḷ〕 形 可怕的，令人毛骨悚然的
horrify horror + ify	▶	〔ˋhɔrə͵faɪ〕 動 使恐懼，使驚懼 be horrified at～「對～感到恐懼、害怕」

The police were horrified at the brutality of the murder.
警察對那宗謀殺案件的殘忍感到驚懼不已。

332

hostile	▶	〔ˋhastɪl〕 形 敵人的，懷敵意的，不友善的
hostility hostile + ity	▶	〔hasˋtɪlətɪ〕 名 敵意，敵視，戰鬥 have hostility to～「對～抱有敵意」

Robert could not get rid of the feelings of hostility he had for the person who stole his car.
對偷了他的車子的人，羅伯始終沒法消除敵意。

human	▶	〔ˋhjumən〕 名 人 形 人的，人類的，有人性的 human being「人類」
humankind human + kind	▶	〔ˋhjumən͵kaɪnd〕 名 人類
humane human + e	▶	〔hjuˋmen〕 形 有人情味的，人道的，仁慈的
humanism human + ism	▶	〔ˋhjumən͵ɪzəm〕 名 人道主義，人本主義，人文主義

humanitarian
human + ian
▶ 〔hju͵mænəˋtɛrɪən〕 形　人道主義的，博愛的
名　人道主義者，慈善家

humanitarianism
humanitarian + ism
▶ 〔hju͵mænəˋtɛrɪənɪzəm〕 名　人道主義，博愛

humanity
human + ity
▶ 〔hjuˋmænətɪ〕 名　人性，人道，慈愛

utting a man on the moon was one of humankind's great achievements.
把人送上月球是人類的偉大成就之一。

humid
▶ 〔ˋhjumɪd〕 形　潮濕的

humidity
humid + ity
▶ 〔hjuˋmɪdətɪ〕 名　濕氣，濕度

When Barbara visited Japan in August, she had a hard time because she was not used to such high humidity.
芭芭拉8月拜訪日本時過得不太好，因為她不習慣這麼高的濕度。

humor
▶ 〔ˋhjumɚ〕 名　幽默感，幽默

humorous
humor + ous
▶ 〔ˋhjumərəs〕 形　幽默的，詼諧的，滑稽的，可笑的

aula said that what she liked most about Scott was his sense of humor.
寶拉說她最喜歡史考特的地方就是他的幽默感。

hungry
▶ 〔ˋhʌŋgrɪ〕 形　飢餓的，渴求的
be hungry for～「渴望（得到）～」

hunger
hungry + er
▶ 〔ˋhʌŋgɚ〕 名　飢餓，食慾，饑荒，渴望

Rosemary had to work through her lunch break, so by 4:00 PM she was very hungry.
蘿絲瑪莉午休的時候必須工作，所以到了下午4點時她肚子很餓。

hygiene
▶ 〔ˋhaɪdʒin〕 名　衛生，衛生學，保健法

hygienic
hygiene + ic
▶ 〔͵haɪdʒɪˋɛnɪk〕 形　衛生（學）的，保健的

The restaurant was closed down because it didn't meet the hygiene standards of the health department.
那間餐廳由於未能達到衛生署的衛生標準而停業。

⭐
333

hypothesis	▶	〔haɪˋpɑθəsɪs〕名　假說，前提
hypothetical hypothesis + ical	▶	〔͵haɪpəˋθɛtɪk!〕形　假設的，假定的

Let's talk about the hypothetical situation in which you have won four million pounds in the lottery.
我們來聊聊假設你中了樂透四百萬英鎊的情況。

idea	▶	〔aɪˋdiə〕名　主意，打算，構想，概念，意見
ideal idea + al	▶	〔aɪˋdiəl〕名　理想 　　　　　形　理想的，完美的
idealism ideal + ism	▶	〔aɪˋdiə͵lɪzəm〕名　理想主義
idealist ideal + ist	▶	〔aɪˋdiəlɪst〕名　理想主義者，空想家
idealistic idealist + ic	▶	〔aɪ͵diəlˋɪstɪk〕形　理想主義的，空想的

Simeon says he won't get married until he finds the ideal woman.
賽門說在找到理想的女性之前，他是不會結婚的。

idle	▶	〔ˋaɪd!〕形　懶惰的，無所事事的，無目的的， 　　　　　　無聊的，空轉的
idleness idle + ness	▶	〔ˋaɪd!nɪs〕名　懶惰，閒散，安逸，失業（狀態）

You should not let your car idle because it wastes gasoline and the emissions are harmful.
你不應該讓汽車空轉，因為除了浪費汽油，排放出的氣體也有害。

illusion	▶	〔ɪˋluʒən〕名　錯覺，幻覺，假象
illusionist illusion + ist	▶	〔ɪˋluʒənɪst〕名　幻想論者，幻術家
illusory illusion + ory	▶	〔ɪˋlusərɪ〕形　幻覺的，夢幻似的，迷惑人的
disillusion dis + illusion	▶	〔͵dɪsɪˋluʒən〕動　使醒悟，使不再抱幻想， 　　　　　　　使…的理想破滅

The large mirror on the back wall gave the illusion that the room was very large.
掛在內牆上的大鏡子營造出房間很大的錯覺。

illustrate ▶	〔ˋɪləstret〕 動 （用圖、實例等）說明，闡明，插圖於（書籍等），圖解 illustrate～with...「用…說明～」
illustration illustrate + ion ▶	〔ˌɪlʌsˋtreʃən〕 名 說明，圖解，圖例，實例，插圖，圖表
illustrator illustrate + or ▶	〔ˋɪləsˌtretə〕 名 插圖畫家，說明者，有實例作用的事物

He gave a detailed example to illustrate his point.
他舉用詳細的例子來說明他的論點。

impudent ▶	〔ˋɪmpjədn̩t〕 形 厚顏無恥的，放肆的，無禮的
impudently impudent + ly ▶	〔ˋɪmpjədəntlɪ〕 副 無禮地，放肆地
impudence impudent + ce ▶	〔ˋɪmpjədn̩s〕 名 厚臉皮，傲慢

The headmaster was infuriated by the impudence of the students.
校長被學生們放肆的態度給激怒了。

★
334

indifferent ▶	〔ɪnˋdɪfərənt〕 形 不感興趣的，不關心的，冷淡的 be indifferent to～「對～冷淡（不關心）」
indifference indifferent + ce ▶	〔ɪnˋdɪfərəns〕 名 漠不關心，冷淡，不感興趣，無關緊要

Santa Clause looked out with indifference at the freezing, blowing snow.
聖誕老人冷漠地望著外頭冰冷的吹雪。

indulge ▶	〔ɪnˋdʌldʒ〕 動 沈迷，放縱自己，使…高興，讓…享受 be indulged in～＝indulge oneself in～ 「放縱（自己）於～」 indulge in～「沈迷於～，放縱於～」
indulgent indulge + ent ▶	〔ɪnˋdʌldʒənt〕 形 縱容的，放縱的，溺愛的
indulgence indulgent + ce ▶	〔ɪnˋdʌldʒəns〕 名 沈溺，放縱，縱容，寬容

Each time Nellie finishes her homework, she indulges in a dish of ice cream.　每次奈莉做完功課，她都會吃一客冰淇淋讓自己享受一下。

industry	▶	〔ˋɪndəstrɪ〕 名 工業，企業，行業
industrial industry + ial	▶	〔ɪnˋdʌstrɪəl〕 形 工業的，產業的
industrious industry + ous	▶	〔ɪnˋdʌstrɪəs〕 形 勤勉的，勤奮的，勤勞的

Nagoya is a very industrial city, but it's a nice place to live.
名古屋是一座非常工業化的城市，但也很適合居住。

inferior	▶	〔ɪnˋfɪrɪə〕 形 （地位等）低等的，下級的，低於…的，較差的，次於…的 （反義）superior be inferior to～「比～差，不如～」 be superior to～「比～好，優於～」
inferiority inferior + ity	▶	〔ɪnfɪrɪˋɑrətɪ〕 名 劣勢，次級

This bicycle is cheaper than that one, but it is inferior in quality.
這輛腳踏車比那輛便宜，但是品質比較差。

install	▶	〔ɪnˋstɔl〕 動 任命，使就職，安裝，設置 install～in...「在…安裝～」
installment install + ment	▶	〔ɪnˋstɔlmənt〕 名 分期付款，分期交付，設置 buy～on installment「分期付款買下～」

Gwen will pay for the computer in ten monthly installments.
葛雯將以十個月分期付款買下那台電腦。

He installed a smoke detector in every room.
他在每個房間都安裝了煙霧探測器。

instinct	▶	〔ˋɪnstɪŋkt〕 名 本能，天性，直覺
instinctive instinct + ive	▶	〔ɪnˋstɪŋktɪv〕 形 （出於）本能的，（出於）天性的，（來自）直覺的
instinctively instinctive + ly	▶	〔ɪnˋstɪŋktɪvlɪ〕 副 （出於）本能地，憑直覺

As soon as she walked into the room, she instinctively knew that someone had been there.
她一走進房內，憑著直覺就知道有人來過。

interpret	▶	〔ɪnˋtɜprɪt〕 動 解釋，詮釋，口譯，翻譯
interpreter interpret + er	▶	〔ɪnˋtɜprɪtə〕 名 口譯員，解釋者

interpretation
interpret + tion

▶ 〔ɪnˌtɝprɪˋteʃən〕 名　解釋，闡明，翻譯，口譯

The data is all in; now we need to analyze and interpret the results.
數據已經齊全了，現在我們需要分析並解釋結果。

335

intrude

▶ 〔ɪnˋtrud〕 動　侵入，闖入，侵擾，打擾，
　　　　　　把…強加（在），把…硬擠（入）
intrude～on（人）「把～強加給（人）」

intrusion
intrude + ion

▶ 〔ɪnˋtruʒən〕 名　侵入，闖入，打擾

I don't mean to intrude, but Ruth, you are needed in the main office.
我無意打擾，但是露絲，總部辦公室現在需要你。

intuition

▶ 〔ˌɪntjuˋɪʃən〕 名　直覺，敏銳的洞察力

intuitional
intuition + al

▶ 〔ˌɪntʊˋɪʃənḷ〕 形　直覺的

intuitive
intuition + ive

▶ 〔ɪnˋtjuɪtɪv〕 形　直覺的，有直覺力的，
　　　　　　可以靠直覺得知的

You shouldn't make decisions based solely on intuition.
你不應該單憑直覺做決定。

invest

▶ 〔ɪnˋvɛst〕 動　投資，入股，投入（時間、金錢等）
invest one's money in～「投資金錢在～」

investment
invest + ment

▶ 〔ɪnˋvɛstmənt〕 名　投資，投資額，投資物，
　　　　　　（精力、時間等的）投入

He made some very wise investments and was able to retire early.
他做了一些非常聰明的投資，所以能提早退休。

investigate

▶ 〔ɪnˋvɛstəˌget〕 動　調查，研究

investigation
investigate + ion

▶ 〔ɪnˌvɛstəˋgeʃən〕 名　研究，調查
FBI = Federal Bureau of Investigation「聯邦調查局」

irksome

▶ 〔ˋɝksəm〕 形　令人厭煩的，令人厭倦的

irksomeness
irksome + ness

▶ 〔ˋɝksəmnɪs〕 名　厭煩，厭倦

He found their blatant disregard for the rules irksome, so he complained to the management.
他覺得他們公然藐視規定很惹人厭，因此他向管理部門投訴。

Irony	▶	〔ˋaɪrənɪ〕 名 反語，冷嘲，諷刺
ironical irony + ical	▶	〔aɪˋrɑnɪk〕 形 冷嘲的，挖苦的，具有諷刺意味的， 用反語的，愛挖苦人的

The irony is that three years ago Frank was accused of the same thing that he is accusing Nora of.
諷刺的是，三年前法蘭克被指控的理由正和他現在指控諾拉的理由相同。

irritate	▶	〔ˋɪrəˏtet〕 動 使惱怒，使煩躁
irritating irritate + ing	▶	〔ˋɪrəˏtetɪŋ〕 形 令人惱怒的
irritation irritate + ion	▶	〔ˏɪrəˋteʃən〕 名 激怒，惱怒，生氣

am couldn't sleep due to the irritation of a mosquito flying around her room all night.　潘因為一隻蚊子整晚在房間四處飛而被煩得睡不著。

jealous	▶	〔ˋdʒɛləs〕 形 嫉妒的，吃醋的 be jealous of～「嫉妒～」
jealousy jealous + y	▶	〔ˋdʒɛləsɪ〕 名 嫉妒，猜忌

Tammy is insanely jealous, and always accuses her boyfriend of going out with other girls.
泰咪異常愛吃醋，而且總是指控她的男朋友和其他女生出去。

⭐ **336** **keen**	▶	〔kin〕 形 熱心的，熱衷的，渴望的，敏銳的， 強烈的 be keen about～「對～很熱心」
keenly keen + ly	▶	〔ˋkinlɪ〕 副 敏銳地，強烈地，熱心地

We are alive thanks to his keen sense of smell; he smelled smoke before we did, and got us all out of the building.
我們能活下來得感謝他那敏銳的嗅覺，他早在我們之前就先聞到煙味，讓我們從那棟建築物逃出。

lament	▶	〔ləˋmɛnt〕 動 哀悼，悲痛，痛哭，悲嘆
lamentation lament + tion	▶	〔ˏlæmənˋteʃən〕 名 悲歎，哀悼，慟哭

Tim lamented the death of his favorite aunt.
提姆為他最愛的阿姨死去而悲痛。

laugh	▶	〔læf〕 動　笑，嘲笑
laughter laugh + er	▶	〔ˋlæftɚ〕 名　笑，笑聲

The laughter from the next room kept Emmy awake all night.
來自隔壁房間的笑鬧聲讓艾美整個晚上都無法入睡。

launch	▶	〔lɔntʃ〕 動　發射，發動，發起，開始
launcher launch + er	▶	〔ˋlɔntʃɚ〕 名　發射者，發射器

The ketchup company has just launched a huge advertising campaign to try to boost sales.
為了提高銷售量，那間番茄醬公司正積極地舉辦大型廣告活動。

lazy	▶	〔ˋlezɪ〕 形　懶散的，怠惰的，使人倦怠的，緩慢的
laziness lazy + ness	▶	〔ˋlezɪnɪs〕 名　怠惰，懶散，徐緩

Betty enjoyed a lazy Saturday morning, doing nothing but drinking coffee and filling in a crossword puzzle.
貝蒂渡過了一個悠閒的禮拜六早上，什麼事也沒做，就只是喝咖啡和玩填字遊戲。

leisure	▶	〔ˋliʒɚ〕 名　閒暇，空暇時間，悠閒，安逸
leisureless leisure + less	▶	〔ˋliʒɚlɪs〕 形　無暇的，無空閒的

Many people like to sing karaoke in their leisure time.
很多人喜歡在閒暇的時候唱卡拉OK。

little	▶	〔ˋlɪtl〕 形　小的，小巧可愛的，幼小的，瑣碎的，少，不多的
less	▶	〔lɛs〕 形　(little的比較級) 較少的，較小的
least	▶	〔list〕 形　(little的最高級) 最小的，最少的，最不重要的，地位最低的
lessen less + en	▶	〔ˋlɛsn̩〕 動　變小，變少，減輕

We've had less rain than normal this year, and the farmers are worried about the rice crop.
今年的雨量較往年要來得少，所以農民對稻米的收成量感到憂心。

337 limit ► [ˋlɪmɪt] 名 界線，界限，限制，限度，極限，範圍
動 限制

limitation
limit + tion ► [ˏlɪməˋteʃən] 名 限制，限制因素，局限，極限，限度

In most cases, hard work makes it possible to overcome one's limitations.
在大多數情形下，努力可讓一個人克服自身的侷限。

linguistic ► [lɪŋˋgwɪstɪk] 形 語言的，語言學的

linguistically
linguistic + ly ► [lɪŋˋgwɪstɪkəlɪ] 副 語言（學）方面

linguistics
linguistic + s ► [lɪŋˋgwɪstɪks] 名 語言學

linguist
linguistic + ist ► [ˋlɪŋgwɪst] 名 語言學者

Although there is some ethnic diversity, Japan is linguistically homogeneous.
雖然日本在種族上稍具多樣性，但在語言方面是單一的。

liquid ► [ˋlɪkwɪd] 形 液體的，液態的，流動的
名 液體
（反義）solid

liquor
liquid + or ► [ˋlɪkə] 名 酒，含酒精飲料，烈酒

As the temperature rose, the solid melted into a liquid.
溫度一升高，固體隨即融化成液體。

loose ► [lus] 形 鬆的，鬆散的，未受控制的，散裝的，散漫的

loosen
loose + en ► [ˋlusn] 動 鬆開，解開，放鬆（限制等），鬆開，鬆弛，變鬆

After eating six cups of ice cream, Jo had to loosen her belt.
吃了6杯冰淇淋後，喬必須鬆開她的腰帶。

lunar ► [ˋlunə] 形 月的，月球上的，陰曆的，月亮似的，新月形的

lunatic
lunar + tic ► [ˋlunəˏtɪk] 形 瘋的，精神錯亂的，瘋狂的
名 瘋子，瘋傻的人

The man was a genius, but he was also a lunatic.
那人是個天才，但他也是個瘋子。

luxury ▶ 〔`lʌkʃərɪ〕 名　奢侈，奢華，奢侈品，享受，樂趣

---

luxurious
luxury + ous

▶ 〔lʌg`ʒʊrɪəs〕 形　奢侈的，豪華的

By booking on-line we were able to stay in a luxurious 5-star hotel for a fraction of the regular price.
我們用網路預訂，可以用比一般低的價格住進豪華的五星級飯店。

---

machine ▶ 〔mə`ʃin〕 名　機器，機械

machinery
machine + ry

▶ 〔mə`ʃinərɪ〕 名　機器，機械，機械裝置

To get the gumball, you need to put the coin into the machine and turn the handle.
你必須把硬幣放到機器裡，然後轉動把手，才能買到口香糖球。

---

main ▶ 〔men〕 形　主要的，最重要的

mainly
main + ly

▶ 〔`menlɪ〕 副　主要地，大部份地

Although their imports come mainly from Italy, they do get some from France as well.
雖然他們的商品大多進口自義大利，但他們也從法國進口一些商品。

338

malice ▶ 〔`mælɪs〕 名　惡意，敵意，怨恨

malicious
malice + ous

▶ 〔mə`lɪʃəs〕 形　惡意的，懷恨的

The rumor is just malicious gossip, and it should be ignored.
謠言只是存心不良的閒話，應該要不予理會。

---

mare ▶ 〔mɛr〕 名　母馬，母驢

nightmare
night + mare

▶ 〔`naɪt،mɛr〕 名　夢魘，惡夢，夢魘般的經歷，恐怖的事

Ellen had a terrible nightmare, and couldn't get back to sleep.
艾倫做了一個惡夢，然後就睡不著了。

demerit
de + merit
▶ 〔di`mɛrɪt〕 名　缺點，過失，罪過

While owning your own car has many merits, you also need to consider the inconveniences such as paying for maintenance, parking and gasoline.
儘管擁有自己的車有很多好處，你還是需要考慮到像是維修費、停車費以及汽油費等等的不方便。

metaphor
▶ 〔`mɛtəfə〕 名　隱喻，象徵

metaphorical
metaphor + ical
▶ 〔ˌmɛtə`fɔrɪkl〕 形　用隱喻的，比喻的

The metaphor "to kill two birds with one stone" is used in many languages.
「一石二鳥」這個隱喻在許多語言中皆有使用。

mischief
▶ 〔`mɪstʃɪf〕 名　頑皮，淘氣，胡鬧，惡作劇
get into mischief「惡作劇，搗亂」

mischievous
mischief + ous
▶ 〔`mɪstʃɪvəs〕 形　惡作劇的，調皮的，淘氣的，有害的，惡意傷人的

Someone should be watching the children so they don't get into mischief.
應該要有人看顧那些孩子，這樣他們才不會搗亂。

★
340

misery
▶ 〔`mɪzərɪ〕 名　痛苦，不幸，悲慘，窮困，苦難

miserable
misery + able
▶ 〔`mɪzərəbl〕 形　痛苦的，不幸的，淒慘的，悲哀的

Alice has a miserable cold, so she won't be coming in today.
艾莉絲得了重感冒，所以她今天不會進來。

mix
▶ 〔mɪks〕 動　混合，結合，調製，混淆

mixture
mix + ture
▶ 〔`mɪkstʃə〕 名　混合，混和，（感情的）混雜，混合物

moist
▶ 〔mɔɪst〕 形　潮濕的，微濕的，多雨的

moisture
moist + ure
▶ 〔`mɔɪstʃə〕 名　濕氣，水分

In order for a sponge to work properly, it has to be moist.
要有效使用海綿，應該要將它沾濕使用。

moment	► [ˋmomənt] 名 瞬間，片刻，時機，重要時刻，關頭 at any moment「隨時」 at every moment「不斷地」
momentary moment + ary	► [ˋmomən‚tɛrɪ] 形 短暫的，瞬間的，隨時會發生的
momentarily momentary + ly	► [ˋmomən‚tɛrəlɪ] 副 短暫地，隨時，立刻
momentous moment + ous	► [moˋmɛntəs] 形 重大的，重要的

The doctor will be with you momentarily.
醫師馬上就來。

moral	► [ˋmɔrəl] 形 道德（上）的，講道德的，品性端正的
morality moral + ity	► [məˋrælətɪ] 名 道德，倫理，品行，道德觀， 道德規範
immoral im + moral	► [ɪˋmɔrəl] 形 不道德的，傷風敗俗的，邪惡的， 淫蕩的

Some religions believe that consuming alcohol is immoral.
有些宗教認為飲酒是不道德的。

muscle	► [ˋmʌsl̩] 名 肌肉，體力
muscular muscle + ar	► [ˋmʌskjələ] 形 肌肉的，肌肉發達的，健壯的

He worked out at the gym every day in order to develop his muscles.
為了讓肌肉發達，他每天都去健身房運動。

mutual	► [ˋmjutʃʊəl] 形 相互的，彼此的，共有的，共同的
mutually mutual + ly	► [ˋmjutʃʊəlɪ] 副 互相，彼此
mutuality mutual + ity	► [‚mjutʃʊˋælətɪ] 名 相互關係，共同性，親密

They were introduced through a mutual friend.
他們經由一個共同的朋友介紹而認識。

myth	► [mɪθ] 名 神話，虛構的人（事物）， 沒有事實根據的觀點（或理論）
mythology myth + logy	► [mɪˋθɑlədʒɪ] 名 （總稱）神話，神話學，神話集

It's a complete myth that it's difficult to learn how to use chopsticks.
學習使用筷子很難是沒有事實根據的說法。

⭐
341

narrate	▶	〔næˋret〕 動　敘述，講（故事）
narrator narrate + or	▶	〔næˋretə〕 名　解說員，敘述者，講述者
narration narrate + ion	▶	〔næˋreʃən〕 名　敘述，記述體，解說
narrative narrate + ive	▶	〔ˋnærətɪv〕 形　敘事的，敘事體的，故事形式的 名　記敘文，故事，敘述，講敘

The story is narrated by a 12-year-old girl.
故事由一個12歲的少女講述。

necessary	▶	〔ˋnɛsəˏsɛrɪ〕 形　必要的，必需的，必然的
necessarily necessary + ly	▶	〔ˋnɛsəsɛrɪlɪ〕 副　必定，必然地，必需地，必要地
necessity necessary + ity	▶	〔nəˋsɛsətɪ〕 名　需要，必要性，必需品，必然（性）

Just because the clothes are expensive does not necessarily mean they are well-made.
衣服昂貴不一定代表它們的做工精良。

negotiate	▶	〔nɪˋgoʃ⌣et〕 動　談判，協商，洽談 negotiate with（人）about～ 「和（人）談判（洽談）關於～的事」
negotiator negotiate + or	▶	〔nɪˋgoʃ⌣etə〕 名　磋商者，交涉者
negotiation negotiate + ion	▶	〔nɪˏgoʃⁱˋeʃn〕 名　談判，協商

After the strike, the workers were able to negotiate a pay increase.
在罷工過後，工人們得以談判要求提高薪資。

nerve	▶	〔nɜv〕 名　神經，神經過敏，憂慮，焦躁 get on one's nerve「惹人心煩，使得人神經緊張」
nervous nerve + ous	▶	〔ˋnɜvəs〕 形　神經質的，緊張不安的

That constantly barking dog is getting on my nerves.
那隻時常在狂吠的狗搞得我很心煩。

noble	▶	〔`nobḷ〕 形　高貴的，高尚的，宏偉的，貴族的，顯貴的 名　貴族
nobly noble + ly	▶	〔`noblɪ〕 副　高貴地，高尚地，貴族出身地
ignoble ig + noble	▶	〔ɪg`nobḷ〕 形　卑鄙的，不光彩的，可恥的，出身卑賤的

Jordon nobly volunteered to do the extra shift.
喬登高尚地自願承擔額外的輪班。

noise	▶	〔nɔɪz〕 名　聲響，喧鬧聲，噪音
noisy noise + y	▶	〔`nɔɪzɪ〕 形　喧鬧的，嘈雜的

The children filled the room with noisy, cheerful chatter.
孩子們喧鬧、興高采烈的說話聲充滿整個房間。

★
342

nominate nomin + ate	▶	〔`nɑmə‚net〕 動　提名，任命，指定 nominate（人）for～「提名（人）做～」 nominate（人）to～「任命（人）做～」
nomination nominate + ion	▶	〔‚nɑmə`neʃən〕 名　提名，任命，提名權，任命權

He has been nominated by his colleagues to receive the employee of the year award.
他被同事提名為年度最佳員工獎的受獎者。

nuclear	▶	〔`njuklɪə〕 形　核心的，中心的，原子核的，原子能的 a nuclear weapon「核武器」nuclear war「核子戰爭」 nuclear freeze「核子武器凍結」
nucleus nuclear + us	▶	〔`njuklɪəs〕 名　（原子）核，細胞核，核心

More and more countries are utilizing nuclear energy.
有越來越多的國家利用核能源。

obscure	▶	〔əb`skjur〕 形　黑暗的，朦朧的，模糊的，難懂的 動　使變暗，使難理解，使不顯著
obscurity obscure + ity	▶	〔əb`skjurətɪ〕 名　暗淡，朦朧，難懂，不引人注目

The written agreement was so obscure that Carol didn't even bother to read it, she just signed it.
那份手寫契約書非常難懂，所以卡洛兒甚至沒費心讀它就簽名了。

odd	▶ 〔ɑd〕 形　古怪的，奇數的，剩餘的，額外的 odd numbers「奇數」 even numbers「偶數」 the odd money「多餘的錢，額外的錢」
oddity odd + ity	▶ 〔`ɑdətɪ〕 名　奇怪，古怪，怪人，怪事

It seems very odd that you slept through the loud thunderstorm last night and didn't hear anything.
那似乎很奇怪，昨晚暴風雨聲那麼大，你就這麼睡著沒聽見半點聲音。

optimism	▶ 〔`ɑptəmɪzəm〕 名　樂觀，樂觀主義 （反義）pessimism
optimist optimism + ist	▶ 〔`ɑptəmɪst〕 名　樂觀者，樂觀主義者
optimistic optimist + ic	▶ 〔ˌɑptə`mɪstɪk〕 形　樂觀的

Today is a good day and I feel full of optimism.
今天是個好日子，我感到非常樂觀。

own	▶ 〔on〕 形　自己的，特有的 動　有，擁有
owner own + er	▶ 〔`onɚ〕 名　物主，所有人

I've never owned my own car.
我從未擁有過自己的車。

paradox	▶ 〔`pærəˌdɑks〕 名　似非而是的議論， 自相矛盾的人或事
paradoxical paradox + ical	▶ 〔ˌpærə`dɑksɪkl〕 形　似是而非的，自相矛盾的

It seems a paradox that you want to live in Spain but you don't want to learn Spanish.
你想要住在西班牙卻不想學西班牙文，似乎有點矛盾。

pay	▶ 〔pe〕 動　支付，償還，付出代價 pay for～「為～付出代價，付～的帳」

payment
pay + ment

▶ 〔ˋpemənt〕 名　支付，付款，支付的款項（或實物）

You will receive payment upon delivery of the goods.
你將在這批貨物交付時收到款項。

⭐ 343

peculiar

▶ 〔pɪˋkjuljə〕 形　奇怪的，獨特的，特殊的

peculiarity
peculiar + ity

▶ 〔pɪ͵kjulɪˋærətɪ〕 名　奇特，古怪，怪癖，特質

She thought the milk tasted a little peculiar, and realized why when she looked at the expiration date.
她覺得牛奶喝起來怪怪的，看了保存期限才知道為什麼。

perpetual

▶ 〔pəˋpɛtʃuəl〕 形　永久的，長期的

perpetuate
perpetual + ate

▶ 〔pəˋpɛtʃu͵et〕 動　使永久存在，使不朽

Her perpetual optimism is an inspiration to us all.
她時時保有樂觀，激勵了我們大家。

person

▶ 〔ˋpɝsn̩〕 名　人

personal
person + al

▶ 〔ˋpɝsn̩l〕 形　個人的，私人的

personality
personal + ity

▶ 〔͵pɝsn̩ˋælətɪ〕 名　人格，品格，個性，性格

personnel
person + nel

▶ 〔͵pɝsn̩ˋɛl〕 名　（總稱）人員，員工

It's not polite to ask personal questions.
詢問私人問題是不禮貌的。

pessimism

▶ 〔ˋpɛsəmɪzəm〕 名　悲觀，悲觀主義
（反義）optimism

pessimist
pessimism + ist

▶ 〔ˋpɛsəmɪst〕 名　悲觀者，悲觀主義者

pessimistic
pessimist + ic

▶ 〔͵pɛsəˋmɪstɪk〕 形　悲觀的

It's been demonstrated that optimists live less stressful lives than pessimists.
事實證明，樂觀的人比起悲觀的人生活過得比較沒那麼緊張。

philosophy	▶	〔fəˋlɑsəfɪ〕 名	哲學，哲理，人生觀，哲人態度，達觀
philosopher philosophy + er	▶	〔fəˋlɑsəfə〕 名	哲學家，思想家，學者，賢哲， 達觀的人
philosophical philosophy + ical	▶	〔͵fɪləˋsɑfɪkl̩〕 形	哲學的，哲學家的，達觀的， 有理性的
philosophically philosophical + ly	▶	〔͵fɪləˋsɑfɪklɪ〕 副	哲學上，賢明地，冷靜地

It seems paradoxical that Don says he is philosophically opposed to violence, but he likes hunting pheasants.
唐說他理性上反對暴力，但是他又喜歡獵野雉，這好像自相矛盾。

physics	▶	〔ˋfɪzɪks〕 名	物理學
physicist physics + ist	▶	〔ˋfɪzɪsɪst〕 名	物理學家
physician physics + ian	▶	〔fɪˋzɪʃən〕 名	醫師，內科醫生，治療者
physical physics + al	▶	〔ˋfɪzɪkl̩〕 形	身體的，肉體的，物理的，物理學的
physically physical + ly	▶	〔ˋfɪzɪklɪ〕 副	按照自然規律，身體上，實際上， 完全地，全然

Regular physical activity such as sports is essential for good health.
規律的體能活動，例如運動，對良好健康是不可或缺的。

☆
344

pity	▶	〔ˋpɪtɪ〕 名	憐憫，同情，可惜的事，憾事
pitiful pity + ful	▶	〔ˋpɪtɪfəl〕 形	可憐的，令人同情的
pitifully pitiful + ly	▶	〔ˋpɪtɪfʊlɪ〕 副	可憐地
pitiless pity + less	▶	〔ˋpɪtɪlɪs〕 形	無同情心的，無情的，冷酷的
pitilessly pitiless + ly	▶	〔ˋpɪtɪ͵lɪslɪ〕 副	無情地，冷酷地

Christine found the tiny bird shivering pitifully in the snow.
克莉絲汀發現一隻小鳥在雪地中可憐地顫抖。

planet	▶	〔ˋplænɪt〕 名	行星

planetarium planet + ium	▶	〔͵plænə`tɛrɪəm〕 名　天象儀，行星儀，天體運轉模型 （或圖），天文館

The planet Mars will be very bright in the months of July and August.
火星將在7月和8月時變得非常明亮。

plant	▶	〔plænt〕 名　植物，農作物，工廠 　　　　動　種植 a power plant「發電廠」
plantation plant + tion	▶	〔plæn`teʃən〕 名　農場，大農場，造林地，新開墾地

Carol planted a banana seed several years ago, and is now eating bananas grown in her own living room.
卡洛兒幾年前種了顆香蕉種子，所以她現在吃得到自己客廳裡種的香蕉。

poet	▶	〔`poɪt〕 名　詩人
poetic poet + ic	▶	〔po`ɛtɪk〕 形　詩的，詩人的，愛好詩歌的， 充滿詩意的，富有想像力的
poetry poet + ry	▶	〔`poɪtrɪ〕 名　（總稱）詩，詩歌，韻文

We will be studying the major English poets this semester.
這學期我們會研究英國主要的詩人。

poison	▶	〔`poɪzn̩〕 名　毒，毒藥，毒物，有害之物， （對社會的）毒害，弊害
poisonous poison + ous	▶	〔`poɪznəs〕 形　有毒的，有害的，惡毒的，有惡意的

There are poisonous snakes in the forest, so proceed with caution.
森林裡有毒蛇，要小心行進。

polite	▶	〔pə`laɪt〕 形　有禮貌的，客氣的，文雅的，有教養的
politeness polite + ness	▶	〔pə`laɪtnɪs〕 名　有禮貌，客氣，文雅
politely polite + ly	▶	〔pə`laɪtlɪ〕 副　有禮貌地，客氣地，委婉地
impolite im + polite	▶	〔͵ɪmpə`laɪt〕 形　無禮的
impoliteness impolite + ness	▶	〔͵ɪmpə`laɪtnɪs〕 名　無禮，粗魯
impolitely impolite + ly	▶	〔͵ɪmpə`laɪtlɪ〕 副　不客氣地，無禮地

She was really hungry, but she refused a second helping out of politeness.
她其實很餓，但是基於禮貌，她拒絕接受第二份食物。

⭐ **345**

politics	▶	〔`palətɪks〕名 政治，政治學，政治信條，政見，政治活動
political politics + al	▶	〔pə`lɪtɪkl〕形 政治的，政黨的，對政治感興趣的
politician politics + ian	▶	〔͵palə`tɪʃən〕名 從事政治者，政治人物

The politicians are all getting ready for the upcoming election.
所有的政治人物都正為了即將到來的選舉而準備中。

pollute	▶	〔pə`lut〕動 污染，弄髒，玷污，敗壞
polluted pollute + ed	▶	〔pə`lutɪd〕形 受污染的
pollution pollute + ion	▶	〔pə`luʃən〕名 污染，污染物，污染地區
pollutant pollute + ant	▶	〔pə`lutənt〕名 污染物，污染源

In many countries, noise pollution is taken just as seriously as air and water pollution.
在許多國家，噪音污染被認定和空氣污染以及水質污染一樣嚴重。

| possess
poss + sess | ▶ | 〔pə`zɛs〕動 擁有，佔有，懂得，掌握，支配，控制
be possessed of～「擁有～」 |
| possession
possess + ion | ▶ | 〔pə`zɛʃən〕名 擁有，所有物，財產，領地，殖民地
have～in possession「擁有～」 |

His most prized possession is a music box he got from a girl he loved in high school.
他最珍貴的東西是高中喜歡的女生送給他的音樂盒。

possible	▶	〔`pasəbl〕形 可能的，有可能的，合理的，合適的
possibility possible + ity	▶	〔͵pasə`bɪlətɪ〕名 可能性，可能的事，發展前途
impossible im + possible	▶	〔ɪm`pasəbl〕形 不可能的，辦不到的

Janet didn't dream that going abroad was even a remote possibility before she won a scholarship to study in Germany for a year.
在珍妮特贏得去德國留學一年的獎學金之前，她做夢也沒想過有出國深造的可能。

potential	▶	〔pə`tɛnʃəl〕 形　潛在的，可能的 名　潛力，潛能
potentiality potential + ity	▶	〔pə‚tɛnʃɪ`ælətɪ〕 名　潛在性，（發展的）可能性，潛力

They tried to consider and prepare for every potential problem before they put the plan into action.
在實行計劃之前，他們設法考量到任何可能發生的問題並加以準備。

poor	▶	〔pʊr〕 形　貧窮的，蹩腳的，缺少的，體弱的，可憐的 be poor at～「不擅長～」
poverty poor + ty	▶	〔`pɑvətɪ〕 名　貧窮，貧困，貧乏

A common theme in Hollywood films is "rags to riches;" meaning people born into poverty in the end enjoying financial success.
好萊塢電影常見的主題是「由貧致富」，就是指出身貧困的人最終能享受賺大錢的成功。

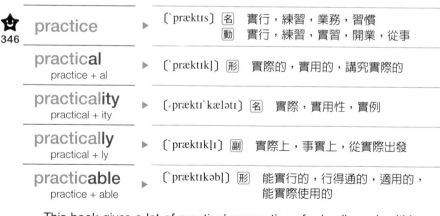

☆ 346　practice	▶	〔`præktɪs〕 名　實行，練習，業務，習慣 動　實行，練習，實習，開業，從事
practical practice + al	▶	〔`præktɪk!〕 形　實際的，實用的，講究實際的
practicality practical + ity	▶	〔‚præktɪ`kælətɪ〕 名　實際，實用性，實例
practically practical + ly	▶	〔`præktɪk!ɪ〕 副　實際上，事實上，從實際出發
practicable practice + able	▶	〔`præktɪkəb!〕 形　能實行的，行得通的，適用的，能實際使用的

This book gives a lot of practical suggestions for leading a healthier lifestyle.
這本書為引導更健康的生活方式，提出了許多實用的建議。

pray	▶	〔pre〕 動　祈禱，祈求，請求，懇求

prayer[1]
pray + er
▶ 〔prɛr〕 名 祈禱，禱告，祈禱式，祈禱文

prayer[2]
pray + er
▶ 〔`preə〕 名 祈禱者，懇求者

She said a quick prayer before she began her meal.
她在開始用餐前做了個簡短的禱告。

present
▶ 〔`prɛznt〕 名 現在，禮物 形 出席的，現在的
〔prɪ`zɛnt〕 動 贈送，描述，提交，呈現

presence
present + ce
▶ 〔`prɛzns〕 名 出席，在場，面前

presentation
present + tion
▶ 〔͵prizɛn`teʃən〕 名 贈送，提出，表現，口頭報告

He stayed up all night preparing his presentation.
他整晚熬夜準備他的口頭報告。

prestige
▶ 〔prɛs`tiʒ〕 名 名望，聲望，威望

prestigious
prestige + ous
▶ 〔prɛs`tɪdʒɪəs〕 形 有名望的

The garbage collector did not care that there was little prestige associated with his job.
那位垃圾清潔工並不在乎他的工作不太體面。

previous
▶ 〔`priviəs〕 形 先的，前的，以前的

previously
previous + ly
▶ 〔`priviəslɪ〕 副 事先，以前

Some foods that were previously thought to be unhealthy are now thought to be healthy.
一些以前認為不健康的食物，現在被認為是健康的。

private
▶ 〔`praɪvɪt〕 形 私人的，非公開的，私立的

privately
private + ly
▶ 〔`praɪvɪtlɪ〕 副 私下，不公開

privacy
private + cy
▶ 〔`praɪvəsɪ〕 名 隱私，私事，獨處，隱居

He always made a clear division between his private and professional lives.
他總是將私生活和工作區分得很清楚。

☆
347

privilege ▶ 〔ˋprɪvḷɪdʒ〕名　特權，優待

privileged ▶ 〔ˋprɪvɪlɪdʒd〕形　享有特權的，特許的，幸運的
privilege + ed

I once had the privilege of having lunch with a famous singer.
我曾經有幸和一位有名的歌手共進午餐。

profit ▶ 〔ˋprɑfɪt〕名　利潤，盈利，收益，紅利，利益

profitable ▶ 〔ˋprɑfɪtəbl〕形　有利的，盈利的，有益的，有用的
profit + able

He bought the vase for a small price at a flea market, and made a nice profit selling it to a museum.
他在跳蚤市場以低價買下這只花瓶，然後轉手賣給博物館賺了不少。

prompt ▶ 〔prɑmpt〕形　敏捷的，及時的，迅速的
動　促使，激勵，激起，提示，提詞
prompt（人）to V「激勵（人）～」

promptly ▶ 〔prɑmptlɪ〕副　敏捷地，迅速地，立即地，正好
prompt + ly

Failing the test has turned out to be a good thing, as it prompted Ken to study a little more.
考試不及格結果是件好事，因為那激勵肯要再用功一點。

propel ▶ 〔prəˋpɛl〕動　推進，推，推動，驅策，激勵
propel（人）to V「激勵（人）～」

propeller ▶ 〔prəˋpɛlə〕名　螺旋槳，推進器
propel + er

The boat is propelled by an outboard motor.
這隻船靠一台尾掛發動機發動。

prosper ▶ 〔ˋprɑspə〕動　繁榮，昌盛，成功

prosperous ▶ 〔ˋprɑspərəs〕形　興旺的，繁榮的，昌盛的，富足的
prosper + ous

prosperity ▶ 〔prɑsˋpɛrətɪ〕名　興旺，繁榮，昌盛，成功
prosper + ity

eople are hoping for peace and prosperity in the New Year.
人們在新年許願和平與繁榮。

provoke	▶	〔prə`vok〕 動 對⋯挑釁，煽動，激怒，激起，誘導 provoke（人）to V「刺激（人）～」
provocative provoke + tive	▶	〔prə`vakətɪv〕 形 氣人的，挑撥的，刺激的

Wolves are usually not dangerous unless they are provoked.
野狼通常是無害的，除非牠們受到挑釁。

prudent	▶	〔`prudṇt〕 形 審慎的，小心的，精明的
prudence prudent + ce	▶	〔`prudṇs〕 名 審慎，慎重，精明，深謀遠慮

It would be prudent of you to keep this information to yourself.
你應該謹慎點，不要告訴別人這個消息。

psychic	▶	〔`saɪkɪk〕 形 精神的，心靈的，超自然的，通靈的
psychiatrist psychic + ist	▶	〔saɪ`kaɪətrɪst〕 名 精神病醫師，精神病學家

She is seeing a psychiatrist to come to terms with her problems.
為了解決問題，她正接受精神科醫師的治療。

☆
348

punctual	▶	〔`pʌŋktʃuəl〕 形 嚴守時刻的，準時的，（表達方式等）正確的，精確的
punctuality punctual + ity	▶	〔͵pʌŋktʃu`ælətɪ〕 名 嚴守時間，正確，規矩

"You should be more punctual" the boss scowled as Norman came in late for the third time that week.
那個禮拜諾曼第三次遲到的時候，老板一臉不悅地說：「你應該要更準時一點。」

punish	▶	〔`pʌnɪʃ〕 動 罰，懲罰，處罰
punishment punish + ment	▶	〔`pʌnɪʃmənt〕 名 處罰，懲罰，刑罰

Although corporal punishment was once common, it is illegal now in many countries.
雖然體罰曾經很普遍，但是現在在許多國家卻是違法的。

pure	▶	〔pjʊr〕 形 純粹的，純淨的，純潔的
purity pure + ity	▶	〔`pjʊrətɪ〕 名 純淨，清潔，純潔
purely pure + ly	▶	〔`pjʊrlɪ〕 副 純粹地，完全，全然，僅僅，純潔地

purify
pure + ify
▶ 〔`pjurə،faɪ〕 動 使純淨，清洗，淨化

Puritan
pure + an
▶ 〔`pjurətən〕 名 清教徒

Be sure to purify the water before you drink it.
喝水之前，請務必先淨水。

pursue
▶ 〔pəˋsu〕 動 追趕，跟隨，追求，進行，從事

pursuit
pursue + it
▶ 〔pəˋsut〕 名 追求，尋求，從事

Louise intends to pursue a career in interior design.
路易絲想要從事室內設計的工作。

puzzle
▶ 〔`pʌzl〕 名 難題，迷惑，猜謎
動 使困惑，使不解

puzzled
puzzle + ed
▶ 〔pʌzld〕 形 困惑的，搞糊塗的，茫然的

What puzzles me is how the skunk got into the house when the door was locked.
讓我不解的是，當門鎖上時，臭鼬是怎麼進入房子的。

quality
▶ 〔`kwɑlətɪ〕 名 品質，特性，音質
形 優質的

qualify
quality + ify
▶ 〔`kwɑlə،faɪ〕 動 使具有資格，使合格
be qualified as～「具備～的資格」

qualification
qualify + tion
▶ 〔،kwɑləfəˋkeʃən〕 名 資格，能力，資格證書，執照

Carter has only one more exam for his teaching qualification.
卡特只剩一次考試，就可以得到他的教師資格證書。

quarter
▶ 〔`kwɔrtə〕 名 四分之一，四等分之一，季度，一刻鐘

quarterly
qurter + ly
▶ 〔`kwɔrtəlɪ〕 形 季度的，按季度的

It'll take about a quarter of an hour to get there.
到那裡大概要花15分鐘。

quote
▶ 〔kwot〕 動 引用，引述，把…放在引號內，報價

quotation
quate + tion
▶ 〔kwoˋteʃən〕 名 引用，引證，引文，語錄

The newspaper quoted him as saying he would run for re-election.
報紙引述他的話，說他會再次出馬競選。

⭐ **349**

race	▶	〔res〕 名　賽跑，競賽，種族，民族
racial race + ial	▶	〔ˋreʃəl〕 形　人種的，種族的，種族之間的 racial discrimination「種族歧視」

Although the city is ethnically diverse, there is little racial tension.
雖然這是座種族多元的城市，但是卻很少發生種族關係造成的緊張。

radiate	▶	〔ˋredɪ͵et〕 動　散發，輻射，情感流露，發射
radiation radiate + ion	▶	〔͵redɪˋeʃən〕 名　發光，發熱，輻射，放射物

Selma radiated with happiness when Stephen told her he loved her.
當史帝芬對莎瑪表示愛意時，莎瑪洋溢著幸福之情。

radical	▶	〔ˋrædɪkl〕 形　根本的，徹底的，極端的，激進的
radically radical + ly	▶	〔ˋrædɪklɪ〕 副　根本地，徹底地，完全地，激進地， 極端地

It's interesting that two people with such radically different beliefs can be such close friends.
有趣的是，兩個信仰完全不同的人竟然能夠成為那麼親密的朋友。

random	▶	〔ˋrændəm〕 形　胡亂的，隨便的，隨機的，無規則的 at random「隨便地，任意地」
randomly random + ly	▶	〔ˋrændəmlɪ〕 副　任意地，隨便地，胡亂地
randomness random + ness	▶	〔ˋrændəmnɪs〕 名　隨意，無安排，無目的

The researchers surveyed a random sample of three thousand residents of Zurich.
研究人員隨機調查了蘇黎世3000位居民。

rate	▶	〔ret〕 名　比例，率，速率，費用 at any rate「無論如何，至少」
ratio rate + io	▶	〔ˋreʃo〕 名　比，比率，比例 at the rate of three to two = in the ratio of three to two「3比2」

The Japanese yen to British pound ratio has recently been in favor of Japanese travelers.
近期日圓對英鎊的匯率對日籍旅客較有利。

rapid rap + id	▶	[ˋræpɪd] 形　快的，迅速的，動作快的
rapidly rapid + ly	▶	[ˋræpɪdlɪ] 副　很快地，立即，迅速地
rapidity rapid + ity	▶	[rəˋpɪdətɪ] 名　迅速

If you take the rapid service train, it'll take you there in less than two hours.
如果搭乘特快車，你不到兩小時就會抵達那裡。

He is furiously applying hair tonic to his rapidly receding hairline.
他急躁地將生髮水塗在他急速後退的髮線。

rational	▶	[ˋræʃənl] 形　理性的，明事理的，合理的
rationalism rational + ism	▶	[ˋræʃənl͵ɪzm] 名　理性主義
irrational ir + rational	▶	[ɪˋræʃənl] 形　無理性的，不合理的，不明事理的，荒謬的

On some level, she knew her behavior was irrational, but she couldn't seem to stop herself from throwing a fit.
在某種程度上，她知道自己的行為很不理性，但她似乎無法克制脾氣。

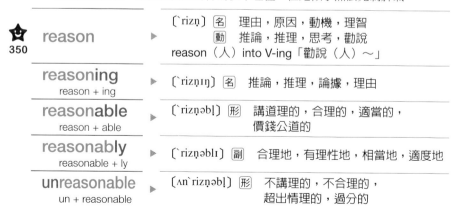

⭐ 350　reason	▶	[ˋrizn] 名　理由，原因，動機，理智 動　推論，推理，思考，勸說 reason（人）into V-ing「勸說（人）～」
reasoning reason + ing	▶	[ˋriznɪŋ] 名　推論，推理，論據，理由
reasonable reason + able	▶	[ˋriznəbl] 形　講道理的，合理的，適當的，價錢公道的
reasonably reasonable + ly	▶	[ˋriznəblɪ] 副　合理地，有理性地，相當地，適度地
unreasonable un + reasonable	▶	[ʌnˋriznəbl] 形　不講理的，不合理的，超出情理的，過分的

Carmella didn't think the demands being put upon her were reasonable.
卡蜜拉認為施加在她身上的請求是不合理的。

rebel	▶ 〔ˋrɛbl〕[名]　造反者，反叛者 　　　　[形]　反叛（者）的，造反（者）的 〔rɪˋbɛl〕[動]　造反，反叛，反抗，嫌惡 rebel against～「反抗～」
rebellious rebel + ous	▶ 〔rɪˋbɛljəs〕[形]　造反的，不法的，難控制的，難治療的 rebellious stage「反抗期」

Colette went through a rebellious stage when she was a teenager, and would never wear the clothes her parents bought for her.
柯蕾特青少年的時候經歷了反抗期，她絕不穿父母買給她的衣服。

recent	▶ 〔ˋrisn̩t〕[形]　新近的，最近的，近來的，近代的
recently recent + ly	▶ 〔ˋrisn̩tlɪ〕[副]　最近，近來

Recently, Lisa has done nothing but work, and she really needs a vacation.
最近麗莎的生活只有工作，她真的需要去渡個假。

reckless	▶ 〔ˋrɛklɪs〕[形]　不注意的，不在乎的，不顧後果的 be reckless of～「不在乎～」
recklessly reckless + ly	▶ 〔ˋrɛklɪslɪ〕[副]　不在乎地，魯莽地，不顧一切地

He recklessly leaned out of the window of the high-speed train.
他魯莽地將身子探出高速列車的窗外。

recreate	▶ 〔ˋrɛkrɪ͵et〕[動]　消遣，娛樂 recreate oneself by～「藉著～娛樂自己」
re-create	▶ 〔͵rikrɪˋet〕[動]　改造，改製，重新創造
recreation recreate + ion	▶ 〔͵rɛkrɪˋeʃən〕[名]　消遣，娛樂，遊戲

The village manages to re-create the atmosphere of colonial North America.
那座村莊設法重現殖民時期的北美風情。

recur	▶ 〔rɪˋkɝ〕[動]　再發生，復發，再現，重提
recurrence recur + ence	▶ 〔rɪˋkɝəns〕[名]　再發生，重新提起，再現，回憶

For weeks before her wedding, Sandy had a recurring nightmare of the hairdresser shaving off all her hair.
在婚禮的前幾週，珊蒂一直夢到美髮師把她頭髮給剃光的惡夢。

351

refrain ▶ 〔rɪˋfren〕 動　忍住，抑制，節制，戒除，克制
refrain from V-ing 「忍住不～，避免～」

refrainment
refrain + ment ▶ 〔rɪˋfrenmənt〕 名　抑制，節制

lease refrain from smoking in this area.
請不要在這個區域抽菸。

I refrained from making any comment on his unreasonable suggestion.
我忍住不對他無理的提議做出任何評論。

refuge ▶ 〔ˋrɛfjudʒ〕 名　躲避，庇護所

refugee
refuge + ee ▶ 〔ˏrɛfjʊˋdʒi〕 名　難民，流亡者

The picnickers huddled under their umbrellas trying to take refuge from the thunderstorm.
野餐的人們在雨傘下縮成一團躲避大雷雨。

register ▶ 〔ˋrɛdʒɪstɚ〕 名　登記，註冊，登記簿，收銀機
動　登記，註冊，申報
registered mail 「掛號郵件」

registration
register + tion ▶ 〔ˏrɛdʒɪˋstreʃən〕 名　登記，註冊，掛號，登記人數

Registration for classes will start next week.
上課登記將從下週開始。

regret ▶ 〔rɪˋgrɛt〕 動　懊悔，因…而遺憾，痛惜，哀悼

regrettable
regret + able ▶ 〔rɪˋgrɛtəbl〕 形　使人悔恨的，令人遺憾的，可惜的

regrettably
regrettable + ly ▶ 〔rɪˋgrɛtəblɪ〕 副　抱歉地，遺憾地

regretful
regret + ful ▶ 〔rɪˋgrɛtfəl〕 形　懊悔的，遺憾的，惆悵的

When Bob got older, he regretted getting the tattoo that covered his back.
當鮑伯年紀漸長，他便後悔當初刺了覆蓋整個背部的刺青。

Regrettably, the missing hikers could not be found, and the search was called off.
很遺憾地，失蹤的登山客沒能被找到，就此結束了搜索。

| relax | ▶ | 〔rɪˋlæks〕 動 放鬆，緩和，鬆懈 |

| relaxation
relax + tion | ▶ | 〔ˏrilæksˋeʃən〕 名 鬆弛，放鬆，緩和，休息，消遣 |

Johnny and Candice are going to Guam for some rest and relaxation.
強尼和坎蒂絲要去關島休息放鬆。

| relevant | ▶ | 〔ˋrɛləvənt〕 形 有關的，切題的，恰當的，
有意義的，關係重大的
be relevant to～「與～相關」 |

| relevance
relevant + ce | ▶ | 〔ˋrɛləvəns〕 名 關聯，適宜，中肯 |

| irrelevant
ir + relevant | ▶ | 〔ɪˋrɛləvənt〕 形 不恰當的，無關係的，不對題的
be irrelevant to～ 「與～不相關」 |

Be sure to give the police all the relevant information.
切記要將所有相關的情報告訴警察。

| religion | ▶ | 〔rɪˋlɪdʒən〕 名 宗教，教派，宗教團體，宗教信仰 |

| religious
religion + ous | ▶ | 〔rɪˋlɪdʒəs〕 形 宗教的，宗教上的，篤信宗教的 |

 eople should not be discriminated against because of the ir religious beliefs.
人們不應該因為他們的宗教信仰而遭受歧視。

🌟
352

| reluctant | ▶ | 〔rɪˋlʌktənt〕 形 不情願的，勉強的
be reluctant to V「不願～」 |

| reluctance
reluctant + ce | ▶ | 〔rɪˋlʌktəns〕 名 不情願，勉強 |

Sam was reluctant to go to the amusement park because he was secretly afraid of roller coasters.
山姆不願意去遊樂園，因為他內心對坐雲霄飛車感到恐懼。

| remark | ▶ | 〔rɪˋmɑrk〕 動 談到，評論，說，議論
名 言辭，談論，評論，注意，察覺 |

| remarkable
remark + able | ▶ | 〔rɪˋmɑrkəbl〕 形 值得注意的，非凡的，卓越的 |

| remarkably
remarkable + ly | ▶ | 〔rɪˋmɑrkəblɪ〕 副 引人注目地，明顯地，非常地 |

Besides making a remark about the weather, he said nothing through the whole meal.
吃飯的時候，除了談到天氣以外，他其餘什麼也沒說。

He made a remarkable recovery from a disease that had killed everyone in his family.
他奇蹟地從害死他全家的疾病中復元了。

renew	▶	〔rɪˋnju〕動 使更新，使恢復，重新開始，繼續
renewable renew + able	▶	〔rɪˋnjuəbl〕形 可更新的，可恢復的，可繼續的
renewal renew + al	▶	〔rɪˋnjuəl〕名 更新，復原，恢復，復興

I almost forgot to renew my driver's license.
我差點忘記更新我的駕照。

rent	▶	〔rɛnt〕名 租金，租費，出租的財產 動 租用，租入，租出，出租 rent～to... 「出租～給…」 rent～from... 「向…租借～」
rental rent + al	▶	〔ˋrɛntl〕名 租金，租賃，出租 形 租賃的，供出租的

How much is rent for a typical apartment in New York City?
紐約市一般公寓的租金是多少錢？

replace	▶	〔rɪˋples〕動 把…放回（原處），取代，以…代替，歸還，償還 replace～as... 「代替～當…」 replace～with... 「用…代替～」
replacement replace + ment	▶	〔rɪˋplesmənt〕名 代替，更換，接替，代替者（物）

Be sure you have the switch turned off before you replace the light bulb.
更換燈泡之前，務必確認已經關掉開關。

Jane is retiring, so we need to hire a replacement.
珍要退休了，所以我們必需雇用一個人替代她。

represent	▶	〔͵rɛprɪˋzɛnt〕動 表現，象徵，表示，代表，演出
representation represent + tion	▶	〔͵rɛprɪzɛnˋteʃən〕名 代表，代理，表現，演出

representative
represent + tive
▶ 〔͵rɛprɪˋzɛntətɪv〕 名　典型，代表物，代表，代理人
be representative of～「～的典型代表」

The lawyer representing the defendant has a reputation for getting the sympathy of the jury.
代表被告的律師以擅長獲得陪審團同情而聞名。

He said that the scattered bricks in his painting are representative of the buildings in a city.
他說他畫中散佈的磚塊象徵一座城市的建築物。

353

repute
▶ 〔rɪˋpjut〕 名　名氣，美名，聲望，名譽
動　把…稱為，認為
be reputed～「被認為是～」

reputable
repute + able
▶ 〔ˋrɛpjətəbl〕 形　聲譽好的，可尊敬的

reputation
repute + tion
▶ 〔͵rɛpjəˋteʃən〕 名　名譽，名聲，聲望，信譽

I don't really believe the rumor, because it didn't come from a reputable source.
我其實不相信那起謠言，因為那不是出自可靠的情報來源。

research
▶ 〔rɪˋsɝtʃ〕 名　（學術）研究，調查，探究
動　作學術研究，調查，探究

researcher
research + er
▶ 〔rɪˋsɝtʃɚ〕 名　研究員，調查者

In some disciplines, qualitative research is more important than quantitative.
在某些學科，質的研究比量化研究要來得重要。

reside
▶ 〔rɪˋzaɪd〕 動　住，居住，歸於

residence
reside + ence
▶ 〔ˋrɛzədəns〕 名　居住，住所，住宅，官邸

resident
residence + ent
▶ 〔ˋrɛzədənt〕 名　居民，定居者，僑民，住院醫生

residential
resident + ial
▶ 〔͵rɛzəˋdɛnʃəl〕 形　居住的，住宅的
residential area「住宅區」

She's been residing in the same place for 35 years.
她住在同一個地方已經35年了。

All the residents of the apartment building were awakened in the night by a large bang.
公寓大樓的所有住戶在夜裡被「砰」的一聲給吵醒。

resource	▶	〔rɪ`sors〕 名　資源，物力，財力 natural resources「天然資源」
resourceful resource + ful	▶	〔rɪ`sorsfəl〕 形　資源豐富的，富於機智的

It's a shame that his ingenious inventions were never developed due to lack of financial resources.
很可惜他創新精巧的發明由於資金短缺的緣故，從來沒有機會發展。

rest	▶	〔rɛst〕 名　休息，休養，休息時間 動　休息，睡
restless rest + less	▶	〔`rɛstlɪs〕 形　煩躁的，受打擾的，得不到休息的，靜不下來的
restlessly restless + ly	▶	〔`rɛstlɪslɪ〕 副　不安地，慌張地，無休止地

The tiger restlessly paced back and forth in its cage.
老虎不安地在籠子內來回走動。

restore	▶	〔rɪ`stor〕 動　恢復，復原，修復，整修，修補
restoration restore + tion	▶	〔͵rɪstə`reʃən〕 名　恢復，復位，復辟，修復，復原，整修，歸還

In his spare time, Marty is restoring a 1968 Mustang convertible.
馬帝有空的時候就在修復一輛1968年的野馬跑車。

☆ 354　retrieve	▶	〔rɪ`triv〕 動　重新得到，收回，使恢復，彌補，（獵犬）銜回（被擊中的獵物）
retriever retrieve + er	▶	〔rɪ`trivɚ〕 名　找回東西者，復得者

The dog retrieved the duck that uncle Emil had shot.
那隻狗銜回了埃米爾叔叔射到的鴨子。

She went back to the restaurant to retrieve the jacket she had left behind.
她返回那間餐廳，拿走她忘記帶走的夾克。

return	▶	〔rɪ`tɝn〕 動　返回，歸還，回復，回報 名　返回，歸還，報答，利潤 return to～「回歸～，返回～」 return～to...「把～歸還給…」

| room | ▶ 〔rum〕名 房間，空間，位置，餘地，機會 |

| roomy
room + y | ▶ 〔`rumɪ〕形 寬敞的，廣闊的 |

He said he chose this model of car because of its roomy interior.
他說他選這一型的車子是因為它寬敞的內部。

| rot | ▶ 〔rɑt〕動 腐爛，腐壞，腐朽 |

| rotten
rot + en | ▶ 〔`rɑtŋ〕形 腐爛的，發臭的，腐敗的 |

I found a rotten hamburger when I cleaned out my refrigerator.
我在清冰箱的時候發現了一個爛掉的漢堡。

| rough | ▶ 〔rʌf〕形 粗糙的，粗製的，粗略的，初步的，粗野的 |

| roughly
rough + ly | ▶ 〔`rʌflɪ〕副 粗糙地，粗暴地，粗略地，大體上，大約
roughly speaking「大致上來說」 |

It takes roughly 2 hours to get there, so you should leave at 10:00 to get there by noon.
到達那裡大概會花2小時，所以你中午要到的話，應該10點就要出門了。

☆
356

| route | ▶ 〔rut〕名 路線，路程，途徑 |

| routine
route + ine | ▶ 〔ru`tin〕名 例行公事，日常工作，慣例
形 日常的，例行的，常規的 |

After finishing some routine chores, she decided to go to the beach for the day. 做完一些例行雜務後，她決定去海邊度過整天。

| royal | ▶ 〔`rɔɪəl〕形 王室的，皇家的，英國的，高貴的 |

| royalty
royal + ty | ▶ 〔`rɔɪəltɪ〕名 皇族或王族（成員），王權，高貴 |

The peasants were required to bow in the presence of royalty.
農夫們必須在皇族成員出現的時候向他們鞠躬。

| rude | ▶ 〔rud〕形 粗野的，粗魯的，無禮的，野蠻的 |

| rudely
rude + ly | ▶ 〔`rudlɪ〕副 冒昧地，無禮地，粗暴地，粗陋地 |

| rudeness
rude + ness | ▶ 〔`rudnɪs〕名 無禮貌，粗野 |

The girl rudely pushed to the front of the line and bought her ticket.
那個女孩沒禮貌地擠到隊伍前方買票。

sail	▶	〔sel〕 名　帆，篷，乘船航行 動　航行，（坐船）遊覽，啓航
sailor sail + or	▶	〔`selə〕 名　船員，水手，水兵，乘船者

The white sail on the boat fluttered in the breeze.
船上的白帆在微風中飄揚。

satisfy	▶	〔`sætɪsˌfaɪ〕 動　使滿意，使高興，使滿足 be satisfied with～「對～感到滿意」
satisfaction satisfy + tion	▶	〔ˌsætɪs`fækʃən〕 名　滿意，滿足，稱心，樂事
satisfactory satisfy + ory	▶	〔ˌsætɪs`fæktərɪ〕 形　令人滿意的，符合要求的
dissatisfy dis + satisfy	▶	〔dɪs`sætɪsˌfaɪ〕 動　使感覺不滿 be dissatisfied with～「對～感到不滿」
dissatisfaction dissatisfy + tion	▶	〔ˌdɪssætɪs`fækʃən〕 名　不滿，不平
dissatisfactory dissatisfy + ory	▶	〔ˌdɪssætɪs`fæktərɪ〕 形　不滿意的，不夠理想的

It is very difficult to satisfy everybody.
要讓每個人都滿意是非常困難的。

savage	▶	〔`sævɪdʒ〕 形　野性的，殘酷的，未開化的，原始的
savagely savage + ly	▶	〔`sævɪdʒlɪ〕 副　野蠻地，殘忍地，粗野地，兇猛地

The tiger roared and growled savagely when she thought her cubs were in danger.
那隻老虎在感覺她的幼虎遭遇危險的時候，兇猛地大聲噪叫。

sterile	▶	〔`stɛrəl〕 形　不生育的，貧瘠的，消過毒的，無菌的
sterilize sterile + ize	▶	〔`stɛrəˌlaɪz〕 動　使無菌，消毒，使不孕，使貧瘠

Make sure the surgical instruments have been sterilized before you start the procedure.
在你開始動手術之前，確保手術器具已經消毒完畢。

★
357

scarce ▶ 〔skɛrs〕 形 缺乏的，不足的，稀有的，珍貴的

scarcity
scarce + ity
▶ 〔`skɛrsətɪ〕 名 缺乏，不足，匱乏，罕見

scarcely
scarce + ly
▶ 〔`skɛrslɪ〕 副 幾乎不，幾乎沒有
can scarcely V「幾乎無法～」

Herbs that used to be found in abundance on this mountainside are now scarce.
過去常在這個山坡發現的大量藥草現在已經很少看到了。

scare ▶ 〔skɛr〕 動 驚嚇，使恐懼，把…嚇跑，受驚

scary
scare + y
▶ 〔`skɛrɪ〕 形 引起驚慌的，膽小的，提心吊膽的

This horror movie is so scary I think it might give me nightmares.
這部恐怖片好恐怖，我覺得好像會做惡夢。

scatter ▶ 〔`skætɚ〕 動 撒，散佈，散播，分散

scattered
scatter + ed
▶ 〔`skætɚd〕 形 散亂的，散佈的

Can you scatter these seeds on the ground for me?
你可以幫我把這些種子播撒到地上嗎？

She's a little scatter-brained, but she has a good heart.
她注意力有一點渙散，但是她的心地很好。

scene ▶ 〔sin〕 名 場面，景象，佈景，（戲劇的）一場，（電影、電視的）一個鏡頭

scenery
scene + ry
▶ 〔`sinərɪ〕 名 風景，景色，舞台佈景

scenic
scene + ic
▶ 〔`sinɪk〕 形 風景的，描繪實景的，舞台的

Their house is nestled in a scenic little valley.
他們的家座落在一個風光明媚的小山谷裡。

scope ▶ 〔skop〕 名 範圍，領域，眼界，見識

microscope
mircro + scope
▶ 〔`maɪkrəˌskop〕 名 顯微鏡

If you look at the table of contents, you can get an idea of the scope and sequence of the textbook.
如果你看了目次，你會對這本課本的授課範圍和內容順序有個瞭解。

scorn	▶	〔skɔrn〕 名　輕蔑，藐視，嘲笑，嘲笑的對象 動　輕蔑，藐視
scornful scorn + ful	▶	〔ˋskɔrnfəl〕形　輕蔑的，嘲笑的

He was scorned for his ideas at first, but was later recognized as a genius.
他最初因為他的想法而遭人蔑視，但後來他被認定是個天才。

seed	▶	〔sid〕名　種子，籽，原因，根源，種子選手， 子孫，後代
seedless seed + less	▶	〔ˋsidlɪs〕形　無核的 seedless grapes「無籽葡萄」

It is amazing to think that this little seed will one day grow into a tree.
想到這麼一顆小種子有一天將長成一棵大樹就覺得很驚奇。

seek	▶	〔sik〕動　尋找，探索，追求，試圖，搜查
seeker seek + er	▶	〔ˋsikɚ〕名　尋找者，搜索者

After they had been fighting for 25 years, the couple finally sought the advice of a marriage counselor.
在吵架吵了25年後，這對夫妻終於尋求婚姻諮詢的建議。

☆
358

selfish	▶	〔ˋsɛlfɪʃ〕形　自私的，只顧自己的
selfishly selfish + ly	▶	〔ˋsɛlfɪʃlɪ〕副　自私地，任性地
selfishness selfish + ness	▶	〔ˋsɛlfɪʃnɪs〕名　自我中心，利己主義，任性

He was so selfish that he ate all the chocolates himself and didn't share with his friends.
他很自私，自己吃掉了所有的巧克力，沒有和他的朋友分享。

senior	▶	〔ˋsinjɚ〕形　年長的，地位較高的，前輩的 名　較年長者，前輩，上司，學長，資深人士 （反義）junior〔ˋdʒunjɚ〕 形　年紀較輕的，資淺的，晚輩的 be senior to（人）by～years「比（人）年長～歲」

seniority
senior + ity

▶ 〔sin`jɔrətɪ〕 名　長輩，老資格，年長，年資

Simply because he has seniority doesn't mean he is any wiser than his younger co-workers.
他只是年資深，不代表他比年輕的同事們聰明。

serious

▶ 〔`sɪrɪəs〕 形　嚴重的，嚴肅的，認真的，重要的

seriously
serious + ly

▶ 〔`sɪrɪəslɪ〕 副　嚴肅地，認真地，當真地，嚴重地

She was a very quiet, thoughtful and serious person.
她是一個非常沈默、體貼、嚴肅的人。

settle

▶ 〔`sɛtl〕 動　安放，安頓，安排，
使（心情）平靜下來，確定
settle in～「適應（或習慣）～」

settler
settle + er

▶ 〔`sɛtlə〕 名　移居者，(糾紛等的)解決者

settlement
settle + ment

▶ 〔`sɛtlmənt〕 名　解決，結帳，安頓，定居

After he was hit by a taxi driver who ran a red light, Jim went to court and got a nice settlement.
吉姆被一輛闖紅燈的計程車撞到後，和對方打官司贏得有利的判決。

severe

▶ 〔sə`vɪr〕 形　嚴重的，嚴厲的

severely
severe + ly

▶ 〔sə`vɪrlɪ〕 副　嚴格地，嚴厲地，嚴重地

severity
severe + ity

▶ 〔sə`vɛrətɪ〕 名　嚴格，嚴厲，嚴肅，嚴重，嚴謹

I don't think the child did anything to deserve such a severe punishment.
我不認為這個孩子做了什麼該受到這樣嚴厲的懲罰。

shade

▶ 〔ʃed〕 名　蔭，陰涼處，陰暗，陰影部分
動　遮蔽，蔽蔭，使陰暗

shady
shade + y

▶ 〔`ʃedɪ〕 形　成蔭的，多蔭的，陰暗的，隱蔽的

When it gets hot I like to sit in the shade of the big oak tree in my garden.
天氣熱的時候，我喜歡坐在我庭院中大橡樹的樹蔭下。

⭐ **359**

shadow ▶ 〔ˋʃædo〕名 蔭，陰暗處，影子

shadowy
shadow + y
▶ 〔ˋʃædəwɪ〕形 多蔭的，有陰影的，蔭涼的，幽暗的

The child tried to jump on his own shadow.
那個孩子試著要跳過自己的影子。

shore ▶ 〔ʃor〕名 岸，濱，陸地

ashore
a + shore
▶ 〔əˋʃor〕副 向岸，上岸，在岸上

I rowed the boat for many hours before he allowed me to go ashore.
在他允許我上岸前，我連續划了好幾個小時的船。

short ▶ 〔ɔrt〕形 短的，矮的，短暫的，短缺的

shorten
short + en
▶ 〔ˋʃɔrtn〕動 縮短，減少，變短

shortage
short + age
▶ 〔ˋʃɔrtɪdʒ〕名 缺少，不足，匱乏

If it doesn't rain soon, we will be facing a water shortage.
如果再不趕快下雨，我們就會面臨水源短缺的問題。

sight ▶ 〔saɪt〕名 視覺，視力，景象，名勝，見解

sightseeing
sight + see + ing
▶ 〔ˋsaɪtˏsiɪŋ〕名 觀光，遊覽

It was a terrible sight to see the town after the bomb exploded.
炸彈轟炸過後的城鎮是一片慘不忍睹的景象。

silly ▶ 〔ˋsɪlɪ〕形 愚蠢的，糊塗的，無聊的

silliness
silly + ness
▶ 〔ˋsɪlɪnɪs〕名 愚蠢

My friends said I would be silly to let this upset me.
我朋友說，如果我因為這件事而心情不好就太笨了。

sin	▶	〔sɪn〕名 （宗教或道德上的）罪，罪惡，過錯
sinful sin + ful	▶	〔`sɪnfəl〕形 罪孽深重的，有罪的，邪惡的
sinfully sinful + ly	▶	〔`sɪnfəlɪ〕副 罪孽深重地，不道德地

This chocolate cake is sinfully delicious.
這個巧克力蛋糕真是好吃得讓人感到罪惡。

sincere	▶	〔sɪn`sɪr〕形 衷心的，真誠的，忠實的
sincerely sincere + ly	▶	〔sɪn`sɪrlɪ〕副 真誠地，誠懇地，由衷地 Sincerely yours「敬上」（信件的結語詞）
sincerity sincere + ity	▶	〔sɪn`sɛrətɪ〕名 真實，誠心誠意

I am not sure if his motive was sincere.
我不確定他的動機是不是真心誠意的。

⭐
360

single	▶	〔`sɪŋgl〕形 單一的，個別的，孤單的，單身的
singular single + ar	▶	〔`sɪŋgjələ〕形 單一的，單數的
singularity singular + ity	▶	〔ˌsɪŋgjə`lærɪtɪ〕名 獨一，唯一，罕有

I have not regretted one single moment of my life.
我從未後悔過人生中的任何一刻。

situate	▶	〔`sɪtʃʊˌet〕動 使位於，使處於 situate～in...「使～處於…」
situation situate + ion	▶	〔ˌsɪtʃʊ`eʃən〕名 處境，境遇，形勢，情況，局面

What would you do if you were in my situation?
如果你處在我的立場，你會怎麼做？

They situated themselves on mats and waited for the fireworks to start.
他們在墊子上坐好，等煙火開始施放。

skeptic	▶	〔`skɛptɪk〕名 懷疑者，懷疑論者，無神論者
skeptical skeptic + al	▶	〔`skɛptɪkl〕形 懷疑論的，懷疑的，多疑的

She was more than a little skeptical about his ghost story.
她對他的鬼故事感到有點懷疑。

skill ▶ 〔`skɪl〕 名 （專門）技術，技能，技藝，熟練性

skilled
skill + ed ▶ 〔skɪld〕 形 熟練的，有技能的，需要技能的

skillful
skill + ful ▶ 〔`skɪlfəl〕 形 有技術的，熟練的，製作精巧

This piece of furniture was clearly made by a skilled craftsman.
這件傢俱很明顯地是出自技術純熟的工匠之手。

skin ▶ 〔skɪn〕 名 皮膚，皮，毛皮

skinny
skin + y ▶ 〔`skɪnɪ〕 形 皮的，薄膜狀的，皮包骨的

My skin burns if I sit in the sun too long.
如果我在太陽底下坐太久，皮膚會曬傷。

slave ▶ 〔slev〕 名 奴隸，奴隸般工作的人，苦工

slavery
slave + ry ▶ 〔`slevərɪ〕 名 奴隸身分，奴役，奴隸制，蓄奴

Although slavery is a violation of human rights, it does still exist.
雖然侵犯人權，但是奴隸制度現今仍存在著。

slight ▶ 〔slaɪt〕 形 輕微的，微小的，少量的，極不重要的

slightly
slight + ly ▶ 〔`slaɪtlɪ〕 副 輕微地，稍微地，纖細地

The warm sun and the slight breeze made it a perfect day to sit at the beach.
溫暖的陽光和徐徐的微風，是個適合坐在海邊的理想天氣。

snob ▶ 〔snɑb〕 名 勢利鬼，自負傲慢的人

snobbery
snob + ery ▶ 〔`snɑbərɪ〕 名 勢利眼，小人言行

snobbish
snob + ish ▶ 〔`snɑbɪʃ〕 形 勢利眼的，自負的

She is such a snob that she won't speak to me because I don't go to a private school.
她真是一個勢利鬼，因為我沒念私立學校她就不跟我說話。

sole ▶ 〔sol〕 形 單獨的，唯一的，專用的，獨占的
名 腳底，鞋底，襪底

361

solely
sole + ly ▶ 〔`sollɪ〕 副 單獨地，唯一地，僅僅，完全

You are the sole inheritor of the estate.
你是這片物業唯一的繼承人。

He fell asleep in the sun lying on his stomach, and the soles of his feet were so burned he couldn't walk.
他背對著太陽睡著了，結果他的腳底曬傷得很嚴重，沒辦法走路。

solemn	▶	［`saləm］ 形 嚴肅的，莊重的，莊嚴的，隆重的
solemnly solemn + ly	▶	［`saləmlɪ］ 副 莊嚴地，嚴肅地，正式地，神聖地
solemnity solemn + ity	▶	［sə`lɛmnətɪ］ 名 莊嚴，嚴肅，莊重，正經， 莊重的儀式

The pop music did not seem to match the solemnity of the occasion.
流行音樂似乎不適合這個場合的莊嚴肅穆。

solid	▶	［`salɪd］ 形 固體的，實心的，充實的 名 固體，固態物 （反義）liquid
solidity solid + ity	▶	［sə`lɪdɪtɪ］ 名 固體，堅硬
solidness solid + ness	▶	［`salədnɪs］ 名 堅硬，厚重，團結
solidarity solid + ary + ity	▶	［ˌsalə`dærətɪ］ 名 團結，團結一致

She wore a solid black suit.
她穿著一套全黑的套裝。

solitary solid + ary	▶	［`saləˌtɛrɪ］ 形 單獨的，獨自的，唯一的，隱居的， 孤獨的，寂寞的
solitude solitary + itude	▶	［`saləˌtjud］ 名 孤獨，寂寞，隱居

When I am sad I prefer to have complete solitude and not speak to anyone.
傷心的時候，我比較喜歡一個人獨處不跟任何人講話。

sophisticate	▶	［sə`fɪstɪˌket］ 動 使懂世故，使複雜
sophisticated sophisticate + ed	▶	［sə`fɪstɪˌketɪd］ 形 世故的，富有經驗的，精通的

sophistication
sophisticate + ion
▶ 〔səˌfɪstɪˋkeʃən〕 名　世故，有教養，複雜，老練

The teenager looked so grown up and sophisticated in her new dress.
那位少女穿著她的新洋裝，看起來很成熟世故。

soul
▶ 〔sol〕 名　靈魂，心靈，精神，精力，氣魄，熱情

soulful
soul + ful
▶ 〔ˋsolfəl〕 形　充滿精神的，精神上的，熱情的

The man on the saxophone played soft, soulful music that fit the scene perfectly.
薩克斯風的演奏者吹出輕柔又充滿感情的樂曲，完美襯托了這個場合。

space
▶ 〔spes〕 名　空間，宇宙，太空

spacious
space + ous
▶ 〔ˋspeʃəs〕 形　寬敞的，廣闊的，無邊無際的

The best thing about my current dwelling is the spacious garden.
我現在住處最棒的地方就是它寬敞的庭園。

362

splendid
▶ 〔ˋsplɛndɪd〕 形　燦爛的，壯麗的，輝煌的，傑出的

splendor
splend + or
▶ 〔ˋsplɛndə〕 名　光輝，光彩，壯麗，壯觀，輝煌

He did a splendid job of cleaning up the house.
他漂亮地把房子打掃乾淨了。

spoil
▶ 〔spɔɪl〕 動　損壞，蹧蹋，寵愛，溺愛，腐敗

spoilage
spoil + age
▶ 〔ˋspɔɪlɪdʒ〕 名　掠奪，蹧蹋，損壞物

lease don't cry because you will spoil the birthday party.
拜託你不要哭，這樣會毀了這場生日派對。

spontaneous
▶ 〔spɑnˋtenɪəs〕 形　自發的，非出於強制的，無意識的，不由自主的

spontaneously
spontaneous + ly
▶ 〔spɑnˋtenɪəslɪ〕 副　自然地，自發地，不由自主地

spontaneity
spontaneous + ity
▶ 〔ˌspɑntəˋniətɪ〕 名　自發性，自然發生

She says that spontaneity makes life fun, so when she goes on holiday, she goes to the airport and takes the first plane, no matter where it is going.
她說順其自然讓人生充滿樂趣，所以休假時她去機場搭乘第一班飛機，不管前往的地點會是哪裡。

starve	〔stɑrv〕 動　餓死，挨餓 ▶ starve to death = die of starvation 「因飢餓而死，餓死」
starvation starve + tion	▶ 〔stɑr`veʃən〕 名　飢餓，挨餓，餓死

It's a shame that there are many starving people in the world when food can be found in such abundance in many places.
當很多地方都有充足的食物時，世界上仍有許多挨餓的人是很遺憾的事。

state	▶ 〔stet〕 名　狀態，形勢，國家，（美國的）州 動　陳述，聲明，說明，確定，指定
statement state + ment	▶ 〔`stetmənt〕 名　陳述，說明，（正式的）聲明，表達方式，陳述方式

"Let me retract that statement," she said, when she saw the look of fury on his face.
看見他盛怒的臉色，她說：「讓我撤回那個聲明。」

statistics	▶ 〔stə`tɪstɪks〕 名　統計，統計資料，統計學
statistical statistics + al	▶ 〔stə`tɪstɪk!〕 形　統計的，統計學的

The statistics show that most students have a mobile phone.
統計資料顯示，大多數學生都擁有行動電話。

steep	▶ 〔stip〕 形　陡峭的，急遽升降的，大起大落的，（價格等）過高的，不合理的
steepness steep + ness	▶ 〔`stipnɪs〕 名　險峻，陡峭

The hill was so steep that she had to get off her bicycle and walk.
斜坡過於陡峭，她只好從腳踏車上下來改用走的。

stern	▶ 〔stɜn〕 形　嚴格的，嚴厲的，嚴峻的
sternness stern + ness	▶ 〔`stɜnɪs〕 名　嚴厲，嚴格

When Larry was young, his father was stern, but as he grew older, they became good friends.
賴瑞年輕的時候，他父親非常的嚴厲，但隨著他年紀增長，他們變成了好朋友。

363

| stiff | ▶ | 〔stɪf〕形　硬的，挺的，（手足等）僵直的，僵硬的 |

| stiffen
stiff + en | ▶ | 〔`stɪfn〕動　變硬，變挺，變僵硬 |

He got a stiff neck from sitting at the computer all day.
他在電腦前面坐了一整天，坐得肩頸僵硬。

| stimulate | ▶ | 〔`stɪmjə͵let〕動　刺激，激勵，使興奮，促使 |

| stimulation
stimulate + ion | ▶ | 〔͵stɪmjə`leʃən〕名　刺激，興奮，激勵，鼓舞 |

| stimulus
stimulate + lus | ▶ | 〔`stɪmjələs〕名　刺激，刺激品，興奮劑<br>（名詞複數）stimuli〔`stɪmjəlaɪ〕 |

It is important to give children toys and books that will stimulate their brains at an early age.
在童年期給孩子能刺激腦部發展的玩具和書籍是重要的。

| stomach | ▶ | 〔`stʌmək〕名　胃
have a sour stomach「胃酸過多」 |

| stomachache
stomach + ache | ▶ | 〔`stʌmək͵ek〕名　胃痛，腹痛 |

I ate too much cake and now my stomach hurts.
我吃太多蛋糕了，所以現在肚子痛。

| storm | ▶ | 〔stɔrm〕名　暴風雨，（政治、社會等的）風暴，
大動盪，（感情的）爆發，激動 |

| stormy
storm + y | ▶ | 〔`stɔrmɪ〕形　暴風雨的，暴躁的，狂暴的，激烈的，
猛烈的 |

The weather man predicts there will be a bad storm tonight.
氣象播報員預測今晚將有一場嚴重的暴風雨來臨。

| stout | ▶ | 〔staʊt〕形　矮胖的，肥胖的，結實的，牢固的 |

| stoutness
stout + ness | ▶ | 〔`staʊtnɪs〕名　堅固，肥胖 |

The woman was very round and stout in stature.
那位女性的體格圓潤結實。

| strange | ▶ | 〔strendʒ〕形　奇怪的，奇妙的，不可思議的，
陌生的，不熟悉的 |

stranger
strange + er
▶ 〔`strendʒɚ〕 名 陌生人，外地人，生手

Not many strangers came to the small town, so when the man with the long black coat came, everyone stopped and stared.
沒有什麼外地人會來這個小鎮，所以當那個穿著黑色長大衣的男人出現時，每個人都停下腳步盯著他看。

strategy
▶ 〔`strætədʒɪ〕 名 戰略，戰略學，策略，計謀，對策

strategist
strategy + ist
▶ 〔`strætədʒɪst〕 名 戰略家，軍事家

The coach had a good strategy about how to win the game.
教練有一個能贏得比賽的好戰略。

strong
▶ 〔strɔŋ〕 形 強壯的，強健的，強大的，強勁的，堅固的，濃烈的

strength
strong + th
▶ 〔strɛŋθ〕 名 力量，實力，強度，濃度，長處

strengthen
strength + en
▶ 〔`strɛŋθən〕 動 加強，增強，鞏固

If you want to strengthen your argument, you need to do a little reading.
如果你想要加強自己的論點，你需要多讀一些資料。

⭐
364

strive
▶ 〔straɪv〕 動 努力，苦幹，奮鬥，反抗，鬥爭
strive to V「努力～」
strive with～「與～鬥爭」

strife
strive + fe
▶ 〔straɪf〕 名 衝突，爭鬥，吵架，不和

She is striving for her goals.
她正朝著自己的目標而努力著。

stupid
▶ 〔`stjupɪd〕 形 愚蠢的，麻木的，無知覺的，遲鈍的

stupidly
stupid + ly
▶ 〔`stjupɪdlɪ〕 副 愚蠢地

stupidity
stupid + ity
▶ 〔stju`pɪdətɪ〕 名 愚蠢，愚笨，愚行，蠢事，蠢話

I stupidly shook the orange juice bottle before I put the cap on tightly.
我很愚蠢地在把蓋子蓋緊前就先搖了柳橙汁的瓶子。

substance
▶ 〔`sʌbstəns〕 名 物質，實質，本質，主旨

substantial
substance + ial

▶ 〔səb`stænʃəl〕形　真實的，實在的，堅固的，結實的

His arguments lack substance, so it's hard to take them seriously.
他的論點沒有主旨，所以很難讓人把他的話當真。

substitute

▶ 〔`sʌbstə͵tjut〕名　代理人，代替物，代用品
　　　　　　　　動　用…代替，代替
　　　　　　　　形　代替的，代用的，替補的
　　substitute～for...「以～代替…，以～取代…」
　　substitute for～「代替～」

substitution
substitute + ion

▶ 〔͵sʌbstə`tjuʃən〕名　代替，代用，替換，代替物

My father often substitutes honey for refined sugar when he is baking.
我父親烤蛋糕的時候，常用蜂蜜代替精製糖。

suit

▶ 〔sut〕名　（一套）衣服，套，組
　　　　　動　適合，中…的意，與…相配
　　suit～to...「使～和…相配」

suitable
suit + able

▶ 〔`sutəbl〕形　適當的，合適的，適宜的

unsuitable
un + suitable

▶ 〔ʌn`sjutəbl〕形　不合適的，不適宜的，不相稱的

The r esident of the United States suited his speech to the young students.
美國總統把演說內容變得適合年輕學生。

Although 300 people applied for the job, there was not one suitable applicant.
雖然有300人申請這份工作，但是沒有半個合適人選。

summary

▶ 〔`sʌmərɪ〕名　總結，摘要，一覽

summarize
summary + ize

▶ 〔`sʌmə͵raɪz〕動　總結，概述，概括

How would you summarize this paragraph in one sentence?
你會怎麼把這一段概括成一句話？

superior

▶ 〔sə`pɪrɪə〕形　上級的，較好的，優秀的，有優越感的
　　（反義）inferior
　　be superior to～「優於～」
　　be inferior to～「比～差，不如～」

superiority
superior + ity
▶ 〔sə͵pɪrɪˋɔrətɪ〕 名　優越，優勢，上等，上級

DVD's are superior to video tapes in many ways.
DVD在很多方面都比錄影帶要來得優秀。

⭐
365

superstition
▶ 〔͵supəˋstɪʃən〕 名　迷信，迷信行為，盲目崇拜

superstitious
superstition + ous
▶ 〔͵supəˋstɪʃəs〕 形　迷信的，因迷信而形成的

My mother is so superstitious that she will never stay on the 13th floor of the hotel.
我媽媽非常迷信，所以她絕對不會住在飯店的13樓。

suppress
▶ 〔səˋprɛs〕 動　鎮壓，平定，壓制，抑制，隱瞞

suppression
suppress + ion
▶ 〔səˋprɛʃən〕 名　壓制，鎮壓，禁止，抑制

Even though the mother knew she had to scold her daughter, she had to suppress a smile while she was doing it.
即使那位母親知道她必須教訓她女兒，但她在責罵的時候還是得忍著不要笑出來。

supreme
▶ 〔səˋprim〕 形　最高的，至上的，極度的，最重要的

supremacy
supreme + cy
▶ 〔səˋprɛməsɪ〕 名　至高無上，最高地位，優勢，主權

This is a matter of supreme importance, so I think we should all get together and talk about it.
這是極為重大的問題，所以我認為我們應該要聚在一起討論。

surgeon
▶ 〔ˋsɝdʒən〕 名　外科醫生

surgical
surgeon + ical
▶ 〔ˋsɝdʒɪkl̩〕 形　外科的，外科醫生的

surgically
surgical + ly
▶ 〔ˋsɝdʒəkl̩ɪ〕 副　外科手術上

He had to have the tumor surgically removed.
他必須動手術切除腫瘤。

sweat
▶ 〔swɛt〕 動　出汗，結水珠
　　　　　名　汗，汗水

sweaty
sweat + y
▶ 〔ˋswɛtɪ〕 形　滿身是汗的，費力的

sweater
sweat + er
▶ 〔`swɛtə〕 名　毛線衣

I sweat a lot when I run fast.
我快跑的時候會流很多汗。

swift
▶ 〔swɪft〕 形　快速的，快捷的，立刻的，即時的

swiftly
swift + ly
▶ 〔`swɪftlɪ〕 副　迅速地，敏捷地

With one swift movement of its tongue, the frog caught and ate the fly.
青蛙飛快地伸出舌頭，馬上就捕捉到蒼蠅吃下肚了。

talent
▶ 〔`tælənt〕 名　天才，天資，天分

talented
talent + ed
▶ 〔`tæləntɪd〕 形　有天才的，有才幹的

As a teacher, he is completely and utterly without talent.
身為一位老師，他可是完完全全沒有半點天分。

tax
▶ 〔tæks〕 名　稅，稅金，負擔，壓力

tax-free
tax + free
▶ 〔`tæks`fri〕 形　免稅的，不付稅的

The government imposes a sales tax on all goods.
政府對所有的商品皆有徵收銷售稅。

366

tear
▶ 〔tɪr〕 名　眼淚，淚珠

tearful
tear + ful
▶ 〔`tɪrfəl〕 形　含淚的，流淚的，哭泣的

Huge tears rolled down the boy's face as he stared in disbelief at his ice cream cone falling on the sidewalk.
男孩不敢置信地望著他掉在人行道上的冰淇淋，斗大的淚珠滑落臉龐。

tease
▶ 〔tiz〕 動　戲弄，逗弄，取笑，欺負，挑逗

teaser
tease + er
▶ 〔`tizə〕 名　戲弄者，嘲弄者，欺負他人者

The boy teased his little sister endlessly, but when she teased back, he went crying to his mother.
那個男孩不停地欺負他妹妹，但她一欺負回去，他就哭著跑去找媽媽。

tedious	▶ 〔`tidɪəs〕 形 冗長乏味的，使人厭煩的
tediously tedious + ly	▶ 〔`tidɪəslɪ〕 副 沈悶地，長而乏味地
tediousness tedious + ness	▶ 〔`tidɪəsnɪs〕 名 乏味，無聊

He watched a soap opera in order to distract him from the tediousness of folding clothes.
為了排解摺衣服的無聊，他看了齣肥皂劇。

temper	▶ 〔`tɛmpə〕 名 情緒，性情，脾氣 be in a bad temper with〜「對〜沒好氣，對〜發脾氣」 lose one's temper with〜「對〜生氣」
temperate temper + ate	▶ 〔`tɛmprɪt〕 形 溫和的，不極端的，有節制的
temperament temperate + ment	▶ 〔`tɛmprəmənt〕 名 氣質，性情，性格，喜怒無常

Although she did an excellent job, her temperament made her difficult to work with.
雖然她在工作上表現很優秀，但是她喜怒無常的脾氣讓人很難跟她一起工作。

tempt	▶ 〔tɛmpt〕 動 引誘，誘惑，勾引，吸引，打動 tempt（人）to V「誘使（人）〜」
temptation tempt + tion	▶ 〔tɛmp`teʃən〕 名 引誘，誘惑，誘惑物

I am on a diet so please don't tempt me to eat dessert.
我現在在減肥，所以請不要引誘我吃點心。

theory	▶ 〔`θiərɪ〕 名 學說，理論，學理
theoretical theory + ical	▶ 〔ˌθiə`rɛtɪkl〕 形 理論的，非應用的

The detective had an interesting theory about who the murderer was.
那位偵探對於兇手是誰有很有趣的見解。

thick	▶ 〔θɪk〕 形 厚的，粗的，濃的，濃厚的，黏稠的
thickness thick + ness	▶ 〔`θɪknɪs〕 名 厚度，濃度，密度

My hair is so thick that I can not get a comb through it.
我頭髮太多了，所以無法用梳子梳開。

⭐
367

| thin | ▶ | 〔θɪn〕形　薄的，細的，瘦的，稀疏的，稀薄的 |

| thinner
thin + er | ▶ | 〔`θɪnə〕名　稀釋劑 |

It is a big problem these days that girls who are already thin want to go on diets.
原本就很瘦的女生還想節食減肥是現今一個重大的問題。

| thirst | ▶ | 〔θɜst〕名　渴，口渴，渴望 |

| thirsty
thirst + y | ▶ | 〔`θɜstɪ〕形　口渴的，乾旱的，缺水的，渴望的 |

Ice water is very good to quench your thirst on a hot day.
天氣熱的時候喝冰水最能解渴。

| thorough | ▶ | 〔`θɜo〕形　徹底的，完全的，周密的，完善的 |

| thoroughly
thorough + ly | ▶ | 〔`θɜolɪ〕副　徹底地，認真仔細地，完全地，
非常地，極其 |

| thought | ▶ | 〔θɔt〕名　思維，思考，考慮，想法 |

| thoughtful
thought + ful | ▶ | 〔`θɔtfəl〕形　細心的，體貼的，考慮周到的 |

| thoughtless
thought + less | ▶ | 〔`θɔtlɪs〕形　欠考慮的，粗心的，輕率的 |

She gave a very thoughtful gift of bath salts and aromatherapy oils.
她很體貼地送了裝浴鹽和芳香精油當禮物。

| threat | ▶ | 〔θrɛt〕名　威脅，恐嚇，構成威脅的人（或事物） |

| threaten
threat + en | ▶ | 〔`θrɛtn〕動　威脅，恐嚇
threaten（人）into V-ing「威脅（人）～」 |

| threatening
threaten + ing | ▶ | 〔`θrɛtnɪŋ〕形　脅迫的，險惡的 |

The terrorist activities pose a threat to tourists in that country.
恐怖攻擊活動對該國的旅客構成威脅。

tide	▶	〔taɪd〕 图 潮，潮汐，潮水，浪潮，潮流
tidal tide + al	▶	〔`taɪdḷ〕 形 潮汐的，受潮汐影響的 tidal wave「滿潮」

The tidal wave was sizeable, but fortunately, it didn't do any damage.
海嘯相當大，但幸運地並無造成任何破壞。

tidy	▶	〔`taɪdɪ〕 形 整潔的，整齊的，井然的 動 整理，收拾 tidy up～「收拾～，使～整潔」
untidy un + tidy	▶	〔ʌn`taɪdɪ〕 形 不整潔的，不修邊幅的，凌亂的

lease tidy up your room immediately!
請馬上收拾你的房間！

tie	▶	〔taɪ〕 動 繫，打結，束縛，與…打成平手 tie up～「繫住～，綁住～」
untie un + tie	▶	〔ʌn`taɪ〕 動 解開，解除，使自由，解決，鬆開

lease tie up your laces because you might trip over them.
請把鞋帶繫好，因為你可能會被絆倒。

☆
368

timid	▶	〔`tɪmɪd〕 形 膽小的，易受驚的，怕羞的，羞怯的
timidly timid + ly	▶	〔`tɪmɪdlɪ〕 副 膽小地，羞怯地

She walked up to the door and knocked timidly.
她走到門前，然後怯生生地敲了敲門。

tiresome	▶	〔`taɪrsəm〕 形 使人疲勞的，令人厭倦的，討厭的
tiresomely tiresome + ly	▶	〔`taɪrsəmlɪ〕 副 累人地，令人討厭地

It is so tiresome to have to do the same thing over and over again.
一再重複做相同的事情是如此令人厭煩。

tolerate	▶	〔`tɑlə‿ret〕 動 忍受，容忍，寬恕，容許
tolerable tolerate + able	▶	〔`tɑlərəbḷ〕 形 可忍受的，可容忍的
tolerant tolerate + ant	▶	〔`tɑlərənt〕 形 忍受的，容忍的，寬恕的 be tolerant of～「對～寬容，對～有耐性」

He is very tolerant of people who are different from him.
他對和他不同的人非常寬容。

trade	▶	〔tred〕 名 貿易，交易，商業 動 交換，做買賣，進行交易 trade with～「和～作貿易，和～交易」 trade～for... 「用～換得…」
trader trade + er	▶	〔`tredɚ〕 名 商人，商船

My brother and I traded jackets because his was too small, and mine was too big.
我哥哥和我交換外套穿，因為他的外套太小，我的則是太大。

tradition	▶	〔trə`dɪʃən〕 名 傳統，傳統思想，慣例，常規，傳說
traditional tradition + al	▶	〔trə`dɪʃənḷ〕 形 傳統的，慣例的，因襲的，傳說的

We carry on a family tradition of taking baked goods to neighbors around Christmastime.
我們家維持著一個傳統，聖誕節時我們會將烤好的食物分送給附近鄰居。

tragedy	▶	〔`trædʒədɪ〕 名 悲劇，悲劇性事件
tragic tragedy + ic	▶	〔`trædʒɪk〕 形 悲劇的，悲劇性的，悲慘的

Shakespeare wrote many plays and they were usually about historical facts, comedy or tragedy.
莎士比亞寫了許多齣戲劇，他們大多關於史實、喜劇和悲劇。

tranquil	▶	〔`træŋkwɪl〕 形 平靜的，安靜的，安寧的
tranquilize tranquil + ize	▶	〔`træŋkwɪˌlaɪz〕 動 （使）平靜，（使）鎮定
tranquilizer tranquilize + er	▶	〔`træŋkwɪˌlaɪzɚ〕 名 鎮定劑，精神安定劑

It is so peaceful and tranquil on this little island.
這座小島是如此的平靜安寧。

transplant	▶	〔træns`plænt〕 動 移植，移種

transplantation
transplant + tion
▶ 〔͵trænsplæn`teʃən〕 名 移植，移植法，移居，移民

All of her green plants were getting too big for their pots so she transplanted them.
因為她的植物長得都比花盆還大了，所以她把它們移植到別的地方。

⭐
369

trend
▶ 〔trɛnd〕 名 趨勢，傾向，時尚

trendy
trend + y
▶ 〔`trɛndɪ〕 形 時髦的，流行的

He was wearing jeans and a trendy shirt.
他穿著一件牛仔褲和時髦的襯衫。

treasure
▶ 〔`trɛʒɚ〕 名 財富，貴重物品
動 珍愛，珍視，珍藏

treasurer
treasure + er
▶ 〔`trɛʒərɚ〕 名 會計，司庫，出納員，財務主管

treasury
treasure + y
▶ 〔`trɛʒərɪ〕 名 金庫，寶庫，資金

I treasure every moment I spend with my good friends.
我很珍惜和我的好朋友一起度過的每一段時光。

triumph
▶ 〔`traɪəmf〕 名 勝利，成功
動 獲得勝利
triumph over～「擊敗～，戰勝～，克服～」

triumphant
triumph + ant
▶ 〔traɪ`ʌmfənt〕 形 勝利的，成功的

triumphantly
triumphant + ly
▶ 〔traɪ`ʌmfəntlɪ〕 副 耀武揚威地，得意洋洋地

He smiled triumphantly as he saw a way to checkmate his opponent.
當他發現能將死對手的方法時，他得意地微笑了。

trivia
▶ 〔`trɪvɪə〕 名 瑣事

trivial
trivia + al
▶ 〔`trɪvɪəl〕 形 瑣細的，不重要的

This is not a trivial matter that will go away in a few hours.
這不是短時間內就能解決的小事。

true
▶ 〔tru〕 形 真實的，確實的，真的

truth
true + th
▶ 〔truθ〕 名 事實，真理，誠實，真實性

You are a true friend.
你是個真正的朋友。

| trust | ▶ | 〔trʌst〕名　信任，信賴
動　信任，信賴，依賴
trust in～「信任～」 |

| trust**worthy**
trust + worthy | ▶ | 〔`trʌst⸝wɝðɪ〕形　值得信賴的，可信的，可靠的 |

Can I trust you to keep my secret?
我能信任你會保守我的祕密嗎？

| type | ▶ | 〔taɪp〕名　類型，形式，樣式，典型 |

| typ**ical**
type + ical | ▶ | 〔`tɪpɪkl̩〕形　典型的，有代表性的 |

Singing karaoke is a typical pastime of Japanese college students.
唱卡拉OK是日本大學生典型的娛樂活動。

| tyranny | ▶ | 〔`tɪrənɪ〕名　暴政，專制，暴虐 |

| tyr**ant**
tyranny + ant | ▶ | 〔`taɪrənt〕名　暴君，專橫的人，嚴酷的事物 |

Unfortunately, too many countries are controlled by tyranny.
很不幸地，有太多國家被暴君所統治著。

⭐
370

| ugly | ▶ | 〔`ʌglɪ〕形　醜的，難看的，可怕的，討厭的 |

| ugli**ness**
ugly + ness | ▶ | 〔`ʌglɪnɪs〕名　難看，醜陋，醜陋的東西 |

Bart doesn't read the newspaper because he says he doesn't want to know about all the ugliness in the world.
巴特不讀報紙，因為他說他不想要知道世界上所有醜惡的事情。

| ultimate | ▶ | 〔`ʌltəmɪt〕形　最後的，最終的，基本的
名　終極，極限 |

| ultimate**ly**
ultimate + ly | ▶ | 〔`ʌltəmɪtlɪ〕副　最後，終極地 |

Although it is impossible to predict the ultimate outcome, we have high hopes for our plan of action.
雖然最終的結果無法預測，但是我們對我們的行動計劃有很高的期望。

| uneasy | ▶ | 〔ʌn`izɪ〕形　不安的，擔心的，拘束的，不自在的 |

uneasiness
uneasy + ness

▶ 〔ʌnˋizɪnɪs〕 名 擔心，不安，侷促，拘束

She had the uneasy feeling that someone was watching her.
她有種被人注視的不安感覺。

unite	▶ 〔juˋnaɪt〕 動 聯合，團結，混合
united unite + ed	▶ 〔juˋnaɪtɪd〕 形 聯合的，統一的，團結的，一致的
unity unite + y	▶ 〔ˋjunətɪ〕 名 單一性，團結，聯合，一致性
reunite re + unite	▶ 〔ˏrijuˋnaɪt〕 動 再結合，再聯合，重聚

The sisters were reunited after being apart for 15 years.
分離了15年後，姊妹們重聚在一起。

usual	▶ 〔ˋjuʒʊəl〕 形 通常的，平常的，慣常的 as usual 「照例，像往常一樣」 as is usual with（人）「（人）如同往常一樣」
usually usual + ly	▶ 〔ˋjuʒʊəlɪ〕 副 通常地，慣常地
unusual un + usual	▶ 〔ʌnˋjuʒʊəl〕 形 不平常的，奇特的，非凡的
unusually unusual + ly	▶ 〔ʌnˋjuʒʊəlɪ〕 副 不尋常地，非常

As usual, Brenda is late.
像往常一樣，布蘭達遲到了。

utter	▶ 〔ˋʌtə〕 形 完全的，徹底的，十足的 動 發出（聲音），說，講，表達
utterance utter + ance	▶ 〔ˋʌtərəns〕 名 發聲，表達，言論，話語

on't utter a single word! They might hear us!
一句話都別說！他們可能會聽見！

vaccine	▶ 〔ˋvæksin〕 名 牛痘苗，疫苗
vaccinate vaccine + ate	▶ 〔ˋvæksn̩ˏet〕 動 種牛痘，注射疫苗，接種疫苗
vaccination vaccinate + ion	▶ 〔ˏvæksn̩ˋeʃən〕 名 接種

Have you had your flu vaccination yet?
你打了感冒疫苗嗎？

⭐ **vain**[1]
371
▶ 〔ven〕形　徒然的，無益的
in vain「徒勞，白費」

vainness
vain + ness
▶ 〔ˋvennɪs〕名　徒勞

Lance tried his best to fix the television on his own, but his efforts were all in vain, and he ended up paying the repairman.
藍斯盡全力想自己修好電視，但是他的努力只是徒勞，最後還是得花錢請修理工人修理。

vain[2]
▶ 〔ven〕形　愛虛榮的，自負的，炫耀的

vanity
vain + ity
▶ 〔ˋvænətɪ〕名　虛榮心，無意義

Narcissus was so vain that he fell in love with his own reflection.
納西斯是如此自負，以至於他愛上了自己的倒影。
【註】源自希臘神話，現解為「自戀」。

vapor
▶ 〔ˋvepɚ〕名　水汽，蒸汽，煙霧

vaporize
vapor + ize
▶ 〔ˋvepɚˏraɪz〕動　蒸發

If you have a cold it is helpful to breathe in the vapor from a steamy bath.
如果你患了感冒，呼吸熱水澡的蒸汽會很有幫助。

vast
▶ 〔væst〕形　廣闊的，浩瀚的，廣大的，巨大的

vastly
vast + ly
▶ 〔ˋvæstlɪ〕副　龐大地，巨大地，極大地，廣闊地

vastness
vast + ness
▶ 〔ˋvæstnɪs〕名　廣闊，龐大，巨大，無邊無際

The cattle rancher owned vast areas of land.
那位牧場經營者擁有廣大面積的土地。

vertical
vert + ical
▶ 〔ˋvɝtɪk]〕形　垂直的，豎的，立式的

vertically
vertical + ly
▶ 〔ˋvɝtɪk]ɪ〕副　垂直地，直立地

The tree was no longer in a vertical position after the storm.
暴風雨過後，那棵樹不再是直立的了。

victim ▶ 〔`vɪktɪm〕 名 犧牲者，遇難者，受害者，受災者

victimize
victim + ize
▶ 〔`vɪktɪ͵maɪz〕 動 使犧牲，使痛苦

That boy is the victim of bullying in his class.
那個男孩是他班上霸凌的受害者。

vigor ▶ 〔`vɪgɚ〕 名 體力，精力，活力
with vigor「精力充沛」

vigorous
vigor + ous
▶ 〔`vɪgərəs〕 形 精力充沛的，強有力的

vigorously
vigorous + ly
▶ 〔`vɪgərəslɪ〕 副 精神旺盛地，活潑地

vigorousness
vigorous + ness
▶ 〔`vɪgərəsnɪs〕 名 朝氣蓬勃，強有力

She tackled the cleaning with vigor.
她精力充沛地開始打掃。

virtual ▶ 〔`vɝtʃʊəl〕 形 事實上的，實際上的，實質上的

virtually
virtual + ly
▶ 〔`vɝtʃʊəlɪ〕 副 實際上，事實上，差不多

It is virtually summer already.
幾乎已經是夏天了。

☆
372
virtue ▶ 〔`vɝtʃu〕 名 善，美德，優點

virtuous
virtue + ous
▶ 〔`vɝtʃʊəs〕 形 有道德的，善良的，貞潔的

My grandmother always told us that patience is a virtue.
祖母總是告訴我們，耐性是一項美德。

voluntary ▶ 〔`vɑlən͵tɛrɪ〕 形 自願的，志願的

involuntary
in + voluntary
▶ 〔ɪn`vɑlən͵tɛrɪ〕 形 非自願的，非出本意的，
不由自主的

volunteer
voluntary + er
▶ 〔͵vɑlən`tɪr〕 名 自願參加者，義工，志願兵

She decided to do some voluntary work to help others in need.
她決定要做一些志工活動，好幫助有需要的人。
The heart is an involuntary muscle.
心臟是不隨意肌。

wander	▶	〔ˋwɑndɚ〕 動　漫遊，閒逛，流浪，徘徊
wanderer wander + er	▶	〔ˋwɑndərɚ〕 名　漫遊者，流浪漢，迷路的動物

I had an hour to kill before my plane left, so I wandered around the airport.
我的班機起飛前有一個小時的時間要打發，所以我在機場閒晃。

warrant	▶	〔ˋwɔrənt〕 名　授權，批准，（正當）理由，根據
warranty warrant + y	▶	〔ˋwɔrəntɪ〕 名　保證書，保單，認可，根據，理由

The police got a warrant to search the house where the fugitive was hiding.
警察獲得搜查令，得以搜索逃犯躲藏的房子。

waste	▶	〔west〕 動　浪費，濫用 名　浪費，濫用，廢棄物
wasteful waste + ful	▶	〔ˋwestfəl〕 形　浪費的，揮霍的

Throwing away half of your meal is very wasteful.
飯吃了一半就丟掉非常浪費。

weak	▶	〔wik〕 形　弱的，虛弱的，衰弱的，軟弱的
weaken weak + en	▶	〔ˋwikən〕 動　削弱，減弱，減少
weakness weak + ness	▶	〔ˋwiknɪs〕 名　虛弱，軟弱，弱點

The astronauts' muscles had grown weak during their time in space.
太空人停留在外太空的期間肌肉會變得無力。

wealth	▶	〔wɛlθ〕 名　財富，財產
wealthy wealth + y	▶	〔ˋwɛlθɪ〕 形　富裕的，豐富的

His wealth is inherited; he has never worked a day in his life.
他的財富是繼承而來的，他這輩子從沒有工作過一天。

weapon	▶	〔ˋwɛpən〕 名　武器，兵器
weaponless weapon + less	▶	〔ˋwɛpənlɪs〕 形　無武器的

She chased the bear out of the house, using a rolling pin as a weapon.
她用一根桿麵棍當武器，把熊從家裡給趕了出去。

weary	▶	〔`wɪrɪ〕形　疲倦的，厭倦的，厭煩的，乏味的

wearily weary + ly	▶	〔`wɪrɪlɪ〕副　疲倦地，厭倦地，令人厭煩地

weariness weary + ness	▶	〔`wɪrɪnɪs〕名　疲倦，困乏，消沈，厭倦

She sighed wearily as she picked up the dirty socks from the living room floor.
她從客廳地板上揀起髒襪子時，疲倦地嘆了聲氣。

weigh	▶	〔we〕動　稱…的重量

weight weigh + t	▶	〔wet〕名　重，重量，體重 lose weight「體重減輕」 gain weight「體重增加」

Ben is trying to lose weight because his doctor said he was at risk for heart disease.
班正嘗試要減肥，因為他的醫生說他有得到心臟病的風險。

☆
373

wheel	▶	〔hwil〕名　輪子，車輪 動　滾動，轉動

wheelchair wheel + chair	▶	〔`hwil`tʃɛr〕名　輪椅

Mandy used a wheelchair for several months after her operation.
曼蒂手術後坐了好幾個月的輪椅。

wholesome	▶	〔`holsəm〕形　合乎衛生的，有益健康的

wholesomely wholesome + ly	▶	〔`holsəmlɪ〕副　衛生地，有益健康地

wholesomeness wholesome + ness	▶	〔`holsəmnɪs〕名　有益健康，增進健康

unwholesome un + wholesome	▶	〔ʌnæholsəm〕形　不衛生的，不健康的，有害身心的

laying board games is good wholesome fun for the whole family.
玩紙板遊戲是有益全家身心健康的娛樂。

wise	▶	〔waɪz〕形　有智慧的，聰明的，明智的，博學的

wisely wise + ly	▶	〔`waɪzlɪ〕副　聰明地，英明地，明智地

wisdom
wise + dom

▶ 〔`wɪzdəm〕 名　智慧，才智，明智，知識，學問

Sharon has wisely been saving a little money every month for 25 years.
25年以來，雪倫有智慧地每個月都存一小筆錢。

---

withdraw

▶ 〔wɪðˋdrɔ〕 動　移開，收回，提領，取消，撤銷，撤退，退出

withdrawal
withdraw + al

▶ 〔wɪðˋdrɔəl〕 名　收回，撤回，撤退，提款

To make a withdrawal, you will need your cash card.
要提款的話，你需要準備好你的提款卡。

---

worth

▶ 〔wɝθ〕 介　值…，值得…
be worth V-ing「有～的價值」

worthy
worth + y

▶ 〔`wɝðɪ〕 形　有價值的，相稱的，值得的
be worthy of V-ing「有～的價值」

worthless
worth + less

▶ 〔`wɝθlɪs〕 形　無價值的，無用的，不重要的

worthwhile
worth + while

▶ 〔`wɝθˋhwaɪl〕 形　值得的，有真實價值的

This is an antique worth a lot of money.
這是件很值錢的古董。

---

wound

▶ 〔wund〕 名　創傷，傷口，傷疤，傷害，創傷
動　傷害，打傷

wounded
wound + ed

▶ 〔`wundɪd〕 形　受傷的

Jason carefully placed the wounded bird into a box and took it to the veterinarian.
傑森小心翼翼地把受傷的小鳥放進箱子裡，然後帶著小鳥去看獸醫。

第 3 章

不能拆的單字

374

address

〔əˋdrɛs〕 名　住址，演說，致詞
動　在…上寫收件人姓名地址，向…發表演說

You should usually not address people by their first name unless you are invited to.
你通常不該直呼別人的名字，除非他們要求你這麼做。

---

affair

〔əˋfɛr〕 名　事件，事情，戀愛事件，風流韻事，男女不正常關係

Many people are interested in the daily affairs of movie stars.
很多人對電影明星的日常生活感到興趣。

He was falsely accused of having an affair with his sister-in-law.
他遭到不實的指控，說他和他的小姨子有外遇。

---

aid

〔ed〕 動　幫助，救助，支援，有助於
名　幫助，救援，援助
aid～with...「幫忙～關於…的事」

It's customary for countries to send aid to other countries where natural disasters, such as floods and earthquakes, have occurred.
一般國家習慣派遣救援幫助發生水災、地震等自然災禍的國家。

---

alike

〔əˋlaɪk〕 形　相同的，相像的

John and his sister looked so much alike when they were children that people often got them mixed up.
約翰和他的妹妹小時候長得非常像，人們常常把他們兩個搞錯。

---

ape

〔ep〕 名　猿，大猩猩

Some anthropologists think that studying the behavior of apes will give insight into human behavior.
一些人類學者認為研究猿類行為能幫助了解人類行為。

---

area

〔ˋɛrɪə〕 名　地區，區域，領域，範圍，方面

This is a safe area of town, so you don't have to worry about your belongings.
這裡是鎮上的安全區域，所以你不需要擔心財物的安全。

---

arrest

〔əˋrɛst〕 動　逮捕，拘留，阻止，制止

The police arrested five suspects in connection with the burglaries.
警察逮捕了5名與搶案有關的嫌犯。

---

aspect

〔ˋæspɛkt〕 名　方面，觀點，方向，方位

Learning the customs and habits of another culture is an important aspect of learning a language.
學習其他文化的風俗和習慣是學習語言重要的一部分。

375

attempt ▶ 〔əˋtɛmpt〕 動　試圖，企圖

The magician who sawed the woman in half first cautioned his audience, " o not attempt this at home!"
把那女人鋸成兩半的魔術師首先警告觀眾：「勿在家裡嘗試！」

average ▶ 〔ˋævərɪdʒ〕 名　平均，平均數
形　平均的，一般的
動　算出平均數，平均分配

The man the police are looking for is of average height and build, with blond hair.
警察在找的男人是中等身高、體型，金髮。

bend ▶ 〔bɛnd〕 動　使彎曲，使致力(於)，使屈服

Glass will not bend very far before it breaks.
玻璃碎裂之前不會彎曲得太厲害。

blame ▶ 〔blem〕 動　責備，指責，把…歸咎(於)，歸因於
blame（人）for～
「把～歸咎於（人），指責（人）～」

One should never blame others for one's own actions.
人不應該把自己的行為歸咎在他人身上。

branch ▶ 〔bræntʃ〕 名　樹枝，分店，分局，分部，
（語系的）分支，（學科的）分科
動　出枝，分支

The branches of the trees were decorated with a thousand beautiful colored lights.
樹枝上裝飾著一千個美麗的彩色燈泡。

His main business is producing wine, but he has recently branched out into micro brewed beer.
他主要的工作是釀葡萄酒，但是他最近著手製造精釀啤酒。

breathe ▶ 〔brið〕 動　呼吸，呼氣，吸氣
breath ▶ 〔brɛθ〕 名　呼吸，氣息

Taking a deep breath of air, she dove into the water to save the drowning child.
她深深吸了一口氣，然後潛入水裡救溺水的孩子。

burst ▶ 〔bɜst〕 動　爆炸，破裂，衝，闖，突然出現
burst into tears/laughter　突然哭起來／突然大笑起來

When the economic bubble burst, many people lost their jobs.
當泡沫經濟破滅，許多人都失去他們的工作。

★
376
chat ▶ 〔tʃæt〕 名 閒談，聊天
動 閒談，聊天
chat with（人）「和（人）聊天」

chatter ▶ 〔`tʃætə〕 動 喋喋不休，嘮叨
名 嘮叨，饒舌

Many people chat on the Internet these days.
現今有許多人在網路上聊天。

The speaker could not be heard above the chatter of the crowd.
演講者的談話被底下群眾喋喋不休的嘈雜聲給蓋住聽不見。

choke ▶ 〔tʃok〕 動 使窒息，哽住，阻塞，噎住

Since marbles can be a choking hazard, they should be kept away
from small children.
彈珠有可能會讓人窒息，所以應該要放在小朋友拿不到的地方。

cloth ▶ 〔klɔθ〕 名 布，織物，衣料，布塊

clothe ▶ 〔kloð〕 動 給…穿衣，為…提供衣服

clothes ▶ 〔kloz〕 名 衣服，服裝

clothing ▶ 〔`kloðɪŋ〕 名 （總稱）衣服，衣著，覆蓋物

Judy bought some silk cloth in Thailand to make herself some clothes.
茱蒂在泰國買了一些絲綢布料替自己做衣服。

clue ▶ 〔klu〕 名 線索，跡象，提示

The detective was unable to find any clues that would help solve the
case.
那位偵探無法找到能幫助解開案件的任何線索。

cosmic ▶ 〔`kɑzmɪk〕 形 宇宙的，廣大的，無限的

Cosmic rays are atomic nuclei that come to Earth from outer space.
宇宙射線是從外太空來到地球的原子粒子。

curse ▶ 〔kɜs〕 名 咒語，詛咒，咒罵，罵人的話
動 詛咒，咒罵

Alfred cursed himself for making a mistake that rendered all his hard
work useless.
艾佛烈因為犯錯讓所有努力變成白費而咒罵自己。

⭐
377

decade ▶ 〔ˋdɛked〕 名　十，十年
in the last decade「過去十年間」

She has been living overseas for over a decade.
她住在國外已經超過10年以上了。

deep ▶ 〔dip〕 形　深的，位於深處的

depth ▶ 〔dɛpθ〕 名　深度，厚度
be in the depths「在極度絕望之中」
in depth「全面地，深入地」

The analysis was not incorrect, but it lacked depth.
這項分析並非不正確，只是缺乏深度。

degree ▶ 〔dɪˋgri〕 名　度，度數，程度，等級，學位，地位，
身分，階層

To people who are used to it, -20 degrees does not feel cold.
對習慣的人來說，負20度並不算冷。

He has degrees in History, English, and hilosophy.
他有歷史、英文以及哲學的學位。

dim ▶ 〔dɪm〕 形　微暗的，模糊的，朦朧的，看不清楚的
動　變暗，變模糊

The lights grew dim as the band came onto the stage.
樂團上台的時候，燈光隨即變暗。

discard ▶ 〔dɪsˋkɑrd〕 動　拋棄，摒棄，丟棄

Be sure you have assembled all the parts before you discard the instructions.　丟棄說明書前，請確認你已經組裝好全部的零件。

disease ▶ 〔dɪˋziz〕 名　病，疾病，弊病

The researchers are working on developing a cure for that disease.
研究人員正致力於發展那類疾病的療法。

divine ▶ 〔dəˋvaɪn〕 形　神的，神性的，天賜的，神聖的，極好的
名　神學家，牧師

This ice-cream pie with caramel sauce is divine.
這個焦糖醬調味的冰淇淋派實在是太好吃了。

drown ▶ 〔draʊn〕 動　把⋯淹死，淹沒，浸濕，溺死，沈沒

Even good swimmers can drown if they aren't careful.
如果不小心的話，就連擅長游泳的人都有可能會溺水。

She likes her pancakes drowned in maple syrup.
她喜歡把鬆餅浸在楓糖漿裡。

due ▶ 〔dju〕 名　應得之物，應得權益，應付款，稅金
　　　　　　　　 形　應支付的，欠款的
378　　　　　　　 due to～「由於～」
　　　　　　　　 due date「期限，到期日」

Because he forgot to pay his dues, he was kicked out of the club.
因為忘記付會員費，他被俱樂部取消會籍了。

---

dull ▶ 〔dʌl〕 形　陰沈的，昏暗的，乏味的，笨的，遲鈍的

The knife is dull, so you don't need to worry about getting cut.
刀子鈍了，所以你不需要擔心會被割到。

The television program was dull, so Jen decided to read a book.
電視節目很無聊，所以珍決定要看書。

---

empty ▶ 〔ˋɛmptɪ〕 形　空的，無意義的，徒勞的

The cookie jar was always empty after Tom came for a visit.
每次湯姆拜訪過後，餅乾罐總是空的。

---

encounter ▶ 〔ɪnˋkaʊntɚ〕 動　遭遇，遇到，偶然相遇

In your life as a university student you will encounter many pleasures
as well as problems.
大學生的生活不光是會經歷許多樂趣，也同樣會遭遇到許多的問題。

---

enter ▶ 〔ˋɛntɚ〕 動　進入，參加，加入，開始從事，
　　　　　　　　 開始進入，將…輸入
　　　　　　 enter for a contest「報名參加比賽」

Margaret suspected something was going on, because as soon as
she entered the room, everyone stopped talking.
瑪格莉特懷疑有什麼正在進行，因為當她一進入房間，所有的人都停止了
談話。

---

epoch ▶ 〔ˋɛpək〕 名　時期，時代，新紀元

Although he delivered his speech in a very dramatic way, his ideas
were hardly epoch-making.
雖然他以非常戲劇化的方式發表演說，但他的論點沒什麼劃時代的創見。

---

evil ▶ 〔ˋivl〕 形　邪惡的，罪惡的，討厭的
　　　　　　　　 名　邪惡

The theme of the story is the triumph of good over evil.
這個故事的主題是良善戰勝邪惡。

379

exchange

▶ 〔ɪksˋtʃendʒ〕 [動] 交換，調換，兌換
　　　　　　　　[名] 交換，交流，交易，匯率
exchange～for... 「用～交換…」
exchange ideas with～ 「和～交換意見」

If you send your C -ROM into the company , you can exchange it for a newer version of the software.
如果你把你的CD-ROM送到公司，你可以把它的軟體換成較新版本。

exploit

▶ 〔ɪkˋsplɔɪt〕 [動] 剝削，利用，開發
　〔ˋɛksplɔɪt〕 [名] 功績，功勳，輝煌的成就

Francine quit her job because she felt that her talents were not fully appreciated or exploited.
法蘭欣辭掉她的工作，因為她覺得自己的才能沒有充分地得到賞識或利用。

external

▶ 〔ɪkˋstɜnəl〕 [形] 外面的，外來的，表面的
externally 〔ɪkˋstɜn̩ɪ〕 [副] 外部地
（反義）internal 〔ɪnˋtɜn̩〕
　[形] 內部的，內在的，固有的，本質的
internally 〔ɪnˋtɜnəlɪ〕 [副] 內部地，內在地

Vitamin E can be taken internally, or applied externally to the skin.
維他命E可以內服，或是外用塗在皮膚上。

fade

▶ 〔fed〕 [動] 凋謝，枯萎，顏色褪去，變微弱

famine

▶ 〔ˋfæmɪn〕 [名] 饑荒，飢餓，缺乏

The country was plagued by drought and famine for nearly a decade.
那個國家近10年來為了乾旱與饑荒所苦。

fatigue

▶ 〔fəˋtig〕 [名] 疲勞，勞累，勞累的工作
　　　　　　[動] 使疲勞

Rest is the only way to overcome fatigue.
休息是恢復疲勞的唯一方法。

fit

▶ 〔fɪt〕 [形] 適合的，恰當的，健康的，強健的
　　　　[動] （衣服）合身，相稱，適合

The suit jacket fit well, but the trousers were too short.
那件西裝外套很合身，但是褲子就太短了。

flavor

▶ 〔ˋflevɚ〕 [名] 味道，風味，香料
　　　　　　[動] 給…調味，給…增添風趣
flavor～with... 「用…給～調味」

These potato chips are pizza flavored.
這些洋芋片是比薩口味的。

☆
380

focus ▸ 〔`fokəs〕 图 焦點，中心，集中點，重點
動 使聚焦，調焦距，聚焦，集中
focus on～「集中在～上」

If you focus on your goal, you can definitely achieve it.
如果你專注在目標上，你絕對可以達成目標。

---

forecast ▸ 〔`for͵kæst〕 图 預報，預測，預料
動 預測，預報，預示，預言

The weather forecast for tomorrow is sunny and warm.
氣象預報明日天氣晴朗溫暖。

---

foretell ▸ 〔for`tɛl〕 動 預言，預示

No one could have foretold that there would be a huge blizzard in
Sao aulo, Brazil.
沒有人能料到巴西聖保羅會有暴風雪。

---

funeral ▸ 〔`fjunərəl〕 图 喪葬，葬儀，出殯行列

They are all dressed in black for the funeral.
為了葬禮，他們全部的人都穿著黑色服裝。

---

gain ▸ 〔gen〕 動 得到，獲得，贏得，增加，獲利

You won't gain anything by lying, so you may as well tell the truth.
說謊不會讓你得到任何好處，所以你最好說實話。

---

gaze ▸ 〔gez〕 動 凝視，注視
gaze at～「注視～」

He sat gazing out the window, fantasizing about being somewhere else.
他坐著凝視窗外，幻想自己身在其他地方。

---

germ ▸ 〔dʒɝm〕 图 微生物，細菌，病菌

" on't eat dirt!" Glenda scolded her child, "it's full of germs."
「不要吃泥土！」葛蘭黛訓斥她的孩子：「那都是細菌。」

---

gigantic ▸ 〔dʒaɪ`gæntɪk〕 形 巨人的，巨大的，龐大的

The child stared wide-eyed at the gigantic lollipop.
那孩子睜大雙眼，望著那支巨大的棒棒糖。

---

glance ▸ 〔glæns〕 動 看一下，掃視，瞥見，簡略提及
glance at～「掃視～」

Without a backward glance, she left the room and slammed the door.
她連回頭看一眼都沒有，就這樣砰的一聲關上門離開房間。

381

goods
▶ 〔gʊdz〕 名　商品，貨物

The company manufactures electronic goods.
那間公司製造電子產品。

grain
▶ 〔gren〕 名　穀粒，穀類，細粒

The farmers in this region raise small grains like wheat, barley and oats.
這個地區的農夫種植像是小麥、大麥以及燕麥等的細穀類。

grant
▶ 〔grænt〕 動　同意，准予，給予，授予，承認
take～for granted「把～視為理所當然」

The blue fairy granted inocchio's wish, and he became a real boy .
藍色妖精實現了小木偶的願望，讓他變成一個真正的小男孩。

When he started doing his own cooking and cleaning, he realized that he had always taken his parents for granted.
當他開始自己煮飯打掃，他才了解一直以來總把父母的存在視為理所當然。

grasp
▶ 〔græsp〕 動　抓牢，握緊，抱住，領會，理解

If you find it difficult to grasp the ideas of the lesson, you should be sure to ask your teacher for help.
如果你覺得授課內容難以理解，你應該要向老師尋求幫助。

guess
▶ 〔gɛs〕 動　猜測，推測，猜中，認為

If I had to guess, I'd say he's about 23.
要猜的話，我認為他大概是23歲。

impact
▶ 〔`ɪmpækt〕 名　衝擊，碰撞，衝擊力，影響，作用

I could never have predicted the impact my words would have on her.
我從沒預料到我的話對她的影響。

impose
▶ 〔ɪm`poz〕 動　徵（稅），加（負擔等）於，把…強加於

The government imposed a 15% tax on imported goods.
政府針對進口商品課收15%的稅金。

inborn
▶ 〔ɪn`bɔrn〕 形　天生的，天賦的

Roger has an inborn talent for music.
羅傑天生就有音樂才華。

☆
382

incentive ▶ 〔ɪnˋsɛntɪv〕 名 刺激，鼓勵，動機

The cash reward was extra incentive for the citizens to find the person who was vandalizing public property.
現金獎賞是額外的獎金，鼓勵市民找出任意破壞公共財產的人。

---

income ▶ 〔ˋɪnˏkʌm〕 名 收入，收益，所得

Shelby almost forgot to pay her income tax.
雪兒碧差點忘記繳她的所得稅。

---

input ▶ 〔ˋɪnˏput〕 名 投入，輸入，輸入功率，輸入信息
　　　　　　動 將（資料等）輸入電腦
（反義）output〔ˋautˏput〕
名 生產，產品，輸出，輸出功率，輸出信息

Without proper input, a computer cannot provide accurate output.
沒有適當地輸入資料，電腦無法提供正確的運算結果。

---

insight ▶ 〔ˋɪnˏsaɪt〕 名 洞察力，眼光，洞悉，深刻的理解

After talking with him, I was given some insight as to why he left his home.
和他談話過後，我大概能理解他為什麼要離家出走。

---

instead ▶ 〔ɪnˋstɛd〕 副 作為替代，反而，卻
instead of～「代替～」

He was too tired to play football, so he took a nap instead.
他太累了，沒辦法踢足球，所以他改成小睡片刻。

---

insult ▶ 〔ɪnˋsʌlt〕 動 侮辱，羞辱，辱罵

Hal didn't mean his comment as an insult, but it made Cheryl angry.
豪爾的評論沒有侮辱的意思，但卻惹惱綺麗兒了。

---

interest ▶ 〔ˋɪntərɪst〕 名 興趣，利益，感興趣的事物或人，
利息，股權

Although he generally has little interest in sports, he always watches the Olympics.
雖然他平常對運動不太感興趣，但他總是會看奧運比賽。

---

issue ▶ 〔ˋɪʃjʊ〕 名 問題，爭論，爭議，發行（物），
一次發行量，（報刊）期號

This issue of the nature magazine has fabulous pictures of Mt. McKinley.
這期的自然雜誌刊登了很棒的麥肯萊山照片。

---

jail ▶ 〔dʒel〕 名 監獄，拘留所，監禁
動 監禁，拘留

383

job
▶ 〔dʒɑb〕 名 工作，職業

He has a job as a gas station attendant.
他的工作是加油站服務員。

join
▶ 〔dʒɔɪn〕 動 連結，與…會合，加入，參加

joint
▶ 〔dʒɔɪnt〕 名 關節，接頭，接合點
形 連接的，共同的，合辦的

The push to decrease crime in the city is a joint effort of politicians and law enforcement.
要推動降低市內的犯罪率，需要政治人物和法律執行的共同努力。

lack
▶ 〔læk〕 名 欠缺，不足，沒有，缺少的東西
動 缺少，需要，不足

As all the guests' faces puckered, it became obvious that what was lacking in the apple pie was sugar.
當客人的臉都皺了起來時，很明顯是蘋果派少加了糖。

landscape
▶ 〔`lænd‚skep〕 名 風景，景色，風景畫
動 造園，從事景觀美化（或園藝）工作

The landscape was vast and rugged, and it gave the settlers a feeling of insignificance.
這片遼闊險惡的景色，讓拓荒者們感到自己的渺小。

late
▶ 〔let〕 形 遲到的，晚的，已故的，前任的

later
▶ 〔`letɚ〕 形 （late的比較級）較晚的，以後的

latter
▶ 〔`lætɚ〕 形 （late的比較級）後面的，
（兩者中）後者的

last
▶ 〔læst〕 形 （late的最高級）最後的，僅剩的，
最不可能…的，最近的，最新的

He saw leftover pizza and soup in the refrigerator; he decided to have the latter for lunch.
他看見冰箱裡面吃剩的比薩和湯，他決定把後者當午餐吃。

lean
▶ 〔lin〕 動 傾斜，傾身，屈身，依賴，依靠
lean on～「依賴～」
lean against～「靠在～上」
lean over～「從～探出身體」

He leaned over the bridge to look at the ducks in the water.
他從橋上探出身子看水面上的鴨群。

384

leap

▶ 〔lip〕動　跳躍，迅速進行，立即著手

He made sure the bungee was securely fastened, and leapt off the bridge.
他確認繩子已經安全地固定好了，然後就從橋上一躍而下。

lightning

▶ 〔`laɪtnɪŋ〕名　閃電，電光
（類似）thunder〔`θʌndɚ〕
名　雷，雷聲，轟隆聲

We couldn't see the flashes of lightning very well, but the cracks of thunder were spectacular.
我們沒能很清楚地看見閃電，但是打雷的轟隆聲非常驚人。

lose

▶ 〔luz〕動　失去，喪失，輸掉，損失（金錢），迷失
lose one's way「迷路」

loss

▶ 〔lɔs〕名　喪失，遺失，損失，虧損（額），輸

I lost my keys and had to pay to get the locks on my apartment replaced.
我把我的鑰匙弄丟了，所以得花錢把我公寓的門鎖換掉。

matter

▶ 〔`mætɚ〕名　事情，問題，事件
動　（常用於否定句和疑問句）有關係，要緊

I don't think we will discuss anything important, so it doesn't matter if you can't make it to the meeting.
我不認為我們會討論任何重要的事情，所以你趕不上會議的話也沒關係。

melt

▶ 〔mɛlt〕動　融化，熔化

The snowman slowly melted away when the weather turned warm.
當天氣變得暖和，雪人就慢慢地融化了。

mention

▶ 〔`mɛnʃən〕動　提到，說起
on't mention it.「別客氣」

id I mention that there is a party on Wednesday evening?
我有說過禮拜三晚上會有一場派對嗎？

naked

▶ 〔`nekɪd〕形　裸體的，光身的，暴露的，無覆蓋的

The seeds are so tiny, they cannot be seen with the naked eye.
這些種子非常小，肉眼是無法看見的。

385

opportunity ▶ 〔͵ɑpə`tjunətɪ〕 名 機會，良機

He waited for the right opportunity to ask his girlfriend to marry him.
他等待恰當的時機要向他的女朋友求婚。

ornament ▶ 〔`ɔrnəmənt〕 名 裝飾品，裝飾

I have an antique ornament on my mantlepiece.
我有一件古董裝飾品放在壁爐架上。

otherwise ▶ 〔`ʌðə͵waɪz〕 副 否則，不然，除此以外，用別的方法，在其他方面

lease hurry up otherwise we will be late.
拜託快一點，不然我們會遲到。

outcome ▶ 〔`aut͵kʌm〕 名 結果，結局，後果

Citizens waited anxiously for the outcome of the election.
市民焦急地等待選舉結果出來。

outlook ▶ 〔`aut͵luk〕 名 觀點，看法，展望，前景，景色，風光，注視，瞭望

He has such a positive outlook on life that everyone loves to be around him.
因為他對人生的看法是如此的正面，所以每個人都喜歡待在他身邊。

owe ▶ 〔o〕 動 欠錢，把…歸功於

on't forget that you owe me fifty dollars.
不要忘記你欠我50元。

ozone ▶ 〔`ozon〕 名 臭氧
ozone layer「臭氧層」

There is a large hole in the ozone layer caused by pollution.
由於污染，臭氧層破了一個大洞。

pant ▶ 〔pænt〕 動 喘氣，劇烈跳動

The dog lay on the porch, panting and slobbering in the heat.
酷暑中，那隻狗趴在門廊上喘息流口水。

parallel ▶ 〔`pærə͵lɛl〕 形 平行的，同方向的，類似的
名 平行線，平行面，類似的人(或事物)，相似處，比較

Although they are geographically far apart, England and Japan have some cultural parallels.
雖然地理上距離遙遠，但是英國和日本有某些文化上的相似處。

386

parliament ▶ 〔`pɑrləmənt〕名 議會，國會，
（英國、加拿大等的）國會

arliament has approved the policy, and it will probably become a law.
國會已經通過那條政策，很有可能會成為一項法律。

phase ▶ 〔fez〕名 階段，時期，面，方面

When Jody was a teenager, she went through a phase where she wouldn't talk to anyone but her best friend.
裘蒂青少年的時候，經歷過一個只和最好的朋友說話的時期。

pile ▶ 〔paɪl〕名 堆，一堆，大量，大數目
a pile of～＝piles of～「一堆～」

I'm sorry, I can't go out tonight, I've got piles of work to do.
很抱歉，我今晚不能出去，因為我有一堆工作要做。

polar ▶ 〔`polə〕形 極地的，兩極的，正好相反的

There is some concern that global warming is causing the polar ice caps to melt.
近來人們對全球暖化將導致極地冰帽融化感到擔憂。

portion ▶ 〔`porʃən〕名 （一）部分，（食物等的）一份，一客

Robert has spent a considerable portion of his inheritance on remodeling his parents' home.
羅伯花了相當多繼承的財產在改建他父母的房子上。

posterity ▶ 〔pɑs`tɛrətɪ〕名 後裔，子孫，後代，後世

"We'd better get this on film for posterity," he said, as his baby took her first steps.
當孩子踏出第一步時，他說：「我們最好把這拍下來給後代子孫看。」

potent ▶ 〔`potṇt〕形 有力的，有效力的，有效能的

This medicine is very potent, and might make you sleepy.
這種藥效力很強，有可能會讓你想睡覺。

pour ▶ 〔por〕動 倒，傾注，傾吐，（雨）傾盆而降

She poured a perplexing amount of chocolate syrup over her ice cream.
她倒了分量驚人的巧克力糖漿在她的冰淇淋上。

presume ▶ 〔prɪ`zum〕動 假定，假設，推測，認為，推定

purchase ▶ 〔`pɜtʃəs〕名 買，購買，所購之物
動 買，購買，贏得，獲得

The salesclerk painstakingly wrapped all my purchases.
店員小心翼翼地包裝好所有我買的東西。

387

quarrel

▶ 〔ˋkwɔrəl〕 名　爭吵，不和，吵鬧
　　　　　　動　爭吵，不和，埋怨
pick a quarrel with～「挑釁～，找～的碴」

Helen was in a bad mood, so she decided to pick a quarrel with her brother.
海倫心情不好，所以她決定要找她弟弟的碴。

quit

▶ 〔kwɪt〕 動　離開，退出，放棄，停止
quit V-ing 「放棄～」

Lenny quit the job he had for 10 years, and went to school to get qualified to be a physical therapist.
藍尼辭掉他做了10年的工作，並為了取得物理治療師的資格去上學。

rage

▶ 〔redʒ〕 名　狂怒，盛怒，狂暴

The bull snorted and pawed in rage.
那隻公牛又噴鼻息又憤怒地踢蹄。

range

▶ 〔rendʒ〕 名　排，行，幅度，範圍，區域
　　　　　　動　排列，將…，把…分類，使系統化
range from～to...「範圍從～到…」

Reactions to the new items on the menu ranged from enthusiasm to disappointment.
對菜單上新菜色的回應，從熱情到失望都有。

rattle

▶ 〔ˋrætl〕 動　發出喀喀聲，使窘迫不安，使驚惶失措

My car has had a funny rattle lately, I'd better have it looked at.
我的車最近會發出一種奇怪的喀噠聲，我最好把車送去檢查一下。

raw

▶ 〔rɔ〕 形　生的，未煮過的，未加工的，無經驗的

A healthy diet includes plenty of fresh, raw vegetables.
健康的飲食包含大量的新鮮生菜。

recall

▶ 〔rɪˋkɔl〕 動　回想，回憶，召回，收回

If I recall correctly, the movie starts at 7:00.
如果我記得沒錯，電影是7點鐘開始。

The computer manufacturer had to recall one of its newest products due to faulty manufacturing.
由於製造上的錯誤，那間電腦公司必須回收一項他們的最新產品。

388

reign

▶ 〔ren〕 動　統治，支配，統治時期

The reign of Queen Victoria was the longest of any of the British monarchs.
維多利亞女王在位期間是所有英國君王中最長的。

release

▶ 〔rɪ`lis〕 動　釋放，解放，鬆開，發射，發行

Fans are anxiously waiting for the movie to be released.
影迷們急切地等待電影公開上映。

relieve

▶ 〔rɪ`liv〕 動　緩和，減輕，解除，使寬慰，使放心

relief

▶ 〔rɪ`lif〕 名　緩和，減輕，解除，寬心，慰藉

The doctor gave the patient morphine to relieve the pain.
醫師給病患嗎啡以舒緩疼痛。

Barbara gave a sigh of relief as she saw her passing test score.
當她看見考試分數及格時，芭芭拉安心地鬆了口氣。

rescue

▶ 〔`rɛskju〕 動　援救，營救，挽救
　　　　　　名　援救，營救

St. Bernard dogs are often used in rescue teams.
聖伯納犬經常被利用於救援團隊。

resume

▶ 〔rɪ`zjum〕 動　重新開始，繼續，恢復，重返

Classes will resume on the 15th of January.
課程將會在1月15日重新開始。

riot

▶ 〔`raɪət〕 名　暴亂，騷亂，大混亂，喧鬧

The police were unable to control the crowds when the riot broke out.
暴動發生的時候，警方無法控制群眾。

role

▶ 〔rol〕 名　角色，作用，任務

Joshua played the role of a sheep in the school play.
約書亞在學校話劇裡扮演一隻羊的角色。

ruin

▶ 〔`ruɪn〕 名　毀滅，崩潰，毀壞，廢墟，遺跡
　　　　　　動　毀滅，毀壞

We went to see the ruins of the ancient castle.
我們去看了一座古城的遺跡。

on't eat chocolate before dinner！You'll ruin your appetite!
不要在晚飯前吃巧克力！你會沒有食慾的！

389

rural ▶ 〔`rurəl〕 形 農村的，田園的，鄉村風味的

The little village was set in beautiful rural surroundings.
那座小村莊坐擁一片田園美景。

scale ▶ 〔skel〕 名 刻度，比率，縮尺，等級，規模

He realized it was time to lose a little weight when he couldn't see the scale because his belly was in the way.
當他因為被肚子擋住而看不見體重計時，他知道該是時候要減肥了。

On a scale of one to ten, I'd say this restaurant is an eight.
滿分是10分的話，我認為這間餐廳有8分。

scheme ▶ 〔skim〕 名 計劃，方案，詭計，陰謀

espite all his scheming and planning, he could still not manage to get his parents to let him buy a car.
儘管他有所謀劃與盤算，他還是沒能說服父母讓他買車。

scold ▶ 〔skold〕 動 責罵，斥責

Billy knew that if he got caught wearing his muddy shoes in the house he would be scolded, so he took them off at the door.
比利知道要是他被抓到在家裡穿著沾滿泥巴的鞋子會被罵，所以他在門口就脫掉鞋子了。

scratch ▶ 〔skrætʃ〕 動 抓，抓破，劃傷，潦草地塗寫，亂劃
名 抓痕，擦傷，刮擦聲，亂塗，亂劃

The cat yawned, stretched, and began to scratch his ears.
那隻貓打了個呵欠，伸了伸懶腰，然後開始搔牠的耳朵。

scream ▶ 〔skrim〕 動 尖叫，放聲大哭，放聲大笑
名 尖叫，尖銳刺耳的聲音，呼嘯聲

She let out a loud scream because she thought she had seen a ghost.
她以為她看見鬼了，所以放聲大叫。

search ▶ 〔sɝtʃ〕 名動 搜查，仔細檢查，探究，調查
search somewhere for～「搜尋某處找～」
search for～「尋找～」

I only found one black sock and now I have to search for the other one.
我只發現一隻黑色襪子，現在我必須要找到另外一隻。

sentence ▶ 〔`sɛntəns〕 名 句子，判決，宣判
動 宣判，判決

He was sentenced to five years in prison.
他被判入監服刑5年。

390

shelter
▶ 〔`ʃɛltə〕 名　躲避所，避難所，遮蔽，庇護
動　遮蔽，庇護，保護，躲避，避難
shelter～from...「保護～遠離…」

She stood in the little shelter to stay out of the rain.
她站在一個小遮蔽處下躲雨。

shiver
▶ 〔`ʃɪvə〕 動　發抖，打顫，發出顫聲
名　顫抖，寒顫

The weather is so cold it is making me shiver.
天氣太冷了，冷得我直發抖。

site
▶ 〔saɪt〕 名　地點，場所，選址，網站

This is the site where the UFO was seen.
這就是幽浮被目擊的地點。

soil
▶ 〔sɔɪl〕 名　土壤，土地，國家，領土，農業

The soil was a dark color and just perfect for growing flowers.
土壤顏色很深，非常適合種花。

solar
▶ 〔`solə〕 形　太陽的，日光的，源自太陽的，利用太陽光的
the solar system「太陽系」

Solar power is an important energy source that is still underused.
太陽能是一項尚未被充分利用的重要能源來源。

sound
▶ 〔saʊnd〕 名　聲音，響聲，喧鬧聲
動　發聲，響起，發音，聽起來

I couldn't sleep well last night because I heard a strange sound in the middle of the night which scared me.
我昨天晚上睡不好，因為半夜的時候有個奇怪的聲音嚇到我。

source
▶ 〔sors〕 名　源頭，根源，來源，消息來源，出處

The Internet can be a great source of information.
網路可說是一個重要的資訊來源。

span
▶ 〔spæn〕 名　跨度，一段時間，全長

These batteries have a life-span of about eight hours.
這些電池可以維持8小時。

spare
▶ 〔spɛr〕 動　分出，挪出，分讓，節省，吝惜
形　多餘的，剩下的，空閒的，備用的

o you have a　spare pen? I forgot mine.
你有多的筆嗎？我忘記帶我的筆了。

391

spread ▶ 〔sprɛd〕動　使伸展，使延伸，展開，攤開，散佈

Rachelle spread all her photos over the table and chose the best ones to send to her parents.
瑞秋莉把她所有的照片攤在桌上，然後挑出最好的寄給她父母。

stare ▶ 〔stɛr〕動　盯，凝視，注視
stare at～「盯著～看」

The mother scolded the child for staring at the people at the next table.
那個母親因為孩子盯著隔壁桌的人看而責備他。

startle ▶ 〔`stɑrtl〕動　使驚嚇，使驚奇

The sudden clap of thunder startled her so much that it took a few minutes for her to calm down.
突如其來的雷聲嚇著她了，直到好幾分鐘後她才平靜下來。

static ▶ 〔`stætɪk〕形　靜的，靜態的，靜止的，停滯的

Language is not static, but dynamic, ever changing.
語言不是靜態，而是動態的，而且總是在改變。

statue ▶ 〔`stætʃʊ〕名　雕像，塑像

They are going to build a statue of the Emperor.
他們要建一座皇帝的雕像。

stem ▶ 〔stɛm〕名　莖，樹幹，葉柄
動　抽去…的梗（或莖），給…裝柄，起源於
stem from～「起源於～，由～造成」

She cut the stem of the rose before putting it in the vase.
她把玫瑰花放入花瓶前，先把莖切掉了。

Most of the problems in the workplace stem from inadequate communication among coworkers.
大多數職場的問題來自於同事之間的溝通不足。

struggle ▶ 〔`strʌgl〕動　奮鬥，鬥爭，努力，掙扎
名　奮鬥，鬥爭，努力，掙扎
struggle for existence「為生活而奮鬥」

She wanted to laugh, but she struggled to keep a straight face.
她想笑，但是她努力板著臉孔。

sum ▶ 〔sʌm〕名　總數，總和，總計

She has saved a rather large sum of money to use for starting her own coffee shop.
她為了開一間自己的咖啡店，已經存了一筆數目頗為可觀的錢。

392

surplus ▶ 〔`sɝpləs〕 名 過剩，剩餘物，剩餘額，盈餘
形 過剩的，剩餘的

We got rid of the surplus textbooks by giving them away as bingo prizes.
我們把剩下的教科書當作賓果遊戲的獎品解決掉了。

surrender ▶ 〔sə`rɛndɚ〕 動 使投降，使自首，交出，放棄

The soldiers had no choice but to surrender to the enemy.
除了向敵人投降，士兵們沒有別的選擇。

survey ▶ 〔sə`ve〕 動 俯視，全面考察（或研究），概括論述，
審視，調查
〔`sɝve〕 名 調查，調查報告，全面的考察

The survey indicated that one in three people don't eat breakfast on a
regular basis. 這份調查報告指出，有三分之一的人早餐不規律。

swallow ▶ 〔`swɑlo〕 名 吞，嚥，一次吞嚥之物
動 吞下，嚥下，吞沒，吞併

My throat hurts and I find it difficult to swallow.
我的喉嚨痛，而且我覺得吞嚥困難。

tail ▶ 〔tel〕 名 尾巴，尾部，尾狀物

The peacock seems to be very proud of his tail feathers.
那隻孔雀似乎很驕傲牠的尾羽。

tale ▶ 〔tel〕 名 故事，傳說，敘述
fairy tale「神話故事，童話」

The little girl loves Grimm's fairy tales so much that the cover of her
favorite book is completely worn out.
那個小女孩喜歡格林童話喜歡得不得了，以致於她最愛的故事書封面已經
完全磨損了。

temperature ▶ 〔`tɛmprətʃɚ〕 名 溫度，氣溫，體溫

The temperature rose to a high of 34. 氣溫上升至34度高溫。

theme ▶ 〔θim〕 名 論題，話題，題目，主題，題材

What is the theme of the movie you are going to watch?
你打算要看的電影是什麼主題？

throat ▶ 〔θrot〕 名 咽喉，喉嚨

The girl had a cold and a sore throat.
那個女生感冒喉嚨痛。

tongue ▶ 〔tʌŋ〕 名 舌，舌頭，說話能力（或方式），語言
one's mother tongue「本國語言，母語」

He bit his tongue while he was eating a carrot.
他吃紅蘿蔔的時候咬到自己的舌頭。

393

tool ▶ 〔tul〕名　工具，器具，用具，方法，手段

You'll find him out in the tool shed, looking for a screwdriver.
你會發現他在工具室裡找螺絲起子。

traffic ▶ 〔`træfɪk〕名　交通，交通量，貿易，運輸

I'm sorry I'm late but there was a lot of traffic on the roads this morning.
很抱歉我遲到了，因為今天早上路上的交通流量很大。

transient ▶ 〔`trænʃənt〕形　短暫的，一時的，瞬間的

This may be uncomfortable, but the pain will be transient.
這可能會不舒服，但是疼痛很快就會過去了。

trap ▶ 〔træp〕名　陷阱，圈套，詭計，陰謀，困境

The fly flew right into the spider's trap.
蒼蠅直接飛進蜘蛛網內。

troublesome ▶ 〔`trʌblsəm〕形　令人煩惱的，討厭的，麻煩的，棘手的，困難的

It may be troublesome, but you will get good results if you follow the instructions carefully.
那可能會很棘手，但如果你小心遵守指示的話，會得到好成果的。

tuition ▶ 〔tju`ɪʃən〕名　講授，教學，教誨，學費

The tuition fees have gone up in price.
學費漲價了。

tutor ▶ 〔`tjutɚ〕名　家庭教師，私人教師，輔導教師

The girl needed a math tutor because that was her weakest subject in school.
那個女孩子需要一個數學家教，因為那是她在學校裡最頭痛的科目。

twilight ▶ 〔`twaɪ.laɪt〕名　微光，黃昏，黎明，模糊狀態

I could just about make out her features in the twilight.
微光之中，我只能勉強辨認出她的容貌。

twin ▶ 〔twɪn〕名　雙胞胎之一，孿生兒
　　　　　　　　　形　孿生的，非常相似的，成對的

I would love to have a twin sister that looked just like me.
我希望能有一個和我長得一模一樣的雙胞胎姊妹。

⭐ **394**

undergo
▶ 〔͵ʌndɚˋgo〕動　經歷，經受，忍受，接受（治療、檢查等）

In order to be accepted into the military, you need to undergo a series of tests.
要進入軍隊的話，你需要先接受一連串的測試。

undertake
▶ 〔͵ʌndɚˋtek〕動　著手做，進行，從事

Organizing the party was not as easy an undertaking as Elly had expected.
策劃派對不像艾莉當初所想的是項簡單的工作。

uniform
▶ 〔ˋjunə͵fɔrm〕形　相同的，一致的，不變的
名　制服，軍服

Military officers are required to wear uniforms.
軍官被要求穿著軍服。

unify
▶ 〔ˋjunə͵faɪ〕動　統一，聯合，成一體

After the civil war finished, it took a long time to unify the country again.
內戰過後，這個國家花了很長的時間才又再度統一。

unique
▶ 〔juˋnik〕形　唯一的，獨一無二的，獨特的
be unique to～
「只存在於～，獨一無二存在於～的」

Koalas are unique to Australia.
無尾熊是澳洲特有的生物。

Each person's fingerprint is unique.
每個人的指紋都是獨一無二的。

unit
▶ 〔ˋjunɪt〕名　單位，單元，（全體中的）一個，一員

You will find that information in unit three in the textbook.
你會在課本的第三單元找到那項資訊。

upset
▶ 〔ʌpˋsɛt〕動　打翻，攪亂，使心煩意亂，使（腸胃）不適

Leila was upset about not being able to get a ticket to the concert.
蕾拉很失望沒能拿到那場演唱會的票。

vanish
▶ 〔ˋvænɪʃ〕動　消失，消逝，絕跡

I wish all the problems of the world would simply vanish.
我希望世界上所有的問題可以就這麼消失。

395

vehicle ▶ 〔`viɪkl〕 名　運載工具，車輛，飛行器，太空火箭

The vehicle turned left at the traffic light.　車子在紅綠燈那裡左轉了。

---

virus ▶ 〔`vaɪrəs〕 名　病毒，濾過性病毒，病毒感染

The common cold is caused by a virus, and not by being cold.
一般感冒是由病毒所引起，而不是由於天氣寒冷。

---

voyage ▶ 〔`vɔɪɪdʒ〕 名　航海，航行，航空

They went on a long boat voyage to the next island.
他們坐了很久的船到隔壁的島嶼。

---

wheat ▶ 〔hwit〕 名　小麥

Wheat is the main crop grown in many states in the Midwest US.
小麥是美國中西部許多州的主要作物。

---

whisper ▶ 〔`hwɪspə〕 動　低語，私語

You should not talk in the library, but if you must talk, please whisper.
你不該在圖書館內說話，但如果你一定得說話，請輕聲低語。

---

whole ▶ 〔hol〕 形　全部的，所有的，整個的

I can't believe I ate that whole apple pie.
我不敢相信我竟然吃光了整個蘋果派。

---

witness ▶ 〔`wɪtnɪs〕 動　目擊，為…作證，證明
　　　　　　　　　　　 名　目擊者，證人，證詞

The star witness for the murder trial is in protective custody.
這起謀殺案件的主要證人現正接受保護性拘留中。
【註】protective custody 保護性拘留：為了避免遭受被告家屬報復而接受
警方保護。

---

workaholic ▶ 〔ˏwɝkə`hɔlɪk〕 名　工作狂
　　　　　　　　　　　　　　　　 形　醉心於工作的
alcoholic 〔ˏælkə`hɔlɪk〕　形　全酒精的，酗酒的
　　　　　　　　　　　　　　 名　酒精中毒的人，酒鬼

Being a workaholic is not a very healthy lifestyle.
過度工作並不是非常健康的生活方式。

---

worry ▶ 〔`wɝɪ〕 動　使擔心，使發愁，憂慮
　　　　　　　　　 名　煩惱
worry about～「擔心～」
be worried about～「為～憂慮」

The parents were weary with worry when their children didn't come
home for three days.　孩子們三天沒回家，那對父母擔心得疲憊不堪。

worship ▶ 〔`wɝʃɪp〕 名 崇拜，敬仰，敬神，禮拜
動 崇拜，敬重，信奉，敬神，做禮拜

eople of many dif ferent religions came together to worship and pray for peace.
許多不同宗教的人聚在一起為了和平向神明祈禱。

wrong ▶ 〔rɔŋ〕 形 錯誤的，不對的，不正常的

The quiz show champion never gave a wrong answer.
那位猜謎節目冠軍從來都沒答錯過。

yell ▶ 〔jɛl〕 動 叫喊，吼叫，叫喊著說
yell at～「對～吼叫」

"Watch out!" he yelled as he saw the bicyclist heading straight for a pole.
當他看見騎腳踏車的人直直往柱子撞去，他大叫：「小心！」

yield ▶ 〔jild〕 動 出產，服從，屈服，投降
yield to～「屈服於～」

Rose yielded to her impulse and bought the dress.
蘿絲向她的衝動屈服，買下了那件洋裝。

索引

A

附錄1 60個常用字首字尾・字首

1 ex- e- ef- 往外的，往外側的

■ export　ex (往外) + port (港口)
　　動 出口 (＜從港口外出去)
■ eject　e (往外) + ject (丟：字根67)
　　動 逐出，將CD等物從播放機中取出
■ efficient　ef (往外) + fic (做) ent (變形容詞：字尾37)
　　形 有能力的，有效率的 (＜具有向外拓展的能力)

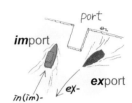

2 in- im- em- 往內的，往裡面的

■ income　in (往內) + come (來)
　　名 收入，所得
■ import　im (往內) + port (港口)
　　動 進口 (＜從港口進來)

3 in- im- 表否定 (不，無，非)

■ incorrect　in (否定) + correct (正確)
　　形 不正確的，不對的
■ impossible　im (否定) + possible (可能的)
　　形 不可能的

4 un- 表否定 (不，無，非)

■ unhappy　un (否定) + happy (快樂的)
　　形 不快樂的
■ unlucky　un (否定) + lucky (幸運的)
　　形 不幸運的

5 pre- pro- 之前

- ＊置於前方 preposition
  pre (之前) + position (置於)
  名 介系詞
- ＊預先 prepay pre (之前) + pay (支付)
  動 預先付款
- ＊延長 prolong pro (先) + long (使長)
  動 延長

*pre*pay

pre position
pre + position
之前　置於
in
at　　school → 學校=名詞
for

6 post- 之後

- postwar post (之後) + war (戰爭)
  形 戰後的
- postgraduate post (之後) + graduate (畢業生)
  名 研究生

pre- war post-

7 re- 又,再,回復到原來,往後面的

- recycle re (再) + cycle (循環)
  動 資源回收,再利用
- rewrite re (再) + write (寫) 動 再寫一次

*re*cycle

8 en- 作動詞

- enchain en (動詞化)+ chain (鎖)
  動 加鎖鍊
- enlarge en (動詞化) + large (大的) 動 擴大

*en*chain

9 di(s)- 表否定 (不,無,非),遠離,完全

- discover dis (否定) + cover (覆蓋)
  動 發現 (＜將覆蓋物掀開)
- disaster dis (遠離) + aster (星星)
  名 災難,慘事 (＜遠離幸運的星星)
- direct di (＜完全) + rect (直的) 形 直的,直接的

*dis*cover

10　**extra-**　額外的，超過的

- extra-large　extra（超過）＋ large（大的）
  形 特大的

11　**a- ac- ad- af- an- ap- as- at-**　往～的方向

- adverb　ad（往～的方向）＋ verb（動詞）名 副詞（＜往動詞的方向）
- awake　a（往～的方向）＋ wake（醒：字根82）動 喚醒（＜從睡眠往醒的方向）
- affirm　af（往～的方向）＋ firm（堅固的）動 斷言（＜心往堅定的方向）
- assist　as（往～的方向）＋ sist（站）動 幫助，協助（＜站在～那側）名 幫助，協助（的行為）

12　**syn- sym-**　同樣的

字根 ㉒

- sympathy　sym（同樣的）＋ pathy（心：字根205）
  名 同情

*sym*pathy

13　**ant- anti-**　反，非，逆

- antipathy　anti（反）＋ pathy（心）名 反感，厭惡

14　**ir- il-**　表否定 (不，無，非)

- irregular　ir（不）＋ regular（規則的）
  形 不規則的
- illegal　il（非）＋ legal（合法的）形 非法的

regular

*ir*regular

15　**co- con- com-**　① 共同，協力，一起　② 整體的，完全的

字根 ㊶

- ①cooperate　co（共同）＋ operate（行動，操作）
  動 合作（＜共同行動）
- ②complete　com（完全）＋plete（滿足）
  形 完成的，齊全的

*co*operate

16 **inter-**　在～之間

字根 **5**

- internet　inter (在～之間) + net (網路)
  - 名 網際網路 (<在電腦網路間來去)

17 **dia-**　在兩者(點)之間

字根 **25**

- diameter　dia (兩點之間) +
  meter (公尺=距離：字根26)
  - 名 直徑 (<穿過圓心連接圓上兩點的線段)

18 **sub- suf- sus-**　下面的，下方的

字根 **68**

- submarine　sub (下面) + marine (海)
  - 名 潛水艇 (<在海的下方行走)
- suffer　suf (下面) + fer (搬運)
  - 動 受苦 (<在行李下方搬運)

19 **de-**　① 遠離，除去　② 往下　③ 完全地

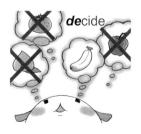

- ① decide　de (遠離) + cide (切：字根57)
  - 動 下定決心，決定 (<切斷猶豫)
- ② decline　de (往下) + cline (傾向)
  - 動 謝絕，婉拒 (<心情往下方傾)
- ③ depend　de (完全地) + pend (吊掛)
  - 動 信賴 (<完全交給對方)

20 **ob**　往～的方向，往～的前方

字根 **69**

- object　ob (往～的方向) + ject (丟：字根67)
  - 名 東西，目的，對象 (<丟到眼前的東西)

*ob*ject

附錄1 60個常用字首字尾・字尾

1　**-ing**　① ～正在做
② ～的 (當形容詞)

■ a crying baby　哭泣的嬰孩 (crying修飾baby)
　→ 動詞可以加上-ing當形容詞使用
■ an embarrassing question 令人難堪的問題

2　**-ing**　做～的事 (作動名詞)

■ Singing is a lot of fun. 唱歌是一件有趣的事。
　→ 動詞可以加上-ing當動名詞使用

3　**-ing**　做～用的

■ a walking stick 拐杖（＜走路用的木棒）
■ drinking water 飲用水（＜作為飲用的水）

4　**-ness**　作名詞 (接於形容詞、分詞後)

■ happiness　happy (快樂的) + ness 名 快樂

5　**-an -ian**　人 (作名詞)，～的(作形容詞)

■ American　America (美國) + an 名 美國人 形 美國的
■ comedian　comedy (喜劇) + ian 名 諧星，喜劇演員

6　**-ance -ence -(i)ce -se**　作名詞

■ resistance　resist (抵抗：字根17) + ance 名 抵抗
■ obedience　obedient (順從的：字根155)+ ence 名 順從

7　**-ous**　作形容詞

*主要是「具～的特徵」之意。
■ continuous　continue (繼續：字根283) + ous 形 連續的，不間斷的

8　-ful　作形容詞

＊「富於～」之意。

■ powerful　power（力量）＋ ful 形 強有力的

9　-less　作形容詞

＊「沒有～的，不足的」之意。

■ careless　care（注意：字根27）＋ less 形 粗心的

10　-(c)y　-(e)ry　作名詞

■ delivery　deliver（運送）＋ y 名 運送
■ bakery　bake（烤）＋ ry 名 麵包店

11　-ion　-tion　作名詞

■ contribution　contribute（貢獻）＋ ion 名 貢獻
■ repetition　repeat（重複）＋ tion 名 重複，反複

12　-ic　-tic　作形容詞

■ poetic　poet（詩人）＋ ic 形 詩的

13　-(i)fy　作動詞

＊「～化」之意

■ simplify　simple（簡單的）＋ ify 動 將～簡化

14　-ist　-er　-or　～的人(或物)

■ pianist　piano（鋼琴）＋ ist 名 鋼琴演奏者，鋼琴家
■ sticker　stick（黏）＋ er 名 貼紙
■ visitor　visit（訪問）＋ or 名 訪問者

15　-ize　-en　作動詞

＊「使～」「～化」之意。

■ specialize　special（專門的）＋ ize 動 將～專門化
■ weaken　weak（虛弱）＋ en 動 使虛弱

16 -(t)ure 作名詞

■ pressure press（壓縮）+ ure 名 壓力

17 -ism 作名詞

＊「～行為」「～主義」之意。

■ criticism criticize（批判）+ ism 名 批判
■ realism real（現實的）+ ism 名 現實主義，寫實主義

18 -al 作名詞

＊附加於動詞之後，有「使～」之意。

■ renewal renew（更新）+ al 名 更新，復原

19 -(i)al -(i)cal -ual 作形容詞

■ national nation（國家）+ al 形 國家的，國立的
■ economical economy（經濟）+ ical 形 經濟的，節儉的

20 -(t)ive 作形容詞

■ supportive support（支持）+ ive 形 支持的

21 -ly 作形容詞

＊附加於名詞之後，有「如～般的」之意。

■ sisterly sister（姊妹）+ ly 形 如姊妹般的
■ monthly month（一個月）+ ly 形 月刊的，每月的

22 -ly 作副詞

＊附加於形容詞之後當作副詞。

■ slowly slow（緩慢的）+ ly 副 緩慢地

23 -ment 作名詞

■ development develop（成長）+ ment 名 成長

24 -(i)ty -ety 作名詞

■ equality　equal（平等的）＋ ity 名 平等

25 -able -ible 作形容詞　　　　字根❶

＊附加於動詞或形容詞後，有「可能的」「應該的」「適合的」之意。
■ respectable　respect（尊敬：字根7）＋ able 形 值得尊敬的
■ reversible　reverse（反的：字根171）＋ ible 形 可逆的，可反轉的

26 -ed -en 作形容詞

＊作為動詞的過去分詞，多為「被～的」之意的形容詞，也適用於不規則動詞。
■ reserved seat 預約席（＜被預約的座位）
■ spoken English 口語英語（＜被說的英語）
■ sold items 賣完的商品（＜被賣完的商品）

27 -y 作形容詞

■ lengthy　length（長度）＋ y 形 極長的，冗長的

28 -ship 作名詞

＊加於名詞或形容詞後，表示「狀態」「性質」「資格」「技能」之意的名詞。
■ friendship　friend（朋友）＋ ship 名 友誼，友情
■ leadership　leader（領導者）＋ ship 名 領導才能

29 -graph(y) -gram 文書，圖表　　　字根❺⓿

■ telegram　tele（遠離：字根21）＋ gram 名 電報（＜從遠方送來的書信）
■ pictograph　picture（繪畫）＋ graph 名 圖象文字，象形文字（＜繪畫的文字）
■ pornography　porn（色情）＋ graphy 名 色情書刊

30 -ary 作形容詞

■ primary　prime（最好的：字根112）＋ ary 形 主要的

31 -ary 人，物

■ secretary　secret（秘密）＋ ary 名 秘書

32　-ant　-ent　人，物

- assistant　assist（協助：字根17）＋ ant　名　協助者，助手
- student　study（讀書）＋ ent　名　學生
- recipient　receive（接受）＋ ent　名　受領者，容器

33　-ory　作形容詞

- sensory　sense（感覺：字根42）＋ ory　形　感覺的
- advisory　advise（勸告：字根4）＋ ory　形　勸告的

34　-ory　場所

- observatory　observe（觀測：字根72）＋ ory　名　觀測所
- lavatory　lava（洗）＋ ory　名　洗手間，廁所

35　-ate　作動詞

- activate　active（活潑的：字根78）＋ ate　動　使活潑，使活化

36　-ate　作形容詞

- affectionate　affection（感情）＋ ate　動　充滿感情的

37　-ent　-ant　作形容詞

- different　differ（不同）＋ ent　形　不同的
- important　import（進口：字根106）＋ ant　形　重要的（＜物資進入港口的重要性）

38　-age　作名詞

- marriage　marry（結婚）＋ age　名　結婚

39　-logy　-ic(s)　學問，思想　　　　　　　字根 52

- zoology　zoo（動物園）＋ logy　名　動物學
- physics　phys（自然）＋ ics　名　物理學（＜自然現象的原理）

40　-ar　作形容詞

- circular　circle（圓形：字根36）＋ ar　形　圓形的